Sock Monkey Blues

a Joe Box mystery

by

John Laurence Robinson

AmErica House
Baltimore

First printing

ISBN: 1-59129-020-1
PUBLISHED BY AMERICA HOUSE BOOK PUBLISHERS
www.publishamerica.com
Baltimore

Printed in the United States of America

"Do you know? Do you wonder what's going on down under you?"

Deja Vu
Crosby, Stills, Nash, and Young

"Science!"
She Blinded Me With Science

Thomas Dolby

For Barb

All my love,
all my life

Acknowledgments

To all who prayed it through:

My wife Barb, my sons Mike and Josh, my daughter-in-law Julie and my grandson Caleb

Mitch and Judy Paris

Jack and Sharon Schrudder

fellow authors James Scott Bell and Karen Kingsbury

and to those who believed:

Tom and Karen Couch
Tom and Karen Howard
Mike and Tania Davis
Bill and Brenda Carr
Odell and Bonnie Brown
Fred and Patty Dye
and Pastor Sam Luke and the staff and members of Princeton Pike Church of God in Hamilton, Ohio

...the dream lives.

PROLOGUE

With a shriek of tortured metal another bullet went slashing past my face, tumbling end-for-end by the sound of it. Ricochet.

Lord, that was close.

I tucked myself further back into the dinky little cubbyhole at the end of the hall, and not for the first time in the last ten minutes I cursed my inability to say no to pie. No doubt about it, if I got out of this alive, I was going to buy a Stairmaster. Maybe two. In circumstances like these, inches could mean death. A saner man would have known that already.

I checked my piece again. Still empty. I know it's weird, but six rounds just don't seem to last as long as they used to. I lay the blame for that squarely at the feet of Rosie O'Donnell.

It sure would have been sweet for a bullet fairy to come flitting in, Disney-like, to bring me some fresh ammo, but even that wouldn't help much. Smith and Wesson make a dandy .38, but right now I needed a rocket launcher.

Running gun battles with nameless men who wish to do me harm is a game for fools. You think I would have learned that lesson back in the war. Stuff like that should be left to guys like James Bond. He's used to it; I'm not.

No, I was just a somewhat honest PI trying to do a job, and look where it got me.

"Mr. Box?"

Boneless Chuck again. Him and that pukey, reedy voice of his. I don't care if he *HAD* been born that way, it didn't make me feel sorry for him one bit, though I don't suppose he cared. Boneless liked his voice, I knew. He liked it a whole lot as a matter of fact. In his heart of hearts--assuming he possessed one--I think that crazy genetic freak truly believed he sounded like a white Johnny Mathis. To me he wheezed like a man with a twig lodged in his larynx.

"Earth to Mr. Box. Hello?" Boneless sounded awfully relaxed, reedy voice or not. He and his boys were nicely ensconced at the other end of the hall, safe from anything short of a tactical nuke. Safe enough from no-bullets me, at any rate.

"Come on, speak up," Boneless rasped. "That last one was close, I'll admit, but you're still alive and with us. For the moment." Simpering yahoo. I hated this guy.

His voice became expansive and mocking. "So as the thumpers like to proclaim in their pear-shaped tones, come, let us reason together. And Mr. Box, here's some reasoning, if you can handle it. I *believe* you're completely out of ammunition, and have been for the last few minutes. I haven't rushed you or had one of my men roll a hand grenade down your way only because you have something of mine, and I wish it back unharmed. You, on the other hand are what we in the trade call a useless eater." Boneless sighed companionably. "So let's take a moment for itemization. You're hurt. You're scared. And you and I both know there's no rescue coming, not in this lifetime. There's only one way out of this hallway. That's towards me." Boneless then laughed, "And that'll make a feller pucker, as your kinfolk might put it.

"Now let me really brighten your day and tell you something I'll bet you aren't aware of. Listen. Do you hear it? A sad and muffled sort of crying?" He whispered the name. *"Felicity."*

What? But she was safe! How in the-?

"Yes, I have her," Boneless murmured. "Life is just plain old chock full of surprises, isn't it? She was caught before she even made it to Level Five. Poor kid. She's standing with me now, shaking like she has the plague. I've talked things over with her. She's really hoping you'll make the right choice and not only save your life, but hers too." His voice brightened. "Say, I would imagine old Felicity has a few words she'd like to say to you, if you'd care to chance peeping your head out for a quick look."

This was lame. I didn't believe it, not for a second.

"Oh, but something in my knower tells me you don't believe me, Mr. Box," Boneless said. "Or may I call you Joe?"

Call me anything you like, jerk. And take your time about it. You'll be calling for your mother when I park a round in your chest. Then my swaggering bravado sank like a brick as I once again remembered I was out of ammo.

And was this man psychic or what? No, Boneless Chuck was worse than psychic. A lot worse.

I heard the smile in his voice as he continued, "I feel we've become fast friends, Joe, but I don't think your ego could take the strain of knowing you've failed, yet again. Story of your life."

Ego. Right. He was a good one to talk.

"But I'll prove I'm telling the truth," Boneless said. "I've heard tell your friend is a marvelous singer, really something special." His voice faded slightly as he turned to her. "Felicity, would you sing for Joe? Make it something...pretty."

There was pause, and then whatever Boneless did to Felicity next caused her to erupt with a shriek that nearly froze my blood. The note climbed straight up into the stratosphere, and then some. It was an awful sound: terrified, pain-filled, lost and alone; the agonized entreaty of someone completely bereft of comfort or hope; the heart-rending wail of a little kid floating in the dark in a flooded basement while snakes dropped in through the broken windows, and mommy's not coming back, ever.

I've heard a lot of horrifying things in my nearly fifty years on this planet, combat included, but nothing like that. I wouldn't have thought it possible that a human throat could make such a sound.

And with that scream I vowed again that somehow, someway, Granny Box's wayward boy was not going to end his life in this lousy corridor. Not today.

Not until Boneless and I had an accounting.

Because you know what they say about payback. And payback dictated that I would make sure before Boneless killed me I had blood enough and nerve enough and hate enough left to send that smirking maniac screaming straight to the harp farm.

No doubt about it, Boneless was *going* to die.

I heard him clapping his hands appreciatively as the young girl wept. "That was lovely, Felicity, really sweet. But what do you say? Let's try it once more, this time with *feeling."*

Felicity moaned her horror and denial, "No no no PLEASE God", then I heard the sound of something tightening around her throat. She began to sob and gag, and my fingers twitched in impotent fury.

God help me, what was I going to do?

Only one other time in my life had I felt so helpless, and that had been the day I was walking point on a trail in the Ia Drang valley, not watching, and had tripped that Bouncing Betty.

I felt now like I had then: all I could do was watch drymouthed as the thing leaped into the air and blew the universe apart. But that was then. *Surely* I had some options...

Then I looked up, drawing a breath, and noticed something.

The twin industrial fluorescent lights running the hall were long, extremely so, spanning nearly twenty feet, but were spaced only three inches apart. And my .38 had a four inch barrel and weighed in at nearly two pounds...

Inspiration doesn't strike me often; when it does, it usually disguises itself as madness.

Okay, Boneless. See what you do with this.

I hefted my gun in my hand, closed my eyes, and with a quick muttered prayer to the God of the desperate, I hurled the thing straight up into those lights.

There was a crash and a flash. The hallway was instantly plunged into darkness.

And howling what I hoped was a feral war cry I barreled straight at Boneless and his troops, hands up like claws, screaming incoherently all the way.

My plan's simplicity was trumped only by its stupidity: I couldn't see a thing, but then neither could they. The idea I had was that the sheer terror of my maniacal shrieks would strike panic into their cowardly, weaselly hearts and send them all scattering like so many field mice before a goshawk. Then I would scoop Felicity up and somehow we could both beat feet to safety. As I said, not a world-class plan, but it was all I had. The devil was calling this dance.

And shazam, as Gomer would say---it didn't work.

As I charged the line the blackness around me exploded into brilliant, deafening balls of light and sound. Boneless's men not only hadn't run, but they opened up on me in a deadly fusillade.

I really shouldn't have been surprised. My nemesis had told me earlier in the evening, though it seemed like a million years ago now, that the security forces under him were made up of former SEALS, ex-Delta Team guys, and Russian Spetznatz troops who had whiled away their misspent youth terrorizing Afghan villagers. Mercs all. No wonder they hadn't run.

But I was committed now--like I should have been when I first agreed to this job--so I just kept running towards them, juking and jiving this way and that, bellowing a rebel yell like one of Bobby Lee's finest boys in butternut brown, as I skittered right down the pipe.

God almighty, how did I ever get myself into this mess?

Oh yeah, I remember...

Chapter 1

Mr. Yee/Lee gazed owlishly at me over the tops of his spectacles, but I wasn't about to be rushed. It isn't every day a man changes his business cards; I wanted these to be perfect.

He smiled, "This one, vetty nice," and pushed one across the desk towards me. It had a picture of Sherlock Holmes smoking a pipe on it, with room for my name and phone number. Nice, simple, and understated, but a bit stiff for this transplanted hilljack.

I shook my head, and he picked up another. "Next cahd also vetty nice. Eyeball nice and big."

Now we were getting somewhere. This one sported a large oversized eyeball--private eye, get it?--but still had plenty of room left for my name, number, and even a motto. The only problem was, I think Pinkerton's had already patented something like this a hundred years ago. Nuts. I shook my head again. "Closer, Mr. Yee, but-"

"Lee."

"Huh?" Here we go again.

"The name is Lee."

"Okay."

We've been having this same conversation for the last six years. Mr.Yee/Lee runs a printshop right below my office, and has been supplying me with my cards ever since I had taken this space. Our building is actually an old apartment house that someone had turned into offices way back when Carrie Nation was still busting up Kelsey's saloon...and sometimes Kelsey. Rumor had it that William Howard Taft had kept a mistress here back in his heyday,but you couldn't prove it by me. The building boasts four tenants: The Allenby Insurance Agency, Whizzer Jokes and Novelty, Pronto Printing, and Box Investigations, starring me, Joe Box.

The Box Investigations name...perhaps that was the reason things had gotten a bit draggy of late. You can't believe how many people thought I was with a trucking company. Either that or Customs.

The problem was, I liked the name Box. It was a good old family name, a Southern name, a name that had never known dishonor, as General Nate Forrest might have put it. That name had stood strong during the War of Northern Aggression, or, as my

Granny used to call it, the Late Unpleasantness. You might know it as the Civil War. You would be wrong.

But back to the problem with Mr. Yee/Lee. In my opinion he ran one of the finest printshops in the city--which in my case translated into good and cheap--and his delivery was fast. The thing is, his was a cash-only business, no checks or credit cards (something fishy there, but none of my beeswax, another Granny-ism), his hours were strange, stranger than mine, even, and I think he was a closet communist. But that wasn't the best: to top it all off, Mr. Yee/Lee sported one of the most terrific hairlips I had ever seen.

So giving him cash when it came time to redo my cards wasn't a problem, but understanding him sure was. And the most maddening thing was he kept changing what I thought was his last name. Maybe to him it was funny. Maybe he believed he was a stitch. Maybe he thought he was really giving this imperialist yellow running dog what-for. Anyway.

"Mr. Lee, what I'm looking for is-"

"Yee."

"Hah?"

"The name is Yee."

I cleared my throat and leaned back in my creaky old chair. "Ohhh...kay. See, what I'm looking for is something with some pizzazz."

"What is...pizzazz?"

"You know. Pizzazz. A grabber. How's this sound?" I leaned forward excitedly, my fingers forming a rectangle. "A light gray card stock. The name Box Investigations in big block letters at the top. My name and phone at the bottom. And right in the middle...a smoking machine gun."

A pause. "Machine gun?"

I rubbed my hands together. I was really seeing it now. "Yeah, an old Thompson, but with a round magazine. One like Elliot Ness had."

"Mistah Box..."

"Sure! The Untouchables, a great old show. Robert Stack, Walter Winchell. Didn't you watch The Untouchables as a kid?"

"No. We were not allowed to view such things."

"We did. We all loved it, Granny and my dad and me. Anyway, that's what I want." I scooted my chair closer. "And could you maybe take a laser and drill some tiny holes in a jagged pattern across it, so that the light shows through? Like Al Capone had just shot back?" I grinned. "I'll bet something like that would make my clients feel they were getting a tough guy, somebody who could really take it. You know, value for their dollar."

"Mistah Box." Mr. Yee/Lee's tone was infinitely patient, and he tapped the Sherlock Holmes one with his finger. "Whom do you wish to attract? Gangstahs oh nice people?"

I saw his point...I guess. We dickered around for a few more minutes on the price and details, then he stood.

"I will have them foh you in three days." He gathered up his samples and left.

"Thanks, Mr. Yee," I called out to him as he started down the back stairs. "And come on up anytime. Don't be a stranger."

He was already on the landing. "Lee."

****

It was nearly an hour later that my phone rang, startling me so badly I almost knocked over the house of cards I was building on my desk. That would have really ticked me off, because I was doing it the hard way, using pinochle cards, and those babies are *slick.*

Wait a minute. Before you get the wrong impression about me, I'd better clarify something: I may have been in a business slump right about that time, but it had nothing to do with my skills as an investigator. *Au contraire,* as the snail-eaters say. It was because I was good at my work that I found myself with a silent phone and too much time on my hands.

My problem had begun simply enough: three months ago I had been approached by a distraught orthodontist who said he was badly in need of help. My middle name, I told him. Well, it isn't really. It's really Jebstuart--yes, spelled just that way--but that's another story.

Anyway, the doctor told me he had only come to me because he had started at the top of the Yellow Pages listings of private investigators and the phone at the first listing, Ace Detective, had kept ringing without anyone ever picking up.

Ace Detective, Billy Barnicke... I know Billy; we've been friendly competitors for a couple of years now. As a matter of fact, Billy's been after me for a while to join agencies. He says the alliteration in the names alone--Barnicke and Box--would be enough to reel 'em in, but I don't know.

The reason Billy's phone kept ringing was I knew he was in the Caymans at the time, betting--and losing--the five grand he had won in a lucky Ohio Lotto drawing last week just as fast as he humanly could. Knowing Billy's luck at the tables, that would take him less than a day...probably less than five hours, truth be told, and then he would happily crawl into a bottle for the rest of the week. But who was I to clue the doctor in on that?

The doctor went on to tell me that since I was the next agency listed, I was the next one he called. He seemed to feel an inordinate need to go out of his way to make it clear that I was not his first choice. Blunt enough, but I'm a big boy. Plus I needed the money. I told him to please proceed.

The doctor suspected that his wife, who was a secretary at a real estate office in Blue Ash, was having an affair, but he needed proof, such proof as would consist of pictures and a journal of times, places, dates, the usual. Classic.

He also felt compelled to tell me his wife had kept her maiden name. Odd, but not uncommon. What was odder was he said that in a fit of pique after their last fight he had moved out and taken an apartment in town. Rather wimpy on his part, I thought, but I try not to judge my clients, at least until the check clears.

I gave him my rates--three hundred per day, plus expenses, with a thousand dollar retainer--and he never blinked. I wasn't gouging him; that's standard anymore. I told him if the job takes less than a week I'll refund the difference, if it takes longer I'll ask for more; seems to work. He agreed and wrote me a check.

The job itself was a snap; within three days I had all the proof the good doctor would need. It was childishly simple, and that in itself should have warned me. Not to put too fine a point on it, but it was almost as if Mrs. Orthodontist and her paramour had never even heard the word 'discretion.' They bar-hopped, rode in cabs, took in shows, visited the Newport Aquarium, gawped at the Cincinnati Art Museum, and so on. She even stayed at his house. All in all, they seemed to be having a fine old time of it. And that's when my internal radar started flashing Code Blue. I mean, insouciance was one thing, but these two really, truly could have cared less who saw them. Like a dark centipede a thought began crawling its way up between my shoulder blades and planted itself firmly in my skull. I know I'm not the brightest crayon in the box, but even I had finally come to realize Something Was Not Right

Here. It still galls me to think somebody sharper than I am probably would have figured it out sooner.

So I called the doctor, who happened to be on the links that day--Tanglewood was his club--and asked him a simple question: what's the date of your wedding anniversary? Why? he asked me, his tone just a bit snotty. A good sleuth must have good information, I replied. There was a pause, and then he told me the date was September 12, 1987. Thanks very much, Doctor.

Then I called his wife at her office. I told her I was with Bride's Magazine--just a teeny fib--and said we were taking a survey for a future issue. What was her anniversary? May 15, 1989, the lady replied. And with no hesitation at all. Thanks very much I said again, then I called my client back on his cell.

"Doctor, that last bit of info helped. The case is finished."

"Already?" he asked. "Three days, that was fast work. Say, do I get any kind of a refund? I remember you mentioned that."

"We'll talk about it. Can I meet you right away?"

"Now? I'm just lining up a putt on the 17th hole."

"I'll meet you at the clubhouse. Say forty-five minutes?"

He sighed. "I suppose. This really can't wait until tonight?"

"No, Doctor," I told him. "It really can't."

So forty-five minutes later I found myself pulling up the long sloping drive of the Tanglewood Country Club. Cincinnati has a lot of really nice golf courses, and Tanglewood is one of the toniest. Spotless landscaping, greens that go for miles, award-winning clubhouse and tennis courts, the works. A really gorgeous place.

They wouldn't have taken me in as a member on a bet. I believe there's an unwritten rule there excluding people born south of the Ohio river from ever being asked in. Unprovable I know, but still a good hunch. Also it cost something like fifty thousand dollars to join, then ten thousand dollars a year dues after that. In addition, you have to be recommended by a member, then voted in. All this was vouchsafed to me by a former Tanglewoodian who had lost his shirt in Japanese tech stocks, of all things, and was summarily booted out on his keister when he couldn't come up with the scratch for his dues. When it comes to money, the rich don't horse around. But as I said, the place was rather nice, in a *Stepford Wives-Westworld* sort of way.

I pulled my 1968 Mercury Cougar--425 cubic-inch big-block Hemi, Holly carb, sport suspension, and Glasspacks that made it sound like a Tyrannosaurus in heat--into the lot, expertly parking it right between this year's Beemer and a Range Rover so new it still had those little black sticky-out things coming off the tires.

Call me a cynic, but I would bet the statistical chances of that Rover ever coming near a mud puddle, much less going off-road, were about the same as me waking up to find Sigourney Weaver singing in my shower.

I had just gotten out and was pocketing my keys when a blond, sandy-haired android, er, lot guy nervously trotted over and asked if he could help me. That's what he asked me, but his tone had said something entirely different.

I looked at the guy as if he were simple. "No, you can't help me, son, but thanks for asking. As you can see, I managed to park my nasty old car without scraping those on either side of it. Plus I've already put my keys in my pocket without once having to read the directions, and I've been walking since I was a year old, believe it or not. I'm not here to gawk, visit, picket, or even, God forbid, become a member. But I do have legitimate business here, none of which concerns you, so why don't you trundle yourself on back into your hut and power-down or recharge your dilithium crystals or whatever it is you do and let me get to it?"

Maybe I was a bit nasty with the kid--okay, more than a bit--but I didn't appreciate the way he had sneered at both me and the Green Goddess, as I call my sweet old ride, when I had pulled up. Too bad. Let him deal with the riff-raff occasionally. It builds character twelve ways, like Wonder Bread.

I had been lied to by the man I was here to meet, and that just isn't done with me...my fib notwithstanding. As Granny used to say, "There's only two things in this world I can't abide: a liar and a cheat." The good doctor was at least one, and maybe both; I knew that now. I was ticked and I wanted some answers.

I breezed on into the clubhouse, right past a maitre d' with a lousy Boston Blackie mustache, and stopped when I located the orthodontist's table. He and the rest of his foursome were seated dead-center in front of the immense plate-glass window overlooking the fairway (figures) and my client had positioned himself so that the sun was streaming through it and landing on him, the better to show off his George Hamilton tan and TV-game-show-host teeth (figures again). They were laughing over a joke one of them had just told when the doctor looked over and spotted me. He frowned in annoyance as I strolled up to them.

And as he put his gin rickey glass down on the table I noticed just the slightest trembling in his hand.

Mercy. A bit nervous are we?

"Good afternoon," I smiled ingratiatingly. "How was the game?"

"Fine," the doctor muttered. He picked his glass back up and took a healthy pull. No doubt about it, the boy was rattled.

But I remained courteous. "I have that information we spoke about, Doctor. If you gentlemen would excuse us?"

There was a lot of hrumph-hrumphing and certainly, certainlies from his buds as I took the doctor by the elbow and escorted him outside into the warm spring sunshine. You'd have to have looked pretty closely to notice I was squeezing the life out of his arm.

I must say, though, I have to give the devil his due: the doctor was still game, grinning like a Chihuahua at passing acquaintances even though we both knew his game was finished.

"Well, Mr. Box?" The man jerked his elbow once before I released it. We found ourselves standing in the shade under a spreading chestnut tree, and not a village smithy to be seen for miles. "What is it that's so important that it couldn't wait until this evening?"

"Simple," I said. "We're meeting here now because I think that tonight could be when you might try to cause Mrs. Stanton harm."

The doctor blanched, but said nothing.

"That is her name, isn't it?" I went on. "And not her maiden name, either. Stanton is her married name. As a matter of fact, she's married to that pleasant-looking fella I've been tailing the past three days. Stop me if any of this is news to you."

When the doctor finally found his voice, it was low and in a whisper. "How did you know?"

"Because I'm an investigator, dimwit." My patience with this man was running low. Nobody likes to be made a fool of, me included. "It's what I do. This whole thing sounded weird right from the get-go with that 'maiden name' horse pucky. And she and the mister just seemed entirely too unconcerned to wonder if their goings-on were being noticed. I've heard of sexual freedom and all, but this was nuts. I guess the capper came when I discovered that you and she gave two entirely different dates for your wedding anniversary." I glared at him. "So what gives, hoss?"

The doctor licked his lips nervously like a salamander for a moment, then he spoke. "Franklin Stanton is my cousin. He and I had both dated Marian off and on ever since college. When she picked him to marry, I was heartbroken, although I kept a good face about it. But three weeks ago I found out from Franklin she was due to come into some inheritance money soon. I'd had him over for drinks, and he was a bit in his cups;otherwise I don't think he would ever have let it slip. He also let me know there was going to be quite a bit coming, enough to make sure that he and Marian were going to be set for life. And this news came to me just as I was coming off the worst year my practice has ever suffered. There had been sexual accusations from some of my female patients-"

"Hold it." This last made no sense. A few years ago a dentist here had gotten into some deep trouble over this very thing. Since then, the media have gone out of their way to uncover stories just like this. So how come I hadn't heard a peep on the news about our good doctor and his restless hands? "You're telling me more than I need to know. I just want to understand where I come into this."

The doctor seemed to be recovering a bit of his frostiness. "It's really very simple, Mr. Box. I needed to ascertain Franklin's and Marian's patterns so when the time was right I could have my cousin...handled."

"Handled?" Good grief. I felt like the winner in a Who's The World's Biggest Idiot contest. "So my job was to give you enough information to have him KILLED?"

"Hardly killed." Doctor Squeezeum was becoming more sure of himself every second. This was not good. "Merely roughed up a bit. I understand such men can be found relatively inexpensively."

"The end result being what, pray tell?'

The doctor smiled. "The end result being that the weeks Franklin was recuperating in a hospital were weeks I could woo Marian back into my camp, and then her fortune would be mine."

I shook my head. "My God. How utterly tawdry."

A digression: when I was still a rookie back on the force my partner and mentor there--cops call them rabbis--was a rough-cut sergeant named Mulrooney. That canny old Irishman, who has long since retired to Florida, had told me many things my first year in uniform that helped me out, but none so important as his observation that all human wickedness could be traced back to the desire for three things: money, sex, or power. It seemed that this bird had a need for all three.

The doctor smirked, "Tawdry? Perhaps you're right." He seemed awfully amused, and my blood pressure shot up another fifteen points. "At any rate, Mr. Box, I'll expect a full written report delivered to me no later than tomorrow afternoon."

"You have got to be kidding." This guy had more brass than a sailboat. "I'm supposed to furnish you with the info to have some poor schlump beaten into gravy just so you can get next to his wife and her money? I don't think so." Now it was my turn to smile. "Matter of fact, Doctor, my next order of business will be to tell this whole sordid story to the cops. They're gonna love it."

He sucked in a breath. "I wouldn't."

"Well, bucko, you just stand there and watch me." I turned to go and suddenly a gun was in his hand, pointing straight at my heart. How did he do *that?* Who was this guy, Matt Dillon?

"You'd better stand quite still." His voice was low and even.

"What, you're gonna shoot me?" I couldn't believe this. "Here? Right next to the eighteenth green, in front of God and everybody?"

The look in the doctor's eyes was glazed. "F. Scott Fitzgerald said it best: 'The rich are different.'"

I shook my head. "Not that different. Who knows what a busboy might see?"

"And who knows what you might have done to provoke me? I am, after all, a member in good standing here. You're just a...guest."

He made it sound like pool slime. "So now what?"

"So now I will accompany you to your office, where you will turn over all the notes and photographs you have concerning this."

"Or?" I wasn't sure I wanted to hear the answer.

"Or I shoot you here, now, and by the time the police arrive I will have ten members swearing you were threatening me. I took the only avenue available. You see, Mr. Box," the doctor murmured, "not only am I a well-respected pillar of the community, my father is the county commissioner."

Caramba. No wonder I had thought his name sounded familiar; guess old Dad had also bought him immunity from the media. But I'd grown tired of Doctor Feelgood and his ways. Time to end this. So before he could draw a breath to give me another taunt, I snapped the fingers on my left hand twice, drawing his glance. Then I lanced my right foot up and kicked him square in the throat. The doctor gasped once and dropped like he'd been poleaxed.

This also deserves some clarification. When I had served in Vietnam I had come into contact with many colorful characters, none more so than Sergeant Peter Smithers. Peter was a Marine Force Recon instructor in the middle of his third tour, and on leave in Saigon. I was on leave too, even though I wasn't due for R and R yet; I was a green Army rifleman, PFC, and had only been in-country four months. But I had just come off a horrendous three-week patrol, searching for a VC we called Sammy the Sniper, and had witnessed something I shouldn't have; my Saigon leave was a present from some grateful higher-ups for keeping my mouth shut. More on that later. Maybe.

Anyway, I was packing too much money and not enough sense when I met Peter. We had both found ourselves in an off-limits bar--badly misnamed The Crystal Sparrow, a real bucket of blood just off Bring Cash Alley--and started the evening buying each other drinks. We had begun by toasting one another's respective branches of service, good health, and revered ancestors, here and gone, then lifted a glass or three to hot lead, cold steel, absent friends, good music, Ernest Tubb, Patsy Cline, Hank and Buddy and Jimi and Janis, the good that had died too young, lousy CO's, popinjay generals, horrific mothers-in-law (being single at the time, I had to take Peter's word on that one), and then moved weepingly on into who was the more swell fella, by God Peter, you are, I mean it, man, no I'm not, Joe, YOU are, becoming progressively more raucous and drawing stares and muttered oaths from the patrons. It's true, cussing sounds the same the world over. By then we blearily realized we were the only two Americans in the place; I found out later that even the MPs gave the place a wide berth. And for good reason: the fight we proceeded to mix up with the Crystal Sparrow's aforesaid patrons was so noteworthy it not only made the Saigon dailies, but Stars and Stripes as well.

Anyway, for some reason the sergeant had taken a shine to me, and I spent my whole week of leave--which we enjoyed in a roasting, airless jail cell, courtesy of the Saigon PD, while our respective CO's palavered with them over our fate--learning things from the man that I had not been taught in basic.

Including that little move there.

While I bent down and removed the .32 from the doctor's nerveless fingers, he clawed at his throat, gasping like someone with sawdust packed in their gullet. I noticed a few people beginning to look our way, but nobody made a move towards us. Wonder why.

I squatted down next to him. "I know it hurts, but believe me, nothing permanent has been damaged. For now. What I'd suggest is that you go home, wrap a warm towel around your throat, and reconsider your stupid plan. And don't let me catch you around my office, Doctor, or the next time I crush your voicebox."

I stood to go, and he finally managed to croak something at me. I was expecting him to say anything but what he did. "What about my refund?"

I shook my head as I walked away. "Pound sand, yankee."

****

So that explains why I was unemployed. As soon as the good doctor recovered, he started pulling some strings, and when he did my business began to dry up. I don't suppose it helped that I had gone to Mulrooney's son, who was also a cop, a vice squad detective as a matter of fact, and told him what my client had in mind for Franklin Stanton.

Whatever Mulrooney Junior had done and however he had done it, the doctor and his scheme made the news. Finally. I guess being the son of the county commissioner can only take you so far. But I found out the rich and mighty really do have long arms to match their long memories; thus my new career as a house-card builder.

And now here my phone was ringing again. Hallelujah. If I'd had been half as smart as I was desperate for work, I would have ripped the plug from the wall.

Chapter 2

But I picked it up anyway; my cable bill was due, and I just can't go long without the Animal Planet channel. "Good afternoon, Box Investigations."

The voice was a woman's. "Please hold for Mr. Taylor."

I hung up.

If Mr. Taylor, whoever he was, couldn't dial his own phone, he wasn't someone I wanted to talk to. But I'd met this type before, so I folded my hands under my chin, stared at the phone, and waited. Twenty seconds later, it rang again, and I picked up. "Good afternoon, Box Investigations."

"PLEASE hold for Mr. Taylor." She sounded a bit miffed at me.

I hung up again.

I leaned back in my chair and stared at the stain on the ceiling. It had started growing four months ago, just when the spring rains had begun in earnest. When I had first moved in a few years back it was only a brownish patch, maybe three inches across, and had looked a little like the island of Malta. But after that frog-strangler we had gotten last month it had started spreading; I guess something in the shingles on the roof had let go.

I had been following the stain's progress like a proud papa these past couple of weeks as it had kept constantly changing and shifting, like a really slow, nasty kaleidoscope. Now it was a foot across and looked a bit like Tom Brokaw having a gas attack.

The phone rang again. This time I let it go four times before I answered. "I can keep this up as long as you want."

"Who is this?" The guy was breathing like a steam engine and sounded mighty belligerent. "Is this Box Investigations?"

"Yep. Joe Box, at your service."

"Why did you hang up twice on my secretary?"

"Because she ragged me off twice with that 'please hold for Mr. Taylor' stuff." I started fooling with a dummy hand grenade I keep on my desk. "What's the matter, can't you dial your own friggin' phone?"

There was a pause of a few seconds, while I presumed the caller was composing himself; my wife Linda used to say I had that effect on people.

"Mr. Box," the man said then, "I apologize."

Son of a buck. He sounded like he meant it.

"My name is Michael Taylor," he went on. "I'm R & D director at Castle Industries, here in town. I've been under some stress lately, and I'm hoping you can help me."

"Maybe I can," I said. "What's R & D?" (Just kidding).

"Research and development." He sounded like he was breathing easier now. "I'm what you might call an idea guy."

"Is that right? Well, beats dog-catchin', as my Granny used to say."

"The reason for my call is that I saw you on the news last month when you testified about that stalking-doctor case. Your integrity impressed me. I didn't have need of your services then, but I sure do now."

"I'll be happy to help you if I can, Mr. Taylor," I said. "Why don't you stop by my office here in a little bit and we'll see?"

He agreed and said he could meet me in an hour. I thanked him, gave him directions, and hung up the phone. Then I left to go eat a sandwich at the deli up the street, figuring to bring my dessert back with me. When I returned Taylor was standing at my office door, waiting. It had only been forty minutes since we had spoken. Maybe this man really did need some help.

"Mr. Taylor?" I asked him. He nodded and smiled, and I shifted my dessert--pie again--and iced tea to my left hand and held out my right. "Joe Box." We shook and I fished my keys out and opened the door. "Please, won't you come on in?"

"Thanks."

We both walked in and I surreptitiously watched him while I put my food on my desk. This is always an interesting time, observing how a prospective client gazes around my office. All the years I've been in this business I've found something repeatedly fascinating: how a person views my workplace quite often determines how well we're going to get along. It's not a hard and fast rule, mind you, but it works more often than not. Roughly, I've placed them into three categories: Say-nothings, Nodders, and Thin-lips. Say-nothings is pretty self-explanatory: these types could care less whether we're meeting in a dark-leather-and-plush-carpet suite on the fortieth floor of the Carew Tower or the steam room at the Y; they're all business, God bless 'em, and are my kinda folks.

Nodders are a bit harder to read. You aren't sure right off the bat if they're thinking, "Unpretentious office, guy must be a straight-shooter", or "My God, look at this place, I should have brought a flea bomb." You just have to let them talk for awhile to see which way they're leaning.

And then we come to Thin-lips. Ah, Thin-lips...you know the type. They come in and stare around, gauging, measuring, and then the eyebrows lower, the shoulders tighten, and the lips...grow thin. Appearance is all-important to these people, and I just know from the start we aren't going to get along. It's at this point I usually say something to discourage them from wanting to do business with me, something on the order of, "I hope I can do you some good, Mr. Jones. You're the first client I've had since I've gotten out of prison." A swirl of air and they're gone.

So using these categories may be one reason why I haven't dressed the place up more; my office seems to work fine as my very own client barometer.

But Michael Taylor threw me. As I sat behind my desk and pushed my food to the side, I motioned for him to take the visitor's chair across from me. Taylor did, and then he began looking around the room, giving it the fish-eye. His mouth grew taut.

Here it comes, I thought. I was about to give him a variation on the line about prison when suddenly the man relaxed and smiled.

"Mr. Box," Taylor said, "this place is a dump. But I have the feeling that in spite of having such a ratty office, you must be an honest man." Taylor laughed at his own joke, such as it was.

And then the oddest thing happened.

I can't explain it, but the air surrounding me abruptly seemed to crystallize. A weird fluttering, almost like the wings of a moth, began to vibrate around the walls of my heart.

And unbidden, an icy dread gripped me...and didn't let go.

Like the sulphurous blackstrap molasses I remembered as a kid, a dark conviction slowly started pouring into me, a conviction that this laughing man was bringing something big into my life, something more than a problem to be solved or a situation to be handled. A lot more.

Something monstrous.

In an unknown, unforeseen way I suddenly knew that whatever Michael Taylor was about to involve me in was going to escalate uncontrolled into a nightmare neither of us could have conceived, something awful, and that I simply had no choice in the matter. None at all. Even if I refused the case, it wouldn't vary a thing. Events had shifted into motion that could no more be changed than I could alter the rotation of the earth.

My Granny used to say that all the Box clan was fey, in one

degree or another. I never really knew what fey meant, and as a kid I thought maybe it meant sissified. But Granny had explained to me one day that fey meant foreknowledge. As far back as she or anyone could remember, she said, a Box would sometimes know beforehand what was going to happen. Not psychic exactly, and nothing definite, but rather a feeling.

For instance, she once told me a story about my Uncle Jimmie Ray, that as a little boy of eight he had inexplicably grown morose during a Saturday afternoon birthday party at a friend's farm. Nothing could console him. The cake went bitter in his mouth, she said, and the milk turned sour. A terrible sadness had gripped him, the worst part being he knew it was a sadness that couldn't be reversed and had to be faced. Jimmie Ray went home sobbing, and the very next day a Western Union kid on a bicycle wheeled up to that farm and told the old man that his only son had been killed during a fierce battle on some island called Iwo Jima.

And here it had happened to me. I was forty-eight years old, a world-weary, card-carrying cynic, and had never experienced anything even close to what Granny had described.

Until now.

But here was the strangest part. Even though I knew, beyond anything stone-cold reason could have told me otherwise, that I was about to be plunged headlong into a dark vortex, an arena of madness more demonic than anything I could ever have imagined on my worst day in Vietnam...in the end it was all going to turn out okay.

That even if I were to die in this, *die* being the operative word, in some strange way that would be all right too. In spite of my death--or maybe even because of it--things were going to work out fine.

Joe, I thought to myself with a shudder, you are about to embark on one whale of a ride.

Chapter 3

"Are you all right?" Taylor was looking at me with some alarm. If the thoughts caroming across my brainpan had transmitted themselves to my face, I couldn't say I blamed him.

"Yeah," I croaked. I cleared my throat and tried it again. "Yes." I smiled at him wanly. "My Granny might have said that I had a sudden attack of the vapors. But I'm fine now."

And I was; the tickling fingers of my feeling were beginning to withdraw themselves from my mind. I figured it would be fine with me if they never came back; that was Granny's world, not mine.

"Mr. Box, I-"

"Mr. Taylor," I interrupted, more gruffly than I had intended, "I don't mean to appear rude, but could I ask you to please cut to the chase and tell me why you're here?"

For a second I thought the man was going to take umbrage with me, but then he smiled. "Okay, fair enough." Taylor clasped his hands on his knee, and I noticed for the first time how big his hands were. The wrists, the hands themselves, the fingers, the knuckles, all seemed to belong to a much larger man. Taylor himself appeared to be a rather tightly-constructed gent all over, as if he spent an inordinate amount of time in the gym. I wondered if being an idea guy generated a lot of stress.

Taylor leaned forward and looked me square in the eye. "Mr. Box," he said, "I'm about to ask you what you may think at first is an impertinent question. But believe me, there's a reason for me asking." His gaze never wavered. "Are you a spiritual man?"

Holy smokes. After my little visit into the *Twilight Zone* a few moments ago Taylor couldn't have gotten me more uncomfortable if he had tried. I cleared my throat again. "Well-"

"Please, Mr. Box." Taylor seemed deadly earnest. "No dissembling. I need you to answer me truthfully." I was rather pleased that he figured I knew what 'dissembling' meant...which in fact I did. But I had to gather my thoughts for a moment before I spoke.

"Well," I said again, "I was raised Baptist and went to church with my Granny as a kid-"

"Mr. Box." Taylor's eyes were still drilling me like a laser. "I'm not asking about then. I'm asking about now."

"Then I would have to say the answer is no," I told him evenly.

"Does that make a difference?"

"It might. It just might." Sudden pain filled Taylor's face. He leaned forward even further and placed both his hands flat on my desk. "My daughter is missing."

This apparent non-sequeter threw me for a second, while I processed what he had just said. Spirituality, missing daughter...now I knew what Taylor wanted: he must have figured the kid had gone and joined a cult. And I began to see my fee flying out the window. Finding missing kids is not my strong suit, and that goes double when they join themselves to cults. I had been pulled into these searches three times in the past, and had struck out exactly three times. In every case the kid was perfectly happy sitting at the feet of Swami Rubadub or whoever, and had strongly resented my efforts to make them see the light, as it were. Unless the person in question was a minor, the cards I held were few.

Plus there was always the factor of trying to consider what kind of home life the kid was running away from. The monsters weren't all out there, past experience had told me. Sometimes the monster was called dad.

"Mr. Taylor," I told him, "I'm sorry, but I'm not so sure that I can give you any help with this."

"What?" There was just the hint of panic coloring his tone. "Why not? I thought PI's did this sort of thing all the time. If it's a matter of money-"

"Money's not the issue here," I smiled. "Well it is, but not the main one. You see, I think you're confusing what I do with what's found on TV." I held up a hand to cut him off. "I know, I've seen those shows too. Some private investigator gets called in to help locate a missing person--which they invariably do, and in only an hour. But Mr. Taylor, this isn't TV. It's real life, and in real life you'll find that one man simply isn't enough for what you need done. It may sound trite, but going to the police will give you a lot better results than you would get with just me. They have the time, the resources, and the manpower, not to mention the experience."

"But I can't go to the police with this," Taylor said intently, his steel-blue eyes holding mine. "Only you have a prayer of getting her back."

Now he had me intrigued. "Okay, Mr. Taylor, I'll bite. Why is that?"

"In order to answer you I'll need to give you some background," he replied. "I'll start with this. My daughter's name is Francesca.

She's just turned eighteen." Taylor smiled a little, his heart not in it. "She's our only child, our baby, and she still lives with us. That is until she starts at UC this fall. It was Sophia who named her, after her grandmother...Sophia's, I mean. Not Francesca's. Sophia's my wife. Her family is Italian. This is killing her by inches...Sophia. And Francesca's been gone for four days. We-" Taylor suddenly stopped and dropped his face into his hands. "My God, I'm really jumbling this up, aren't I?"

"Just take your time, Mr. Taylor," I said, beginning to feel for him. Linda and I had never had kids of our own, but I had seen this pain before. "I'm listening. Can I make you some coffee?"

"No," Taylor mumbled, then he pulled his hands away from his face and stared at me. "I guess I'm kind of a mess."

"You're doing fine. So about Francesca," I prompted.

"All right." Taylor drew a breath and started again. "Our daughter has always been headstrong. Willful. Opinionated." He rushed on, "Not in any really bad way, you understand, but she has her own way of looking at things. And sometimes it caused problems between us. Her changing her name, for instance."

"She changed her name?" I interrupted.

"Yes. Well, not legally, but last year she started singing at some small teen clubs around the area, and began calling herself Felicity Smith. We figured it was just a phase, although it kind of hurt Sophia's feelings, her having named her after her grandmother and all."

"Is she any good?"

Taylor gave a wry grimace. "Not really. The raw material is there, if you know what I mean, but she needs training. Sophia and I asked her if she wanted us to help her look into getting some lessons, but she became insulted."

I smiled at him. When you're eighteen it doesn't take much to do that. Taylor went on, "She's had all the usual teenage angst: school, boyfriends, career choices, you name it. But at heart Francesca's a wonderful girl. She has a tender side that she lets few people see; as a matter of fact she's even spoken more than once of becoming a medical missionary. She hates suffering in all its forms." Taylor reached into his breast pocket and pulled something out, some kind of paper. "Which makes what my wife and I found on her desk the day she disappeared so upsetting."

He slid it across to me. It was an ad, obviously torn from the newspaper, and was for some medical testing lab out on the west side. The gist of it went like this, paraphrased: Women, if you're eighteen to twenty-five, single, in excellent health and pre-menopausal, here's a chance to do some good in the world, and get paid for it to boot. Discretion always. Screening done at our facilities, a Struble Road address, and then the phone number.

I began to give it back to him. "Sounds like a fertility clinic."

"Keep it, please," he said. "I've made copies. And you're right, it does. But the director there told me they've never heard of Francesca!"

I frowned. "You've called them?"

"Yes." Taylor's voice was anguished. "When I saw the ad I thought that this sounded just like something Francesca would do. Donating eggs to some infertile woman. But that doesn't explain her vanishing, and where in God's name she is."

I pulled a notepad over. "Maybe you'd better give me the chronology of what happened."

"All right," Taylor said again, and he began to unconsciously rub his hands together. "Francesca works at a B. Dalton not too far from us, making some spending money for fall. As I said before, she's due to start at UC then. And she always seemed like she enjoyed her job, and got along well with her co-workers. Francesca gets along with everyone, she always has..." Taylor realized he was beginning to wander again and with an effort got himself back on track. "Last Friday morning, she left earlier than normal. They were doing inventory that day, she said, and they needed her there by eight. She was supposed to be home by four that afternoon, because she and Ted were going to Armorbearers."

"Who's Ted?" I asked. "And what's Armorbearers? A club?"

Taylor gave me a tired smile. "Ted Whittaker's a friend from church. He would like to be more than a friend, I'm sure, but Francesca is popular, and really isn't ready for a steady boyfriend yet. Armorbearers is the name of the college-and-careers group there."

"At church," I nudged.

"Yes. Harvard Pike Church in Hamilton."

I was scratching notes onto the pad. "That's where you and your family live? Hamilton?"

"No," he replied. "Milford."

I looked up at him. "Long way to go to church."

"Not really." Another tired smile. "Not when it's the right church."

I let that one slide by with no comment, then said, "So four o'clock came and no Francesca?"

"That's correct. Sophia and I figured it was just Friday afternoon traffic; Milford is really starting to grow. But by five we were becoming concerned. Ted was due to pick her up at six and Francesca always likes to get a shower when she gets home before she goes back out. So I called her work and they said she had clocked out at three forty-five. We thought maybe she had car trouble, but were unable to raise her on her cell phone." Taylor's voice thickened. "Now we were really starting to become frantic. Where could she be? When Ted showed up at six we sent him right back out to see if he could spot her car on the road."

"The boy didn't have any luck?"

"None. He must have traveled the route three times and didn't spot a thing. That's when I left in our own car to see. But she was gone." Taylor drywashed his face with his hands. "By eight o'clock we contacted the Milford police and the state troopers.They said they would keep their eyes open, but that we couldn't file a missing person's report for twenty-four hours."

"They're right," I said. "And they can be the longest twenty-four hours of your life."

His voice cracked. "She could be anywhere by then!"

"I know," I said softly. "So the next day did you and your wife file the report?"

"We did." Taylor's reply was hollow. "And that's been the end of it. We've called them every day since then, but it's like... like she never was. They're good people, but..." He trailed off miserably.

"So now you're here," I said.

He swallowed hard. "And now I'm here."

"Mr. Taylor." I laid my pencil down and folded my hands in front of me. "You said a few minutes ago that I was the only one who had a prayer of finding your daughter. I'll ask again: why me?"

"You really want to know?" he asked, his tone a bit guarded. "Some people might find the answer amusing."

"Sir," I said, "I may laugh at a lot of things. But not at this."

"All right." Taylor drew a long, shuddering breath, then let it go. "God told me you're the one He's chosen to find our baby."

There was a long pause while I just stared at him. *That* I hadn't expected. What do you say to a statement like that? I was completely at a loss, but felt I had to make some kind of a reply to Taylor, if for no other reason than to disabuse him of the idea that

Joe Box was on call for God. I finally opened my mouth. "So you prayed, and God told you to call me."

Taylor simply nodded with a sad look in his eyes, as if I had, with my tone, confirmed my opinion of him. I shook my head. I had a hundred withering comebacks ready to fire at this man, but suddenly they died unsaid. They died because like a distant, forgotten whisper, I was feeling that strange otherness beginning to niggle at the outer edges of my consciousness again. Talk about an unwelcome guest. With a will I shook it off, then I cleared my throat and looked pointedly at him. "Does God speak to you on a regular basis, Mr. Taylor?"

"Yes He does." Taylor's voice was calm, and I had to hand it to him; the guy certainly didn't seem to fit the profile of your garden-variety nut. "Every day."

"Huh." I wriggled my fanny around on my chair; odd that it had never felt so uncomfortable before. "How about that." I fiddled with my pencil again, trying to get my mind to settle down. "Sir," I said then, "I'm still having a problem here. A little while ago you asked me if I was a spiritual man. And I believe I told you I'm not. So assuming what you say is true, why on earth would God have someone like me take this case?"

Even as I said the words, the weird prickling running up and down my spinal column began to increase. This bizarre business was harder to get rid of than a summer rash, and was just about as pleasant.

"I have no idea," Taylor answered. "All I know is Sophia and I have prayed harder these last four days than we've ever prayed about anything in our lives. This morning the answer came to us both."

"Answer?" I leaned back in my creaky old chair and it screeched like the demons of hell; even as I said the words I knew the reply he was going to give me. "What kind of answer?"

"Your name," Taylor said evenly. "That's all. Just your name. And for the first time in the last four days, my wife and I felt peace."

Chapter 4

The traffic was surprisingly light as I tooled on down Hamilton Avenue towards home, and I used to the time to mull over the events of the last few hours. Granny, I thought silently, wherever you are, I hope you're taking notes, because your number one grandson is in way over his head.

After that last comment Michael Taylor had given me, I was convinced the day could not have gotten any weirder; it turned out I didn't even know the half. I had simply given the man what I was sure was a superior look and told him, "An answer to your prayers, huh? I've never been that to anyone before. I'm not so sure I like it."

"Mr. Box," Taylor replied with a sad smile, "I think at this point we both know it really doesn't matter what either of us likes. The only salient question is, will you do it? Will you help us find our daughter?"

And what do you know? Even as I opened my mouth to tell him thanks, but no thanks, round yourself up another PI, I found myself simply saying instead, "Yes. I will." What was I, some kind of ventriloquist's dummy? Not likely.

"Good." Taylor didn't cry in relief or anything, just slapped both hands down hard on his thighs and nodded. "Good."

"You realize, of course," I told him in a wry voice, "you're getting damaged goods here. In the missing kid department I'm batting 0-for-three."

"That's all right," Taylor said with a smile, for once a genuine one. "You've never had God coaching you before."

I laughed, "Mr. Taylor, you're a piece of work, I'll give you that."

"Call me Mike," he grinned.

"Joe," I replied. "And Mike, I hate to sound mercenary, but..."

"But we need to talk payments and contracts, of course," he finished for me. I was glad I hadn't had to draw him a map regarding this; some of the folks that have come in here for help are either laboring under the delusion I work gratis, or that I negotiate fees. I never negotiate fees--that way I can truly give every one of my clients equal service--and while I have done a few pro bono cases in the past, right now I was up against it, and Michael Taylor's retainer check was going to spend just fine.

We spent the next few minutes going over my standard

agreement, which he said was more than satisfactory, and then he wrote me a check to cover a week's worth of work. I think the unsaid thing between us was we both knew a week would tell the tale; in seven days Francesca would either be safe at home, or she would never be. Likely they would never know what had become of her. The very thought of such a horror made my mouth go dry.

After we stood to shake hands, the deal consummated, I said, "I'll need a recent photo of Francesca, if you have one on you."

"A photo." Taylor shook his head in frustration. "I knew I was forgetting something. I do have one, but I left it back on my desk at work. If you'll follow me over we can get it."

"Fine," I nodded. "Just give me the address in case we get separated."

He agreed, then we both walked out my door, down the flight of stairs to the main landing, and out into the sunlight.

Taylor craned his neck up, squinting into the bright, dry, cobalt-blue sky. The mid-August humidity here usually requires gills, but for once the weather was pretty good. "It's turning into a gorgeous day, Joe," Taylor said, then he looked back down at me and grinned. "In more ways than one. I feel like a weight has been lifted off my shoulders, like I'm a new man."

And he did. Taylor did look considerably better now than he had an hour earlier when we had first met. But I felt some caution was called for here; one of us had to be the adult voice of reason, and I guessed that was me. "Don't get too laid back yet, Mike. I still have to find her."

"You will," he said. "I have faith."

Good. That made one of us.

Taylor had parked his car, a Mercedes, in the parking space on the street right behind the Green Goddess. He looked startled when he saw me put my key in the old gal's door.

"That's yours?" he asked, his eyes bulging.

Yeah, and what of it? I almost snarled, but then Taylor surprised me.

"A sixty-eight Cougar," he breathed reverently. "Big-block four twenty-five? Holly carb?"

"Of course," I said, giving him a look. "And Glasspacks."

"Glasspacks." Taylor came over and ran his hand lightly over the flawless Junebug green paint job. "I had a Cougar like this when I was eighteen, but mine was candy-apple red." He grinned at me again. "When this is over, I'm going to buy another one. To celebrate."

It occurred to me about that time that Michael Taylor was a man of many parts, not the least of which were his implicit confidence in both me and his God; I couldn't speak for God, but I sincerely hoped Taylor's trust in my tracking skill wasn't misplaced. Even though I was sure it was.

****

We hopped on I-74 and took it on around as it wound down the hill where it connects onto I-75 south. After a few more minutes of me following him, we exited onto Seventh Street, finally pulling into the underground garage beneath the thirty-story Whittaker Building. I had lived in Cincinnati a good many years, but this was going to be the first time I had come in here.

I idly wondered if the thing was owned by Ted Whittaker, Francesca's almost-boyfriend. Naah, probably not; it's been my experience that eighteen-year-old boys rarely own office buildings. His daddy, on the other hand...

My musings were cut short as Taylor pulled into a slot marked with his name. I was about to drive past him on my way to a visitor's spot when he waved me into the next empty slot over. The nameplate on that one read Gary Kilgallen, Vice-President of Operations, Castle Industries. Whoever he was, I was pretty sure he wasn't me, but then I noticed Taylor's nameplate on his spot read Michael Taylor, Director of Research and Development, Castle Industries. The title was longer, and maybe that counted for something. Mentally I shrugged; if in Taylor's mind a director trumped a vice-president, who was I to argue?

We got out of our cars and walked over to the bank of elevators. Taylor pushed the button and immediately the door to one of them opened, like the thing had just been sitting there, patiently waiting for us. After we got in he reached over and punched thirty. We began to rise smoothly.

"All the way up, huh?" I said.

"Yes," Taylor smiled at me. "The view's great up there. Castle Industries takes up the whole thirtieth floor."

I whistled. "We're talking some serious bucks here."

"I know," he replied, "but the business really didn't take off until Nick assumed control after his father's death fifteen years ago."

"Nick?"

"Nick Castle. His father Henry started the company back in the late 1930's. Hence the name, Castle Industries. I hope Nick is still in the building." Taylor grinned over at me. "I think you'd like him, Joe. Nick's down to earth, but he has the business savvy of any ivy-league MBA you'd care to pit him against."

I smiled at my new client. "You sound like the head of his fan club."

Taylor was about to reply when the elevator slowed, then stopped. The doors opened and we got out. I found myself standing in a very large, nice lobby, done up in muted brown and green earth-tones. I noticed the beige carpet beneath my feet was a Berber, plush, and there were plenty of plants around. They were live ones too, not like those dusty plastic things that decorate my office. Soothing classical music--Bach's *Air on a G String*--was playing from hidden speakers. (Sometimes a hilljack will fool you with what he knows.) The indirect lighting was recessed, but somehow the place was still well-lit. All in all, very, very nice.

There were only two jarring notes. Jarring note number one was the sign above the receptionist's desk. I had almost stumbled over my own feet when I saw it because it read, bold as you please, *Castle Industries-God Is Our High Tower.* Say WHAT? Definitely lost some PC points there. As a matter of fact, with today's enlightened thinking regarding religion I wasn't sure if it was even legal to display such a thing. Mightn't the wording on a sign like that cause some innocent atheistic salesman, who had just wandered in, to have a heart fit or something?

And jarring note number two was the receptionist herself. The woman was modestly dressed in a conservative business suit, but she was--Lord, how does one put it? just say the words, I guess--one of the most supremely homely people I had ever seen. I wouldn't say she was horse faced, but My Friend Flicka had nothing on this gal. That fact was intensified when she saw Taylor and smiled. The woman's teeth were an absolute wonder--the seven of them that I could see, that is--every one sporting a handsome chocolate brown coloration and no two pointing in the same direction. I later found out she had been homeless only a year ago.

"Meester Taylor!" the woman squealed in heavily accented Spanglish. "I thought jew hab lef' for thee day!"

"Hi Rita," Taylor smiled. "No, I just had to take care of something. Say hello to Joe Box. Joe, Rita Ybarra."

Rita turned the full wattage of her smile on me. "Hello, Meester

Box!"

"Hello yourself." Egads. I turned toward Taylor. "Say, about that picture..."

"Sure, right this way."

We turned to the left and began padding down the long hall, passing door after open door. You could hear the sounds of people talking on phones, computer keys being clacked, the squeak of dry-tip felt markers on wipe-off boards, printers whirring. The place was as busy as a fiddler's convention, but the people working here for the most part were smiling and seemed happy. Some were even singing. Singing?

"Either Nick Castle pays his employees very well," I remarked to Taylor as we walked, "or everybody that works here smoked some wacky tabbacky during their lunch break."

Taylor laughed. "Not that, I can assure you, Joe. As I said, Nick Castle is a singular man, and working here is a singular experience."

"Must be." I motioned with my chin back over my shoulder. "Is that sign back there on the level?"

"Yes it is," he smiled.

"So you have to be a Christian to work here, huh?" Even I knew that such a requirement had to be illegal.

"Not at all," Taylor answered evenly. "All we care about is that the people here simply do the work we pay them to do. Most of our employees are Christians, but certainly not everyone." He laughed again, "We don't make anybody sign a loyalty oath, if that's what you're asking."

"I guess the question still remains then," I said. "Why do so many Christians choose to work here?"

Taylor's reply was enigmatic. "Why indeed? Okay, here we are." He opened his office door and we strolled on in.

I gave the place my own version of the Say-Nothings, Nodders, and Thin-lips treatment. The room, like the man, was neat almost to the point of fastidiousness, and was done up in a pleasing dark cherry paneling that contrasted nicely with the cream carpet. Diplomas and civic awards dotted the walls, and a large plate-glass window behind the desk looked out over the city. Taylor walked over to that desk, which wasn't any bigger than a medium-sized aircraft carrier, and plucked off one of those three-fold gold picture frames like your great-aunt keeps on the mantle. He held it up with a smile, then moved aside so I could see it better.

The end picture was one of Taylor and two other women, whom I assumed were his wife Sophia and their daughter Francesca. Both were dark-haired beauties, showing well their Italian ancestry. The graininess of the picture revealed it was a snapshot blown up to five-by-seven size, and was of the three of them on some recent Christmas. Francesca was holding up some keys--car keys?--Sophia a string of pearls, and Taylor clutched what had to be one of the world's ten most hideous ties. All three were grinning, but it didn't have a forced look; they genuinely appeared happy.

The next picture was a simple two-shot of Taylor and his wife done at a studio somewhere, and the last one was of Francesca alone, with the same studio look.

Taylor smiled as he gazed at them, then he looked at me. "The first picture was taken last Christmas Eve by Ted. He and Francesca were going out to a church party later that evening with their friends." Taylor looked back down at the photo and his smile grew wistful. "Our baby looks happy, doesn't she? The car we gave her that year wasn't much, a used Toyota Celica, but you would have thought Sophia and I had given her the keys to a Lexus. And you know what? Francesca used that old car to carry people back and forth to the homeless outreach that our church runs. She really was a wonderful girl..." Taylor must have realized what he had just said, because he glanced up at me, stricken. "IS! Is a wonderful girl! My *GOD* Joe..." Taylor slapped a hand over his mouth, and for a second I thought he might keel over.

"Mike!" My tone was sharp. "You okay?"

"What kind of a slip of the tongue is that?" Taylor shuddered. "Or is something trying to tell me...to prepare me..."

I didn't like where this was going at all. "Right the first time, Mike. Just a slip is all it was, nothing more." I pointed to the other two pictures, trying to get his mind off of morbid thoughts. "Those are nice shots. A local studio?"

"No." Taylor seemed to have gotten himself under control now, his panic banked with a strong will. "No, those were taken in the chapel. The church had a professional come in to get pictures taken of everyone in the congregation for the directory."

"A directory?" I grinned at him crookedly. "Just how big is this church of yours, anyway?"

"Four thousand and growing," Taylor answered.

Four THOUSAND? Caramba. There weren't four thousand people in our whole town when I was a kid...probably not that many in the whole county. What could possibly entice four thousand people all to attend one church?

About that time we heard a knock on his door. "Yo, Mike," a low voice rumbled, "any news about Francesca yet?"

We both turned, and I had to stifle a yelp. Standing not ten feet away from me was the biggest, broadest, meanest-looking black man I had ever seen. As best I can describe him, take Mr. T, remove the jewelry, give him some hair, stretch him to seven feet tall and have him tip the scales at three hundred and fifty pounds and you start to get the picture.

"Oh, hi, CT," Taylor said. "No, nothing yet, but this is the private investigator I told you and Nick about. Say hi to Joe Box. Joe, CT Barnes."

The giant stepped over to me, hand outstretched, grinning at me like I held the cure for cancer. The teeth crowding his jaws were as yellow as Indiana feed corn, and the thought hit me, maybe I ought to call Doctor Feelgood, my old orthodontist pal, and set him loose on this floor. Between the receptionist and this guy, I could guarantee at least a year's work. Or maybe not.

"So you're Joe Box," Barnes rumbled again. "I remember you now from the news. That crazy doctor thing wasn't it?" I averred that was true. "You look smaller in person," he said.

I grinned up at him. "Mr. Barnes, I bet that's one of the two most common things you say each day."

He frowned. "What's the other one?"

"That's easy," I said. " 'Who stole my Pepsodent?' "

Barnes looked at me hard for a second, as if he was sizing me up for the proverbial pine box. I was mentally kicking myself when suddenly he threw back his head in a roar of laughter. "Mike, I like this guy," Barnes huffed. "Ya gotta give him a G for guts, anyway. The only person I usually let tease me is my momma."

This man had a momma? What was she, a yeti?

Taylor was smiling as he turned to me. "I guess you pass, Joe. CT is the head of security here, and if he likes you, you're golden."

"Glad to hear it." I motioned to the picture of Francesca in the frame. "If you'll slip that out I can get cracking."

"Sure thing." Taylor clumsily fumbled with the back of the frame for a second. Finally it came off and he handed me the picture. Then he glanced at me, over to Barnes, and finally back at me, a funny look on his face. "Joe, before you leave, I wonder if we could do just one more thing. It won't take long."

"Okay," I shrugged. "You're paying the freight."

Taylor stared at Barnes again. "Is Nick in?" The giant nodded. Taylor then said, "Let's all go to his office." Barnes nodded again, and it seemed as if an unspoken communication had passed between the two.

The three of us left Taylor's office and went down two more doors to the end of the hall. We stopped at the last office there, this time a corner one. The small brass plate on the door read simply Nicholas J. Castle, President. Taylor rapped a couple of times. "Nick? Do you have a minute?"

"Sure, Mike," a voice behind the door said. "Come on in."

We all entered, and I gazed around approvingly. Now *this* was an office. The place was not a whole lot bigger than Taylor's, but where his had looked to be preternaturally austere, this office, though understated in its elegance, had a comfortable, lived-in feel to it. Hanging on the walls with the usual diplomas and such-like as I had seen in Taylor's office were framed pages of what appeared to be ancient books, intermixed with bits of old, yellowed parchment containing faint scribbles of indecipherable writing. There was also a tall bookcase holding some small intricate statuary and what looked to be a carved olivewood manger scene of unknown age. Was this guy an amateur archeologist? And where Taylor's desk approximated only a medium-sized aircraft carrier, the one in front of me was a big daddy, a full-blown Nimitz class.

The man behind that desk stood and smiled. He was pleasant-looking, in his late forties and around six feet tall. He had salt-and-pepper hair and boasted a rugged, outdoorsy good look that some women--and men, for all I know--would find attractive.

Taylor broke the ice for me. "Nick, I'd like you to meet Joe Box, the investigator I told you about. I've hired Joe to find Francesca. Joe, Nick Castle."

Castle smiled at me and held out a hand. We shook, and as I felt Castle's hand I noticed it was rough, dry, and calloused; I knew I had been right in pegging him for an outdoorsman.

"Joe, it's a pleasure," Castle said. "I hope you're as good as your reputation. Mike's really pinning his hopes on you."

"Yeah, well, we've discussed that," I replied. "All I can say is, I'll do my best."

"That's the reason we stopped by," Taylor broke in. "I was hoping the three of us, and Joe, if he wants, could pray before he sets out."

PRAY?

"Hold the phone here, Jackson," I spluttered. "Mike did I, or did I not specifically tell you in my office, not an hour ago, that I wasn't a spiritual man? I'll repeat myself: that's your deal, not mine."

"You did say that, Joe." Taylor's gaze on me was calm. "And I also believe I told you it didn't matter. God is going to use you in this, like it or not. We're both on the potter's wheel, my friend, and there's no getting off until he's had his way with us."

I looked beseechingly at both Barnes and Castle, hoping for some sympathy, but all I got from them was the same serene look that was on Taylor's face. Then it struck me: all three of them were on the same page here, and I was an outsider.

Outsider...

I started to speak, and wham! just like that, the strange feeling suddenly roared back, only this time stronger, darker, and more virulent than ever. With a rush I felt the room spin. A cold wind started to whistle shrieking through me, unstoppable, and then I sensed...something...beginning to tear around in my mind, noxious and mad and laughing. With a sick feeling I felt that fluttering once more start up inside, but now it was no longer a moth.

It was a raven.

I pictured it in stark reality, its beak reddened with my blood, as it flapped and slashed inside my rib cage, desperately trying to rip its way through. It opened its mouth to screech... and black bile came pouring out. But that wasn't the worst.

Suddenly it felt as if steel bands had encircled my skull, inexorably tightening down. Then they grew spikes that punched inward, cracking through bone and driving deep into my brain.

You're doomed, a voice hissed. *Why try? You'll fail...*

God almighty, what WAS this? Was I going crazy? Rapid-fire thoughts began assailing me. What was I even doing here? Who was I fooling? The girl was long since dead, and everybody knew it except for her poor sap of a father. She had in fact been dead since late Friday night, and was beyond my help or anybody's. And what was I, anyway? Just a broken down PI, with an empty wallet and an emptier future. An aging ex-cop and former combat soldier, not good to anybody, a failure. Who was I to hold out hope to anyone? I couldn't even save my own wife from dying... Oh God!

Immediately I was gripped by the insane desire to rush out of this office, down the hall, out of this building and never, ever come back. Just keep running, never stop, just keep going, stuff those memories back inside, Linda, Linda, please don't die...

"Man, Nicky, the tiger's really got him," I heard Barnes say, as if from a distance.

"It's nothing we haven't seen before," Castle replied, then he said forcefully, "Satan, leave him alone, in Jesus' name!"

And like the sluice gates on a dam springing open, the voices ceased, the pain lifted, and the blackness rushed out just as fast as it had come.

I staggered to a chair behind me and sat down heavily, gasping for air. Castle leaned down over me, concern filling his face.

"CT, get him some water," Castle said, his eyes never leaving mine. Then he said to me, "Joe, I'm not even going to ask you how you feel, because I already know. You feel like hell. Literally."

I could only nod dumbly. Barnes shambled back over and handed me a full glass. I snatched it from him with trembling hands and drank it down greedily, as if I had been hiking the Gobi.

Castle went behind his desk and got his chair and brought it around, placing it directly in front of me. He sat, and then leaned forward, still gazing at me steadily. I don't think I have ever seen a more intense look on anyone, before or since.

"Joe, CT and Mike will be the first to tell you I'm not one to mince words," Castle said, "so I'll say this straight. You've just gone a full round with the prince of the power of the air, Lucifer himself. And I'll bet you didn't like it. At all."

"No bet," I wheezed. "How did you know?"

"A little something called the gift of discernment," Castle answered, his voice even. He looked over at Taylor. "Mike, shut that door. The four of us are going to talk."

That had an ominous sound, and also sounded strongly like a cue for me to leave. I began to stand. "Guys, I'd love to. But I'm feeling better now. Really." I wiped my mouth with the back of my hand. "And I really do need to get started..."

"Sit. Down." Castle's words were not a request. Then he softened his look and smiled. "Please."

Wordlessly I did.

"Joe," he began, "you're a free moral agent, and so you have the right to accept or reject what I'm about to tell you. But it bears hearing: there's something about this case you don't know."

That got my attention. "Such as?"

"Such as the fact there's a spiritual side to Francesca's

disappearance that frankly has all of us on edge."

"Spiritual side?" I frowned. "I'm afraid I don't follow you."

"'Afraid' A good choice of a word." Castle folded his arms across his chest. "Joe, have you ever listened to how people use that word, in all its forms, every day? 'I'm afraid your son might need an operation.' 'We're afraid the stock market is headed down.' 'So, are you going to go to the party? No, I'm afraid not'" He went on, grinning humorlessly. "And let's not forget death. 'Tickle me to death.' 'Scare me to death.' 'This job is going to be the death of me.'" Castle shook his head. "Ours is a culture of fear and death, Joe, and has been since the Fall. But lately it's been getting worse."

"Worse? How so?"

Barnes broke in, "Come on, man, you aren't stupid. What are you, close to fifty?" I nodded, and he said, "So don't tell me you haven't noticed how weird things have been gettin' lately."

"Check the news, Joe," Taylor added. "There's a factor of fear that's permeating everything these days, and it goes deeper and is much worse than anybody has ever seen in the past."

"All this was predicted centuries ago in the Bible," Castle said. "These times we're in are known as the last days, the summation of history. It's just our bad lot--or good one, depending on how you look at it--that we're alive right now."

"Very interesting," I said, looking at the three of them. "But what does all that have to do with finding the girl?"

"Everything," Castle replied. "Here's the point I was getting to. When Mike called me at home Saturday and told my wife Maryann and me about what had happened, we both felt in our spirits that something even more malevolent than the disappearance of a healthy, vital young woman had occurred. So I called CT at his house right away, and he told me that during their prayer time early that morning both he and his wife had felt a heaviness that was unexplained. When I told him what Mike had told me, that mystery, at least, was solved..." Castle paused.

"Go on," I said.

Castle looked up at Taylor, his expression unreadable. "Did you tell him the rest?"

"Not yet," Taylor replied. "I was hoping you would. You're better with words than I am."

This whole thing was starting to slither into the realm of the bizarre, and my tone reflected, I'm sure, how upset I was getting. "You want to cut the Agatha Christie crap and get to it?"

"Okay," Castle said. "Here it is: Mike feels, and CT and I agree with him, that whoever took Francesca did so by mistake."

"What?" That was unexpected. "What do you mean?"

"I mean," Castle said evenly, "that whoever has her doesn't know--or at least didn't know when they kidnaped her or seduced her or whatever--that Francesca is a Christian. Maybe not the strongest one that ever was, granted, and as full of silly ideas as most eighteen-year-old girls are, but a believer nonetheless."

I frowned at him again. "Yeah? So?" I simply wasn't tracking with him at all.

"So that's your edge, man," Barnes broke in again. "Because of the fact that Francesca's a Christian, that means we can apply spiritual force to gettin' her released."

"'Spiritual force?'" I snapped. "What are you talking about? And what's this 'we' stuff? I told you I don't buy any of it."

"After what happened to you not two minutes ago," Castle said softly, "maybe you should start."

He had me there, I'll admit. "Okay," I said, "just for grins let's say all three of you are right. That a satanist or a cultist or some such has the girl. How does that information help us?"

Castle looked at me. "First off, we don't think that a satanist or a cultist does have her, Joe. There's something darker working here. More subtle. Something that could take a girl like Francesca and her natural love for people and turn them to its own ends without her even noticing."

"Like what, for God's sake?" I jumped out of the chair and pushed past the three of them, shaking my head. I was completely off the charts by now and had no idea where all this was going. I whipped around and faced them with a scowl. "And what would be the point? Or hasn't your angel or whatever told you that?"

"Don't crack wise, Joe," Barnes rumbled menacingly at me, his expression dark. "Nicky's just tryin' to tell ya how things are."

"All right, and how are they? Let me see if I have this straight." I began to crack my knuckles, one of my least endearing traits, or so Linda used to tell me. "Sinister forces, but NOT satanists or cultists, have lured a loving, trusting, but immature young girl into their clutches. And for what purpose? We don't know, but it ties in with some fertility clinic here in town. And it turns out that said sinister forces don't even *want* Christian girls, but by God, they have one now, although they may or may not know it. And IF they don't know it, the very fact she's a Christian may hold the key to her release. How am I doing so far?"

"You're battin' a thousand," Barnes said. "Keep goin'."

"Yes, but here's the best part!" I was trying not to gibber like an idiot. "Plunked right in the middle of this cosmic battle between good and evil is me, Joe Box, a lapsed Baptist who's not even sure if he believes in God anymore and for *real* sure doesn't believe in your brand of Christianity. But that doesn't matter, because out of all the six billion people crawling across this tired old globe God Himself has picked this same Joe Box to do mortal combat with Dark Forces Beyond The Pale and rescue the girl. That about sum it up? Did I leave anything out?" I was breathing heavily as I glared.

The three of them didn't say anything for a minute, then Castle spoke up, a half-smile on his face as he looked at me. "Are you finished?"

"Yeah. In more ways than one." I began to head for the door. "I won't say this hasn't been fun...because it hasn't." I shot my final remark over my shoulder as I walked. "Mike, I'll tear up our contract and mail your check back to you. I left it in my desk."

Taylor jumped to his feet. "You're going to WHAT? WHAT?" Before I got to the door Barnes stepped between me and it, blocking my way. He folded his arms tightly over his massive chest, scowling at me like we suddenly weren't friends anymore.

"And you can move it, Godzilla," I snapped. "I've taken down bigger guys than you." Which was a lie, but as I've heard it said, when you can't fix 'em with facts, baffle 'em with bushwah.

Castle stood as well. "Everybody shut up. My God, you can cut the testosterone in here with a chain saw." He pointed at his two employees. "Mike, you be quiet, and CT, you take it down a notch." Then he looked at me. "And Joe, stop...please."

I did, and turned to face him.

Castle smiled at me. "I'll ask you nicely. As a personal favor. Would you please sit back down?" He looked at Barnes and Taylor. "Could we all sit down? Talk about this?"

I blew a breath at him, trying to get my swirling emotions under control. "Okay. I guess." I walked back over and sat down again heavily in the same chair. "Mr. Castle, say your piece."

"Seems to me he already said it," Barnes muttered. I ignored him.

Castle smiled, "Joe, during this whole business these past few minutes I've been trying to put myself in your shoes, trying to imagine how crazy all this must seem to you."

"You've got *that* right," I told him darkly.

"But just because it sounds crazy," Castle went on in a soft voice, "doesn't necessarily mean it isn't real." He paused, and I nodded for him to continue.

"I'm only going to scratch the surface of this," Castle said, "for time's sake. When I'm done then you can tell Mike if you want to go on with the case. If not, I'm sure he'll understand."

Out of the corner of my eye I saw Taylor start to open his mouth in protest, but Castle shot him a look and he closed it; I was starting to get an inkling of just how the man managed to run a place like this simply through the sheer force of his personality.

"Okay, let's start with the basics." Castle held up three fingers. "God is a trinity: Father, Son, and Holy Ghost. Right?"

I nodded again, remembering this much from Sunday school lessons I had as a kid.

"And it says in Genesis God made mankind in His own image, after His own likeness, which means we have three parts also." Using his other hand, Castle ticked the points off on his fingers. "Man has a physical body, with its attendant five senses, a body we can see and touch, a body which can know pain and pleasure; a soul, which consists of the mind, will, and emotions; and a spirit, which is the life-force inside, the real you."

"Okay, I'll grant you that much," I said. "Make your point."

"You know, you were right, before," Castle answered obliquely. "There *is* a battle raging. A battle of the spirit. And it may be invisible, but this battle is as real and as solid as the asphalt on the street outside." He smiled at me. "Truth be told, the victory was won on a cross two thousand years ago. But the enemy is stubborn, and he's still fighting for all he's worth. You're a part of that battle, Joe...maybe a bigger part than you knew. You always were, but only now you're becoming aware of it. And the grand prize of this conflict is the life of every person on earth." Castle stopped for a second and let that sink in.

"I never asked for this," I said then.

"I know."

"I'm just a PI." I was trying to keep my voice from pleading. "Just a man. *Why me?*"

"Joe, that's been the cry of every man that ever went to war down through the ages," Castle said softly. "They said it as their horses were shot out from under them. They said it as they went over the tops of trenches into withering machine gun fire. They said it as their ships went down or their planes fell from the sky. I know I said it. I'll bet you did too." I swallowed, staring at him. Castle smiled at me, his eyes infinitely sad. "And the answer has always been the same. Because they had to."

I swallowed again and didn't speak. Neither did Barnes or Taylor. All of us were looking at Castle.

"So, yeah, you can leave here," he said. "Walk away. Leave the whole thing on the table. Go stroll in the sunshine. But remember this." Castle's voice then took on an odd quality, scolding and gentle at the same time. "There's a young girl out there somewhere whose world has fallen in. She's scared, alone, and wondering what's happened to her." I could hear Taylor gulp. "God alone knows why you were chosen to bring her home," Castle said. "But Francesca needs her life back...and so do you. You need to do this, Joe. For Francesca. And for yourself."

Chapter 5

So that's how the day had gone. After a bit more wangling, I had agreed to work the case. Now all that was left was strategy. Besides, I thought, it's only for a week. What could go wrong in a week? I was about to find out, and that's what you get for thinking, as Granny used to say.

I suppose that I should have headed right on over to the fertility clinic to see what was what, but I didn't. By now it was nearly five p.m. and honestly, I was too fried from everything I had been through so far to be much good to anybody. My body hurt, a headache was sullenly kicking at my brainstem, and my eyelids felt packed with grit. I figured I would start Mike's clock for the week's work first thing in the morning. Right now nothing sounded better than to slip into a nice scotch, a warm bath, and bed, in that order. Guess I'm a wimp.

Hamilton Avenue grew narrow as it approached the Mount Healthy area--so named after the village had proved itself immune during a cholera outbreak in the late 1800s; why, I have no idea--then I turned left from it onto Riley, my street, and at last into the Agnes, where I lived. That name requires some explanation.

When I was sixteen my dad and Granny and I had moved from Picklebutt (don't ask), Kentucky to Cincinnati so my dad could take a job working on the line at the old GM plant in Norwood, building Pontiacs...a job which would kill him a year later.

Three things immediately struck me as strange when we arrived in this town: what Cincinnatians call "chili" to me it tastes like sloppy joe sauce with cinnamon mixed in; when the folks here don't understand what you just said they say "please?" instead of "huh?", like normal people do; and lastly the apartment buildings here sometimes have ladies' names. Old ladies' names. But it's okay. Cincinnati has slowly had its way with me: over the years I've grown rather fond of their weird chili, and for a while now I've been living in an apartment building with the same name as my aunt. I still say "huh", though. You have to draw the line somewhere.

I pulled the Goddess through Agnes's pothole-strewn parking lot and then into the first slot I came to. I shut the car off, got out, and glanced up. I stifled a half laugh with a shake of my head. Quite a comedown from the Whittaker Building.

Old Agnes, like most dowagers her age, had certainly seen better days since her birth in the art-deco thirties. The building's bricks were grimy and chipped, the mortar in them between was badly in need of patching, and the only air-conditioning to be had was what was cranked out by leaky old window units that cooled only intermittently and wheezed like German submariners trapped on the floor of the Atlantic. But the heat was free and the rent was cheap, so I called it home.

I wearily trudged up the four steps to the main door and let myself in. When I had moved in six years ago the door still had a lock on it, and if you were visiting somebody they would have to buzz you in. But a while back the lock got broken and was never fixed, and not too long after that vandals ripped out the buzzer system. So now any old sleaze-king can wander in anytime he wants. Like me.

I climbed the darkened stairwell up to the second floor and then to 2-B, my place. I slipped my key into the lock, wrestling with it, and when I finally opened the door I saw the only thing in the whole dump that could make me smile: Noodles, my cat. Noodles is a shorthair tabby of uncertain ancestry, and he and I have sort of adopted each other. How I found him bears telling.

Two years ago I was working per deim for an insurance company on a disability fraud case. It seemed they had a man who had fallen off a ladder and was now unable to work, so he said. If the company allowed the claim the guy stood to net a hundred and fifty dollars a day of disability income that would be coming in for quite some time, so naturally they wanted to make sure he was really hurt. My job was to tail the man and try to find out, even if it meant staking out his place in my car all night.

I gave it my best, but by the fifth night I had had it. Everything I had seen seemed to prove the man's injuries were for real: he always wore a back brace on the outside of his shirt, he walked using one of those metal canes that have those four little feet on the bottom, and he looked to be in constant pain. I had yet to photograph him through his living room window dancing the lambada with a redhead.

It was now nearly midnight and I was ready for home. The sandwiches I had brought were just a fond memory, and frankly using a Mason jar as a restroom had long since lost its charm. I was inclined to finish this and tell my employers they ought to pony up and pay the man, which it later turned out they did.

Twelve-thirty came and I left.

It was nearly one when I pulled into the parking lot at the Agnes. I had just gotten out of the car and was pocketing my keys when I heard a strange noise coming from around the back of the building. Strange noises in this neighborhood weren't that unusual, but this was. It sounded like men's voices laughing, followed by a curious yowling. Normally I would have shrugged it off and headed on inside, but something about that yowling compelled me to check it out. So I walked around to the back of the building, where the Dumpster is, and came upon an odd tableau.

There in the shadows squatted two guys in their mid-thirties. They were laughing and obviously drunk, and were holding down a bedraggled-looking cat. But it was what they were doing to the cat that stopped me cold.

They were burning off its fur with lighters.

The cat yowled again, piteously. Then it saw me and redoubled its screaming, as if I was its only hope in the world. The look in the cat's eyes spoke of pain, terror, and blank confusion as to what it could have done to deserve this.

That did it.

"Hey!" I yelled. "What do you think you're doing?" Yeah, I know, pretty lame, but it's what I said.

The younger of the two stopped what he was doing long enough to laugh at me. "Up yours, man. It's just a cat."

Which was the wrong thing to say, at the wrong time, to exactly the wrong guy.

I'm not proud of what happened next. Suffice it to say the wrongs were righted, the feline was freed...and I used my bare fists to beat those two poor drunks half to death.

And that's how Noodles became my friend.

He purred loudly as he rubbed around my feet, saying howdy and how's about a cat treat and scratch my head while you're at, all in the same breath. The places on his body where he had been burned never did grow any hair back, and his nude, scarred tail stuck straight out off his rear end like a twisted pink Slim Jim. Every time I see that tail I remember the feeling of those drunks' bones as they snapped under my hands and Lord help me, I still smile.

I checked his food bowl. Half full yet, but what the heck. I went to the cupboard and got out a can of chicken Pounce treats. (Noodles prefers chicken, but will accept tuna; finicky he's not.) As soon as Noodles saw the can his purr became louder, making him sound like a B-17 warming up on an English runway in an old *Twelve O'Clock High* rerun. I gave him five treats, then went to the fridge and poured an ounce of milk into his saucer. Next I went back to the cupboard and pulled out a bottle of Cutty Sark-- for me, not him. I poured a healthy slug for myself into a Kroger's jelly glass and drank it down neat as I stood at the sink.

When I was done I plodded into my living room and sank listlessly down into my old sofa. Noodles hopped up on my lap, purring for all he was worth. He kneaded my stomach for a few seconds, then curled up with a sigh and closed his eyes. After a bit, my own eyes did the same.

So cat and human, both well-lubricated and content with each other's company, quietly conked out while the late afternoon sun gently lapped in through the slats in the blinds.

We both slept till morning, and I never did get my bath.

Chapter 6

In any missing persons case the logical place to start is with those who saw the person last. In Francesca's case that meant the folks she worked with at the B. Dalton in Milford. The problem with that was the store didn't open until ten, and I didn't want to waste the earlier morning hours. So logic be hanged: I decided to visit the fertility clinic first.

As I mentioned before, the Agnes was located just off Hamilton Avenue in Mount Healthy, and as luck would have it the Brighter Day Clinic was on Struble Road, only a mile away as the crow flies. Unfortunately I wasn't a crow and had to drive, but even so it was only a couple of miles and I was there in ten minutes. This was a bit of a gamble on my part, being here at eight-thirty, and not having called first to check on their hours, but I thought I would chance it.

I pulled into the newly-recoated--judging by the blackness and smell--parking lot the clinic shared with a dry-cleaner's and a pony keg. Crazy name, pony keg...that's what Cincinnatians call a carry-out. Why? Lord knows. I always thought that with a moniker like "pony keg" you might expect to see Seattle Slew or Mr. Ed behind the counter, selling beer and Lotto tickets. Weird, huh?

Anyway, I shut the Goddess off and as I got out the heat immediately slammed me. Sometime during the night the weather gods had pulled the plug on the cool, dry air of the last few days--"Hah! Fooled ya!"--and Cincy's climate had once again reverted back to the sticky August blast furnace all of us here know and love. The sky above me was already bone white at this early hour, heat waves shimmering off the parking lot and the road it fronted like a waterfall turned on edge. Across that road the cicadas were tuning up in the trees, and underneath my shirt I could feel hot sweat beginning to form a small lake in my navel. I also could sense my deodorant breaking down. Idly I wondered if I would need to change shirts before lunch. Oh well. That's just part of the price we pay here for enjoying summer weather that would make a Louisiana shrimper cry for mercy. Of course it's not always like this: in winter we get snowfalls so deep and icy that the citizens of Buffalo gaze upon us with ill-disguised envy.

As I walked up to the clinic's door I noted the hours posted: Monday through Friday, eight a.m. to five-thirty p.m., closed

Saturday and Sunday. Smiling, I opened the door and went in. On the way over here I had considered how best to approach this, straight up or on the sly. I didn't wrestle with it for long before I decided to take the sly road, as it were. Here's why: if I went in and told the people there why I was there and who I was looking for, any element of surprise was obviously lost. And who knows, I might have need of it later. So that left sly.

I felt I could take this in a couple of directions. The first would entail me passing myself off as a man wanting information on how to become a sperm donor...but that carried its own problem. Delusions of grandeur notwithstanding--such a question would presuppose some woman would actually *want* the genes of a transplanted hillbilly coursing through her child's body--the age factor was working against me. I had read somewhere that these clinics didn't want the seed of any man over thirty-five, and I was well past that; call it creeping geezer-itis. And in this age of informed consent and privacy laws I couldn't very well say I was seeking fertility info for my wife or daughter, so that left the second direction, and the one I had chosen: reporter.

This wasn't as hard as it sounds. I had minored in journalism in college so I knew the language, enough to fool most people anyway, and awhile back I had Mr. Yee/Lee make me up some fake business cards stating that I was, depending upon the need, either Stanley Niven, special affairs correspondent with the *Hillsboro Democrat-Advocate,* or Thomas Balizet, political beat journalist for the *Northern Kentucky Observer.* I'd only had to use this ruse a few times in the past, and thankfully no one had ever checked to see if these newspapers even existed--which they didn't, except in the fevered mind of yours truly. I also had a third set of cards I had yet to use, even though they had been in my desk drawer for the past three years. There's a reason why they remain there to this day.

One night Mr. Yee/Lee and I were working our way through a case or two of Tsing Tao beer a cousin of his had gotten at cost somewhere, and along about the ninth--or was it tenth?--beer I had the brilliant idea--at least that's what I thought at the time--of having my old printer buddy make me up a set of cards saying I was Herman Greenbaum, human interest editor with the *Zionist Weekly.* Why Herman Greenbaum? And why the *Zionist Weekly?* God alone knows; that Tsing Tao is vicious stuff.

Anyway, upon regaining consciousness in the cold gray light of the following morning (and how did I end up on the fire escape, anyway?) it blearily occurred to me that my idea for a third identity, a Jewish identity at that, probably wasn't as great as those beers had led me to believe. Hadn't Alexander Pope once said something about alcohol's delusions causing us to mistake guile for knowledge? Something along that line...maybe it was Shakespeare. Or Milton. Could be it was Granny. Whoever said it was pretty smart, though.

Because the thought also occurred to me right about then that I knew exactly nothing about Israeli politics, and that as far as ethniticity was concerned, Andy Griffith looked more Jewish than I did. My smart idea made about as much sense as going fishing in a bucket. I had decided to tell Mr. Yee/Lee not to bother, but it turned out the damage was already done. The crafty old commie had outdone himself this time.

In the center of my desk lay a boxed set of three hundred of the prettiest cream-colored, custom-engraved cards you ever saw... and free, to boot (Mr. Yee/Lee gets generous when he drinks Tsing Tao, and obviously holds it better than most people). It must have taken him hours. I've never had the heart to throw them out.

As I walked in the clinic I gave it a quick glance. It was nothing fancy, just a square waiting room decorated with the same type of cruddy plastic plants I had at my own office. Four or five chairs against the walls, a coffee table covered by last year's magazines; all in all pretty ordinary. But then I did a double-take as I saw on the walls what passed for art around here: graphic posters of VD-encrusted genitalia, along with equally vivid pictures taken from inside some woman's womb of a developing baby. Yecch. That'll throw a feller off his feed.

At the back of the room stood a counter topped by a frosted glass wall that reached from its surface to the ceiling. There was an open sliding glass window in the center of it, and behind it sat an overweight fiftyish nurse-type who scowled at me as I strode up; my guess was that they didn't get too many men in here.

"May I help you?" the woman frowned, as if helping me was the last thing she wanted to do.

"Hi there! I sure hope so, Miss..." I read her nametag. "Blutarski."

Blu-TAR-ski? I almost broke out laughing at that handle, and stifled it only with difficulty. The only person I ever heard with the name Blutarski was John Belushi's character Bluto Blutarski in the movie *Animal House*. But as I looked at the woman again, it fit; she could have been his sister.

Her reply was frosty. "My name is MRS. Blutarski." (Married in a moment of weak abandon, no doubt.) "And I asked you if you needed help." As she glared at me, a faint furze of mustache above her lip quivered with annoyance. My goodness, what a pleasant woman. Mr. Blutarski, whoever you are, you're a lucky, lucky man. Okay, time to load up the charm gun; I figured it couldn't hurt.

Mentally I went into my 'Joe Box, cub reporter' mode. "Yes, you can help me, ma'am," I said. "At least I hope so." I handed her a card. "My name is Stanley Niven. I'm a special affairs correspondent with the *Hillsboro Democrat-Advocate."* As the nurse scowled at my card I craned my head around, grinning. "Gosh, this is a sure nice place you have here." Yeah, sure it was. If you could somehow get past those nasty posters on the walls the thing looked like the waiting room of any third-class dentist's office, but I kept that to myself.

"You're a reporter?" Sharp as a razor, this gal was. Didn't I just say that?

"That's right. May I ask you some questions?"

Bluto narrowed her eyes. "What about?" Her cordiality had dropped another ten degrees, and she couldn't spare it.

"Well, my paper is developing a story on family planning in the 21st century. I was hoping to speak to your boss about that." I flipped open a small spiral notebook, clicked my pen, and looked down, ready to write. "May I have his name, please?"

"I'm sure he won't want to speak with you," the nurse said. "He's a very busy man."

I looked back up at her. "Golly, that's discouraging," I sighed, and tried to look crestfallen. "But how about we let the doctor decide that, okay?" I smiled in what I hoped was a boyish way; sometimes it works with these types.

"No, that's not okay." Bluto glared at me again. "And unless you have business with this clinic, I suggest that you leave."

Rats. My Jimmy Olsen persona was going down in flames. Time to punt.

"Say, are any of these posters for sale?"

"Wha-a-t??"

I motioned at them. "These posters. Are they for sale? My Granny just moved into a rest home in Florida and I've been racking my brains for a house-warming present." I wished with all my heart she had been; my granny's been gone for almost twenty years now. "Granny likes hospital dramas, the gorier the better. Any of these would do." I peered back at one, a particularly oozing putrescent thing that looked like seafood gone bad. "How do you pronounce this? Is it cla-MID-i-a or cla-mid-EE-a?" I sat down in one of the chairs with a sigh. "Oh man, that's better. Hotter than a Teamsters meeting out there. The AC in here feels great."

Bluto stood up, frowning, her knitted eyebrows making one long black caterpillar of distaste. "What do you think you're doing?" she huffed, pointing at me. "Get out!"

I tucked my pen behind my ear and placed my notebook in my lap. Then I laced my hands behind my head and stretched back, grinning. "No, I don't think I will."

"You'll get out or I'll call the police!"

"Do that," I said, and my grin faded. "I'm sure your employer will love the publicity. Especially the way I'll write it up. Can't you see the headlines? 'Reporter arrested in neighborhood clinic: many issues raised, doctor questioned.'" I sat up and folded my hands in my lap. "Ma'am, I'm not your enemy. Truly I'm not. And if you don't want to tell me your boss's name, that's all right; public records are called that for a reason. I just think that in the interests of general goodwill, if nothing else, you'd see your way clear to help me out a little."

Bluto's lips were a thin compressed line--Thin-lips!--and you could tell she just hated it, but she was stuck. I had her by the short ones, well and truly, and we both knew it. "What do you want to know?" she hissed.

"Same as before," I smiled. "Your boss's name, and what time he comes in."

"All right." If dirty looks were bullets, I'd have been as perforated as the earthen berm at a gun club. "His name is Mangold, Doctor Ernest Mangold. He comes in at nine this morning."

I stood smiling, and cocked my head at her. "There now, Mrs. Blutarski, that wasn't so bad, was it?" I cranked up the charm a bit. "Could I make an appointment with him? Could you set that up for me?"

The nurse sighed now, the fight gone out of her. It's terrible to see a foe humbled. Later, after I'd talked to Dr. Mangold, maybe I'd understand better what had set her off. "As I said, he's due to be here at nine to go over some files. I suppose he can see you then."

"Thank you." I looked at my watch; it was ten till. "Mind if I just wait for him here?"

"Suit yourself," Bluto answered, and snorted a laugh. "That's what people usually do in a waiting room."

Maybe she wasn't as humbled as I thought.

Chapter 7

At nine straight up the door opened and Mangold stomped in. I sat up in my chair and laid the magazine I had been reading down on the end table in grateful relief. No doubt about it, when I become emperor there's going to be some changes made.

The first decree I'm going to enact will be directed at every doctor, dentist, orthopedist, ophthalmologist, proctologist, oncologist, head-shrinker, boil-lancer, joint-cracker or worse, every student of Hippocrates, all medicos of whatever stripe of the human anatomy, head to toe, skin to bone, horn to hoof, and require that they provide plenty of sure-enough, up-to-date reading materials for their patients, upon pain of death. I figure with this one simple act I'll endear myself to the populace forever.

Oh yeah, I'll also make sure they have some fishing magazines too, so the men can have something to read besides all those *Better Ladies' Homes and Sassy Madamoiselle Journals.*

Mangold frowned at me. "Who are you?" He was a wizened old croc, rather tall, in his seventies or thereabouts, with a balding head and spectacles so thick you could have used them as glass coasters. The slack skin covering Mangold's face was loose enough that I wondered if the nerves underneath had been severed, and the wattles under his chin jiggled unnaturally, like the man was packed with nightcrawlers. His purplish lips were full, but it didn't seem he possessed the muscle tone to be able to lift them very high; smiling appeared to be as alien to this boy as marital fidelity had been to Bill Clinton. Mangold's great big old buggy eyes took my measure, not liking what he found, and I had the unsettling thought that I knew him from somewhere. Then I realized I did. I remembered him from childhood.

He was the boogie-man.

I began to answer him but Bluto beat me to it. "His name is Niven, Doctor. He's a reporter." The way she said it, I should have been wearing a bell and yelling "Unclean!"

"Yes, but what does he WANT?"

She curled a lip. "He says he has some questions for you."

"Regarding what?"

"I have no idea, Doctor. He seems quite adamant."

I snapped my fingers at them both. "Uh, excuse me? Hello? The two of you seem to have me confused with one of your potted ferns," I smiled. "But it's no problem. I get that stuff all the time."

Mangold mashed his lips together in annoyance, with the unfortunate result of making them look like two pieces of old liver caught between pinch-rollers. He snapped his head once in the direction of a closed door next to the counter. "Come on," he growled. "Let's get this over with." He stalked off, leaving me to follow. I'll bet Mangold always wondered why his graduating class hadn't voted him Mr. Congeniality of 1946.

I entered his office behind him, and immediately something made me sneeze. Whether it was dust, mold, pollen, or recycled B.O. I have no idea, but the one I let go was a sinus-clearing, gold-medal winner. Mangold frowned at me. "Do you mind not doing that?"

"Not at all, Doctor," I smiled. "Sorry. That one caught me by surprise too. But haven't you ever heard a good sneeze temporarily stops, then restarts your heart? It's better than a vacation."

"That's as may be," he said. "Although I don't really wish to discuss your nasal problems, Mr. Niven. Just ask your questions and leave."

"Okay." Enough bantering with this ghoul. To work. I flipped open my small notebook. "What is it exactly that you do here, sir?"

"Didn't Mrs. Blutarski tell you that?"

"No. Frankly this is the first reproductive clinic I've ever visited. All my paper did was give me a list of several for the story, and Brighter Day was the closest."

Mangold jerked his head up at that, peering at me closely. "Oh? What are the names of the other clinics?"

Wups, struck a nerve with that one. What's worse, I didn't know of any others. I hadn't planned on him asking this, and frantically I wondered how to answer him.

"Um, I can't tell you that, Doctor. I'm afraid that's privileged information."

"What in the world does THAT mean? That makes no sense."

You're telling me. "What I mean is, other reporters are covering the other clinics. My editor gave me this one because it was closest to where I lived." My God, that sounded lame, even to me.

"I thought you said your paper had given you a list of clinics."

"No, just the name of the closest one to me. Like I said." I hoped he wasn't taping this. And was it getting hotter in here?

"So you don't know the names of the other clinics."

"No, sorry." I had to get Mangold off this. I smiled at him

disarmingly; maybe it would work better on him than it had on Bluto. "That's why I'm hoping I'll do well here." I lowered my voice conspiratorially. "My editor is a troglodyte."

"I don't care if he is the Piltdown Man," the doctor said hotly. "Chust ask your questions. Then go."

Was it my imagination, or had Mangold suddenly let slip a bit of a Teutonic accent right there? Curious...

And deep in my hindbrain, alarm bells began to clamor. Way down in the viscera, where the dark things dwell, I think I knew, even then.

Chapter 8

Mangold must have caught his slip of speech, because his accent disappeared as quickly as a politician's promise in December. "Mr. Niven, will you *please* ask your questions. I have a patient arriving in fifteen minutes." He tapped his pen in staccato on his desk to emphasize his displeasure.

I hate that.

But hold on. Something wasn't adding up here. I didn't think Mangold's pen-tapping was simply annoyance: as he continued to stare at me, sweat had begun to bead up and pop on the man's forehead like oil drops on a hot driveway. His great gray slug of a tongue shot out and quickly ran around the surface of his lips. Mangold was, as they say, as nervous as a scarlet lady in church. Why? Surely not on my account...unless he was hiding something. Was it because he was German? Did that figure into this? And obviously, Mangold *was* German, and had just as obviously worked long and hard to eliminate his accent; even his idioms sounded authentically Midwestern. But again I wondered, to what purpose?

As if in answer, that prickling began to tickle my spine again. Oh no. Not here. Not now. Not *again.*

"Right." I cleared my throat and gritched around on my chair, buying some time until the feeling passed. It did. To be back later, I was sure. "Sorry. So Doctor Mangold, is this clinic only for women?"

"For the most part, yes." Mangold had also gotten himself under control somehow. "We do get the occasional man in here requesting a sperm count, but by and large our clientele is women."

"I see." I figured I could go my whole life without ever knowing what my sperm count was, but I wrote down his quote anyway; you never know what'll come in handy during an investigation. "So Brighter Day primarily dispenses fertility information?"

"That is correct. We are also licensed to do medical work, when required, on our patients."

"Blood tests and such?"

"Yes."

"Abortions?"

"Never!" Mangold shouted, making me jump. Blue veins popped on the sides of his neck in stark relief to his pallor. The man's vehemence had surprised me. "We do NOT perform abortions here! Human life is valuable!"

Valuable. Now wasn't that interesting. In his agitation Mangold had used the word "valuable", instead of "sacred" or "precious." On my pad I wrote, *valuable to whom? Commodity?*

"All right," I said. "So your main function is helping women become pregnant?"

"No." For the first time, Mangold smiled: a ghastly sight. "We are not gigolos here, Mr. Niven. At Brighter Day we simply help women maximize the experience of their pregnancies."

I smiled back at him as I wrote, *said 'we' twice. Editorial we? Or others?* "Maximize?" I asked. "In what way?"

Mangold leaned back in his chair and tented his fingers. "Vitamins, exercise, holistic therapies, self-actualization...there are many paths. You see, Mr. Niven, we simply wish to trigger the realization of the full potential of not only every woman that comes to us, but of the unborn child they are carrying as well."

Lord-a-mercy. What WAS the man babbling about? "I see," I said again, not seeing at all. "Could you tell me the approximate ages of your patients, Doctor?"

"Why?" The doctor's eyebrows had lowered in suspicion.

I smiled and cocked my head. "No reason. Simply statistics for my story."

"Very well," Mangold answered grudgingly. "They range from the young to the middle-aged. Some are as old as sixty. There have been many advances in extending a woman's fertile years, you know."

"Yes, I know." Pedantic blowhard. Mangold's pontificating was starting to wear on me. "You said the word 'young' a moment ago. How young? As young as say, eighteen?" I watched him closely.

And there it came again, the lip-licking. Nerves.

"Sometimes." Mangold shifted his rear. "Is that germane to your story, Mr. Niven?"

"Oh golly, Doctor, I don't know," I smiled. "It might be. It's like throwing spaghetti against the walls. You just see what sticks." I couldn't, of course, ask him what I really wanted to know: do you recall seeing a patient by the name of Francesca Taylor? So I made as if I was finishing up. "Anyway, Doctor, thank you for your time. You've been most helpful. May I call you later if I happen to think of any further questions?"

He sighed, wanting to end this. "If you wish."

"Thank you." I stood, closing my notepad, then I motioned to the file cabinets behind him. "This is sure some place you're running. All these patients. You should be proud." I had thrown out the bait, to see if Mangold would acknowledge that those cabinets did indeed contain his patient files. He took it.

"That's right, I am," the doctor said, standing as well in dismissal. "Most proud. Good day, Mr. Niven."

"And to you, sir." I left his office and passed back through the waiting room. As I did I smiled dazzlingly at Bluto. "And thank you too, Mrs. Blutarski."

She just glared. Battle-ax.

"Come again," she said coldly.

"Oh, you bet I will," I said with a wave as I walked out. I'd be coming back, all right, and sooner than they wanted. I knew I would return here later tonight--much later--for some entertainment I rarely get to enjoy.

A little burglary.

Chapter 9

But that would need to wait until after midnight. Right now, next on the agenda was a trip to Milford and Francesca's place of employment, the B. Dalton there. I hopped on 275 east and was at the U.S. 28 exit in about twenty minutes. I turned north on it, away from the town, and as I did I landed smack in the middle of Dante's fifth circle of Hell.

Michael Taylor had told me Milford was growing. From the construction traffic I found myself snarled in I could believe it. As soon as I had made the turn off the ramp there was a guy in a hardhat stopping all the cars, making us wait while a Caterpillar D-7 heavy dozer slowly backed out onto the highway. The thing paused, then made a ponderous, grinding turn before moving back off the road. Hardhat vigorously waved us on, and we all traveled about a foot before a stoplight got us.

Caramba. This was gonna take awhile.

The road was washboard-rough from the heavy equipment abusing it eighteen hours a day, and it seemed there were traffic lights spaced at fifteen-foot intervals. The drivers I saw were either heedless of the mess and yakking on car phones, or gritting their teeth at it all in helpless frustration. I was right with them. Country boy that I was, congestion like this made me want to leap from the Goddess and run screaming through a cornfield...provided I could find one. Where in the world was the land? Gone forever, I reckon. Everything this side of the 275 loop appeared to be either hamburger joints, strip malls, or car dealerships. Oh, baby. Heartburn, tacky junk, and Japanese iron: America at its best.

It took me nearly forty-five minutes to go a mile, but finally I located the shopping center where the B. Dalton was located. I gratefully pulled off the road and into the parking lot, at last shutting my poor overheated ride off.

As I walked into the store I was immediately greeted by the wonderful, papery smell of books. Books of all shapes and sizes, colors and subjects...Lord, how I love 'em. Even as a kid you were as likely to find me haunting our local library on a summer day as you would the swimming hole or the ballfields, and to their eternal credit both my dad and Granny encouraged my reading. I think they realized that expanding my horizons would be the only ticket that would ever get me clear of Picklebutt.

They were right. Books gave me wings, up and away from our poverty-cursed town, and into the great wide world. And my love of reading has held me in good stead all my life. Politics, fiction, nonfiction, reference, histories, biographies, classics, you name it--books have always been meat and drink to me, and always will. I feel that any part of the book business, from the writing of them to the printing and the selling, is as near to nobility as I'm ever likely to see.

Smiling, I strode up to the counter, which was manned--womaned?--by a slack-jawed androgynous member of some species.

Well sir. Maybe nobility is too strong a word.

I looked closely at this critter. His/her name badge read "Pat". Figures.

"Uh. Can I help you?"

"Hi Pat," I smiled. "I'd like to speak to the manager."

"Huh?"

I said it slower. "The manager."

"Uh." Gum-popping. Cud-chewing. "How'd you know my name, anyway?"

Ah, the young. So bright. So alert. I leaned in. "Look down on your shirt, Pat, and you tell me."

Pat frowned. "...what...?"

This place was a bookstore, all right, but I wasn't so sure that books would help Pat.

Right about then I heard a man's deep voice behind me. "Is there a problem?" I turned and nearly laughed out loud. Before me stood a man, probably my age or older, of average height and weight, but whose face was anything but average. I'll put it this way: I'd heard of body-piercing, but this was insane. The guy had a ring in each nostril, as well as one in his septum, like Ferdinand the Bull. Both earlobes sported pirate rings, and there was a huge safety pin in his left cheek. Two little silver horns hung dangling from the corners of his mouth. Frankenstein staples danced merrily in a lightning zigzag across his forehead, there were six studs in his right eyebrow, and through the bridge of the man's nose I counted four long things with balls on each end, like those skewers you use to hold a turkey butt together.

I suppose the guy thought he looked hip and with-it. I thought he looked like he'd been attacked by a rivet gun.

"You're the manager?" I asked.

"That's right. Reynaldo Phillips."

I stuck out my hand. "Hi, Mr. Phillips. My name is Joe Box. I'm a private investigator."

"Investigator?" Phillips frowned as we shook. "What's going on? What's this all about?"

I glanced at Pat, who blinked at us slowly, once, mouth agape. I couldn't tell if Pat was either shocked by my statement of who I was or was just a natural mouth-breather. Smiling, I gave Phillips a look. "Could we talk somewhere?"

He stared at me a second, then jerked his head over his shoulder, causing his face jewelry to catch the light. It still didn't look good. "I guess so. This way."

I followed him to the back of the store, and then into a tiny office fairly overflowing with undone paperwork. On Phillips' dinky desk sat a cooling Styrofoam cup of Micky D's coffee, alongside a breakfast sandwich that had a huge bite missing. I idly wondered if the man's mouth-horns ever jabbed his tongue. I guessed he wouldn't care. The high price of high fashion.

Phillips went around his desk and sat in a chair that was rattier than the one I used at my own place. He didn't offer me a seat, but to be fair, there wasn't another one, unless I wanted to pull up a box. Which I didn't. Phillips flipped open his hand and held it out to me, palm up. "Got any ID?"

What, he expected me to lay my license on it, like he was a cop that had just pulled me over? I didn't think so. He waited expectantly. I suppose I could have slapped my own hand down on his in a low five, but why start out on the wrong foot? So I drew my wallet out of my back pocket and dropped it open with a careless flick, exposing my Ohio PI license, just the way I used to do it when I was a cop myself and was badging somebody. Behind that license was another which gave me the right to conceal-carry, but ol' Reynaldo didn't need to know that. Yet.

He leaned over and peered at it, then sat back, satisfied. "Okay, you're legitimate. You can't be too careful these days."

Yeah, that's true. Book selling is a profession known for its seedy and dangerous elements.

"So, Mr. Box," Phillips continued, "what I can I do for you?" He took another huge bite of his sandwich, chewing it in a lazy side-to-side motion, like a camel.

"I've been retained by the Taylor family," I said. "I'm trying to get a lead on Francesca. Your store is the last place she was seen."

"I figured it was something like that," Phillips nodded. "Francesca's dad footing the bill. Because it's a sure bet the freaking cops won't break a sweat trying to find her."

"Why do you say that?"

He lazily closed one eye. "I don't think much of the police here. Never have. My Camaro and I aren't too well-liked in this town. I've had a few run-ins with Milford's finest in the past."

With his appearance and demeanor? Shocking.

"But I'll be happy to tell what I know," he finished. "We all liked Francesca, even if she was a little weird."

Weird? This from a guy with a face like a golf shoe? "Tell me about her, Mr. Phillips."

"Not much to tell," he shrugged. "She's been here about a year. Good worker. Prompt. Good with the customers, and my other employees seemed to like her. If she hadn't been so pushy about that stupid religion-"

"Religion?" I interrupted. "What kind?" Of course I knew, but I wanted his take on it.

Phillips curled a lip in distaste. "The worst kind. Francesca was one of those 'born-again' types. You know. Hoop-hallelujah! Her and that holy roller church she went to. She was always talking about it or God or Jesus or something."

"You mean in an offensive manner?"

"No." Phillips shook his head. "Not really. She was more subtle about it. But it always came out. Always. I mean, Francesca could take the most innocent or inane comment you would make about, say, the weather, and turn it straight into talk about God." The man's voice rose to a falsetto. " 'Oh, I agree! Isn't that sky something? And to think, God made it all just because he LOVES us!' " Phillips dropped back down into his normal speech. "It got a little tiresome, I can tell you. But other than that, she was fine."

I stared at him, trying to get my brain to re-engage. Phillips' crack about the sky... A memory was trying to rise. With an almost physical effort I pushed it firmly back down, and I cleared my throat. "Did Francesca ever discuss anything... private...with you or her co-workers?"

"Private? You mean other than her religion? Like what?"

"Like anything. Her life, what her plans were, did she ever want to get married. That sort of thing."

"Not with me," Phillips said. "Probably not with anyone else here, either. I keep the kids hopping, if you know what I mean.

They earn their money." He chuckled nastily.

What a jerk. If I had been Francesca I sure wouldn't have wanted to work for him. Unless maybe she had taken him on as some sort of project.

I pointed back out into the store. "How about Pat? Think she might know anything?"

"He." Pat was a he? Great-googly-moogly. "And I doubt it. Pat's only worked here since Saturday. I needed somebody to replace Francesca, and I mean like yesterday."

"So there's nothing really you can add."

"Nope. Francesca was in here Friday for inventory at eight, took a lunch at eleven, and clocked out at three forty-five." Phillips spread his hands. "That's all I can tell you. Sorry."

I leaned over and shook his hand. "Well, thanks for your time, Mr. Phillips. I'd like to call you again if I have any further questions."

"Hey, no problem," he smiled. "And good luck. I'd love to see you win this one instead of the cops."

I'll just bet you would, Speed Racer. I started to go, then turned back to him. "So did it take?"

He frowned again. "Did what take?"

"Francesca's... God-talk. Did any of it ever take with you?"

Phillips snorted dismissively. "Not hardly. I'm a self-made man."

The sad thing was, he looked it.

I left the store, shaking my head. This had been a useless trip. And it hadn't gotten any cooler out here. By now it had to have been at least ninety-five and heading higher. No doubt about it, we were going to be experiencing another day of Cincinnati under a slow broiler. Even Felicity--it was becoming easier to think of her by that name--would have had a hard time turning this weather into God-talk. Unless she wanted to talk about hell.

I glanced up at the unforgiving whiteness. In this heat it was like staring up into an immense inverted china bowl baking in a kiln. Yeah, wasn't that sky something...

And in a rush that almost made me gasp, my mind went back to Linda.

Chapter 10

We had met in Columbus nearly twenty-five years ago, while I was there on police business. I was working on what had started out as a local internal affairs problem.

The dilemma concerned a cop in our district who had been giving us fits. He was a plainclothes detective--never mind the name, it doesn't matter, call him Dirty Dan--whom the Captain suspected had been involved in what he termed "dereliction of duty." That really didn't say it. What the detective was in fact doing was allowing the drug dealers that congregated down at the corner of Eleventh and Vine to skate in exchange for a little product. "Dereliction" my foot. Dan was as dirty as a bus station men's room.

But I'll have to say he knew his stuff, because he was also as slick as an eel in butter, always staying two steps ahead while he continued to draw a city paycheck. Then one day IA and the Cap had an idea: a sting. We'll catch him in the act, they said, and make it airtight. (Remember, this was twenty-five years ago, when stings were considered cutting-edge.) Cap asked Sergeant Mulrooney and me to coordinate with IA in setting it up.

Why us? Simple. Our drug-dealing cop had been recruited by the Sarge nine years earlier, and was like a son to him. To the brass it was a no-brainer: Mulrooney had been there at the beginning of this man's career. Now he would be there at the end.

To a civilian mind that sounds cruel. I guess it is, but it didn't matter. The brass was adamant--Sarge was to be in on the arrest. Maybe they thought it would bring Mulrooney closure...or maybe they just wanted Sarge to pay for the mistake in delivering them this bad apple in the first place. Who knows.

Arranging the sting wasn't all that hard. What the IA had done was ask the Fourth District to send over a detective that our dirty friend didn't know. We then loaded the guy's pockets with a dozen or so glassine packets of cocaine we had gotten from the evidence room and placed him downtown on a corner that we knew the dealers frequented. Now all we had to do was wait.

Sure enough the crooked cop showed up a half-hour later, scowling and swaggering down the sidewalk in a loose-jointed gait. His eyes slid from side to side and he held his arms slightly away from his body, like a gunslinger. Maybe Dan thought that stride made him look tough. To me he waddled like a man with a hemorrhoid problem.

Sarge and I sat low in an unmarked car across the street, watching Dan as he came and snapping pictures of him with an old Pentax.

We saw Dan saunter up to our guy and badge him. A few words were exchanged, and our guy put up both his hands and shook his head. Dan sneered at him, then in a flash the crooked cop spun our guy around and slammed him flat up against the alley wall. For the longest time Dan kept him like that, all the while whispering something in the fake dealer's ear.

After a bit our guy nodded, reached into his windbreaker pocket, and held out two of the cocaine packets. Dan quickly glanced around him, then took them. They went their separate ways. We caught it all on film.

And that's how careers die: game, set, and match.

I saw Sarge shake his head almost imperceptibly. Then with a sigh he keyed his mike and said, "Now."

Within eight seconds three squad cars rocketed from out of nowhere, trapping old Dan in a triangle of steel and smoking tires. It was over just that fast.

The shocked expression on Dan's face was exactly that of a twelve-year-old caught peeking at his dad's Playboys. Sick and confused. You could almost hear the sound of Dan's cell door slamming shut.

And Sarge broke down and bawled like a baby.

That should have been the end of it. It wasn't. Now, five months later here the Cap, Sarge, and I were in Columbus, trying to settle what should been a local IA beef. We had thought we had Dan dead to rights, but found out there was more to the story.

It seemed our dirty cop had been piecing off some of the drugs he had stolen from the dealers to his mistress, who happened to be working as a secretary in the statehouse. She was then selling some to her co-workers and splitting the money with him, sixty-forty. Neat and untraceable, so they had thought.

And that just shows to go ya, as Granny used to say. I know that crack makes no sense, but sometimes she was like that.

Between us city cops, our Hamilton County brethren, and the staties the jurisdiction in this whole deal had turned into a real nest of snakes. Everybody was scrapping over poor old Dan like wolves around a deer carcass.

But a half-day of testimony later the decision was finally taken that it was state business after all. Which was fine with me. After four solid hours of depositions even I was ready to confess. At twelve o'clock straight up the assistant Attorney General closed the folder, smiled at us, thanked us, and dismissed us.

So there we were, the Cap, Sarge, and me. We had been given a full day off with pay to attend to this, and now here we were, done at noon.

The Cap and Sarge decided to hang around the AG's office, renewing old acquaintances. To a twenty-three-year-old cop like me, staying inside on such a pretty day and talking crime with old people sounded too much like jail, so I left.

I walked around town for a bit, neck craned up as I gawked at the buildings. I had been a Cincinnati resident for the past seven years--the time I spent humping it overseas for Uncle Sammy, and then my recuperation in the hospital from the same didn't count--but I was still fascinated by tall structures.

Considering my hometown, that wasn't hard to understand. To me, any intersection consisting of more than a church, a gas station, a general store, and a feed-and-grain co-op was Big Stuff.

So there I was, strolling down the street in my freshly starched uniform, head up and mouth open like the archetypical rube I was, when I ran slam into a woman.

We both went "oof!" at the same time, and the woman's papers and folders went flying. The next thing I knew we were both on the sidewalk, she on her side and me flat on my keister. I jumped to my feet and grabbed her hand, pulling her up. I almost started to dust the woman off, but stopped myself at the last second: no sense in making her think I was a pervert as well as an idiot.

My dad and Granny both had always told me as a kid to "suck it up and take it" when I screwed up, so I braced myself for the worst. I expected a torrent of well-deserved invective from this lady...but it never came. She didn't curse me. Instead she laughed, a tinkling, musical sound.

And I can pinpoint that moment as when I fell in love.

As the woman rearranged her clothing, smoothing the wrinkles out of her dress, I gazed at her. I got my first good look at this person I had collided with.

She appeared to be my age and was about my height, which made her pretty tall. In all honesty I really can't say she was beautiful. Striking maybe, with a strong sculpted chin, doe-brown eyes, and long, wavy, honey-colored hair that looked good enough to eat. That hair had come loose on one side, hanging down over the left part of her face, and she reached up long delicate fingers and pushed it back in place with a grin.

I finally found my voice. "Oh my God, ma'am!" I choked out. "Are you all right? I'm so sorry! I wasn't looking-"

"It's all right," the woman laughed. "I'm fine. It was as much my fault as it was yours. Were you looking up too?"

"Looking up?" I shook my head. "I'm afraid I don't-"

"Oh, I thought maybe you had been looking up at the new sign they put on top of Rasmussen's."

"Rasmussen's?"

"The store, silly." She pointed across the street at a five-story building. "That's where I work. They just put a new sign on top." She frowned at me, looking as cute as a puppy. "You really don't know what I'm jabbering about, do you?"

"No, sorry. I'm from out of town. Cincinnati."

The woman took a step back, giving me the up-and-down. I think it was only then that she noticed I was a cop.

"Wow," she laughed. "Do I feel like a ditz! I should have seen it right away. The difference in uniforms, I mean. And Columbus cops don't normally appear so---intimidating." She curled a finger on that sweet chin and smiled. "But I don't know. Maybe it's not just the uniform."

I felt my face turning as red as a kidney bean. Where I came from if a woman began staring at me as frankly as this one was, my Granny would have called her a trollop, or worse.

But I liked it.

"Have lunch with me." I almost looked around. Who said that? Was that ME? Before the last word was out of my mouth I regretted my outburst. This gorgeous creature didn't know me from Adam's off-ox, and here I had just asked her to lunch. That's not how you did it. Lord, I was rotten at this sort of thing.

"What I mean is-" I stammered. "It's noon. Lunchtime. I feel really bad about...knocking... I mean, I just wanted to--"

And that's all that came out. My thoughts had seized up like a tractor clutch in July.

But then amazingly, sweetly, she took pity on this stumbling farm boy and offered me her right hand to shake. Wordlessly I took it. It felt nice in mine. Really nice. Her skin was as warm and smooth and soft as a quilt in winter.

And even without me asking, she knew instinctively what to say next, that's how good she was. "Names first," she smiled. "Then lunch. I'm Linda Nash. And you are-?"

I returned the shake--as gently, I hoped--and released her hand. "Joe. Joe Box." I was stammering again.

"Well, Joe-Joe Box, it's a lovely day, and I'm starving. But it's too lovely to eat inside. Do you like chili dogs? I know a great stand just down the block."

I was smiling, but inwardly I grimaced. Chili dogs...arrgh. I'd never had a chili dog in my life; to me they looked like hot cat food. But if it meant spending lunchtime with this beauty, I'd have eaten tacks with a spoon.

"Sounds great!" I nodded enthusiastically. "Chili dogs would be great! Just down the street, huh? Chili dogs?"

Did I really sound as stupid as I felt? I half wished a bank robber would come backing out right about then so I could shoot him and show her I wasn't a complete incompetent.

But Linda didn't even seem to notice. "I think you'll like them. The owner uses brown mustard instead of yellow. It really gives them zip."

Zip? English language had deserted me, and my mind was racing like a car in neutral. What's zip?

"Come on, Joe-Joe," Linda smiled. She began to turn, then she stopped. "Hey. Will you just take a look at that." Linda angled her face up, pointing. "Isn't that sky something?" I looked up too. It was, and it was only then that I really noticed how nice everything felt. April had never seemed so kind--T. S. Eliot's crack about it notwithstanding.

After a moment we both looked back down at each other. Once again I fell headlong into those soft brown eyes.

"Our nasty old Columbus weather sure has cleared up, hasn't it?" Linda grinned. "It looks like we're getting our Easter present early this year. Isn't today turning out great?" She offered me her arm, just like we were courting.

I slipped my arm around hers. Great. That's how I felt, all right. Deliriously, goofily great.

And don't you know it, Linda laughed again: the music of the spheres. God was in His heaven, all was right with the world, and Joe Box had a lunch date. With her! I felt like dropping one wing and running around in circles.

I glanced over at Linda, and her mischievous eyes danced with hinted-at pleasures. She felt it too. We started to walk.

"Hey, wait a minute, what about your papers?" I asked, turning and pointing at them on the sidewalk.

"Oh, leave them, Joe-Joe." Linda tossed her head, grinning again. "It's spring!"

No doubt about it, I was in love.

*****

Linda and I enjoyed what the blue-haired authors of ladies' books like to call a "whirlwind romance." Cyclone was more like it. I knew from the start I was seriously out-classed, but it was love, and frankly I didn't give a rat's hairy behind.

Linda was from Boston, she told me over those chili dogs--not bad, by the way--and hailed from a long line of Brahmins. Idiot me, I wasn't about to ask her what a Brahmin was; I thought maybe it was some sort of Hindu. But again, Linda was a step ahead of me and told me that's what landed gentry Bostonians were called.

She had gotten her degree a year ago in marketing from Vassar, and "Daddy" had helped her get a position with Rasmussen's department store as a buyer. That made sense to me. I mean, that's what the rich do...buy stuff. So why not get paid for it? Anyway, it hadn't hurt anything that "Daddy" had sponsored one of the Rasmussen kin in his college fraternity years ago, so when it came time to help Linda land a job, Rasmussen stepped up to the plate. Old boy's network, I reckon.

From the start people, mainly Linda's people, said it wouldn't work. There were too many differences between us, they said. She was high-church Episcopalian; I was brush-arbor Baptist. She was Saks and Liz Claiborne; I was K-Mart and Old Spice. She was Chateaubriand and claret; I was brats and beer. She was--well, you get the idea.

In sum and in total, she was rich, and Lord knows I wasn't.

We simply didn't care; we each completed the other, just the way it's supposed to work. So the cyclone commenced. That chili dog lunch was followed by a long walk to I-don't-know-where. Linda and I just walked and talked, talked and walked. Late that afternoon we finally parted ways in front of the statehouse, both of us promising to call each other and both grinning like we'd been sucking helium.

Sarge and the Cap took one look at me as the three of us

climbed into the squad car, and they exchanged knowing glances.

"Joe, my boy," Sarge said, as he started it up, "you've got it bad, and that's a fact. Something tells me this one's gonna go fast."

He was right. Inside of two months Linda and I were engaged. Her folks griped about it some, understandably. They thought she was marrying beneath her station. I was sure of it, but Linda just laughed and gave me a head-noogie.

We were married at Christmastime in Boston, complete with a full-dress-uniform ceremony. Linda's pastor officiated, and Sarge, who had flown up at his own expense, stood with me as my best man. We were accompanied not only by the sweet sounds of Christmas carolers softly singing outside in the snow, but also by Granny on the piano. She swayed and played to beat all. Granny also sang, in a clear contralto, one of my old favorites, *Whispering Hope*. Even Mr. and Mrs. Nash joined in the singing; I guess they had forgiven me for stealing away their daughter. All in all, it was a perfect a wedding as the human mind can conceive.

But the moment didn't hold. A year later, on our first Christmas eve together as man and wife, Linda died.

It happened this way: every Christmas all of us Third District cops drew lots to see who would have to work that shift. This night, of all nights, I pulled one of the short straws. Sarge must have seen the look of abject disappointment on my face, but he didn't say anything until he saw me filling out the squad car requisition form.

"Give me that," Sarge said, sliding the clipboard over to him. "I'll finish the paperwork if you'll go get the car warmed up. Colder'n a well-digger's heinie tonight."

"What are you talking about?" I asked. "I'm the one that has to pull a double shift here, not you. I saw you draw a long straw."

He scowled. "You need glasses. Wish I did. So hurry up, already. You know how much I hate sliding in on that cold vinyl."

I did as Sarge told me, and went out and started the car. After a few minutes I came back in to grab us some coffee for the shift. That's when I ran into Donnelly, another rookie.

"You and Sarge heading out?" he asked. "Man, I hope you're wearing your thermal skivvies. It's brutal out there tonight. Super-frosty. I'll sure be feeling for you guys."

I shot Donnelly a look. "What's that supposed to mean? I saw you draw a short straw, too."

"Yeah, I did," he laughed. "And Sarge switched with me. Big dumb Mick said he wanted to work with you tonight. Ain't that a kick? Looks like a nice Christmas present for me and Sue."

As I watched Donnelly move on down the hall, Sarge came up and took one of the styrofoam cups from me. "Come on, junior. Crime awaits."

I stared at him, and the words finally came. "Listen, Sarge, Donnelly told me what you did. I-"

"Yeah, he's been spreading that tale all over the station house," Sarge snorted. "I'd say the boy needs a checkup. What the Academy's sending us these days, I swear..." Sarge slurped his coffee, then examined me closely. "Well? Are you gonna stand there all night giving me goo-goo eyes or are we gonna go catch crooks?"

"You big, dumb..." My throat closed, and I said huskily, "Donnelly sure pegged you right. Okay, let's go catch crooks."

*****

It was nearly ten p.m. when we caught the squeal. Traffic accident, Harrison and La Feuille, occupant trapped. Sarge and I looked at each other and tensed. The weather tonight had turned truly foul, and in the last hour the temperature had dropped to five degrees with a wind chill of minus-twenty. The streets were now glazed with black ice. A wreck, bad enough at any time, in these conditions could only be horrific.

We flipped on the lights and siren and hit it.

In less than three minutes we were at the scene. The car involved had wrapped itself around a power pole so completely the front end was almost touching the rear. Trashed as it was, I could tell it was a Dodge Cricket, never the safest of cars even on dry pavement. I knew, because Linda and I owned one. I had bought it solely for the reason that it was cheap, and I had stubbornly refused any help whatsoever from Linda's kin.

Pride. Rotten pride...

We pulled the squad as close to the wreck as we could. Sarge had already called an ambulance en route, and in the distance we could hear the scream of the siren as it came. We clambered out of our vehicle, both of us zipping our leather jackets tight against the wind. As we stumbled around the wrecked car's back end I thought I saw, folded into the glass shards of the rear window, what looked like an NRA sticker.

I shook my head. No. Couldn't be. Other Dodge Crickets had

NRA stickers besides ours.

Then I heard Sarge. "Oh. My. God..." He had reached the driver's side door before I did, and had shined his torch inside. "Joe."

My heart died as Sarge said my name. I knew.

I violently shoved him aside as I shined my own light on the driver crumpled over the wheel. It was Linda.

"Oh Jesus!" I wrenched the door open and made a grab for her, but Sarge pulled me back. "Leggo!" I screamed. "It's Linda!"

"I know it is. But don't go yanking on her. You want to kill her? Think! Use your training!"

I must have given Sarge a look of pure despair, for he softened his tone. "Talk to her, Joe. She's still breathing. Keep her with us. The medics'll be here any second."

I leaned back in. "Linda?" My voice was quavering. "Honey? Can you hear me? It's Joe."

"Hm?" Linda pulled her head up off the wheel and looked at me. I had to bite my knuckle to keep from screaming. Her face was a mass of blood. "Joe? ...you...?" She was having a hard time focusing on me.

"Shh, baby, keep quiet, now." I gulped hugely. "The ambulance is coming. Just-"

"I was...buying...present..." Linda's voice sounded distant, disconnected. Worse, blood was bubbling on her lips with every word. "Some...surprise..." So that explained what she was doing out here. We had agreed, for our budget's sake, not to buy presents for each other this year. I had agreed. It was just like her to try to surprise me.

"Oh Joe..." Linda was staring up through the cracked windshield at the night sky, where a billion stars shone. "Isn't that sky...something..." Then her breath fluttered, her eyes closed, and she was still.

A billion stars. Now a billion and one.

*****

We buried Linda two days later.

And two days after that I quit the force.

Chapter 11

Even though it wasn't yet noon, I felt like having a drink. No. That wasn't it: I felt like drinking. There's a difference.

Heading back towards the 275 interchange I saw I was passing any number of small, strip-center-type bars. Some of them even had vehicles parked in front at this early hour, mostly mud-encrusted pickups. Construction guys was my guess, and they were having lunches of the liquid type. I felt like joining them. Inside.

So I wouldn't have to look at the sky.

But I didn't. Maybe it was for Linda's sake I kept on driving. Or mine. I don't go on benders, not anymore. What I did the day I quit the cops cured me of that. Because that was the day I went on my very last world-class, week-long tear.

Linda's death had hit me like a ray. I just could not get past it. Sarge tried to help, but his words fell flat. I couldn't work, and I couldn't stay, so I rented a car and ran. Like a dog that had been clipped by a gasoline tanker, all I could think of was getting home.

And so I did, but not back to our house. I instead had gone to the only place that I thought would still have me, no questions asked: Clay County, Kentucky, and my home town of Picklebutt.

I negotiated the five-hour drive over the snow-covered highway while still in a mental fog. Several times I'm sure I narrowly missed going off the road, but I simply didn't care. I drove with the single-mindedness of a lemming.

Home. I had to get home.

As I finally approached Picklebutt's city limits though, I realized the trip had, in the end, been pointless. I had no kin left here. What had I been thinking? Where would I go now? With grim resolution, as I mashed the gas, I knew.

I drove right through the little town, and kept on going. For miles I drove, over twisty roads, right on up into the hollers. On and on I went, farther and deeper into the hills, finally pushing so far back that where I was headed, the daylight had to be piped in. I was on a mission now, but not on a mission for God, like the line in the old Blues Brothers movie. No. My mission was more simple than that, more gut-level: I wanted 'shine. Moonshine. Good old Kentucky bust-head corn-squeezin's. My whole being was crying out for it. And the oblivion I so desperately sought.

Lem MacElroy, Clay County's most famous citizen, would help me. It was well-known around these parts that Lem made the best 'shine in the state. And weirdly enough he had never been raided, not even once. Maybe it was because people thought he was crazy. Rumor said that Lem and his boys had stuck up on pikes the heads of any revenooer stupid enough to go stomping around their land.

Knowing Lem, I could believe it. He was a florid-faced, whisker-stubbled giant of a man, and it was said of Lem that if he liked you he would share a glass of his concoction with you and tell you stories until the sun came up.

If he didn't like you, you never made it off his mountain.

I had finally driven as far as I could, so I pulled off the road and parked the car. Then I hiked the rest of the way up to his base camp over a slippery, barely-seen path; not an easy task.

As I slowly walked into the clearing, I kept my hands well away from my body. The area appeared deserted, but I knew better, and I felt unseen eyes checking me out as I stopped.

I noticed the still, a huge brass contrivance, and Lem's source of living, was bubbling away on the fire, apparently unattended. Its wood fuel was neatly stacked beside it, and the smell of cooked grain hung heavy in the air.

The utter silence was unnerving. Nothing stirred. An old beat-up Airstream trailer crouched just at the treeline, waiting.

Time hung fire.

I stopped, motionless, expecting the shot.

But it never came; Lem must have still liked me. Instead a few minutes later his sentries simply materialized, like a conjuring trick. With curt, wordless nods they let me pass unharmed. It didn't hurt that one of them, Gary Joe, was Lem's youngest boy, and he and I had wrestled together in junior high.

So that's how I found myself perched on a stump, waiting for Lem, and watching the January snowflakes as they whirled around me.

The door finally opened on his trailer and Lem stomped out. "Heard ya lost yer wife," he grunted at me in greeting, in that snuffling way he had. No hello Joe, how are ya, just that.

"Yeah," I grunted back. "Who told you?"

"I hear things. Ya still with the po-lice?"

"If I was, would I be here?" I guess Lem picked up the raw pain in my voice, because he simply handed me a washed-out gallon plastic bleach bottle that was full, I knew, of his finest.

"'xpect ya need this," Lem said as he handed me the jug. Then he reached down and picked up an old jelly glass off the ground. He held it out. "Use this if ya want, Joe."

I glanced at it as I took it from him. Dirty. Like I cared.

"Thanks." I unscrewed the bottle cap and poured the nearly clear liquid into the glass, almost to the brim. Then I drank it down to the bottom in three gulps. It burned like napalm, and in seconds I could feel my brain synapses beginning to shut down.

"Good as always, Lem," I breathed. "How much?"

"Nothin'. For yer loss."

"Well, thanks again." I lifted the jug at him in salute.

He shrugged. "I know how it is. Losin's what I do best. Lost Ella purt near twenty years ago. Every now and then, of a warm summer day, if the air is clear and the light's right, I can still see her bathin' in the stream and laughin'. She's kinda shimmerin', like. I 'xpect I'll be joinin' her directly."

I didn't answer as I settled back on the stump, pouring myself another not-so-healthy slug as I did.

Lem looked at me. "Ya wanna come on back to the trailer house with me'n the boys, Joe? Warmer there."

"No thanks," I replied, taking another long pull. "Here is fine."

"Ya might freeze."

"Yep." I finished the drink and poured another. "There is that."

Lem nodded in understanding. "I know how it is."

*****

But I didn't freeze. Along around four in the morning Lem, Gary Joe, and Lem's other son Estill came out of their trailer to check on me. What they found was a twenty-four-year-old former cop, covered with snow and drunk beyond reason, propped against the stump. As they hefted me onto their shoulders--they told me later--I was as stiff as cordwood, blue skinned, and very nearly without a pulse.

They brought me into the trailer, cranked up the kerosene heater, covered me with quilts that Lem's dead wife Ella had made as a young woman, and placed me between three blue-tick hounds that shared their quarters. For the first hour or so it was touchy, they said, but when my blueness had finally started to fade and my heart started pumping better, they all breathed sighs of relief.

Not that Lem was a saint. He just told me later that the ground was too hard to dig another grave. Estill suggested the stump-grinder, and Gary Joe had said that maybe they could have thrown me in the lime pit. Lem had allowed that he hadn't considered those things, but if I didn't make it, either was fine with him.

To this day I don't know if they were joking or not.

Before I left I purchased six more jugs of 'shine from Lem. This time he didn't refuse my money, but only parted with solemn words, something to the effect of that I should only try to drink a jug a day, or until the pain left.

I knew I would run out of jugs long before that.

Chapter 12

The next twelve years are a blur as I traveled all over the country, working. Among other things I worked as a rent-a-cop at malls, stood night-watchman duty at warehouses, even parlayed my size into doing body guarding work for some spoiled rock'n'rollers. Anything to keep a few bucks coming in, so I could move on.

That last gig, the rock'n'roll thing, was the worst, although it paid the best. "Spoiled" is too tame a word for the yahoos I babysat. They were sullen momma's boys with minimal musical talent, and their main proclivities were, in order, drinking kegs of beer, trashing more rooms than you could possibly believe, and pursuing any little groupie girl seventeen or under. The whole thing made me sick. As I said, though, the money was good, and the drugs weren't bad, so with a firm determination I buried any self-respect I still possessed even deeper.

But one night the wheels finally came off. It was Christmas eve, and I was at the end. I had rented a room in a ratty, mildewed, peeling-wallpaper hot-pillow joint somewhere outside of Baton Rouge. Nothing unusual there; many a Christmas eve had found me in such places, or worse. But that night would prove to be different, because that was the night I got my life back...sort of. And here's something strange: even though most of my lost years are just a smear in my memory, for some reason I can recall every detail of what happened during those next three hours. Each part stands out in crystal relief.

The time was nearly midnight, as I recall. The concert I had helped control--for a group called Hit The Switch, you may remember them--had been over for an hour. The room I occupied at the Southern Breeze Motel possessed a solitary window, and I had it cranked all the way open, because of the heat. No AC. Across the darkened, cracked parking lot I could smell the fetid odor of a swamp. I don't know the name of it, but I remember gas rising off its surface in ghostly swirls. Off in the swampy distance a nutria screamed, sounding just like a hysterical woman. For a second even the frogs and crickets shut up to listen. There was an old black-and-white TV perched on the cigarette-scorched dresser, and a Christmas movie was playing on it--*The Bishop's Wife.* The scene was where Cary Grant was skating with Loretta Young across an impossibly flawless frozen soundstage pond. A band was playing, I remember, and the two of them were pirouetting like Olympians. Could any Christmas be so perfect? I didn't know; I had the volume off. I was sitting on the bed in my clothes, which I had not changed in six days. In my left hand I clutched a piece of paper. On it was Sergeant Mulrooney's phone number for his retirement condo in Florida. How I got it I have no idea, but I know I had been carrying the thing in my wallet for over a decade. That's what I had in my left hand.

In my right I held my Smith and Wesson .38 revolver. One bullet rested in the chamber, and I had the hammer cocked back. For the longest time I looked back and forth between the phone number and my piece, deciding, deciding.

In the end, I called Sarge.

"Hello?" He still sounded the same.

"...Sarge?"

"Hello? Helen, turn that thing down, willya?...I dunno who it is...Who is this?"

"Sarge..." My voice caught.

"Joe? Joe, is that you, boy?"

"God..." I almost dropped the phone. Why was everything so blurry? My nose was running, and I choked out the rest. "Help me, please..."

"Helen, it's Joe...no, I don't know where... Where are you, son?"

"Baton Rouge." I was finding it hard to breathe. I was seeing nothing but water. Then it all came tumbling out. "I had your phone number on me, I've kept it all these years, I'm sorry to be calling you on Christmas eve, but I had your number, and I've got my piece cocked and I just don't know what to do, Sarge..."

"Your gun? Oh God. Lower the hammer, Joe, and put it down. You done that yet? Okay, we gotta talk..."

*****

And talk we did, for the next three hours. Talked and prayed. That is, Sarge prayed. I listened and vented. It all came out, every bit. The tears, the regrets, the grief for the lost years, even the anger I felt at Linda for dying and leaving me all alone. At the end I was emotionally drained.

"So now what, Sarge?" My breathing was ragged.

"You tell me. It's your life, Joe. Your decision. Would you like to go back on the force? I know the new captain. I could pull some strings. And you know my son Jack is a cop, don't you?"

"Really?" I was breathing better now. "No, I didn't know."

"Yeah, he joined up a year after you left. Made me a proud papa, I can tell you. He worked his way up, got his gold detective shield and everything, and now he's with the vice squad."

"You don't say. Sarge, that's great. Really."

"You said it. So if you wanted me to, I could call him..."

"No, that's all right," I said. "I think my cop days are behind me. Too many memories, and too many miles."

"Okay." I could hear Sarge take a drink. He dearly loved eggnog. Non-alcoholic, of course. "So how's about going private?"

"Me?" I almost sputtered a laugh; it would have been my first in months. "A private eye? Heaven forfend."

"Why, Joe? You've got the temperament, not to mention the smarts."

"Yeah, but not the drive."

"How do you know?"

"Sarge, I haven't had the drive to do much of anything for an awfully long time."

"Well, boy," he sipped again. "Maybe it's time you got off your dead butt and did something about that."

Sarge always did have a way with words. And just maybe... Was it possible he saw something in me no one else did? Could I really do it?

"Are you thinking, Joe, or did you fall asleep?"

"I'm thinking... Sarge, do you really think I could?"

"That's not the question. Do *you* think you could?"

"Maybe." The idea was growing like a flower. "Yeah. I could."

"Good." I could hear Sarge drain the last of his nog. "Now here's the thing. Tomorrow's Christmas day. You sleep in. Get some rest. The next day let me do some phoning. I know some guys in Columbus. Let me call in a few markers. We'll make this work, Joe. You'll see."

I felt the tears welling up again. "Oh God, Sarge, thanks. You just don't know-"

"Yeah I do. Helen and me, we've freely received. Now we're freely giving. The circle stays unbroken." He hung up.

*****

I had always known that Sarge and his wife were Christians,

right from the beginning. They had never pushed their religion on anybody, but they made no bones about it either. I saw that for myself on my first day in uniform.

Sarge had brought me to his house after our shift was over for supper, and Helen made us a great one, everything I liked: meatloaf, mashed potatoes, peas, even apple cobbler for dessert. How had she known? And what was most incredible was that they prayed before we ate; even Granny had never done that. The two of them prayed like they believed God was listening, that He cared.

That night Sarge had proven his Christianity once again, and on a no-good h'aint like me. Amazing. The thought hit me, now as many times before: if I was ever to become a Christian, I wanted to be one like Sarge.

The Mulrooney's love didn't end with me. After I met Linda they went out of their way to include her in their family, too. Sarge and Helen would have us over to watch TV with them sometimes, or to play cards. Or just to talk, whatever. The thing I remember best about them is that they fit together, just like Linda and I did...would have.

They came to her funeral, of course, and two days later when I quit the force Sarge hugged me fiercely and said that he and Helen understood and would keep praying for me, and would never give up. That struck me then as an odd thing to say.

I was to find out much later how strong and lasting those prayers were.

Chapter 13

The interstate loop sped beneath me as I headed west towards Hamilton, and towards Mike Taylor's church, Harvard Pike. I had called the church from my car to set the appointment up, then I called Mike to ask him how to get there. Mike sounded excited that I was going to meet his pastor, a man named Luke Samuels. I was looking forward to it too. So far this investigation was going nowhere; maybe I would find some answers at the church.

I used the drivetime for introspection. I knew a few things for sure, but only a few: one, Brighter Day clinic was a front for something else (a guy like Mangold doesn't sweat like he did over a pap smear); two, Mrs. Blutarski was a real-life Nurse Ratchet, minus the charm; three, the B. Dalton in Milford smelled wonderful; four, Reynaldo Phillips, its manager, was a smirking dictator; and five, his clerk Pat had less sexual identity than David Bowie.

Not much collating for a morning's work, was there?

I took the route 4 exit off I-275 and headed north. After three miles, I took the route 4 bypass, again keeping north. I was following the directions Mike had given me, but it still seemed to me that he and his family lived an inordinately long way from their church. Again I wondered what the attraction could be. Mike had said his church was Pentecostal. Could that be it? I knew nothing about them, except that Granny had warned me about them as a kid. She said the people that went to such places were crazy. I guessed I would find out soon enough.

I finally came to Princeton Road and turned left. Princeton Road, Harvard Pike Church...I almost expected to see a Yale pony keg. What was with the Ivy League names? Cincinnati was a good eight hundred miles from that part of the country. Maybe the developer here had been a big football fan. Cute.

But as I approached the church I saw I hadn't been far off. The building really did sit at the corner of Princeton Road and Harvard Pike, and right catty-ways from it was Yale Boulevard.

Well, hoo-rah. Pass the pigskin.

Mike said his church had a congregation of over four thousand. Seeing the size of the place I could believe it. Contemporary in design and spotlessly landscaped, Harvard Pike Church seemed to fit in well with the upper-middle class neighborhood surrounding it. Considering that Mike said it was Pentecostal, I didn't know if that was a good thing or not.

I pulled the Goddess into the large lot, shut her off, got out, and entered through the big double doors in the front. As I strolled in the lobby I glanced around. The church proved to be as nice on the inside as it was on the out. Mauve carpeting, oak walls, teal and cream accents, high beamed ceilings, skylights... some serious money had gone into the place. This was a Pentecostal church? Incredible. Where did they keep the snakes?

The door marked "Staff" was the first one off a short hall that looked like it led down to some sort of atrium. I opened the door and stepped into a small waiting room. At the back a counter separated it from the offices beyond, and behind the counter sat a young woman who smiled winningly as I walked up.

"Hi!" she chirped. "May I help you?"

I noticed her nameplate read Zoe Gennaro. "Hi, Ms. Gennaro. My name is Joe Box. I-"

"Joe Box!" She almost jumped up. "You're the one that's looking for Francesca, right?"

I guess Mike hadn't wanted it a secret. "That's right."

The young woman pressed a hidden buzzer and the door between us opened.

"Come on in, Mr. Box! Pastor is expecting you."

"Thanks, Ms. Gennaro," I answered as I walked past her.

"Call me Zoe," she giggled. "Any friend of Francesca's is a friend of mine!"

I guess it hadn't occurred to Zoe that I had yet to meet Francesca. Oh well. After enduring the sullen Mrs. Blutarski and the vacant Pat, I was just about in the right mood for a bubbly twenty-something. I grinned at her and pointed. "Which way?"

"To your right, last door on the left. You can't miss it. It says Pastor Samuels right on it!"

I grinned again. Nice kid.

I did as she said, walking the thirty or so feet down the hall and coming to the door. It did indeed say Pastor Samuels right on it. As I knocked I heard a pleasant, country-tinged voice call out "Come on in!"

I gave the office a quick glance as I did. Not nearly as big as Nick Castle's digs, or even Mike's, but nice nonetheless. The oak paneling motif had carried through to here, but the carpet was a muted beige. Oddly enough, on the walls there were more of the book fragments like I had seen Nick have. Maybe they both belonged to the Parchment of the Month Club.

I hoped Mike's pastor wasn't going to be one of those "bless...Gawdd..." stuffed shirts. Nose in the air, hoity-toity, condescending martinets--those dudes chap me. A lot.

But what if this guy was worse? What if he slapped both hands on the sides of my head and screamed? What if he started dancing? Lord help me, what if he pulled out a snake?

I guess it's an understatement to say I was more than a bit tense as Samuels came out from behind his desk to greet me. I was a bit taken aback, though, as I got my first good look at him: he sure didn't look much like a crazy man or truth be told, even a pastor.

Not that I had encountered that many, but the pastors I had met in the past were usually uptight, jugeared, Ichabod Crane stand-ins. Not him. Samuels looked more like a middle-management executive, or maybe the business ed teacher at a community college. In other words, no snakes in sight. Yet.

So far, so good, and I relaxed a bit. As we shook hands, the pastor's affable demeanor put me even more at ease.

"Mr. Box?" he smiled. "Luke Samuels. Have a seat, won't you?" The pastor's smile was open and genuine, and his soft southern drawl made my defenses lower down another notch.

I noticed that Samuels was a bit shorter than I am, but his erect posture more than made up for it. He was about my age, dark-haired and dark-complected, with close-set brown eyes bracketing a strong, Roman nose. Now this next may sound weird, but when I looked at the man I got the quick mental picture of an eagle: confident, secure, and utterly at ease.

More at ease than I was, that's for sure.

But back beneath the pastor's smiling countenance I could sense something else: a core of strength that I had only seen twice before in my life. Sergeant Mulrooney had it. So did Linda.

I would have hated to have gone eyeball-to-eyeball with this man at a poker table. Or faced him down in a gunfight back in the old West. But something told me he would have been a good man to have next to you when you were pinned down in a rice paddy by the VC, like happened to me many moons ago.

I almost laughed: I had sure made quite a judgment of Samuels in less than fifteen seconds.

Smiling, the pastor motioned at me with his hand, but instead of going back behind his desk, he led us to a small round table in the corner. Nice touch. Folksy.

"Thanks." I took one chair as he sat down in the other. I smiled at him. "Your church isn't quite what I had expected."

Samuels grinned at me in return. "Southern boy, Mr. Box?"

"Yep," I allowed. "You can tell? I thought I had lost most of my accent years ago."

Samuels grinned again. "It's like putting white paint on a green wall. What's underneath always shows through."

We both chuckled, and I felt myself relaxing. "You're right. We might as well carry signs."

"Would you like some coffee, Mr. Box?"

"Yes, thanks."

"Just a second." Samuels got up and opened his office door. "DOTTY!" he bellowed at the top of his lungs. "COFFEE!" He turned to me and said in a normal voice, "How do you like yours?"

I was trying to get my pulse to slow down. Samuels' yell had scared the whiz out of me. "Uh, black?"

"MAKE ONE BLACK!" he screamed again.

I heard a faint voice down the hall answer, "Okay..."

Samuels closed the door and rubbed his hands briskly. "Dotty'll be back with our coffee in a minute. Although I make no claims as to how good it'll be." I must have been staring at him, for he continued, "Oh, my yelling. Our intercom system is down again, for the sixth time in the last five weeks. I've about given up on it, and yelling seems to work just as well. As a Pentecostal pastor I'm used to it!"

Before I could answer him his door opened and a tall, elegant-looking older woman entered, bearing two white steaming mugs. "Here, Pastor."

Samuels took them from her. "Thanks, Dotty." He handed me mine, and then sipped from his. He made a snarling face. "Oh, good Lord have mercy. This is awful."

"I know, Pastor," the woman--Dotty--commiserated. "We've tried everything with that old urn. Cleaning it, new filters, even different coffee. Nothing helps. What does it taste like today?"

Samuels sipped again and shuddered. "Like the way WD-40 smells."

Dotty shook her head. "I'm sorry, Pastor..."

"Not your fault, Dotty," he soothed. "Like I've said before, we'll get a better machine when we get in the new house."

Dotty departed, still clucking despondently.

Samuels watched her go and shook his head in admiration as he sat back down. "Dotty Leland." He turned to me. "Dotty's been my secretary forever. She and her husband Fred, one of our elders, practically run this place. Without 'em I'd be dead in the water and sinking fast."

I smiled and took a sip from my cup. And almost choked. Caramba. Samuels was right.

"Bad, huh?" he asked.

"Oh yeah. And I thought army coffee was rotten." I sat the cup down and pushed it aside. Granny didn't raise no fool.

Samuels did the same with his. "When were you in?"

"What, the army? Almost thirty years ago. I can truthfully say it was not the most fun I've ever had."

"It sounds like there's a story there."

"There is," I agreed. "Short and not very sweet. I went in to fight for Uncle Sam in June of '70. Eight weeks after I enlisted I found myself in Vietnam, a rifle company. April the following year I was wounded and I finished my hitch at Walter Reed. You?"

"I was in a year earlier, although I never saw combat. They put me in the Signal Corps. I was stationed at a little base outside of Laguna Hills, California."

"Rough duty."

Samuels laughed, "Wait, it gets worse. You'll never guess what we did there."

I shook my head, and he laughed again. "We made the medical training films for the guys headed overseas. You probably saw my work. They were real cautionary tales."

"That was *you?*" I was laughing too. "We hated those things."

"Aw, come on," he grinned. "You honestly didn't like 'VD: The Whispering Killer'? That was one of our best."

"Nope. And I really hated the sequel, 'Penicillin: Our Powerful Pal'."

We both laughed again, and Samuels leaned back in his chair. "So anyway, Mr. Box, I know you didn't come here to swap service stories."

"Call me Joe."

"Luke."

"And no, Luke, I didn't." I folded both hands on the table in front of me. "How much has Mike Taylor filled you in?"

"Not a bunch. Just that Francesca's been missing since Friday afternoon. That's all it took to get the intercessors going on it, and the church as a whole has been praying for her, too."

There it was again. Prayer. He said it so matter-of-factly. Not even a hint of self-consciousness. Just like Linda and Sarge.

"Is there anything you can add to my understanding of her?" I asked him.

"Maybe. Did Mike mention the Armorbearers?"

"Yeah. College-and-career group here, right?"

"Yes. Francesca never missed an outing with them." Samuels went on with a chuckle, "They've even been good for making matchups. I've conducted five weddings since I've been here that I can trace directly back to the group."

"Mike mentioned a boy here named Ted," I said. "Do you know him?"

"Yeah, Ted Whittaker. He's a good kid. And he's flat nuts about Francesca."

"But Mike also said it wasn't mutual. True?"

"Yeah, as far as it goes," Samuels allowed. "Francesca is really popular, and I suppose she just isn't ready to settle down with a steady boyfriend yet."

I leaned forward. "So in your opinion, Luke, do you think that this Whittaker kid may have something to do with her disappearance?"

Samuels sat back and gave me a hard look. "Wow, Joe, you really cut to it, don't you? Are you normally this blunt?"

"Yeah. My wife used to call it a character flaw. So, do you?"

Samuels was shaking his head even as I asked it. "Nope. You're over in the next county on this one. Ted's had similar crushes on no less than three of our girls here in the last year. In each case the boy's fallen as hard for them as he did for Francesca. I think he's just lonely."

I blew out a breath. "Well, it was a theory, anyway. Okay, how about this? Do you think there's a chance I could talk to some of her friends here? Maybe they might shed some light."

"More than a chance, Joe. How would you like to meet the whole group, right now?"

"They're here?"

"Yep," he smiled. "They're all leaving next week for a ten-day missions trip to Guatemala, getting it done before school starts back up here. They're going to be helping to build a medical clinic, and right now the whole bunch is in the chapel going over some last-minute details. Follow me."

We got up and exited his office through a back door. In two steps we found ourselves walking down another hall.

"The chapel is the original sanctuary," Samuels explained as we went. "Ten years ago we outgrew it and built our present sanctuary, which is quite a bit bigger. But even it's not big enough. That's why we're building yet again."

"Is that the 'new house' I heard you mention to Dotty?" I asked.

"Yeah," he smiled again. "That's kind of our slang term for it. It'll be about a third again as big as what we've got now."

"Luke, not to be impolite," I said then, "but what on God's green earth could cause so many people to come to one church? Are you THAT good?"

Samuels stopped short and doubled over in laughter. I just watched and waited him out. "Oh, good gravy," he finally said as he stood, wiping his tearing eyes. "Joe, you oughtta go on TV."

"So?" I said. "Are you?"

He smiled. "Not even close. Yeah, I suppose I'm a pretty good preacher, but it's God's Spirit Himself that draws people. Any man that thinks otherwise is in for a fall."

"Well. I was just wondering."

Samuels cocked his head at me and gave me a sly look. "Why don't you come Sunday, Joe? See for yourself. Put your mind at ease."

"I'm not wondering that much," I said, and Samuels just laughed again. "What's so funny?"

"My grandpappy used to have a saying," he grinned. " 'Play round the creek bank long enough, son, and sooner or later you're bound to slip in.'"

"My Granny used to say the same thing," I said. "It never has made sense."

"I think it does," Samuels said, and we started walking again. We turned another corner, and then went through two double doors into the chapel.

I saw what Samuels had meant about it being smaller. But I also know smaller can be a relative term. What I saw before me was a largish rectangular room, with cream colored concrete-block walls divided up by skinny stained-glass windows and topped by a high peaked oak-beam ceiling. Rather traditional churchy, I thought, but then I saw that instead of pews bolted to the floor there were folding chairs going from the altar area on back. I estimated there were close to three hundred of those chairs, nearly all of them filled with grinning, chattering young people. A thought occurred to me: this may have been just Harvard Pike's chapel, but I bet some pastors back home would have given up a seat on heaven's bus to be running a crowd that big.

And this was just their young adult group. Mike had said Harvard Pike had a total roll of over four thousand, and Samuels had told me they were building a bigger place to hold a third again that many. Incredible. *Why?* There HAD to be more here than it appeared.

Samuels caught the eye of a tall man up towards the front who was standing behind an acrylic lectern. "Just a minute, guys," the man said, and strolled back to us. "Hi, Pastor," he smiled when he reached us, his eyes not leaving mine. "What's up?"

"Tony," Samuels said, placing a hand on my shoulder, "I'd like you to meet Joe Box. Joe's the investigator Mike Taylor hired to find Francesca. Joe, Tony Jackson. Tony's the associate pastor here, as well as the head of Armorbearers."

We shook hands as I got a better look at him. Jackson was taller than me, older as well, balding but with the unmistakable chiseled features of a Southwest Indian...excuse me, Native American. He had a ready smile though, and kind, deep-set eyes.

"A pleasure, Joe," he said.

"Same here. What tribe?"

Jackson grinned. "Apache. My wife's Cherokee. Between the two of us we'll bring peace to the West yet."

"Yeah?" I said. "I'm a Native American myself. Fifth-generation hillbilly."

Samuels winced, but Jackson just laughed. "Close enough for jazz, anyway. I guess you'd like to talk to the group, huh?"

I noticed the kids were surreptitiously giving the three of us looks. "If I'm not interrupting," I said.

"Nope," he answered. "We're about done. Come on up front."

Samuels and I followed him back up the aisle to the altar. When we got there Jackson held up a hand. "Guys? Could I have your attention for a minute?"

The kids sat up expectantly, but all eyes were on me. The group was pretty evenly split between males and females, and was comprised of at least half a dozen racial types. Rapidly I tried to process everything I was seeing here. Well-kept church property, a self-effacing pastor with a ready laugh, a youth group made up of a rainbow of skin colors and headed by an affable Apache...my preconceptions about Christianity were crumbling by the second.

And suddenly I thought of Sarge.

Jackson went on, "This is Mr. Box. He's a private detective-"

"Investigator," I broke in.

"What?"

"I'm a private investigator. Only cops are detectives. They're a little touchy about the distinction." I nodded. "That's a fact."

"Uh, okay." Jackson turned back to the crowd. "Mr. Box is an investigator looking into Francesca Taylor's disappearance. I'm sure that any help we could give him would be appreciated." He stepped aside. "They're all yours."

"Thanks." I stepped away from the lectern. I wanted to keep this as casual as possible, to keep them from spooking. But I needn't have worried. Those kids were all looking at me in shining wonder, as if I was a new form of life. I guess they had never seen a real PI up close. I cleared my throat. I loathe speaking in front of crowds, no matter what the age. "Hello. As Pastor Jackson said, my name is Joe Box. I want to keep this brief, so I'll start with this: which one of you is Ted Whittaker?"

They began to mutter, and as one their heads all turned to gaze upon the poor unfortunate, who was squirming in exquisite discomfort on the back row. All the kid needed was a red neon arrow flashing over his head screaming, "I'm the guy!" Whittaker was an average-looking young man, solidly built, with football shoulders and a brown crewcut flat enough to carry a plate. If there was any drawback to him, I sure couldn't see it. Maybe Francesca was just plain too picky.

I smiled at the boy in what I hoped was a kind way and asked, "Ted, I understand you had been seeing Francesca. Is there any light you could shed on this?"

"M-maybe," he stammered. "I'm n-n-not s-sure."

I was wondering what could have been making Whittaker so nervous when an acne-plastered youth up on the front row sniggered. "C-calm down, Ted," he mocked. "Th-th-ey'll k-keep the electric chair h-hot for ya."

I frowned at the punk, and was about to give him as good as he dished out when Jackson beat me to it. "Not funny, Alan," the pastor scowled. "You'll learn some Christian charity yet, even if I have to take you outside and teach you myself."

The kid stared down at the floor. "Okay, okay. I was just funnin'..."

Whittaker slumped down further in his chair, not meeting any of the gazes, his face glowing hot crimson. I softened my tone even more. "Okay, Ted. You were saying?"

"I l-like F-francesca," the boy mumbled. "W-we w-w-went out a f-few t-times. She h-hardly ever n-n-noticed m-my st-stut..." Whittaker trailed off miserably. I glanced down at the Alan kid. He was twisting his mouth around, trying not to laugh.

"How about you, handsome?" I barked. "Anything to add?"

"No," he muttered.

"How's that?"

"No," he said, a bit louder.

I looked out at the rest of them. "Francesca's dad told me she's popular around here. Can any of you tell me anything else about her that would help? Anything at all?"

I waited patiently as the kids cleared their throats and shuffled their feet. Then at last one girl about three rows back shyly raised her hand. "I don't know how important this is..." she began.

"You never know," I smiled.

"Well..." The girl kneaded her hands in her lap. "Oh, I dunno... She'd kill me if I told..."

"Come on, Miss," I prompted. "Time's a-wasting."

I didn't think the girl was going to continue, but then she licked her lips. "Our missions trip was just the start," she said softly. She swallowed. "That's what Felicity said. One night she told me what she was going to do, but said I had to keep it a secret." The girl turned tormented eyes to me. "But now that's she's missing, it's okay to tell. Right? It's important, right?" I nodded. The girl was blinking back tears, silently begging for my understanding. "I mean, she could be... Oh God, who cares now. Secrets!" She spat the word. "What good are they?" She shook her head, her face downcast. "Okay, Mr. Box, I'll tell." The girl's voice was almost a whisper. She swallowed again. "You see, Felicity... She had been going to a fertility clinic." The words had seemed to just fall out, and there were gasps and mutters from the crowd. "Oh, not for anything bad," the girl rushed on, louder now. "Felicity told me. She said she was going to be helping people, more people than you could ever believe, she said. And she said it was only the start." The girl kept twisting her hands in her lap. "A new beginning, that's what Felicity called it. She said it was a...a genesis."

"Genesis?" I asked. "That was the word she used?"

"Yes," the girl nodded. "Genesis."

Both pastors gave each other a long, strained look. It was a look of consternation, but also something more.

A knowing.

Chapter 14

"You want to explain to me what all that was about?" We were now back in Samuels' office, sitting at his little round table, and I frowned my question at him.

"All what?" Samuels feigned innocence, but I wasn't buying.

"Why the word 'genesis' made you and Jackson so jumpy," I snapped. "It IS in the Bible, isn't it? Or am I mistaken?"

"No, you're not mistaken, Joe." Samuels' shoulders slumped tiredly. "It's just that if I tried to explain it to you, you might not understand."

"Try me," I said. "You have no idea how open-minded I can be."

"But you're not a Christian. It makes a difference."

"How do you know I'm not, Luke?" I could feel my temper flaring, and that was stupid. After all, he was right. I wasn't a Christian. So why did his observation of that fact nettle me?

He just gave me a slight smile. "*Are* you a Christian, Joe?" Samuels' soft brown eyes held no condemnation of me, but I felt condemned all the same.

"No," I allowed. "So what? You're skirting the issue."

"I'm not, Joe. It ties right into the issue." Samuels sighed and interlocked his fingers before him. "Okay, I'm going to let you in on something, but what I'm about to tell you has to do with spiritual things, so don't get angry with me if you don't get it."

I smiled thinly at him. "You and I are hillbillies, Luke, but that doesn't make us stupid. Don't you hate it when people assume that we are?"

"Did I mention anything about smarts?" he said sharply. "I'm talking about something way beyond that."

"Okay, okay," I said, holding up a hand. "Sorry."

"All right, Joe," Samuels sighed again. "Listen. My staff and I meet every morning at six a.m. for prayer, as well as to go over ministry business. Running a church this size is too much for any one man, especially if he tries to do it in his own strength. Too many lives are impacted here by what we do, or fail to do." Samuels smiled. "How does the old saying go? 'I had so much to do today, I couldn't possibly NOT pray.' So each day we meet in this office for an hour, to seek God's face and inquire of His wisdom."

I didn't say anything, but inside me something stirred. At first

I was afraid; I thought it might be that eerie feeling coming back.

But it wasn't. It was, instead, something else.

Some inner part of me had suddenly jumped up and smacked me upside the head. *LISTEN to this man,* a still, small voice said, insistent. *It's important.* Important? I argued. Why? *Because you need that same wisdom,* the voice said. *You know you do. And also because Joe Box is just about out of gas.*

Whoa. Roses are red, violets are blue, I'm schizophrenic, and so am I. I drew a deep breath and nodded at Samuels to continue.

"Most mornings," Samuels said, "we pray awhile, tarry awhile, fellowship awhile, then get on with our tasks. This morning, though, something unusual happened." He shifted around in his chair. "Right in the middle of our prayer, we all stopped at the same instant and looked at each other. Because it was at that very same moment all of us had been given one word, just one. Genesis. And Joe, that word chilled each and every one of us right to the bone."

"But why?" I asked again. "Like I said before, it's in the Bible, right?"

"Yeah," Samuels said tightly. "It is. But the warning we had been given had nothing to do with the word in its Biblical sense."

"Warning?" Uh-oh. My neck hairs were trembling again. Not a good sign. "A warning about what?"

"I don't know!" Samuels almost shouted, his frustration coming to the surface. He pointed his finger at me. "But I'll say this: the Holy Ghost never, and I mean NEVER, does a move like that without purpose." Samuels blew out a breath and looked down at the floor for a moment. An odd, sad smile flickered on his face. Then he looked up. "Would you like to know another funny thing my grandpappy used to say when I was a kid, Joe?" I nodded. Samuels said, "Sometimes when grandpappy knew something bad was about to happen, he'd shiver, and he'd get this really strange look on his face, and then he'd say son, I feel like somebody just stepped on my grave."

I sat up straight, feeling the color draining from my face.

Samuels glanced at me in concern. "Lordy, Joe, I didn't mean to alarm you." He gave a nervous half-laugh.

I whispered the next. "Your grandpappy was fey."

"Yeah, that he was," Samuels agreed, then he frowned, "What's the matter with you?"

"I know-" My throat closed up. I swallowed and tried it again. "I know just how he felt."

"What?" Samuels sat up with a frown. "YOU?"

"Yeah." My voice felt shaky. "I've been experiencing the same thing. But only just recently." I stared down and nervously began picking at a piece of veneer coming off the pastor's table. Then I looked up and met his eyes, wondering what he thought of me now. "Ain't that a kick in the head?"

"How recently?" Samuels asked, peering at me closely.

"Just since...just since yesterday, when I took this case." I rubbed my hands over my face. "The first time it happened was when Mike Taylor was in my office, telling me about Francesca. I thought it was bad then, but I was wrong. The worst was when I was talking with him and his boss, Nick Castle. It was... I thought I was going crazy. But then Castle said...something, and it left. A few times since then I've felt some weird stirrings, but they always go away."

Samuels nodded, musing. "It all fits, then."

"What fits?"

He gave me a wry grimace. "Joe, my unsaved friend, it seems you've stepped into the biggest cow pie in your life."

"What's THAT supposed to mean?"

"I'll tell you." Samuels leaned back in his chair. "But let me ask you this first. What exactly did Nick Castle say that made your strange feelings subside?"

I rubbed my chin. "I can't rightly remember," I said. "Something about telling Satan to leave, and then he mentioned Jesus... It's all a blur." I went on with a grimace, "I wasn't feeling too well right about that time."

"Did you know Nick goes to this church?" Samuels said then.

"No." I snorted a laugh. "It doesn't surprise me, though."

"Well, he does. So does his security chief, CT Barnes."

"Yeah, I met Barnes. Big ol' mother."

Samuels chuckled at that. "CT makes an impression on folks, that's true. But did you know that almost a third of the people that work at Castle Industries are also members here?"

"Again, I'm not surprised," I said. "Get on with it." Why on earth was I being so gruff with this man? This wasn't like me.

"Why did Mike hire you?" Samuels then asked me, his voice gone as flat as paint.

"You'd have to ask him that," I replied, the same way. "It all has to do with some claptrap about him hearing from on high that I was the one 'God' had picked to find Francesca. Me, an atheist." I shook my head. "Frankly, the further I've gone with this whole business the nuttier it seems."

Samuels drummed his fingers on the table. "Joe, let me ask you something else. Do you know everything there is to know?"

I chuckled in disbelief. What a stupid question. "Of course not."

"How about half?"

"What? Luke-"

But he wouldn't be deterred as he continued to stare at me. "Would you say you know half of everything there is to know?"

I sighed. "I'll say it again. No."

Samuels held up a hand. "I know I'm aggravating you, Joe, but humor me, please. There's a point to this. Just for grins let's say that of all the knowledge that's contained in the universe, you hold exactly half."

"Okay," I smiled at him in condescension. "And that makes me a very smart man. So?"

"So," Samuels said, "would you then at least acknowledge the possibility that God could exist in the half of the knowledge that you don't yet possess?"

I opened my mouth to give him a smart reply. And then shut it. Nuts. He had me. I wasn't about to tell him that, though.

"My position remains clear," I said. "Because I'm thinking right now that the whole lot of you jumped the rails on sanity about a mile back."

"Maybe," Samuels said. "But let's apply some numbers here, okay?" He ticked the points off on his fingers. "One, Mike Taylor approaches you with a simple disappearance job, and you get attacked by satan." I started to open my mouth in protest but the pastor held up a hand, cutting me off. "Call it what you will. Two, you meet Nick Castle and CT Barnes, and the devil or whatever hits you again, harder. Three, you've been having attacks of varying severity, off and on, since yesterday. And four, when Mary Ellen Conroy mentioned the word 'genesis' a few minutes ago, it simply confirmed the warning that I and my whole staff received this morning."

I started to rise. "This is insane..."

"Did Nick say anything about warfare?" Samuels said then, his tone sharp, and those soft brown eyes had now gone hard as quartz as they drilled me.

I stopped, looking down on him. "Yes. He did."

"And did you listen?"

"What are you, Luke, the Grand Inquisitor?" I could feel my face growing hot. "Do I need to remind you that I'm not one of your flock?"

"No, I'm aware of that, Joe," Samuels said, then he smiled. "I'm really ragging you off now, aren't I?"

"Yeah, you are. And if you're that much in need of a workout, let me recommend an hour or two with a heavy bag. Make sure your gloves are filled with steel shot." I turned to go.

"Maybe it's not me," Samuels said, stopping me again.

I blew out an exasperated breath. "What?"

"Maybe I'm not your problem. Maybe you are."

"Oh God. Psychology?" I shook my head. "Forget it, man, I took the course." I began to push past him.

"You arrogant fool!" Samuels had suddenly stood as well, knocking his chair over as he did and blocking my way. He leaned in and put his nose about an inch from mine, locking eyes. The last person that did that was my army DI; I didn't like it any better now than I had then. But something in those eyes was sure different than that sergeant's. Could it be--compassion?

"You have no idea of what you're involved in," Samuels went on more softly. "Joe, you're a natural man, heading into a supernatural fight. A baby trying to stop a freight train." He leaned in even closer. "Do you understand that? Do you?" His voice grew hoarse. "My God, man. Open. Your. Eyes. Don't you see? The devil is real. Believe it. He hates your living guts. He lives for that hate. And if you don't understand that, then failing in your quest to find Francesca won't be the worst thing that will happen to you." Samuels' stare was as piercing as an arc welder. "You'll die, Joe. So will she. Believe that as well."

Chapter 15

What a rotten way to end a meeting. I thought Luke was going to be an ally, and here he had turned out to be just as big a religious nut as Mike Taylor, Nick Castle, and the rest. Then I almost laughed. Big shock, there: Samuels WAS a pastor, after all. We had parted with handshakes, mine cool and distant, his fervent. Samuels' last words had been a harsh whisper: "We're going to be praying for you, Joe. All four thousand of us. Count on it."

Whatever. I mentally promised myself that when this goat-grab was over, I'd never again take on a Christian as a client. Cross my heart.

I checked my watch as I drove back to the Agnes. It was now nearly three in the afternoon. With what I had planned for the Brighter Day clinic tonight, I figured it would be best if I grabbed an early supper and then caught a few hours sleep. Because if everything went according to plan, I knew I would be visiting another place even later tonight, after I was done.

I drummed my fingers on the wheel in frustration. Incredible. Here I was, nearly two days into the case, and I didn't know any more about Francesca than when I had begun. If I didn't strike oil tonight at Brighter Day, I was fresh out of ideas. So then what? Return the balance of Mike's retainer with an apology? "Sorry, Mike, but I crapped out. I told you I would. You and your God-talk. Maybe you should hire yourself a real PI. Provided your daughter's not dead by now, of course."

I shook off that morbid thought. This wasn't my fault. If that's the way it worked out, you couldn't say I hadn't tried to warn him. What was that old line Clint Eastwood had said as Dirty Harry? A man's got to know his limitations...

But then, across my despondent musings, something broke in sideways. A whisper: *There's a strength beyond yours.*

It was that same soft voice from before.

It said it again: *There's a strength beyond yours, Joe. It's yours for the asking.*

Even as part of my mind struggled with what I was hearing, another part was marveling at the difference between the calm assurance that this voice possessed, compared to that vile thing that had been tormenting me for the last two days. How could one voice be so, well, GOOD, and the other be so bad? And how could they both fit into my head, along with me, myself, and I? If this kept up, I'd have to start assigning room keys.

Then I realized something. The good voice wasn't echoing in my head. It was coming from somewhere deeper, further south.

My heart.

I swallowed a lump in my throat the size of a river rock. When Linda died, I thought my heart had died with her. I gulped again. I guess it hadn't... And with that thought, my world imploded. Like a screaming dentist's drill, that other voice began screaming and slashing through my head, howling pure, unshirted hell.

Die!Die!Die!Die!Die!Die!Die!Die!Die!Die!Die!Die!Die!Die!Die!

God! The car fishtailed, insanely whipping back and forth across all three lanes as it did. Horns bellowing, other cars careened out of my way, and I fought the wheel as it flipped around in my hands like a living thing.

Something was trying to kill me.

That knowledge seared as bright as bronze across my frontal lobes. I gasped a scorching breath, wrenching the wheel hard to the right, and when I did I came within a hair of nailing a large white panel truck emblazoned with a sausage emblem on its side.

I cut sharply in front of the thing and a second later I was rocketing down the emergency lane, road debris clanging and pinging off the car's underside like shotgun blasts.

Engine roaring, I clutched the wheel in a death grip, stood on the brakes, and screamed.

I thought the ride would never end. But at last, tires smoking wildly, the Goddess and I shuddered to a grateful stop. I hung my dripping head over the wheel, sucking in air so deeply I was almost sobbing.

The panel truck I had cut off pulled into the lane a few dozen feet ahead of me and the driver leaped out. He looked like a typical trucker as he stomped back my way, large and glowering. The guy was a head taller than me and must have outweighed me by twenty pounds.

When the man reached the side of my car he slammed the flat of his hand on the glass next to me, his face red with rage. "Are you crazy? What do you think you're doing? I oughtta-"

I looked back at him. Whatever the trucker saw on my face caused him to involuntarily stumble back a step. He slapped his mouth closed and dropped his hands. Turning abruptly and muttering curses all the way, he made it back to his truck, shooting me looks over his shoulder as he went. I saw him climb in his truck, start it, and then with a yip of tires and slung gravel he peeled back onto the interstate. A second later his rig was lost in traffic.

I hung my head again. "What's happening to me?" I whispered. "What's happening?"

The voice in my heart answered me simply: *Warfare.*

I knew enough now not to question the reality of this, whatever it was. But I argued back anyway. "War," I mumbled. "I've had enough of war. In Vietnam it was war. On the cops it was war. Fighting Linda's death it was war." I clenched my fists. "All my life it's been war. I'm tired..."

Those were only battles, the voice answered. *THIS is war.*

"I don't want to fight," I groaned.

You won't fight alone, the voice replied. *I'll battle for you. I'll battle with you. All you have to do is ask.*

Didn't it understand? That was a hard thing. For me.

"Tomorrow," I said.

Never comes, the voice whispered back, with a sad finality.

Chapter 16

Don't you hate it when you get a snatch of a melody lodged in your head, and the thing just won't leave? That was happening to me now as I slunk through the back door of the Brighter Day clinic. The song was, of all things, from Gilbert and Sullivan's *Pirates of Penzance,* and it occurred as the aforementioned pirates were sneaking up on General Stanley's castle in the dead of night. They were slinking along, quiet as could be, when suddenly the whole bunch of them began singing at the tops of their lungs, in pure gusto, "WITH CAT-LIKE TREAD...!" I couldn't recall right now what the other part of the verse was, but I know it was screamingly funny. That show had been a favorite of Linda's and mine.

Well sir. It wouldn't do to start laughing now, that's for sure. If the police caught this particular cat, I knew I would have a lot of years in the clink to remember just how the rest of the song went.

I had arrived here twenty minutes before, right about midnight, after I had parked the Goddess a few doors down at a closed gas station. I had then walked the rest of the way along a rear alley, finally coming up to the back door of the clinic. When I got there I wasn't surprised to see a security light high up on a pole, flooding the area in stark relief.

Rule one in burglary: plan ahead. I had dressed for the part before I left home, in black from head to toe. Black sneakers, black socks, black jeans, black sweatshirt, black watch cap. I had even blackened my hands and face with dirt I had gotten off my tires. In retrospect I suppose I looked like some sort of low-rent ninja, but you had to give me this: I was hard to see.

I reached into my black gym bag and pulled out my Crosman air pistol, which I had loaded with steel pellets. Yeah, the gun was black too. I cocked it, and then drew a bead on the globe at the top of the pole. As a kid I could knock the eye out of a squirrel at twenty yards, so putting out that light with one shot was easy work. The only thing I hadn't counted on was how loud the breaking glass was as it fell. I crouched down after the shot and waited. After a minute, though, I realized the sound had gone undetected, so I stood and started moving. In three steps I was standing at the door. I took another quick glance around, then put the gun back in the satchel and pulled out a packet of lock picks.

Now on televison or in the movies you'll see the protagonist draw a wire out of a kit like mine, stick the thing in the lock, give it two wiggles, and then turn the knob. Sorry, but it doesn't work that way. It takes a while, one pick holding the tension bar out of the way while you laboriously use another to turn the tumblers. If the lock is weak and you're very good, you can usually spring it in three or four minutes. If, on the other hand, you're like me, who never was a whiz at this, and you're confronted with a monster lock on a steel door like I was facing now, you might as well hunker down and know you're going to be here for a spell.

Hence the reason I shot out the light.

Did I say I wasn't a whiz at lockpicking? I misspoke. I'm a dud. I squatted there, fooling with the silly thing, penlight between my teeth, for the better part of a quarter of an hour. By the time the last tumbler dropped in place sweat was cooking my eyes and my thighs were vibrating like mad, screaming for relief. I finally stood up with a grateful sigh, my joints creaking and snapping like acorns under a boot.

I had then checked the doorframe for wires before I turned the knob; I didn't want to trip any alarms, silent or otherwise. Okay, it was clean. Good. With one last cautious look around I eased the door open.

So now here I was in Mangold's office. The moving rectangles of light caused by the passing cars outside gave the whole place a surreal feel, and that same funky odor that had made me sneeze earlier in the day was still here, albeit not as strong. Maybe it was Mangold himself that had caused it Maybe his pheromones were as sour as the rest of the man. Whatever it was, there were still enough particles in the air to make my nose tingle and twitch.

I turned to his filing cabinet, expecting it to be securely locked, but I gave the top drawer an experimental tug anyway. To my surprise it slid smoothly out, too smoothly. Either the man had an overweening trust in his door locks, or this cabinet didn't contain anything important. I shone the penlight inside the thing. Empty.

I did the same with the other drawers, then checked the other two cabinets. They were all as hollow as a movie star's head. I slid the last one closed. Well. I guess I really hadn't thought it would be that easy. Had anything on this case been that way yet?

I drew out Mangold's desk chair and sat down, glancing at my watch. Twenty-five minutes after twelve. I really had hoped to be gone in another five minutes, but it didn't look like that was going to happen. The doctor's tough door lock had thrown my schedule to the wind. As I began to open Mangold's desk drawers and examine them one by one, I recalled something that an old cat burglar had said to me years ago.

One dark night as Sarge and I were walking our beat, we had paused at a dry cleaner's, hearing someone banging around so loudly in there it was almost like he hoped he would be heard. We grabbed a rickety old codger as he was backing out of the place, pillow case with the day's take held loosely in his hand. He hadn't fought us as we had each taken him gently by the arm; not that it would have helped. As I reflect back, I think that maybe he felt that he was getting too old for such pursuits, and thought getting caught in the act was the only honorable way he could end it.

Anyway, we were booking the old burglar back at the precinct later that shift when he looked up at me from the prisoner's chair and did something odd: surprisingly, he winked. Sarge was filling out the paperwork and missed it, but I didn't. The old man lifted his hands and crooked one finger at me to bend down. I did, and he smiled at me toothlessly.

"I'm eighty-one years old," he said, "and I've never been caught before tonight. You know why? Speed, boy." The old man nodded in ragged dignity. "Only three rules have guided me in this life I've chosen. Get in. Get it all. Get out." Then he leaned back, still smiling, as if he had just passed on the wisdom of the ancients.

Maybe he had.

I pulled open Mangold's desk's center drawer. At first all I could see was the usual detritus all of us accumulate: paper clips, rubber bands, broken mechanical pencils, dried bottles of Wite Out. But then I noticed something further back. An envelope. I drew it out, seeing it was from a local bank. The stamp cancellation on it showed last week's date. It had already been opened, so I did the same and shone the light on it. Sure enough, it was Mangold's bank statement, and I followed the entries down it with my finger. There were just the usual check deposits from patients, none of them bigger than a hundred dollars, and I started to sigh in disgust. But then, halfway down, I saw another entry. My blood froze. The deposit amount was three thousand dollars.

And the check had been drawn on something called GeneSys.

Bingo, Pastor Samuels.

I let my breath out; I hadn't even realized I had been holding it.

The next few entries were more patient fees, and then two weeks after the first GeneSys deposit on the page, I found another.

Frantically I reached my hand further back in the drawer now, feeling for more envelopes. I found them and pulled them out. They were all from the same bank, and all contained statements going back over the last year. And each and every one showed biweekly deposits for three thousand dollars into Mangold's account from the entity called GeneSys. Mentally I calculated it. The doctor was pulling down over seventy thousand a year from that activity, plus his normal earnings from his practice. Mangold was, as Granny used to say, walking in tall cotton.

Quickly I pulled out my little spiral notebook and wrote down the routing numbers not only from Mangold's bank, but from the one that GeneSys had drawn the checks on as well. I had no idea what they meant, but I would find out. Bank on it. Heh. Heh.

I put the envelopes back where I found them and then turned to Mangold's computer. As I booted it up, I checked my watch again. Going on one a.m. This was taking an obscenely long time, but I was in too deep now, and I sent up a silent prayer to Mike Taylor's God that I would find something on the computer about Francesca. Otherwise this case was over, and she was dead.

But two minutes later, fate was kind. Right where they should have been on the system, I found Mangold's patient files. I resisted the urge to look at my watch again as I typed in Taylor, Francesca, and hit enter.

There was a short whirring, and the screen went blue. I then saw, in neat pica script at the top of the page: Taylor, Francesca, her date of birth, address, blood type, and patient number. Yes! My relief was short-lived, however, when I saw the rest.

Right after Francesca's patient number were the initials PGP, and then the biggest mishmash of letters and numbers you ever saw. What was this? It was if Mangold had let a chimp do his data entry. Could this be right? With a sick feeling, I knew it was.

The doctor had encrypted her file.

But there was no more time to think about this. A feeling of dread was breathing down my neck. Somewhere a game whistle had blown, and I knew that if I stayed here just five minutes longer, I was going to get caught.

There was one more thing that had to be done, however. Before I had left home that evening I had entertained the half-feeling I might run into something just like this, so right before I closed up my gym bag I had thrown in some blank diskettes. Now I pulled one out, shoved it in, and did what I needed to do to make a copy of Francesca's file.

Then, trying not to rush too badly, I shut the system down. I put everything back to where I hoped it went and made my way back outside. The last thing I did was to take some dirt and rub it into the scratches I had made with those picks on Mangold's lock. I leaned back and gave it a critical look. It would have to do.

Three minutes later I was back in the Goddess, heading down the road. I had no idea how to break that computer code, but I knew who could.

Chapter 17

"Ice-cold Stoly." The man in front of me smiled, lifting the bottle. "There's really nothing in the world quite like it, Joseph. But I can't even get you to try."

I regarded my old friend with a shake of my head. Rankin Quintus Blaine: *bon vivant*, *raconteur*, gormand of prodigious appetites, computer genius of the first water. And an unashamed pusher of that vile stuff he daily drank by the fifth, Stolinachaya vodka, served at a mean temperature of no more than thirty-three degrees Fahrenheit. "Keep that liver-dissolver to yourself, Quint," I said. "I'll stick with scotch."

"All right," Quint sighed at me with exaggerated defeat, then he turned back to his well-stocked liquor cabinet. Quint and I were relaxing in his living room, which was opulent enough to impress Marie Antoinette. "And you keep your provincial ways, Joseph. See if I'll ask you again." Quint would, of course; he always did. He and I go back a few years, and we ramble through this vaudeville routine every time I come over, which isn't nearly often enough. He pulled out a bottle of Glenlivet. "I don't keep your brand, Cutty Sark, on hand, but will this do?"

I took it from him with a smile. "That it will, Quint, and the day you stock Cutty Sark is the day I turn Democrat."

We both grinned at each other, and I watched him pour his drink while I did the same with mine. It was now nearly two in the morning, and Quint--rotund, jovial, bearded Quint--was still, or was it yet, dressed in evening finery. I've known him for nearly ten years, going back to the day he and I had been called in as state's witnesses to testify in a particularly twisted case of industrial pollution, and I have never seen the man dressed otherwise. I don't think Quint possesses a pair of jeans or sweat pants; I doubt he even owns pajamas. For all I know he sleeps propped up in the corner. All I can say for certain of him is that he's a dear friend, is a sucker for jazz and blues albums--especially old 78's–and has the sharpest mind I have ever encountered. If there's a computer code that Quint can't decipher, I don't know of it.

The house we were in was his, a meandering little number left to him by his dead sister nearly twenty years ago and nestled deep in the environs of Indian Hill, Cincinnati's richest neighborhood. To this day I don't know what Quint does for a living; with his abhorrence of manual labor and his rich lifestyle, I figure it has to be something to do with either the Mafia or the CIA--same difference.

Quint hadn't said anything about the lateness of the hour or of my showing up here unannounced, or even of the way I was dressed. I knew he wouldn't; my friend has a singularly sanguine approach to letting live and let live. And I knew I would find him here, because for all his finery, Quint rarely steps foot outside his front door. There's a story there, and maybe someday he'll tell it.

Quint's only failing is his insistence on always calling me "Joseph." I think it tickles him to know how much I hate the way he says it.

"Democrat," Quint laughed. "I'll make a liberal of you yet, Joseph."

"When pigs fly," I replied, taking a swig of my drink.

Quint smiled and tenderly put his bottle of Stoly back in its iced bucket. Then he set his glass down. "All right. As to why you're here..."

"Right." I finished my drink and set it down as well. I pulled out the disk. "See what you make of this."

He took it from me. "Well, let's see... Flat plastic square, three inches by three inches or so, little sliding metal door..." He smiled up at me in triumph. "I'd say it's a computer disk."

I scowled at him. "Funny, Quint. Did you ever think of taking your show on the road?"

He barked a laugh, putting his hands out in front of him. "For pity's sake, Joseph. Lighten up."

"Sorry," I said. "But you can't believe how the last forty-eight hours have gone. And my client is desperate."

"So you're on a case, are you? Good. You needed one, I'll be bound." Quint waved the disk at me. "So what's on this? Wandering wife? Unfaithful husband?"

"No," I sighed. "Medical records. I think. I hope."

Quint frowned at me. "Medical records? The law takes a dim view of you having this, Joseph. Unless they're yours."

"They're not," I said. "If I'm lucky, they belong to a young woman I'm trying to find."

"I don't want to know how you came by this, do I?"

"Nope. All I'll tell you is that when you run it, you'll find her name and a few stats, then the initials PGP. And then the screen fills with gibberish."

"PGP?" Quint frowned again.

"Yeah. Why? Are you familiar with that?"

"I am." He rubbed his nose. "PGP stands for Pretty Good Privacy. It's an encryption program." He shook his head. "Very elaborate and very, very tough."

"For you?"

Quint gave me a wintry smile. "Never for me. Although it may take a while." He stood and walked away towards his dining room. That was where he kept, I knew, hundreds of thousands of dollars worth of the most up-to-date computer equipment and its attendant junk in the world.

"With your shield or on it, Quint," I said to him as he left. "Make me proud."

"Help yourself to the Stoly, Joseph," he called over his shoulder.

I got in a final shot. "Only if you have an airsickness bag handy."

Quint waved and chuckled and kept moving.

"But I'll tell you what I will do, old buddy," I muttered, rising. I walked over to Quint's enormous entertainment center and squatted down before his record collection. "I'll drink some more of your Glenlivet and listen to some fine Billie Holiday while you slave away in there." I put my finger on one of hers and pulled it out with a smile. *God Bless The Child.*

It seemed appropriate.

*****

Two hours later I was in a happy haze, and I don't mean from the scotch. I had progressed my way through Quint's excellent music library, going from the aforementioned Miss Holiday to Ella Fitzgerald and Sarah Vaughn, then immersing myself in instrumental geniuses like Bix Biederbecke and Charlie "Bird" Parker. Now I was slumped deep in Quint's custom-made gray leather easy chair, goofy smile on my face, as I listened in awe to Leadbelly tearing his heart out for all and sundry to hear.

My reverie was ended with a sharp tap on my shoulder.

"If you've scratched any of my 78's you'll never make it to my front door alive," Quint said.

"That's what those were? I was using them for coasters."

"Not funny, Joseph." I swear the color had drained from his face. "Don't even joke about such things."

I stood up with a stretch. "So, were you victorious?"

"I'm not sure," he answered, his voice grave. "I guess it all depends on your definition of 'victory.'"

"Yeah, you sound like a Democrat, Quint." Then I peered at him. "You're serious, aren't you?"

"I am." He held up a sheaf of papers. "After I finally broke the code, I printed out what was on the disk." Quint shuddered. "Joseph, if this is real, it's the most monstrous thing I've ever heard of."

"Good Lord. What is it?"

He shoved the papers at me. "Read them yourself. I need a drink." Quint made his way on unsteady legs over to his bar and poured himself a large Stoly. His hands were shaking so badly he battered out a tattoo with the bottleneck on the rim of his glass.

I sat back down in the chair and began to read. It didn't take long to go through the five pages. Ten minutes after I had started I let the last page flutter to the floor and gazed up at Quint through haunted eyes.

"You called it, brother," I croaked. "Monstrous is the word, all right."

Quint took a deep swallow of his drink and regarded me with a stare. "Fetal research. The Human Genome Project. DNA replacement. Clone farming. Nutrition pods." He ran his hand through his hair. "My God, Joseph, what have you stumbled across?"

"Something that God apparently has very little to do with," I answered, my voice shaky. "That's all you could make sense of too, huh?"

"Yes. It's just notes, as you can see. This doctor--Mangold, is it?--evidently felt that even an encryption program like PGP wasn't enough security for this, so he purposely kept his notes vague. But there's enough there to give me nightmares for a year."

"Yeah." I leaned back, feeling a hundred years old. "All I can tell for sure from this is that Francesca Taylor entered what she thought was a program that would help end disease. She had no idea she was going to be a cog in some sort of superman scheme. Poor kid." I swallowed. "Poor, misguided kid."

"What was the title of the program she's in? The Final Triumph?" Quint shuddered again. "Sounds an awful lot like Hitler's 'final solution', doesn't it? That one almost did my people in."

I looked up in surprise. "You're Jewish, Quint? Blaine is a Jewish name?"

"Not Blaine." My friend gave me a sad smile. "Baline. My grandparents were Russian Jews."

"Caramba. No wonder this upsets you so badly."

"It would upset any human with a heart!" Quint said vehemently. Then he leaned down over me and put both his hands on the arms of my chair. "Find them, Joseph. This must not happen again. Do you hear? Find them and end this. I'm begging you."

He didn't have to beg me. The very thought of a young girl like Francesca, whom I hadn't even met yet, in the clutches of people like Mangold made my skin crawl. She was trapped in a nest of termites.

But I was the Orkin man.

Chapter 18

I hate, loathe, and despise nightmares as a general rule--who doesn't?--but the one gripping me now was in a class by itself.

In this particular movie from hell I had found myself back in Vietnam. That alone was bad enough, because any dream I've ever had about my time in that place is excruciatingly brutal. This time, though, the cruelty of it was cranked up several notches.

I again was nineteen and walking point on the same trail in the Ia Drang valley that was to have such an impact on my life. The sun was scorching hot, God's own heatlamp, and the sweat running underneath my cheesecloth-rotted fatigues felt like ants scurrying across my body. My M-16 was slippery in my hands, as if it was still coated in Cosmoline, and my ill-fitting pot kept sliding down over my eyes, its steel rim slamming the bridge of my nose. The savage sawgrass flanking either side of the trail ripped my bare arms afresh with every step I took, and I couldn't even comment to anyone on my miseries, because I was far out in front of the others. That was the idea behind walking point: the guy doing it would be the first one to step on a punji stick, or fall into a tiger pit, or trip a landmine, or run into Charlie. In this way the rest of your troops were alerted. It was, needless to say, a lousy job, and was only assigned by lot.

Today it was my turn.

The sun sat low on the mountain ridge above me, mercilessly refusing to set. What was the matter with it? Didn't it know that once it was dark, I could rest? Rest. My God, I needed rest. I felt like I had been walking for years. Sweat was flowing into the cuts on my arms made by the sawgrass, making them burn like they had been dipped in acid. Maybe...maybe around the next turn I could sit, and get a drink from my canteen, and rest.

But then I heard a noise. It didn't sound like Charlie's chatter. It was...what was it? Whatever it was, it wasn't coming from ahead. Past experience had told me that any new noise was not good. I stopped and listened. If the bugs would just shut up I could hear it better.

Then I did. The sound I was hearing was soft...but it grew. Steadily it grew, and expanded, until it was all around me, until it filled the world. The sound of crying. Babies crying.

Oh God.

I saw them then, the babies. I saw them. I gazed around openmouthed, in silent, unbelieving horror as I saw them.

As far as the horizon the landscape was littered with living, breathing, squalling babies. But something was wrong.

These babies were straight out of the mind of madness.

Some were missing arms, or had three. Some had two heads. Some had no eyes. Some had tongues on their feet, or lips on their thumbs. Some were moving, and some weren't. Those babies all were crying the cries of the damned.

And they all were blaming me.

I dropped my rifle and slapped my hands over my eyes. Blaming me! Why? What did I-?

"Help them, Joe." I knew that voice. I turned to see who it was.

Linda.

She was wearing the same outfit she had died in, and she was drenched in blood. "Help them like you should have helped me..."

My shame was too much. Linda was right. My pride had killed her. I knew it was me. I was the one. I deserved death. The babies said so, pointing their tiny fingers at me.

But maybe I could still make it right. If I could just hold Linda, kiss her, talk to her one more time, I knew I could make it right. I began to run towards her. But my feet didn't obey. To my horror I found I wasn't running towards her, but running back up the trail, and my traitor feet wouldn't stop.

I hadn't gone twenty steps when I heard the double click.

"Bouncing Betty" is the ghoulish name our guys had given to one of the nastier pieces of ordnance. A Bouncing Betty, simply, is a landmine that leaps into the air when you step on it. Only then does it explode. It is an antipersonnel weapon in its purest form. On occasion they've killed, but the Bouncing Betty's primary purpose is to maim. I had seen men lose feet, kneecaps, legs, and their sexual organs to the things. And Bouncing Bettys were unique, known by the double click sound they made when they were stepped on. One click arms it, and a split second later a second click launches it three feet in the air. If you hear that sound, your life is about to change.

And I had just heard it.

I only got a quick glimpse of the mine as it jumped out of the ground in front of me. That glimpse showed it was maybe eight inches across, looking like a black, spinning coffee can. Then it went off, and I screamed. But instead of one boom I heard... four? Boom boom boom boom. The babies were screaming. Linda was screaming. I was screaming. Lost, lost... Boom boom boom boom.

I screamed again and threw the covers off me.

Boom boom boom boom.

God. What-? My heart slammed in my chest. A dream. It had only been a dream after all. I fell back, gasping. What time was it? I sat back up and looked at the clock on my bedside table. Nine a.m. I had only crawled into bed at five.

Boom boom boom boom.

It wasn't a Bouncing Betty. It was my door. Someone was pounding on my door.

Boom boom boom boom.

I leaped out of bed, still disoriented and madder than a dunked cat. Fours hours of sleep, and most of that rotten. This. Had better. Be good. I stalked into my living room and flung open the door.

"What!!" I yelled.

The two young men in front of me were nonplused for a second but quickly recovered. "Hello! Did we wake you?" said one.

Blearily I regarded them. The boys were around twenty years of age, and could have been brothers. Both were middling-height, with short, fair hair and light skin, and they were wearing matching blue suits with some kind of gold plastic nametags. I figured with their appearance they had to have been either Mormons or with the IRS.

"What do you want?" I said, this time in a calmer way.

"Could we talk to you about God?" the other one chirped. I leaned past the two and looked out into the hall and down the stairwell. There on the landing just inside the door I spied two new, snazzy ten-speed bikes, parked side by side. Mormons, all right. I straightened back up and as I did the first one started jabbering again without missing a beat.

"We'd like to talk to you about the Church of Jesus Christ of Latter Day Saints, and your part in the-"

I held up a hand. "Hold it." Back in my college days I had taken a course on comparative religions, and I had studied enough of Mormonism to know that, however they viewed themselves, and however facile they were with the terminology, Christians they weren't. Jesus Christ, as He was traditionally taught, had very little to do with them.

Try telling them that, though.

"Number one, boys, I've had a lousy night, and number two, I just don't care. Thanks for your interest, though." I began to close the door, and that's when Tweedledee decided to stick the toe of his shoe in it. Mistake.

For a second I considered grabbing the huge conch shell I keep on a nearby shelf and slamming it right down on the top of the kid's highly polished black Oxford, but I didn't. His lucky day.

I opened the door back up and looked at them again. I knew how to end this, but quick. "So you guys are Christians?"

"Yes!" They both nodded so quickly and forcefully I thought their freckles were going to fly off.

"Okay. One question then. If you answer it correctly I'll invite you in. Here it comes. Is Jesus God?"

"Why...no." Tweedledum looked at me as if I were simple. "Jesus and satan are angels, created beings, and are in fact brothers—"

"Braaaaak! Wrong answer. But thanks for playing."

And I slammed the door right in their scrubbed, lying faces. Idiots. Even I knew that Christians believed Jesus was God. Luke Samuels would have been proud of me, I bet.

I stumbled back into my bedroom and fell sideways across the bed. In twelve seconds I was asleep again.

Boom boom boom boom.

I opened one bleary eye. No. It couldn't be. I looked at the clock. I had only been back asleep for eighteen minutes.

Boom boom boom boom.

I stalked into my living room with cold-blooded murder in my heart. Freckles or no, these Mormon boys were history. I jerked the door open and yelled, "Who dies first?"

But it wasn't the Mormons.

It was Sarge.

Chapter 19

"Well?" He arched his eyebrows. "Have you taken up catching flies with your mouth or are you gonna invite me in?"

"What the-! Sarge! What are you-?"

"Thanks, I believe I will." He pushed in past me, wearing that same crooked smile I had known so well all those years back.

Sergeant Timothy Mulrooney. He must have been seventy if he was a day, but his posture was still ramrod-straight and his iron-gray crewcut could have passed muster on Parris Island. The only concession Sarge had grudgingly given to age were the character lines crossing his Irish face: they were a bit deeper than when I had last seen him, over a decade ago.

But what was he doing here, now?

As if reading my mind, Sarge grinned. "You look like the man that sat down on his toilet in the dark, forgetting he'd left the seat up earlier. Shocked, you might say."

"You...you'd be right," I stuttered, walking over to him. "After ten years you nonchalantly walk through my door, so yeah, I'd say shocked is the word. How did you find me, anyway?"

"'Nonchalant'," Sarge chuckled. "Joe, you're still a silver-tongued devil. And my son Jack, the cop, gave me your address." Sarge twisted his mouth. "Are we gonna just stand here or what?"

"Uh, no. Have a seat." I was still trying to process what was going on.

"Thanks." Sarge did, sitting down on one end of my ratty sofa. A second later Noodles poked his head out from underneath. My cat is, rightfully enough, skittish around strangers, so I expected him to bolt. Instead Noodles gazed up at Sarge placidly, blinked once, and said "Naow?" Then the rest of him followed. The cat's nose twitched at the odor of this man and his nude tail was swishing like mad, but he didn't run.

Sarge looked down at him. If Noodles' scarred appearance disturbed my old partner, he didn't let on, and he absently reached down and scratched Noodles under the chin. The cat arched his back, groaning in ecstasy, then he began to purr like three cats.

Sarge looked up at me as he continued to scratch. "Where in the world did you find this one? Looks like he had a rough start."

"We kind of found each other." I was still standing as I looked down on him. "Sarge, what are you DOING here?"

"Well, that's the question, ain't it?" His blue eyes twinkled up at me shamelessly, as if he was enjoying my discomfort. "We haven't seen each other for over-"

"Ten years," I finished. "Like I said."

"Yeah, and that last time we didn't exactly part on the best of terms, did we?"

"No, we didn't."

"I remember," Sarge nodded. "It was Christmas eve. Helen and me had flown up here to spend the holidays with Jack and Sharon. Then Helen had the idea of going over to your place, as a surprise. She said she had been feeling a burden from the Lord for you for days. So we did."

"Yeah, I remember, too," I said as I sat down on the opposite end of the couch. "I was still living in that crummy joint in Clifton the night you two showed up."

Sarge looked around. "This place is a step up, I think." He grimaced. "A little, anyway. But you're right, that Clifton apartment was really pretty bad. I remember the wind was whistling so loud around the windows that night it sounded like a siren. We could hardly talk." Sarge settled back. "Helen and me didn't stay too long, as I recall."

"No."

"As I further recall, you threw us out. And on Christmas eve, to boot."

"Sarge, that was a long time ago..." Then I saw him grin, and knew he had only been teasing.

"Ah, I'm just ragging you, Joe. And who knows, maybe you were right for throwing us out. I know Christmases are rough for you, then when Helen wanted you to kneel down with us and pray—"

"I got sore and told you both to beat feet." I leaned over, staring at the floor while I rubbed my hands together slowly. "I'd had a few beers that night, and I wasn't the best of company to start with. Then here you two came knocking, and it just seemed to bring everything to the surface." I looked at him. "I had no call to do what I did, though. You and Helen were the closest thing I had to friends. Have to friends." I looked back down. "Later on I was too ashamed to call you and apologize, then the holidays came and went, and then the years just kind of started stacking up..."

Sarge was shaking his head. "Old news, Joe. And it wasn't just you. Helen had been hurting for you, bad, and that night she saw an opportunity to try to make it better. Sometimes when she gets that way her zeal gets in the way of her thinking."

"And yours doesn't?" I looked back up, giving Sarge a wry smile, and at the same time I sighed in regret. And then, as if on cue, we both stood and looked at each other awkwardly. The moment seemed to hang.

Suddenly Sarge walked over two steps and embraced me. It felt...great. Like home. "Aw, God, Sarge," I mumbled into his shoulder. "I'm sorry."

"Me too," he said, his voice rough. My old friend slapped me several times on the back, while I did the same to him, then he chuckled, "Now this is the greeting you should have given me in the first place," and we broke free with embarrassed laughs.

Manly rituals; ya gotta love 'em.

"Well," Sarge smiled at me. "Now that we've gotten that out of the way..."

"Yeah." I began to head for the kitchen. "Can I get you anything? Coffee? No, wait a minute, I haven't started any yet. How about..." A beer? Some scotch? No, I didn't think so, not unless Sarge had forsaken his religion. "...some water?"

"Sit down, Joe." Sarge took his own advice and planted himself back down on my sofa. "You're making me nervous. I didn't fly all the way up here to drink water. Not hardly. What you and me are going to do is, we are going to have us a talk."

That sounded familiar, then I thought: it should. Nick Castle had said virtually the same thing to me, what was it, just two days ago? Lord. The prospect didn't sound any better now than it had then.

But I sat down anyway. This was, after all, Sarge.

"Okay." I braced myself for who-knew-what. "So we'll talk."

"That we will. And Joe-" Sarge held up a warning finger. "You and me both know we have a history, as they say, so I don't want any prevarication to occur here. Are we fairly clear on that?"

"Prevarication?" I laughed, my heart not in it. "Now who has the silver tongue? Did you buy a dictionary or what?"

But he wasn't having any of it. When Sarge was zeroing in on something, he wouldn't let up until he had found out what he wanted to know; I had seen him do it enough times with recalcitrant suspects. "We'll laugh later, Joe." Sarge closed one eye and squinted at me with the other, like he was lining me up in a gunsight. "Right now I want you to tell me everything that's happened to you in the last forty-eight hours. Leave nothing out, no matter how small you think it may be. Go." And with a frown on his face, still squinting, Sarge leaned back, crossed his legs, and laced his fingers behind his head. I used to call that his 'no-lies-or-you're-dead' pose.

But wait a minute. What little business I still had was due in no small part to my keeping my yap shut about my clients' affairs. My office wasn't quite on par with a priest's confessional, but for me it was close enough. What Sarge was asking me to do went contrary to everything that had guided me these last twelve years. So instead of answering him right away I bent down to fool with my shoe. It's what I used to do as a first-year cop when I was trying to buy time with him over some minor infraction.

Then I remembered I wasn't wearing any shoes.

I looked up at Sarge, a sheepish grin on my face. He was still squinting at me, waiting; he hadn't forgotten my little ploy. Oh well. Maybe he was right. Maybe it was time to pass the burden off. God knew I wasn't doing so well on my own.

So I told him. I breathed out a sigh and I told him.

I told him everything, beginning with Mike Taylor's phone call Monday morning, right up to my nightmare of an hour before. Truth be told, when I was done I'll admit it had felt pretty good to vent it all.

But I wasn't sure Sarge felt the same, because at the end he just stared at me for a few seconds, not saying a word. Then he shut his eyes and violently drywashed his face with his hands. After a few more seconds of that he opened his eyes and leaned over and stared down at Noodles, who had fallen asleep across his feet.

I waited. And waited some more. The silence was killing me.

"Some story, huh?" I said then, just to be talking. "Pretty weird, right?" I was trying to keep my tone light, and failing miserably.

Sarge finally straightened up and looked me squarely in the eye. "Joe, you're nearly fifty, and you know what? You're still a rookie."

What? Of every possible thing he could have said, that was the least expected. Rookie? *ROOK*-ie? I could feel the color flooding my face. "Now wait a minute here, where do you get off-"

Sarge stood, startling Noodles, who quickly scampered back under the couch; I guess the cat had picked up on the vibes. "I said rookie, and I meant it." Sarge was scowling at me, not a pleasant sight, especially before noon. "Joe, you're a smart guy, but you've made the classic rookie mistake. You've gotten cocky."

"Cocky??" My mouth dropped open and I jumped up. "Me?

Cocky? About what, Sarge? What in the world do I have to be cocky about? Look at me! I'm practically broke!" I flapped my arms around. "Look at where I live! Look at my furniture! Look at my clothes! For God's sake, look at my cat! What cocky man would own a cat that looks like that?"

From under the couch, Noodles picked that exact moment to let out a pathetic "Mrowrr-r-r..." Now THAT was weird. Also uncalled for, but I was on a roll.

"Sarge, these last two days have sucked on toast. Nothing is working out the way it's supposed to. Nothing! If anybody would understand that, I think it would be you."

He smiled. "Oh, but I do."

I was breathing heavily. It took a second for it to register that he had spoken; I didn't want to admit how much his words had stung. "Do what?"

"Understand." Sarge was still smiling. "Yeah, I know what you're feeling now, Joe. Exactly. It happened to me, Lord, quite a while ago. In Korea. How does the saying go? Oh yeah, 'Been there, done that, got the shirt.'" He chuckled, "Joe, you're about at the same point I was, all those years back. Just about. I wish Helen was here right now to see this."

"Sarge, I don't have clue one what you're saying."

He was still smiling, like he held a secret. "Sit down, Joe. You're gonna pop a vein." Sarge sat back in his same spot on the couch, but Noodles stayed hidden. I guess he was seeing which way all this was going.

I did, but only because Sarge was right. I felt as if any second I was going to keel over. And then, right on cue, here came that awful voice. Again. *Eat a bullet. Now. In front of him.*

I glanced up at Sarge. I have no idea of the expression on my face, but it was enough to wipe the smile off his. "Oh Jesus," Sarge whispered. "Jesus, Jesus, Jesus..." I realized with a shock what my old friend was doing. He was praying. For me.

And then from my heart I heard the other voice. The softer one. The sweeter one. *Let it go, Joe,* the voice said. *Come home.*

Die now! screamed the bad voice.

Live, said the good.

Die!

Live.

Time to die, Joe!

Your times are in my hands, Joe. Live. Come home.

Boy, you're mine! You're going straight to hell! Die! Die!!

I couldn't take anymore. I was being ripped apart. Blindly I reached out my hands to Sarge and repeated the same words I had groaned on that dark Christmas eve, back in that Baton Rouge motel room, all those years ago. "God... Help me, please..."

And I fainted dead away.

*****

Black... Wet... What? I sat up straight, breathing hard, and the moist washcloth fell off my eyes. I was in my bed. In the far corner sat Sarge, who had pulled one of my two kitchen chairs into the bedroom. He was looking at me closely, and his smile could have been better. "How you feeling?"

"Like I've been enthusiastically kicked by a Peruvian soccer team." I rubbed my face. "How long was I out?"

"Over an hour. I dragged you in here and threw you where you landed." Sarge got up and stood over me. "Lord a'mercy, Joe, you only weigh about two pounds less than a Shetland pony. I almost blew a rivet. What are you are you made of, depleted uranium? You sure don't look fat." I guess he realized he was rambling, because he dropped his banter. "Is that what you meant by the voices?"

"Yeah." I stared at him. "You mean you could hear them too?"

"No. But by the look on your face I knew you could." Sarge shook his head. "Holy Moses, I thought you were just being dramatic when you had told me about them earlier. But you weren't kidding, were you?"

"Not hardly." I flopped back down. "Sarge, I thought this time they had me. That I was really going to die."

He didn't answer for a second, then he smiled. "Well, boy, I think maybe it's high time you did."

"Do what?" I sat back up. "You mean *die??"*

"Sure. Dying is the only thing that saved me. The same goes for Helen. Linda too, and I don't mean in that wreck."

"Now I'm really lost," I groaned.

"Yeah, you are," Sarge said, "but you don't have to stay that way."

I gave him a sour look. Not this again.

Sarge went on, "These people you've run into these last few days...what were their names again?"

"What people?" I wearily climbed out of bed and stood up.

"You know, the Christians."

I sighed, not sure of where he was headed. "Well, there was my client, Mike Taylor, and then there were Nick Castle and CT Barnes, and their pastor, and then some others-"

"Yeah yeah, all them," Sarge interrupted, waving his hands to shut me up. "Do you know what they all have in common?"

"Riddles?" I groaned in exasperation. "Do we have to? Sarge, I'm not in a riddling mood." I started back towards my living room, my old mentor following.

"No riddles, Joe," he said. "What they all have in common is they've all known you less than two days. We go back nearly thirty years."

I went to my cupboard and pulled down the bottle of Cutty Sark. Sarge frowned at that, but I ignored him as I grabbed a glass. If he didn't want to watch me drink, he could avert his eyes. I poured two fingers with deft precision. Only then did I turn, scotch in hand, and face him. "So?"

"So it's like I said before," Sarge said, looking straight at me, and pointedly ignoring what I held in my hand. "You and me, we have a history, Joe. We've been through a lot. We've seen it all, twice over. We've even been under fire together, and you know that'll bond men. So I'm gonna ask you something, and don't lie." He was giving me flat cop eyes. "Why won't you accept the Lord?"

"Getting personal in your old age, aren't you?" I shot back, feeling nasty. Sarge didn't answer, so I shrugged and drained my glass in one shot. It burned like fire. Not as much as Lem MacElroy's 'shine, but respectable. Over the years I suppose I've drunk hundreds of gallons of alcohol; you'd think the pain would have burned away by now. Sarge was still staring, waiting.

"Well," I told him at last, fake smile on my face, "it's like the old song says. He done me wrong."

Sarge frowned again. "Who did?"

"Who do you think, Sarge?" I laughed without humor and pumped my thumb towards the ceiling. "The dream crusher. The big kahuna. The head cheese. The ringleader of this farce. Your friend and his. God."

Sarge shook his head. "Good grief, Joe. I know you've had a rough life, but blasphemy won't help. And I also know losing Linda was terrible, but we all-"

Now it was my turn to interrupt, barking a laugh. "YOU know?"

I lowered my voice, trying not to throttle him. "You don't know squat, Sarge, so don't even pretend you do. Nobody KNOWS, not unless they've hiked across that particular piece of real estate." I squinted at him. "How long have you and Helen been married?" I asked, my tone rough. "What is it, going on forty years now?"

"Forty-five." His answer was soft.

"Forty-five," I smirked. "Well throw him a fish. You know how long Linda and I had? Exactly three hundred and sixty-five days. A bit short of forty-five years, wouldn't you say?" I sneered again. "Terrible? Sarge, old buddy, you don't know the meaning of the word. But I'm about to educate you, yessiree." I was starting to feel the liquor. "Yessiree bob, I'm about to take you to school. Like Paul Harvey says, you're going to be told the rest of the story. And Sarge, it'll blow your Buckeye mind."

Screw it. I turned and poured myself another drink. For what I was getting ready to share, I needed it. I pushed myself away from the counter, drink in hand. "So walk this way, because class is about to start. I'm going to expand your horizons, friend, and stretch your thinking, and share with you the full weight of the word 'terrible'."

I headed towards the bedroom, Sarge right behind. "What are you going to show me, Joe?" Even after the way I had been speaking to him, I could hear the compassion in Sarge's voice for me. First Pastor Samuels, now Sarge; maybe it was my week for it.

"You're about to see something unique, Sarge," I said. "A singularly 'terrible' thing." I stopped by my bed and pointed with my drink. "Reach under there. You'll find a box. Pull it out."

Sarge stared at me in incomprehension for a moment, then he knelt and fished his hand back under the bed.

"Feel it yet?" I sipped my drink, not looking at him.

"All I feel is dust bunnies. You could start a ranch."

"Further back. Down towards the foot."

"Wait a minute," Sarge grunted, moving his hand around. "Hold it. I got it."

Then with another frown he slid the box out. I didn't but glance at it. I already knew what it looked like; after all these years, I should. It was like a shoebox, but bigger, with faded, ripped Christmas wrap still clinging to it. Old Christmas wrap, nearly three decades old. Sarge sat down on my bed with the box in his hands. He looked up at me.

"Open it. Look inside." I took another sip. "Behold the dream crusher's work."

Sarge stared at me another second, then without another word he lifted the lid and peered in. He shook his head.

"Lift it out," I told him.

Sarge did and held it up in his hand. "What is it?"

"What does it look like?"

"It looks like a stuffed monkey." Sarge shook his head again. "I don't get it. A stuffed monkey is your dream?"

I sighed as I sat down in the same chair Sarge had used a few minutes before. I took another sip of my scotch, this time a bigger one, before I spoke.

"That's called a sock monkey, Sarge. They're big down south. It's made out of old socks. Really, it is. You see the red muzzle? That's from the sock's heel. I had one as a kid. Granny made it for me. It's a poor kid's toy."

"This one?"

"No." I breathed out the word, feeling my chest constrict. "No, Linda bought that one the night she died."

I took another sip of my drink and held the glass up to the light. Maybe my answers were in there, in the scotch. I hadn't found them there yet in thirty years, but maybe today it would happen. "The day after we buried Linda I got a call from the salvage yard, the place where they had towed our car. They wanted me to come down and claim some stuff they had gotten out of it. When I got there the guy told me that when they had popped the trunk, they found something with my name on it inside."

Sarge nodded at it. "This box."

I held out my glass to him in salute. "Give that man a cheroot. Yep, that box." Using my left hand so I wouldn't spill my drink, I rubbed my face. "When I got home I sat down on the couch with it, and just...held it for awhile. Maybe an hour. Maybe longer. Somewhere in there I think I even sang to it." I laughed bitterly. "Now that's dumber'n dog poop, isn't it? Truth to tell, Sarge, I don't really remember what I did for that hour. I do know that finally, though, I opened it up. And you know what I found?" I smiled. "Inside the box, on top of some tissue paper, there was a note. It was from Linda." I smiled again, dying a little more. "Man, she loved writing notes. You remember, Sarge." He nodded, not speaking. I went on, "Linda knew my old sock monkey had been my favorite toy as a kid, and she knew I had even named him: Mister Monk. But somewhere along the way she also knew I had lost him. So Linda said in the note that she had been out driving around earlier that evening and had found an Appalachian shop right down in Northside. I didn't know there was a store like that down there, did you, Sarge?" He shook his head. "Well, there is," I said. "I've been in there several times since. Looking for...anyway. And guess what was sitting in the window? Guess what caught her eye?" I pointed. "That. A handmade sock monkey. So Linda bought it, and she put it in that box under some tissue paper, then she put her note on top. Before she did that, though, she had the store make up a little sock monkey nametag, and she hung it around his neck: Mister Monk Junior."

Now I looked at Sarge, straight at him, my eyes glistening, the pain just about to kill me. "Oh, Sarge, that was the best part," I said, "the Junior part. It was Linda's way, her way of telling me. Because down at the bottom of the note was the rest of the news, in big happy letters." I put my hand over my eyes, the grief inside me burning as bright as a supernova. "Telling me that she was two months pregnant."

There was a long pause, then Sarge whispered, "Oh sweet Jesus. THAT was the surprise."

"Yeah." The tears began to finally squeeze through. "Ain't life rich? That sock monkey wasn't for me. It was for our baby."

Chapter 20

Sarge didn't do anything but look at me for a minute. Then with a small shake of his head he tenderly put Mister Monk Junior back in his box and replaced the lid, closing the scraps of wrapping back over it. He gently laid it on the bed. Then Sarge stood with a sigh, shuffled over, and placed a hand on my shoulder.

"Joe," he began, "I don't have...words..." Something seemed to catch in his throat, for he cleared it and started over. "You've carried an awful weight all these years."

"Yeah I did," I snarled, and I roughly wiped my face clean of tears. "And I carried it alone. I guess your pal the dream crusher had other things to attend to besides me." I tossed back the rest of my drink. It tasted lousy.

"Don't call him that," Sarge admonished, his voice still soft. "He wasn't the one that killed your family."

"Really." I stood, pushing Sarge's hand from me. "Now that's interesting, old buddy. I suppose you know who did."

"Sure," he replied. "Satan."

"Satan." I nodded. "Satan. And you believe that."

"I know it."

"Sarge," I said then, "maybe you'd better leave. Because if you don't I'm just liable to beat you to death."

"Feel free to try, Joe," he smiled. "But I'm not the one you're mad at."

"No?"

"No."

"Well then enlighten me, Sarge!" I yelled. "Clue me in! Bring me up to speed on the program! Give me the skinny, or any other way you want to say it! I need an answer, if you've got one! Because I DON'T believe in your God, and I DON'T believe in your devil, so that just leaves blind chance, doesn't it! Blind chance, and a husband TOO! FREAKING! CHEAP! to buy his wife and child a safe car, a car that wouldn't have skidded and...killed..."

Words failed me then. I lost it, just completely folded up like a Chinese fan. I dropped to my knees, and as I did hot tears again started flowing down my face, this time unchecked.

"Let it go, Joe..." Sarge whispered as he knelt down and gently rubbed my neck. "Let it go..."

My crying became a kind of weird laughter, almost hysterical, as I tried to speak an answer. Maybe I really was going insane.

"You know, Sarge," I spluttered and laughed, "I think Linda was carrying my son. And I thought I had cried all my tears all those years ago, but I guess not. After losing Linda and Junior, I find I've still got plenty left. Ain't that a laugh and a half? I've even got enough to share!" My hands began to move and dance, seemingly of their own volition. "So tell me, old buddy, what kind would you like? Tears of blame, regret, shame, what-if...I've got 'em all!" Manically I plowed on, cackling, "Hey, maybe we'll open a store and sell them! You know the market will never run out. Yeah, there's pain and hurt and death aplenty in this nasty old world, and more coming, every day! We'll need all the tears we can get. And who knows, maybe someday we'll have cried enough and bled enough to wash all that pain and hurt and death away..."

"Somebody already did, Joe," Sarge said, but I barely heard him. I simply could not seem to shut up. The venom just kept pouring out.

"And won't that be a wonderful day then, children!" I yelled. "Oh yeah! Sarge's world will be perfect, and mine will still be rotten. But who cares? You and goody-two-shoes Helen, your lovely wife of FORTY-FIVE YEARS will wake up and found that you've inherited paradise, won't you? While I--while I--"

I simply stopped then, out of gas. Just like that, I was done; the voice had said I would be. I was finished, over, kaput. I guess even I had a limit to how much pain I was willing to inflict on an old friend. I stopped my blathering and my venting and I hung my head, spent. "I'm sorry, Sarge. I didn't mean..."

My God, I was weary. Weary of it all. My weariness was so great I felt I would never be able to walk upright again. "I-"

"Shh," Sarge whispered, then he smiled. "You're at the end, now, aren't you, Joe?"

I nodded, exhausted down to my very core.

"You're beaten," Sarge went on. "Or we could use country-type words, words you taught me. What are some of them? Down to the short rows. All done in. At the water's edge."

I nodded again, speechless. How did he know how I felt?

"So do it, Joe," Sarge said softly. "Slip in. Slide on into the river, and let it wash you clean."

But he just didn't seem to get it. "I can't," I whispered. "What I've done-"

"Doesn't matter," Sarge finished, then he smiled again. "You've never seen Helen's and my place in Florida, have you?" I shook my head. "You need to come down sometime, when your case is over," he said. "We'll fish. Anyway, in our living room we've hung a picture. It's called 'Forgiven'. Have you ever seen it?" I shook my head again, and Sarge smiled even wider. "It's a dilly. It shows a guy--much like you, Joe--who's at the end, too. He's had it. Beaten. In one hand the guy is holding a mallet, and in the other, some spikes. But guess who's holding him tight, Joe? Guess who's keeping him up? The man he had just used that mallet and spikes on."

I swallowed. "You mean Jesus."

"That's right," Sarge nodded. "See, the very one you've hurt with your words and indifference is the very one who wants to make you whole again. It's His way." Sarge blew out a breath and rocked his head from side to side. "Joe, I don't know why your life has gone the way it has. I don't know why your wife and child had to die. But I do know this, for true," and he gave me hose eyes again. "Nothing happens that isn't sifted through the hands of the Father first. It's like a, what's it called, a tapestry. On one side all you see is knots and strings, and it's ugly. But turn it over and you see the whole. And then it makes sense." Sarge put both his hands on my shoulders as he gazed at me. "Someday, Joe, this *will* make sense, perfect sense, all of it, and we'll slap our heads and wonder why we never saw it." Sarge's voice grew low. "But until that day, you've got to go on, and you've got to fight. Only you don't have to fight alone. Let Jesus fight for you. Let Him fight with you. All you have to do is ask."

I stared up at Sarge, mouth agape. "Those are the same words I heard that voice in my heart tell me yesterday."

"Well, I don't wonder," Sarge said. "That's God pulling you, boy, wooing you home." My old friend stopped. Then he went on, his voice even lower, "And Joe, Linda and your boy are waiting there for you. Waiting and watching. They're seeing just exactly what it is you're going to do." Sarge nodded. "It's time, son."

I swallowed again, harder. "I don't know how..."

"I do," he smiled. "Just say this..."

*****

And so right there, right in the middle of a cruddy old apartment in Cincinnati, my life started over. I finally got that new beginning I had heard so much about all these years, but had not dared to believe could be mine. And now it was.

But here was something funny. After Sarge and I had finished our prayer, and after I had asked Jesus to take this wreck of a life and somehow get it squared away, I looked down at my now-still hands...and I laughed. These were...baby hands? I laughed again, harder. I guessed they were. There was really no other way to put it: I was a forty-eight-year-old, burly, battle-scarred...newborn.

And then it hit me: newborns scream, don't they? Blamed right they do.

So I let one fly.

I screamed a rebel yell, screamed it right at the top of my voice. I screamed that yell so loud my ceiling fixture buzzed and old Mr. Platz, my upstairs neighbor, pounded on his floor with a broom. A rebel yell...only now I knew who I was rebelling against. And what I was fighting for. Sarge laughed; so did I. It felt great.

Right about then Noodles came out from under the couch to see what all the hubbub was. His ruined tail swished lazily from side to side as he watched my restart. And my rebirth.

How about that, I thought with a grin. My very own cat midwife.

And I swear he was grinning too.

Chapter 21

Twelve o'clock. Lunchtime, and here it was, just Noodles and me. I hadn't been able to persuade Sarge to stay to eat with us. He had told me thanks, but he couldn't, he had to catch his flight back home to Florida, mission accomplished. I guess it was just as well; I had checked my larder and found that all I had to serve were scotch, beer, and cat treats. We had a good laugh over that, but then right at the door Sarge stopped, and his smile faded.

He looked at me, his face grave. I hardly noticed; I was still buzzed over what had just happened to me. Liquor didn't even come in a close second to the high I was feeling. But the gravity I heard in Sarge's voice brought me up short.

"I know you're cranked, Joe," Sarge said. "And that's good. Enjoy it. Because in a little bit it's gonna hit you that something important happened here this morning. No, it was more than that. Lifechanging. And Joe, I know you, I know how you get." Sarge gave me a stern look. "You feel bulletproof right now, don't you?" I grinned, and he shook his head in exasperation. "Yeah, I can see it all over you. I can read you like a book. Hey, and speaking of books..." Sarge reached into his hip pocket and pulled out a thin volume. He handed it out to me.

"What's this?" I asked, taking it. Then I saw what it was: a battered, black New Testament. "Where did you get this?"

"It's mine," Sarge said. "From Korea. The chaplains handed them out to us on the troop ship as we headed over."

I tried handing it back. "You know I can't take this, Sarge. It's got sentimental value for you."

"The value it has is how it helps you walk out your life in the Lord," Sarge answered. "I heard a preacher say that once. Besides, Helen and me have a ton of 'em." Sarge shook his head again. "That woman is a Bible-holic. If we have one translation we must have twenty. You can't swing a dead cat in our house without hitting a Bible." Sarge looked down. "Sorry, Noodles."

Noodles licked his paw, supremely indifferent.

"Anyway, Joe, I want you to have it," Sarge said. "Keep it. But don't just keep it, read it. Plus you need to get yourself a whole Bible when you get a chance. And then find a good, solid church to join. Maybe that one you told me about."

"That'd surprise a few folks," I muttered.

"But you need to do those things, Joe," Sarge went on. "Because it's like I said, I know you like you were my own. You'll be spoiling for a fight next, only this time a righteous one. You'll be wanting a little payback from the devil." I nodded again, still grinning--Sarge knew me so well--and he blew out a breath. "Southern boys. Always wanting to scrap." Sarge stared right in my eyes. "Well, Joe, if you want a fight, you're gonna get one. And it'll be a honey, the devil will see to that. He'll be real eager to accommodate you." Sarge twisted his lips in a scowl. "Satan's a cruddy loser. And right now he is mightily ticked that he lost you. You've crossed him, and he's not the type just to let that lie. I have no idea how all this'll turn out." Sarge's gaze turned soft. "So Joe, will you take some advice from an old man that's stood right in your shoes?"

"Sure," I said, wondering where he was going with this.

Sarge's answer was flat. "Get prayer cover."

"Huh?" What did THAT mean?

"You remember air cover from the war, don't you?"

"Sure," I said again. "We'd call it in, and the F-4's would come screaming in low. They'd strafe the treelines, or drop nape, or whatever we needed, then we would go in and clean up."

Sarge nodded. "And what would have happened if you had tried to 'clean up' before the planes had done their job?"

I laughed. "I guess we would have gotten cleaned up."

"Darn straight," Sarge said, then he frowned. "Joe, you know Helen and me have prayed for you for all these years. And we don't regret a second of it; what you did today makes it all worthwhile. But Joe"--and here, for the first time, Sarge looked his age-- "we're getting old. You may have noticed that. For what you're about to do, you need more people praying for you than just us."

Now it was my turn to nod. "Prayer cover."

"Bingo. You guessed 'er, Chester. And you need it bad. You need prayer warriors, intercessors, fighters. People that are like, what do you call them, Gila monsters."

"*Gila* monsters?" I laughed.

Sarge waved his hand at me. "Sure, you've seen them on those nature shows. Once a Gila monster clamps onto something, it won't let go. Not even if you chop its head off." Sarge closed one eye and nodded at me, a sage of the age. "That's the kind of prayer fighters I'm talking about. People that'll lay down a little scorched earth before you go in on the ground."

"I think I've got some of those already," I said slowly, remembering. "The pastor at that church told me that there would be four thousand people praying for me. At the time that sounded stupid."

Sarge's eyebrows climbed up to his hairline. "Stupid? Four thousand people praying for you? Boy, if the pastor told you that he must feel you're gonna need 'em all."

I gave a slight smile, beginning to feel a bit overwhelmed. "Guess so."

"No 'guess' about it, Joe." Sarge's voice was sharp. "You need to call that pastor, today, and tell him what's happened to you. You also tell him to get those prayers cranking, now."

Suddenly my old friend's face blanched, and his eyes took on a look, as if he was listening to something I couldn't quite hear. And what he was hearing wasn't good.

"Oh my God. Joe, I got sirens going off in me." Sarge's voice thickened, his eyes now as large as plates. "Sirens inside. They're going off in my spirit like crazy. They started up, just now." Sarge turned his gaze back to me, his expression unreadable. What WAS that look? Was it...sadness? No, more than that.

Goodbye.

"Get that prayer chain going, Joe," Sarge whispered hoarsely. "What you've seen up till this point were just the preliminaries. Now get ready for the main event."

Chapter 22

It was a little past one p.m. and I was in my office, getting the phoning I needed to do done before I headed out to see what was what. "Hi, may I speak with Mike Taylor, please?"

"May I ask who's calling?"

"Joe Box."

"He's taking a meeting now, Mr. Box. May I ask what this is in reference to?"

Taking a meeting. Of all the California phrases that have spread like kudzu across our fruited plain, I think I hate that one the most. Taking a pill I can understand. Even taking a sitz bath. But meetings should be 'attended', not 'taken.'

Oh well. Easy, son. I took a breath as I smiled through gritted teeth. "No, it's rather personal. Could I leave a message on his voice mail?" Wasn't it nice that I hadn't snapped Mike's secretary's head off with all her nosiness? Wasn't I being good? Of course I was...or maybe it was the new me coming out.

"Certainly," she said. "I'll connect you."

She did, and I made it short. "Hi, Mike, it's Joe Box, and I was calling to give you an update. I think I may have a lead on Francesca. Now before you get all excited, I'm not going to tell you where she may be, exactly, because I think that might cause you to want to do something silly like tagging along...no offense. So let's just say I think she's somewhere close. I'll call you back when I get the chance." I hung up.

At least, I hoped she was close. And she was, if Quint's information about GeneSys was correct. Right before I had phoned Mike Taylor to update him I had called my old computer pal, to see if he had gotten anything from the bank routing numbers found on Mangold's statements.

Not surprisingly, he had.

"Joseph." Quint had grunted my name when he answered. "I thought it might be you." He sounded awful.

"Rough night?"

"You might say that. Nightmares."

"Me too," I said.

I could hear Quint take a deep draught of something, and I bet I knew what it was. "I dreamed I was at Auschwitz," he said. "I was naked in a room with a hundred other naked people, including my parents. There were shower heads above us, but it seemed I was the only one that knew what they were for. I was trying to jump high enough to snap one off, but I kept missing. My dad laughed at that, and the rest joined in. Then the Zyklon-B gas started hissing out of those heads, and suddenly nobody was laughing." Quint took another swallow. "Anyway. I ran the routing numbers early this morning and I found out where GeneSys is."

I sat up straight. He had said it so matter-of-factly. "You're kidding! Where?"

"You're not going to believe this, Joseph. It's located right over in Indiana, about two hours west of here. The town it's in is called Willisville. I checked the map, and it's on 50, halfway between Versailles and North Vernon."

"Well, I'll be dipped." I shook my head. "I've never even heard of Willisville."

"Probably no one has, that's why they picked it." Quint cleared his throat. "So I assume this is it, you're going to head over there now to rescue the girl, guns blazing?"

"I hope guns won't figure in, Quint, but yeah, I suppose I need to check it out."

"Well, whatever you do, Joseph, please be careful." Quint's voice grew tight. "The friends I have that appreciate the musical transcendence of Muddy Waters I can count on one hand."

"One hand's all you've got, Quint, since you use the other to hold that nasty liquor you favor so much." He laughed at that--good, he needed it--and I went on, "But not to worry, buddy. I've grown too fond of my skin to want to risk it battling Nazis, or whatever they are. I'll just do a little recon, and if it looks like it's going to be too tough to get her out by myself, I'll call in the cops and let them handle it."

"Good." I heard Quint drain his glass. "Your Granny would be pleased to have reared such a wise boy."

We rang off, and then I had called Mike Taylor and left my message.

Now I was facing this last call before I left to go home and pack my gear, and this one was going to be a bit harder: Pastor Samuels. I futzed around for a bit before I picked it up.

Well, here goes. Sarge had always said that Jesus gave you a fresh start. After they way Luke and I had parted, I needed it.

I dialed the number. "Um, hello. May I speak with Pastor

Samuels?"

"Sure, who's calling, please?"

"Uh, tell him it's Joe. Joe Box." Nuts. I was stammering again.

"Mr. Box!" Now I recognized her voice. "It's me, Zoe! Zoe Gennaro! Hi!"

"Hi, Zoe." This kid. I felt a little smile breaking out in spite of myself.

"Gosh, Mr. Box," Zoe rushed on. "You sure turned this place on its ear. Everybody was talking about you! All day long!"

My smile faded. "Everybody?"

"Sure! The Armorbearers, Pastor Jackson, Pastor Samuels, Dotty...oh, everybody!"

"Uh, well then maybe you'd better patch me through, Zoe. To Pastor Samuels."

"Wups, I forgot!" she giggled. "Sorry!"

Immediately Zoe was replaced by the recorded sounds of music and an announcer telling of upcoming events at the church. After a few seconds of that Luke picked up. "Hello, Joe?"

"Uh, hi, Luke." This was going to be harder than I had thought. "Listen, I-"

But his next words floored me. "You're a Christian now, aren't you?"

Say WHAT? "Luke, now how in the h-" I stopped, and started over. "How did you know *that?"*

He was laughing. "Am I right?"

"Yeah you are." I have to admit it, the pastor's laugh was infectious, and I caught the bug myself as I chuckled, "Since late this morning. Ain't that fine? But Luke, how did you KNOW?"

"Don't ask me," he said. "I can't answer that. Some people would call it discernment."

Discernment... Where had I recently heard that word before? Then I remembered: Nick Castle again. It was how he had known what was tormenting me that day in his office.

But wait. Was there a difference between 'discernment', as Christians defined the term, and that other thing I had known all my life, what we hillbillies called 'fey'? I didn't have a clue.

Brother. I had a lot to learn about this stuff.

"Well, anyway," I said, "I wanted you to know. Oh, there was something else. The guy that prayed for me today said to ask you about 'prayer cover'. I guess you know what he means, huh?"

"That I do." Luke cleared his throat. "This is what you've been hoping for, isn't it, Joe? Things are coming to a head."

"You said it," I answered flatly. "And yeah, this *could* be it. I'm heading out now. With any luck Francesca might be back home tonight."

Luke paused. "Do you mind telling me where you think she is?"

I wrestled with it for a second before I relented. Somebody besides Quint should know where I was going; it only made sense. Why not him? "Well...all right. But for God's sake keep it to yourself. If Mike Taylor tries pumping you, don't give in. I don't want some distraught dad messing up the works. Deal?"

"Deal," Luke told me. "Within limits."

That I didn't like the sound of. "Explain, please."

"Joe, this is new territory for you, I know," he said, "so let me answer you this way: if I get a strong leading from the Lord that I'm to tell Mike where his daughter is, I'll have to do it. My first priority is to our heavenly Father, not you. Do you see?'

I didn't really. But I guessed it didn't matter; I would simply have to trust this man to do what was right. "No, Luke, I don't see, but I'm going to tell you anyway. Just remember, though, our butts are in your hands."

"Now that's as grisly as thought as I EVER had," Luke said, in a dead-bang perfect imitation of Groucho Marx, then he laughed.

Son of a gun, now I started laughing too. "Stop it! I'm serious, doggone it!"

Cackling like asylum escapees, we both carried on like that for a few seconds, the tension over what I was about to do easing. At last I calmed down enough to go on. "Anyway, I think she's in a little town just west of here. Willisville, Indiana."

"Willisville. I've never heard of it."

"Join the club. But that's where I'm going, right after I stop back home. So if you get the chance, maybe you and your people wouldn't mind sending up a prayer for me, okay?" Lord, that sounded so strange to say; perhaps it would get easier over time.

Then a sobering thought hit: provided I was granted that time.

"You can count on it, Joe," Luke said, his voice rough with emotion. "Count on it."

Chapter 23

Mile after mile. The eastern part of Indiana is as pretty a section of the country as you're ever likely to encounter...once you get past the casino boats infesting the areas around Aurora and Lawrenceburg. As the old song went, they've been the ruin of many a poor boy; my competitor and pal Billy Barnicke was proof of that. I'll never understand the attraction of pulling a lever over and over, eyes glazed and your breath shallow, or watching a little white ball spin around an inlaid wooden wheel, desperately willing it to drop where you wanted. Now that I was a Christian--that word still tasted strange in my mouth--I understood it even less. If those people on those boats could have just an inkling of what I was feeling now...caramba, indeed.

As I had told Luke that I would, I had gone home right after I had hung up with him. I needed to figure what I was going to take, and I'd made a list in my head as I'd headed back to the Agnes: my .38 revolver, certainly, and shells for the same; my would-be ninja clothes; some regular duds and toiletries; my Visa card and a little cash...oh yeah, and Sarge's New Testament he had given me.

I smiled at that. A pistol and the Good Book: now I truly was that rarity of the old West, a Bible-totin' gunslinger. Was there a dichotomy there? I didn't know. To say that I was new at this would be an understatement.

The last thing I had done before I left was to grab Noodles and go upstairs with him. I wanted to ask Mr. Platz if he would take care of my cat while I was gone, and also give him my key.

"Yah, sure, Joe," the old man said. "I vatch him. But you, no more screaming, eh? I tot you vas gettink killed."

"I kind of was, Mr. Platz," I smiled, and he frowned, not getting it. "Part of me, anyway. I'll explain it when I get back. Thanks for taking care of this useless cat."

"Ah, Noodles." Mr. Platz picked him up, and Noodles head-bumped the old man under the chin, purring. "Vhat Cherman doesn't love them?"

*****

A short two hours after I had said goodbye to my friends, I had finally come to my destination. I had rounded one last easy turn on route 50, and there was the greeting sign for Willisville.

If you've ever taken any two-lane country roads in your time, you'll know the kind of sign I mean; it was as much advertisement from the town fathers as anything else. The one I was seeing now was typical: wooden, white, maybe four feet tall by six feet wide, with "Welcome to Willisville" in bold letters at the top. Underneath that greeting were plaques from the Kiwanis, 4-H, Rotary Club, Lions, area churches and such-like, and then the population: 9,346. "And gro-o-o-wing!" the sign had proudly crowed.

Growing by at least one missing girl, I thought darkly.

As I entered the town I was struck by its simplicity. The whole place couldn't have been more than ten city blocks square. Strangely, that simplicity made me uneasy. But why? The people I saw walking the sidewalks in this crazy heat seemed ordinary enough, and the town itself was rather pretty. The main street was wide and well-kept, with the side streets crossing it at every block the same. I passed a small, neat library, a diner, a police station, a pool hall, a five-and-dime, a dry goods store, a bar and grill, and so on. When I came to the town square I noted it was decked out with the obligatory pillared courthouse, complete with a cannon on the lawn. All this town lacked was Andy and Barney chatting amiably with Floyd. In sum, Willisville was perfect. Unnaturally so.

The feel was like Mayberry had come to life, transported to Indiana. No, worse. The town put me in mind of the village from *Invasion of the Body Snatchers*: cheery, bright, and hollow at the core. It was as if space aliens had ordered a 'town: small: Midwestern' straight from 1950's central casting. As I slowly cruised down Main, I almost expected any second to see Kevin McCarthy lurch from an alleyway and begin pounding on the Goddess's hood screaming, "You're next!!"

Weird, I know, but I couldn't shake the feeling as I kept driving through. A scant ten minutes after I had entered Willisville I left it. I knew what I was after, and it wasn't going to be located in town.

Half a mile later, I found it. I rounded another easy turn, and there it was.

GeneSys.

I don't really know what it was exactly I had expected, but this beat anything I could have come up with. Picture a huge, flattened, elongated silver dome, maybe five hundred feet across by a thousand feet long, all of it surrounded by two rows of twelve-foot-high chain link fence, and that topped by roll after roll of concertina razor wire. In other words, that dome and its grounds covered an area greater than five football fields. In front a jet-black two-lane driveway came off the main road, ending at a guard shack. And right next to that shack was a large sign with the legend: GeneSys--Tomorrow Begins Here. I slowly drove by the facility, trying to silence what I was surely hearing inside.

Sarge's sirens. They were howling like the end of the world.

I could sense...something...flowing out from that dome, flowing out like acid-yellow radiation. I knew now what this was, this awful feeling. It was that old horrible thing from the past few days, only now magnified a millionfold.

Pure, uncut, mad-dog-dripping evil.

But here was something strange. Even though I recognized that sensation, I knew something about it now. I knew it was coming from outside myself this time, not inside.

And then that calm voice spoke up. I guess the word is "sweet", as it whispered to me, *You'll never feel that darkness inside you again, Joe. Never again. It's gone forever. Because today you asked Jesus to come in, and take its place.*

Yeah, I thought with a grin. That's right, I did. And good riddance to the bad. I squared my shoulders. All right, children.

Time to kick this deal into high.

Chapter 24

In any small town there's one sure place for a guy like me to find out what was shaking, and I knew where it was. I reentered Willisville, circumnavigated the square, and turned the Goddess back the other way I came down Main. Pulling up in front of the bar I had passed before, I stopped the car, got out, and walked in. Jerry's Time Out looked and smelled like any other run-down saloon you'll find in America, and it took a few seconds after I had entered for my eyes to adjust to the dim light. The place was small, holding maybe six or eight tables scattered haphazardly through it, with the bar itself on the left and running the length of the room. In the far corner an old Wurlitzer jukebox tiredly squatted, mercifully silent. Above me the ceiling appeared to be darkened punched tin, and on the scuffed floor lay an unappetizing mix of spilled beer, peanut shells, cigarette butts, and something else. What was this? I peered closer at it. It looked for all the world like dried blood. Well. Maybe this wasn't Mayberry after all.

Back behind the bar, up in the corner, the obligatory TV was going with the sound turned off. I glanced at the show: it was some trash-talk episode in the Jerry-Rikki-Sally Jesse Raphael genre. I sincerely hoped the bartender would have enough common human decency to keep the volume down on the thing, because I'll say this as genteel as I can: those shows make me puke.

The said bartender, a medium-built, toothpick-sucking balding guy wearing an earring and a filthy apron, nodded at me noncommitally as I took a seat at the far end of the bar. He then wandered over and lazily swiped the spot in front of me with a malodorous piece of damp, cheesecloth-looking rag that could have been mummy wrappings for all I knew. Scowling, the man asked what for me. No kidding, that's exactly what he said, "What for ya?", like a Damon Runyon character straight out of the thirties.

I almost felt like replying to him out of the corner of my mouth, "Gimme a shot with a beer back, and when do the dames come in?", but I didn't. Instead I said, "You Jerry?"

"Yeah," he answered in a flat monotone. "What for ya?"

Well sir. Jerry seemed to possess all the irresistible charm of a jar of Cheez Whiz, but I kept that to myself. No sense in ticking him off. And at first blush a beer sounded good, I have to admit, but then a part of me spoke up quietly: "Nope. You're done with all that." Oh really? Says who? I and this other me would need to have us a talk about that later. So I found myself saying to the bartender, "I'll just have a Coke."

He grunted and turned, drew one from the tap, and set it down on the bar with an unceremonious clunk. Then, not even looking to see where it went, he slid it down in front of me. A Wharton School of Business grad old Jerry obviously wasn't.

I started to ask Jerry another question, but my stomach picked that exact time to begin growling and muttering, rudely reminding me I hadn't eaten yet today. Granny used to call that sound the 'airy-urps'. Country wit, but think about it, that's what it does sound like. So I asked the man, "What kind of sandwiches do you have? Could you make me a grilled baloney and onion?" My, that sounded fine.

Jerry began walking down towards the other end of the bar, picking his teeth as he went. "Don't got any sandwiches."

A place like this, out of sandwiches? Unless we were well into the second week of a nuclear winter, I found that hard to believe. "What do you mean? The sign out front says bar and grill."

He gave me a lazy look. "The grill ain't worked since the Bay of Pigs. The bar's what ya see in front of ya."

Okay. On second thought, maybe that was for the best. I'd have been willing to bet the health inspector hadn't been in here since the Bay of Pigs either. "Got any munchies, then?"

Jerry sighed at me like I'd asked him to perform differential calculous, then he reached under the bar and pulled out an old chipped bowl. With snap of his wrist he slid it down my way. I have to say, Jerry's technique was pretty good: the thing stopped dead center in front of me, and I looked. Salted peanuts in the shell. Probably the safest things he had to eat, considering. I picked one up, shelled it, popped it in my mouth, then said to him, just to get the ball rolling, "Kind of quiet in here, huh?"

He shrugged. "Guess so."

I swallowed the peanut, took a sip of my Coke, and began shelling another nut. "Not much shaking in mid-afternoon, I suppose."

Jerry sucked his toothpick and didn't answer.

I plowed on. "But I bet it'll pick up later, though. When the day shift at GeneSys gets done, I mean. Lots of thirsty people at quitting time in this town, right?"

Jerry shrugged again and flipped his toothpick to the floor, where it joined, I'm sure, hundreds of its cast-off brethren. He then absently scratched at himself and belched. A class act.

"Yep," I said, as I smacked my lips appreciatively over my Coke, "I'll bet later tonight this place will be jumping. Am I right?" Although with Smilin' Jack here as host, maybe not.

Jerry shrugged yet again, and an odd thought occurred to me: perhaps things weren't as they seemed at this place. Could it be I was selling Jerry short? My tired mind began to wander in weird directions.

Maybe the bartender was really a space alien, a pod person, a thing incapable of human emotion. Or maybe Jerry'd had a lobotomy at some grim, state-run home for the criminally insane, and he owed this job to a halfway house that had helped him after he had gotten out. Or possibly he was an agent from Japan, where a gesture can have many subtle meanings, and been surgically altered just to LOOK like a Caucasian.

Yeah, I bet that was it. Old Jerry was really a cunning spy, sent to infiltrate us and learn our way of tending bar. Then he would tell his masters back home and they could train others to do it, so they could then eavesdrop on our corporate cocktail parties. Those same spies could pass any information they gleaned along, and thus bring to ruin a large portion of the American economy.

I rubbed my eyes. I was obviously more tired than I thought.

In reality, the unadorned truth of it was a lot more straightforward: Jerry really was the crass, uncommunicative dullard he in fact appeared to be.

Enough of this. Trying to pump the bartender this way could take hours, hours I simply didn't have the luxury of wasting. I had shot my bolt with this fool. Nearly ten minutes I had spent grilling the man and for my trouble had gotten the equivalent of two sentences, five shrugs, and a grunt. Compared to him, Cal Coolidge was an unrepentant ratchet-jaw.

I crunched my peanut and shook my head with a sigh. The talky, wisecracking barkeep: another stereotype, shot to perdition. Instead of being the garrulous fount of information I had hoped for, Jerry was, as Quint puts it, *bupkes,* nothing.

And the way the man doled out words...brother. You would have thought they cost him a dollar apiece. He would make a clam look like an auctioneer.

Time to go. I figured I would come back later tonight, and hopefully somebody else would be behind the stick. Or maybe

Jerry would be more talkative with the townsfolk pounding back drinks. Either way, I was finished here for now. I drained the rest of my Coke and set the glass down heavily on the bar.

" 'nother?" the barkeep asked, startling me.

Good Lord, Garbo talks!

"No thank you," I said as I stood, going into a fake British voice; you get your laughs where you can. "I am strictly a one-Coke man. But the peanuts, my good fellow, were absolutely first-rate. My compliments to the chef."

Jerry stared at me like I had just beamed in from the Crab Nebula, then he shrugged again, and I took that as my cue. I flipped a buck on the bar and left.

Chapter 25

Years ago I had promised myself that one day I would own a really good pair of binoculars. But I didn't want the dinky ones. No, I wanted the big, man-sized ones, the kind that would make me look like Glenn Ford peering out at the Japanese fleet from the conning tower of a submarine, the kind that came complete with rubber-coated knobs and a real leather strap. And back last May I had finally made good on that promise when I had purchased a Zeiss from American Science and Surplus. The things were black and massive and the ad had said you could see inside the craters of the moon with them. All of which was fine, but what I needed them to do now was view the workings of GeneSys. Hopefully.

After I had left Jerry's I had driven once more past the place, this time going another half-mile down the road before I found a secure area to pull off and hide my car. I had then jogged back towards the dome, at last coming to a small hummock on the other side of the road. I was now within a hundred yards of the complex. Cautiously I took the glasses from their case and peeped my head over the top with them. What was I looking for? I didn't have a clue; I figured I'd know it when I saw it.

Now I had been here almost two hours, with nothing to show for my efforts. Time had slowed to a crawl as I scanned, and sweat meandered lazily down my back, making the place between my shoulder blades itch like blazes. The air was still blisteringly hot, even at nearly six p.m., and felt as heavy as wet wool. My Granny used to call this stormin' weather, the kind that can change things in a flash. How can you tell? I had asked her as a boy. The trees, she answered. Check the trees when you see climate like this. But check for what, Granny? Leaves showing silver, she had said with a nod. What she meant by that country term was that if the leaves on a tree turned over, showing their silvery undersides, that meant rain was on its way, and also break in the heat. Does it work? Maybe six times out of ten; as good as you'll find on TV. I pulled my eyes away from the binoculars, checking the treeline across the road. No silver there, not yet. Only dark green foliage on the oaks and poplars that grew between the twin rows of fencing around the dome; in this heat the insects covering the branches screamed insanely. The shift at the complex had changed an hour ago, the two guards at the security shack smoking cigarettes and sniggering like eight-year-olds over a private joke while I watched the changeover. A few unmarked trucks had come and gone through the gates, driving slowly. For the fifth time since I had settled in the thought hit me: God, what a forbidding place. And meanwhile the sun relentlessly beat down.

I peered through the lenses once more. What was missing here? All I was seeing were trees, fencing, guards, and that sci-fi dome. Nothing else. *Nothing*. I blew out a frustrated breath. What kind of a factory was this, anyway? What-

Smokestacks. I looked again. That's what was missing. No smokestacks. But so what? In a place this futuristic, smokestacks would have been an anachronism anyway. But now I saw there were no vents of any kind that I could see. So what? I pulled the binocs away, my mind spinning. Why was that important? *Think.*

I found myself whispering a prayer, my first one in many years, besides the Big One I had prayed this morning. "God, I don't understand. Tell me. What am I missing here?"

Incredibly, three letters instantly dropped into my mind: *E.P.A.*

And I slowly nodded in understanding. E.P.A.

*****

"Now tell me again what it is you want?"

I smiled at the printshop owner; I guess my request did sound strange. "Like I said, I'm the new area inspector for the Environmental Protection Agency. The E.P.A. I've been assigned this whole quadrant of the state to make sure it's in federal compliance. My job is to inspect industry sites, landfills, schools, hospitals, and so forth. But I've got a problem. When my flight from Washington landed in Cincinnati this afternoon, I realized I had left my badge back home, and I need a replacement. I'm hoping you can help me."

"Yeah, maybe." The guy lifted an eyebrow. "But how do I know you're really with the E.P.A.?"

My smile left and I gave him a pained look. "Come on. Is that something someone would lie about? Where's the glamor in that? It's like saying you're with the IRS. We're not the most popular people around."

The man rubbed a hand on his chin. "Well, I don't know..."

"Did I also tell you I was assigned to check out all the print and copy places in southeastern Indiana?" I smiled, "Boy, you just can't imagine the stuff we find when we decide to look. What a mess. The stores can be shut down for weeks. Sometimes they never reopen at all." I smiled again.

The owner curled his lip in a snarl. "Okay, okay, I get it. No need to get rough." He slid a pad of paper over to me. "Sketch out what you want. I'll have it done in two days."

"Two days?" I shook my head. "I'm afraid that won't help. I need it now."

The man barked a laugh. "Well, you're out of luck, pal. Two days is the best I can do, inspection or no."

"Gosh." I slumped my shoulders in defeat. "You wouldn't believe how bad that makes me feel. All those delays..." I sniffed, frowning. "Say, what is that I'm smelling? Solvents? I hope you're not using the kind with PCBs or carcinogens. Why, just last week, we-"

The man held up a hand. "Enough. When would you like it?"

I gave him hopeful. "An hour?"

"An HOUR?" He started to shake his head. "For an ID badge I'll need to lay it out, then typeset it, then burn a plate, then-"

Now it was my turn to interrupt as I reached for my wallet. "Did I mention that I was on an expense account?" I pulled out a hundred. "Would this speed things up?"

For the first time the owner looked pleased with me. "Mister, for a hundred bucks I can have it done in forty-five minutes."

I quickly wrote down on his pad what I wanted on the badge, then handed it and the money to him. "Thanks. And your government says thanks as well."

Chapter 26

I gnawed on a fingernail as I looked at the badge. True as gold, the printshop man had gotten it made in forty-five minutes.

He saw what I was doing and frowned at me. "What's the matter? I put on it everything you said. And you told me that you wouldn't need your picture on it, so I-"

"No, no, it's fine. You do good work, sir." And he had. That badge looked as official as all get-out. No, what was bothering me was something I couldn't share with him. Or anybody, really. I looked back up and smiled. "You even put a pin on it. I wasn't expecting that."

The man smiled back. A bit nervously, I thought. "Well, nothing's too good for Uncle, you know?" The man nodded quickly. "I just wanted to make sure I stay on the good side of you guys. Okay?" The owner nodded again and gave me a sick grin, like a baboon eating a rotten banana. That made me feel even worse. Only now I knew what was bugging me.

I had lied to this man. Lied to him, just as cold as an eel.

Here he was, a poor schnook trying to make a buck with his little one-man print shop, and I had come off all tough and bad and had practically bullied him into doing my will. It wasn't a good feeling. But the thing was, I knew I had done far worse things in my line of work over the years, and they had never bothered me. Until now.

Was it because of my new faith? Was this sudden burst of honesty going to hamstring me from here on out? Blamed if I knew; this was going to require some thought. Then I realized the owner was still awaiting some sort of response from me.

"Uh, yeah," I said. "It's fine. Really. We appreciate it." Lord, I had to get out of here before I broke down and confessed all to this man. And that wouldn't help Francesca a bit, would it?

My brain was flying. By my lies--a bad thing--I was trying to free a girl--a good thing. Right?

Or not?

Caramba, this Jesus stuff was confusing. At least to me. But who knew, maybe I'd get better at it as I went. I gave the guy another wan smile and walked out.

*****

Seven-thirty p.m. and Jerry's Time Out was, as the saying went, a happenin' place. But then it would have to be: as near as I could tell, it was the only bar within a radius of fifteen miles. The room was packed with hard-drinking, chain-smoking, laughing-too-loud people. On the television, which everyone was ignoring, ESPN was showing some weird, incomprehensible sport that appeared to be a combination of luge and field hockey. Ratings time again. Predictably, the Wurlitzer jukebox in the corner had come to life since this afternoon, lucky me. The thing was now bellowing out country tunes with a bass line loud enough to loosen plaster. They call that boot-scootin' music, but nobody was dancing: no room. There was a point in my past when I would have felt right at home in such an establishment, but not any more. Especially not since this morning. But I was here to work, so I slid onto the only available barstool and waited my turn. Back behind the bar I noticed my old pal Jerry pouring drinks, only I saw that now he had himself a couple of helpers.

The first guy appeared to be nearly sixty, and was afflicted with blue, watery eyes and a shuffling gait. His ponderous upper lip was buried under a huge, yellow-stained mustache that hung straight down...the kind we used to call a "soup-strainer." I'd have been willing to bet a nickel the man went by the nickname of Pop. I couldn't tell if Pop's squint was due to his old age or the haze of smoke hanging like curtains of studio fog in here.

The other barkeep was a much younger guy, not yet thirty, with a quick smile and an easy banter that the customers, especially the ladies, seemed to eat up. He worked with the economical moves and fluid grace of a wide receiver as he kept up his nonstop chatter. And then there was the third man, Jerry himself. Jerry seemed content to let the other two do most of the work, with the old man keeping the patrons at the bar happy while the young guy served the tables.

During a momentary lull Pop came over my way and raised his eyebrows at me; as good a way as any of asking what I wanted to drink. This afternoon's Coke had been so pleasant I ordered another one.

"A COKE?" The old man looked at me as if he hadn't quite heard me right. "You sure you don't want a beer?"

I smiled at him. "A Coke is fine, Pop."

"Okay..." He bent over and drew one from the tap. Setting it down in front of me, Pop looked at me again. "You're new in town, aren'cha? How'd you know my name, anyway?"

Hah. I owed myself a nickel. "It just figured." I sipped my drink and smiled at him.

Pop shuffled off, muttering.

I half-twisted around in my seat to check out the room. Sarge used to have a saying: "There's three kinds of people, Joe--those who watch things happen, those who make things happen, and those who say 'what happened?'"

I smiled at that, because in a couple of minutes I was going to start asking these folks some questions, and then we would see...what would happen.

As I said, the bar itself, along with every table, was filled, and as I sipped my Coke I was now finding something disconcerting: every so often I noticed that the patrons here would turn their eyes my way, stare frankly at me for a second, then look away. And those looks they were giving sure weren't friendly. A few of the people even frowned at me, and then I would see them lean their heads together, whispering. The air in the room was growing heavy, and it wasn't just the humidity or the cigarette haze. I felt a little bit like Gary Cooper in *High Noon*, or maybe Sean Connery in *Outland* (which was really nothing more than a remake of *High Noon* in outer space). Do not forsake me, oh my darlin'.

Well, here goes. I turned to the patron on my left and smiled. "Some place, huh?"

The man stared down at the bar as he slurped his Seven-and-Seven. "It is what it is."

Oh good, a philosopher. Maybe later we'd discuss the high points of Plato's Republic. I pointed at his drink, still smiling. "You're right about that, friend. Can I buy you another?"

The man turned his attention from his drink to me, and I got a good look at him. It was not a world-class experience. If you were to look up "thug" in the dictionary, you would see his picture beside it. What few hairs remained on the man's head he had glued flat across his bald pate, his grey eyes were as cold and merciless as the north Atlantic, and he'd obviously battled acne in his youth. Just as obviously, he'd lost that war. The guy's face was covered with cratered scars, and I idly wondered if he would mind if I brought in my Zeiss binoculars to explore them. Probably.

"I'm not your friend," the man said in a dead voice. "And no, you can't buy me another. I don't like you." From the way he slurred his speech, I guessed he had been here awhile.

"Hey, no problem," I smiled, my cheek muscles twitching in protest. "Just trying to be neighborly. But let me give you two friendly parting words." I leaned in closer. "Belt. Sander."

For the first time the man smiled back. It wasn't pretty. His teeth were snaggled, tiny, and very white, like broken baby pearls. Not taking his eyes from mine, he addressed the guy on his left, a dark-haired, skinny guy with a profile like the hood ornament on a '37 Plymouth. "Did you hear that, Chet?" Dead-eyes chuckled. "We have us a com-" He belched. "A comedian."

Chet leaned past him and laughed at me, "A-hyuk-hyuk-hyuk", like Jughead.

I grinned back. "Yo, Chet. Betty and Veronica say 'hey'."

Chet quit laughing and looked at Dead-eyes, not getting it. It was clear who was the brains of this duo, and that wasn't saying much.

Dead-eyes squinted at me. "You know, I don't much care for your mouth."

"Neither do I," I said. "But it keeps my nose from flopping down onto my chin."

Dead-eyes frowned at that. "Is that supposed to be funny? Are you some kind of a funny man?"

"Yeah, I am," I admitted. "Funny girl was already taken." Why on earth was I baiting this man? Edgar Allan Poe had called what I was doing the 'imp of the perverse.' As good a term as any.

Dead-eyes sighed and stood, picking up his drink. Plainly feeling I wasn't worth the effort, he began walking away. Chet aped him. These two. "Stay loose, funny man," Dead-eyes said to me over his shoulder as he went. "We'll meet again."

I lifted my glass to his back and sang, "Don't know where, don't know whennn...."

Oh well. I took another pull on my Coke, considering my options. There didn't seem to be all that many. The young bartender sidled up to me about then, tray in his hands. "I'd rethink trying to antagonize Blakey Sinclair if I were you," the kid muttered. "He's one of Gwyllym's goons, and is tougher than any man around here. So he says."

"Could be," I allowed. "But I'm not from around here. And who's Gwyllym?"

"Oh God," the young guy groaned with a shake of his head.

"Whatever you do, just take it outside, huh?"

"Sure," I said. "No sense adding to the blood already on the floor. Is that some of Blakey's doing as well?"

"Come on, mister," the kid pleaded. "I need this job."

I held up a placating hand. "I'll be good. Promise."

Then I heard a movement behind me, and I turned back around and looked. It was Blakey and Chet. They were standing beside a table that held a young, college-age looking kid and his equally young date. Both the guy and his girl didn't appear a day over twenty, and both were studiously ignoring the two men hulking over them.

"Hey, Diane," Blakey said. "Don't you remember what I told you? Didn't I tell you I didn't want you hanging around this guy?" Blakey turned his gaze to the kid. "Leave. Now."

The kid hunched his shoulders and didn't answer. Chet jiggled his fingers and bounced on the balls of his feet, jazzed and obviously getting ready for what was next. The noise level in the bar dropped in half as the patrons watched the drama unfold; the jukebox even picked that time to finish its song.

Blakey reached down and clutched the back of the kid's arm, the thug's knuckles turning white with force. I'll have to give the kid this, he didn't cry out, but merely stared around the room, seeking help. I wasn't ready to throw in, though, not yet.

Blakey bent down. "Did you hear me, yellow?" he growled. "I said leave. That wasn't a request."

Squeezing back tears, the boy violently shook his head, and as he did Diane shot to her feet. "Leave him alone, Blakey. You're bigger and older than Danny. Please, leave us alone!"

"Not just yet," Blakey said. And with that he shot out his right fist and slammed the girl directly under her left eye. She cried out and crashed to the floor. Danny screamed in anguish at it.

And nobody in the bar moved a muscle to help.

Okay. *Now* I was ready.

"Oh, Blakey," I breathed, and the thug looked over at me, dead eyes now burning. "You're mighty tough with children, son," I smiled. "How are you when they're a little bit bigger?"

Chet bobbed his head at that, going "A-huyk-hyuk-hyuk" again. That could grow wearisome over time, I bet. Blakey released the boy with a grin. "Well, let's see."

Out of the corner of my eye I saw the old guy pick up a phone, but that was all the attention I could give him because Blakey suddenly was right there in front of me, his fist rocketing towards my face. Lord-a-mercy, the man was as quick as a king snake. I slipped the punch and danced back, the patrons giving us room. I guess in a small town, entertainment is where you find it.

"Not bad, Blakey," I said, putting my own dukes up. "You've had training." He whistled a left hook at me, missing me by inches. "Just not enough training, I'm afraid." That was a lie. I could tell by the way Blakey was pacing himself he was good, but the liquor was slowing him down, making him miss. Good thing for me.

Blakey growled, "Marine Force Recon, punk," and he grunted with effort as he swung another one at me.

I pedaled back, nearly tripping over somebody's foot, and as I did Blakey's fist grazed my temple. *Clang.* Glancing as it was, there was still enough force behind that punch to make sparks jump behind my eyes. Unless I was very good, or very lucky, old Blakey was going to clean my clock. But I didn't figure to give him that chance as I started to taunt him, still dancing away. I'd make my chance happen.

"Marines, huh?" I said. "Bull. They don't take derelicts." That tore it. With a scream and a curse Blakey brought his right fist flying towards my sternum. I remembered this trick from Sergeant Peter Smithers. That blow done right, the sergeant had told me, can stop a man's heart. Blakey was really not a nice person. I twisted to my right, nearly slipping the punch again, but not quite. It missed my sternum, instead rebounding off my rib cage. Not fatal, but it still hurt like a mother.

I blinked back the pain, dimly hearing Chet in the background. "Take him, Blakey! Kill the sucker!" I'd deal with that boy in a minute. Right now I had a bigger fish. Nastier too.

Because about that time I remembered another trick Peter had taught me, and it was a goodie. If Blakey really had been Marine Force Recon, I hoped he had missed this next lesson.

"Jarheads," I mocked, windmilling my hands. I was watching Blakey's eyes. I would know when the time was right, and I kept up my banter. "Maybe you really were one, dude. But then again, maybe not. Maybe you're really just a lying ape." My hands were still moving hypnotically. "Because a good fighter knows you should never-" Blakey's gaze flickered, and there it was. The moment. My right hand bobbed, and the second it did my left fist launched out and caught Blakey right on the point of his chinny chin chin. An instant later my right followed it, crashing into the man's left ear, John Phillip Sousa gone mad.

Blakey's face went out of round and those dead eyes of his rolled back into his head. With a hiss and a sigh he sank to the floor, gone. I figured he'd regain consciousness somewhere around Arbor Day.

"-assume someone will finish speaking before he hits you," I concluded.

The bar rang with silence, the patrons stunned at Blakey's defeat.

There was a crash. Chet had flung his chair aside, making a dead run for the door. Oddly, he wasn't laughing now.

Picking up my heavy-bottomed Coke glass, I hurled it at him as he ran. The glass struck Chet butt-first at the base of his skull and when it did his arms shot out to either side, like he wanted to hug the world. Then he slammed face-first to the floor and lay unmoving, gone like yesterday's news.

"That's for picking the wrong friends, Chet," I said to him. "And for generally being a jerk."

Danny stared up at me, eyes round as guppies. I smiled at the boy. "On with your date, kids."

Danny ignored me. He pulled Diane, still groggy from her hit, from the floor, and without a backward glance or by-your-leave, they fled.

Oh well.

I settled back down on my barstool and waited for the cops.

Chapter 27

Police cars always smell the same. It doesn't matter if they're city or county, federal or state, big town or small, they all bear the odors of fear, disruption, shame, and lies. Plus every blessed one of them retain, in whatever measure, and regardless of the disinfectant used, the faint reek of vomit.

I know, because I now reposed in the back of Sheriff Elgin Hardesty's Crown Victoria sedan, listening to him read me the riot act. The sheriff's words were barely registering as he rambled on, because I already knew the script. I ought to; I had inflicted it on scofflaws myself in the past. No, what was drawing my attention now was what I was smelling. Was it citrus? Or bleach? Whatever, it was failing to do its job. I still was smelling puke.

"Mr. Fleming," Hardesty chided with a snap of his fingers. "Why do I get the feeling I don't have your full attention?"

"But you do, sir," I answered. That is, James Fleming answered. Fleming was the name on the E.P.A. badge I had showed the sheriff when he had demanded some ID back in the bar; all I had to do now was to remember who I was as long as I was in Hardesty's jurisdiction. "Sheriff, I'm hanging on your every word."

"Hm." Hardesty squinted back at me through the mesh that divided his front seat from the back, where I sat. "So you're sticking with your story, are you? That you were just trying to come to the aid of Danny Demaris and his date, and that Blakey Sinclair threw the first punch?"

"That's right," I said. "If you don't believe me, just ask the people there that saw it."

"I did," Hardesty replied. "Most of them were drunk, though, so their witness doesn't carry a lot of weight with Judge Sanders. Not to mention that most of them work where Blakey and Chet do, GeneSys, and they don't want to get on their bad side."

"So ask Jerry," I said. "Or Pop, or the young guy."

"Mark Fontaine."

"Yeah, him."

"All three were serving customers, so they say, and they missed the whole thing. All Pop can recall is phoning dispatch."

"Well, I know one guy that'll corroborate my story."

Hardesty frowned. "Yeah, who?"

"Blakey Sinclair."

"Him," Hardesty grunted with a laugh. "He's still out. The doc's are saying he may be out for quite a while, too. What did you hit him with, a five-iron?"

"Nope, just little old me. How about Chet? Still out too?"

"No, he's awake," Hardesty said, "and he's blaming you, of course. Not that he carries much weight, either."

"So I guess all that's left are those kids I helped."

"Yeah, and they're your saving grace," Hardesty grunted again. "After I chewed them out for being underage and in a bar, Danny and the girl pretty much told it the way you did. But I don't think they'll be going into Jerry's for awhile."

I smiled at that. "So I'm free to go, right? No one is pressing charges?" Lord, I hoped not. If I was booked, I'd be fingerprinted, and there would go my cover.

"GeneSys might pursue it," Hardesty allowed. "They're the biggest employer around here, and those two are theirs. But I doubt it. Blakey is simply a bullying fool, and Chet is his toady. It was only a matter of time until they were handled. If it hadn't been you, it would have been somebody else." The sheriff smiled thinly. "Maybe even me. Oh well, come on."

He got out of the car and came around and opened my door. I gratefully climbed out and drew in a breath of hot, humid air. Forget the heat, it smelled like freedom to me.

Scowling, Hardesty began to undo my cuffs. "Listen, Fleming-" he started, but I cut him off.

"Is this where I get the 'I run a clean town here, stranger, so watch your step' speech?" I grinned, rubbing my wrists. "Don't worry, Sheriff, I will."

"Oh, but I do worry," he said, his eyebrows climbing up. "I worry like the very dickens. GeneSys has made plenty of money for Willisville, mister E.P.A. man, and has kept a ton of food on a lot of tables. The thought of anything happening to our gravy train is liable to upset certain folks around here. So you just watch your back, Mr. Fleming." Hardesty nodded. "And I'll be watching you."

Chapter 28

The sun was just coming in through the window as I sat up in my bed with a wince. This room at the Willisville Arms was pleasant enough, I suppose, but the way I was hurting, my old bed back home sure would have been more comfortable. Blakey's rib shot from the night before had now blossomed into a half-dozen shades of yellow and blue, and my entire right side throbbed as if I had been worked over with a ball-peen hammer.

Funny. If that punch had landed just three inches more to the left, I might be seeing Linda and Junior again right now, instead of groaning in pain. I shook that off. Someday, yeah.

But not today.

I climbed out of bed and headed towards the bathroom. No, today was the day I entered the lion's den, and I wanted to look my best. After showering and shaving I put on my good dark navy suit. Actually my only dark navy suit. Actually my only suit, period, dark or otherwise. I sighed. Maybe when this was done, and I had returned Francesca to her folks and became the conquering hero, things would start looking up for me. Perhaps I could afford better cat food for Noodles. And get new tires for the Goddess. And buy another suit. The last touch I added was my ersatz badge.

Then I sat back down on the bed and pulled out Sarge's--my--New Testament. What I was about to do seemed stupid, but I was brand-new at this and hoped God would give me a pass. I closed my eyes and opened the Bible, sticking my finger straight down on the page. Then I opened my eyes and looked. My finger was resting right in the middle of Psalm 91. Psalms? I thought Psalms were Old Testament. Weren't they? Keeping my finger there, I flipped it over to the cover. The New Testament, it read, with Psalms and Proverbs. Okay. I didn't want to think that Sarge had given me a dud Bible. I opened it back up, looking to see where my finger had landed, and as I did a chill ran up my back. Because here is what it said, plain as day: "Though a thousand may fall at thy side, and ten thousand at thy right hand, it shall not come near thee."

My throat closed up with emotion. Caramba. God was saying I was going to be all right. Him, personally, to me, Joe. And that was good enough for me. I closed it back up with a smile and left. It was now a little past eight a.m., and last night as I was checking in here I had spied the Good Enough Diner right across the street. Funny name. I hoped the food at least lived up to the billing, because it seemed like a good idea for me to make the time to grab a quick bite before I headed out to GeneSys. Since I was supposed to be an employee of the federal government, I figured it would be bad form if I showed up out there any earlier than nine. Bureaucrats have images to maintain, too.

After strolling into the diner I noticed it was nearly full. Either the food here was better than the name, or the denizens of Willisville had abysmally low standards of dining. I planted myself at a window table, prepared to wait, but I had to give the place points for service; a moment later a craggy-faced, forty-ish waitress materialized at my elbow. With practiced efficiency she whipped a small order pad out of her apron and then, after blowing a strand of unnatural-looking red hair away from her face, she licked the point of her pencil. "What'll you have, hon?"

The woman's voice was low and smoky, the victim of too many cigarettes, and I checked her name badge. Rae Ann. "Hi, Rae Ann." I smiled and put the menu down. In little places like this, if you wanted to know what was good, ask the help. "What's decent today?"

The waitress peered at my own badge and grinned back at me. "Howdy yourself, James." Then recognition seemed to dawn. "James Fleming. The E.P.A., right? I've heard of you." She went on, still grinning, "Man, you sure woke 'em up at Jerry's last night."

I shook my head. "I didn't mean to. All I wanted was a drink and some pleasant conversation, and things kind of got out of hand."

Rae Ann laughed throatily at that. "I'll say! You nailed Blakey and Chet both, nailed 'em but good. It was quite a treat to see, so they tell me. But it's too bad you didn't go for the hat trick, and punch Jerry out while you were at it."

"You don't like him?"

She laughed again, cracking her chewing gum. "Sure, what's not to like? Jerry's rude, he's gross, he stinks, and he's hit on every woman fifty and under in this town."

I smiled. "Rae Ann included?"

"Yeah," she chuckled. "I qualify. Just barely." The waitress's green eyes twinkled with self-effacing humor.

I believed I was going to like Rae Ann just fine. Not only did she seem like the known-it-and-seen-it-all person I had hoped to find here, but she also appeared to be genuinely nice.

"Anyway, James, back to breakfast," Rae Ann said, her tone brisk and her pencil poised. "You like meat? Are you one of them, whattyacallit, car-nee-vores?"

"Sure."

"Then whatever you do, if you value your life don't order the bacon. I gave it the sniff test it when I first came in today, and it smells like your mother's old gym socks." I laughed, and Rae Ann went on, "I'm serious! I think Lou is trying to get rid of it, and he's got a bunch. I believe the new meat salesman that the distributor hired last week knew an easy mark when he saw one, and the guy unloaded some of his old stuff."

Good thing Rae Ann had told me, I thought with a shudder. That would have been a heck of thing to bring the case down at this stage, food poisoning. "How's the sausage?"

"That's okay. Lou bought that at the market just yesterday afternoon. It's fresh-made, right outside of town." Rae Ann snapped her gum again, grinning. "Pink and spicy. Like me."

"And the eggs? Any good?"

She rocked her hand. "How brave are you, James?"

I chuckled. "Not very." I rested my chin in my hand. "Tell you what, Rae Ann, how's about sausage and toast, gravy on top?"

She grinned again. "Good choice, hon. Coming right up."

*****

I wiped my mouth with my napkin; the breakfast had been good and filling. There's something to be said for the simple pleasures of eating meat and bread, and I tried to shut out the saying "the doomed man ate a last hearty meal" from my mind. Instead I thought about that Bible verse, what God had told me. And I also thought about Felicity. Hang tough, child. Help is on the way.

Rae Ann showed up with the coffeepot and pointed to my cup. "Freshen that up for you, hon?"

I slurped down the last of it and shook my head. "No thanks. Everything was great, though. Tell Lou." I began to reach for my wallet but Rae Ann placed her work-roughened hand on top of mine.

"It's on the house, James. My treat." She smiled, shyly it seemed. "For what you did to Blakey and Chet. At least they won't be bothering the Willisville womenfolk for awhile."

So that was it. I guess Jerry wasn't the only pig in town. "Makes me wish now I'd hit them harder," I smiled, and Rae Ann laughed.

"Ahh, you did good," she said, and patted my hand.

Still smiling, I got up to leave, and was heading for the door when Rae Ann called out to me. "You come back and see me now, James. Try our pie." She gave me a wistful look. "It's always here."

Chapter 29

"Yes sir. Can I help you this morning?" The security guard, one of the ones I had observed last night, was smiling at me, but I had caught the flicker of interest he had given the Goddess as we had paused at the gate. Sorry, friend, she's mine. Buy your own.

I slipped my thumb under my badge, lifting it off my lapel an inch. "Fleming, E.P.A."

"Yes sir." He checked his clipboard, still smiling. "I don't see your name here, Mr. Fleming. Do you have an appointment?"

I shook my head. "Nope. I'm the new boy in town. Courtesy call."

"I see." The guard flashed another smile at me, as fake as the first. "Let me make a call."

Drumming my fingers on the wheel, I watched him go back into the shack and mutter something to the other guard, who was reading a porn magazine. They both laughed, then the first guy picked up a phone. I saw him punch in a single digit, wait, then he turned away from me as he spoke. A few seconds later I saw him nod briskly. He hung up the phone and wandered back to the car, still wearing that cheesy grin.

"Yes sir, Mr. Fleming," he said. "You're all set. Just drive through and pull into any slot in the visitor's area."

I put the Goddess into drive, but before I let off the brake I looked at him. "You mind telling me what's so funny?"

"Not at all, sir," the guard grinned again. "We've heard all about you, Mr. Fleming. What you did to Blakey and Chet. Mr. Gwyllym's real anxious to make your acquaintance."

"I see."

The guard pointed. "Anywhere in that lot is fine."

I pulled through the gate and headed the Goddess into the visitor's area. After parking her, I put the keys in my pocket and walked towards what I assumed was the entrance. I mean, what else could it be? Swelling out from the dome's front section was a tunneled archway, perhaps thirty feet long by ten wide, and made of the same shiny material as the rest of the structure. Big as that arch was, it was still dwarfed by the dome itself.

Flanking the walkway towards the doors, and running to either side of the dome as far as I could see, were close-trimmed bushes, flowers, and dark green grass. Those horticultural touches didn't help much; the dome still looked like the mother ship from *Independence Day* parked in rural Indiana.

I reached the opening and pulled on the handle of one of the two large glass doors at this end of the tunnel, which I now saw slanted down. With a click and a hiss the door opened, cold air blowing out. A disembodied voice said, "Welcome to GeneSys."

Welcome to hell is more like it, I thought. Abandon hope, all ye that enter here.

I began walking down the thirty feet towards a matching set of doors at the far end of the tunnel, my footsteps absolutely silent on the black carpet underneath. As I reached the halfway point I heard another hiss and click. I stopped and turned around. The first set of doors were now securely closed. Oh poopie.

We have the subject trapped now, Doctor! Good, good, gas him!

I shook that off. Let's not go there. With more courage than I felt I strolled up to the second set of doors, and when I pulled them open I heard the same click and hiss.

Airlock, I thought. Maybe this really was the mother ship.

I went on through and found myself in a lobby. But what a lobby. The room was huge and well-lit, maybe fifty feet by fifty, all done up in chrome and black leather. Gracing the room's center was a large, circular metallic desk, full of buttons, TV monitors and enough phonelines to reach Mars. Seated at that desk was another beefy security guard, and he smiled at me as I walked up to him. My, what a happy bunch worked here. "Yessir, Mr. Fleming?"

"My fame precedes me," I said.

"I've alerted Mr. Gwyllym, sir. He'll be right out." The guard pointed at a bank of uncomfortable-looking chairs. "Have a seat."

"No thanks," I said. "I'll stand, if you don't mind. Those chairs have 'back-strain' written all over them."

The guard smiled thinly and returned to his viewing. While he did that I gave the room a closer look. Besides the huge desk and those chairs, the room also boasted plenty of real plants. First the ones at Castle Industries, and now here; maybe it was time I joined the crowd and bought some of those myself.

My reverie was ended when I heard a weird, wheezing voice behind me. "Mr. Fleming?"

I turned and came face to face with a human scarecrow. I am not kidding. This fellow appeared to be in his early thirties, standing well over six feet tall, and was as skinny as a broom handle. He was also saddled with sallow skin, a sunken face, and limp, blond hair. But the man looked at me humorously, his blue eyes intelligent, and I felt as if he was taking my measure.

"That's me," I smiled, and the scarecrow returned it.

"I'm Charles Gwyllym, head of security. Nice to meet you."

We shook, and as we did I noticed his hands were bony but strong... unusually so. I also hadn't missed the characteristic knots and callouses across the man's knuckles, common to that of a martial arts student.

We released hands and I looked around. "Some place you have here, Mr. Gwyllym. Who's the head dog?"

The scarecrow smiled again. "That would be my father. He asked me to escort you on back. This way."

We were going to be in for a long hike, I thought, but no. We turned a corner and there sat a row of golf carts. The man picked one out, climbed in, and motioned for me to join him. Once I was in he flipped the switch, stepped on the pedal, and we were off.

We glided down a long, and I mean long, corridor, riding noiselessly on that same black carpet. Maybe they had gotten a deal on it somewhere, I mused, so much off in exchange for doing the whole complex, and the carpet salesman had retired on the commission he had made. We were passing relatively few doors, and they were all closed. For some reason that made me uneasy.

After a few moments of silence my guide spoke up, glancing at me as he drove. "My father is really looking forward to meeting you, Mr. Fleming."

"Meeting me as a representative of the E.P.A., Mr. Gwyllym?" I asked him. "Or as the guy that put two of his men in the hospital?"

The man chuckled and wheezed, glancing again at me. "Both, actually. Many men have tried, and failed, to do what you did with those two. I would imagine you would make a formidable adversary."

"Maybe," I said. "And maybe I was just lucky."

The man smiled at that, more than it deserved, as if he was enjoying a private joke. "Oh, I don't know. We make our own luck, don't you think?" He returned his gaze forward. "Here we are."

We had stopped at the last door at the end of the corridor, and as we got out I gave the door a quick double-take. It carried the grain and color of wood, but I would bet Noodles' last cat treat it too was made of metal, like everything else around here.

"I'll be leaving you now, Mr. Fleming," the scarecrow wheezed again, his voice brisk as we climbed out of the cart. He pointed at a recessed button next to the door. "Just press that and wait. You'll be buzzed in. When you and my father are done chatting, feel free to use the cart to take you back up front."

We shook again, and the man began walking a few steps back down the way we had come, whistling tunelessly. He finally disappeared down a branching corridor. Huh. He was...different.

I turned and mashed my thumb on the button, doing as I was told. There was a pause, then the door slid silently back. I heard a voice call my name. "Mr. Fleming? Come in please."

I did, and found myself in the lair of Ernst Stavro Blofeld. Well, not really, but the headquarters of James Bond's old villain would have had a hard time competing with the room I was presently standing in. Metal again, and plenty of it; not surprisingly, the dome's motif had carried through into here. More chrome, more black leather, more black carpeting, more steel walls; it was if Hal the computer from *2001* had taken up interior decorating.

I had an idea. I bet I knew what would help warm this place up, and make it more inviting: circus posters. Big ones.

"Mr. Fleming?" My attention was drawn from the stark decor to the man standing behind his desk, hand outstretched. "Hello," he smiled. "I'm Alexander Gwyllym."

So this was the guy. Our villain. Gwyllym the father, strangely, bore little resemblance to Gwyllym the son. The man before me was about my height, in his late sixties or thereabouts, and of an average build. But like Blofeld, Gwyllym too was the proud possessor of an erect posture, a bald head, and an expensive suit. All the man lacked was a white Persian cat to carry around.

But Gywllym's best feature was his chin: I had never seen the beat of it. It was a massive chin, smooth and pink, a veritable promontory of a chin, a chin big enough for its own zip code. And dead-center, right in the middle, was the thing's crowning glory: a dimple deep enough to hide a raisin. Mercy, what an object. A chin like that would make Kirk Douglas hang his head in defeat.

Trying not to stare at it, I walked over the ten or so steps to him and gripped Gwyllym's hand. "Sorry. James Fleming, E.P.A."

Gwyllym released my hand with a tight grin. "I know. And don't worry about your reaction, Mr. Fleming. Our little facility has that effect on people." That's not what I was reacting to.

"It sure beats anything I ever saw," I admitted. Yes it did.

Gwyllym motioned to a chair opposite his side of the desk.

"Please, have a seat, won't you?" I did, thankful that the chair he was directing to me to appeared normal, just regular office furniture. A second later Gywllym did the same in his.

He tented his fingers as he regarded me with a condescending smile. "So you're the new field inspector for the E.P.A."

"That's right," I smiled back. "And unfortunately I left quite a bit of my materials back in Washington, so maybe you won't mind me asking." I spread my hands. "What in the world IS this place?"

Gwyllym tilted his head back and laughed at the ceiling, but it sounded artificial, as if he didn't get much practice at it. Then he finished and looked back down at me. "Believe it or not, Mr. Fleming, this is a genetics lab. Albeit a huge one."

I knew it.

"Our name here is simply a play on words," Gwyllym continued, the baron addressing a peon. "GeneSys is shorthand for Genetic Systems." He smiled again. "I came up with that myself."

"Catchy," I said. "But what do you do here?"

"I'll show you. Look here." Gwyllym turned in his chair and directed my attention to two framed photos on the wall behind him; I hadn't even noticed them when I came in. He pointed at the one on the left. "That's a normal tomato plant, the way they've appeared for thousands of years. No surprises. And this-" he pointed at the other one "-is what that same species of tomato plant looks like after we've tinkered with it."

In the left photo a man's thumb--Gwyllym's?--was next to a tomato hanging from the vine, and the fruit appeared normal-sized, about the span of a tennis ball. But in the right photo the same thumb posed beside a genetically-enhanced tomato. And that baby was huge, nearly the size of a pumpkin.

I leaned forward in my chair, my mouth agape. "That's real?"

Gwyllym chuckled. "As real as you, Mr. Fleming. Or me." His voice then grew deep. "As real as famine, or deprivation, or want. The things that have plagued humanity for centuries. But not for much longer. Mr. Fleming, we here at GeneSys intend to end all that, and help to remake the earth into a paradise."

I leaned back and gave Gwyllym a disbelieving grin. Brother. Cue the soprano.

Gwyllym's little speech had sounded so warm and sincere; he must have worked hours on it. But I knew there was more going on here than growing county-fair prize tomatoes. "That's a lofty goal, sir. I wish you the best. I only have one question."

"Yes?"

I grinned, pointing at the picture. "How does it taste?"

Gwyllym frowned, tenting his fingers again. "Taste," he said, shaking his head. Good, I must have hit a nerve. "We're still working on that, night and day. The thing is, Mr. Fleming, we can make vegetables grow to practically any size. There's no real trick to making them big, a simple DNA splice. The only problem we're having is when they reach that mass, they turn poisonous."

Poisonous? I laughed out loud at that, not caring much how Gwyllym felt about it. "Yeah, I can see how that would tend to not go over well with the public. Zow-wee. Remind me never to eat a B.L.T. at your house." I laughed again, harder, but Gwyllym didn't join in. Obviously the man failed to see the humor in having a tomato as big as your head that would kill you if you tried to eat it.

His smile was frosty. "It's really not a joking matter, Mr. Fleming. If we can solve that problem we'll have gone a long way in healing a persistent world malady."

"I'm sorry," I said, hoping he would buy it. Because I wasn't sorry at all.

"Are you working on anything else?"

"Yes," Gwyllym replied. "We've had quite good success with a mold-resistant strain of corn, and within the year you'll see lettuce being sold that can be stored down to a temperature of thirty-four degrees Fahrenheit for up to ten weeks."

Well, wasn't that fine and noble, but what Gwyllym was describing could be accomplished in a facility a third this size. No, there was more here, and I knew it. He was hiding the truth.

But I hid my thoughts as well. "That's terrific, Mr. Gwyllym. Really." I stood. "Well, I need to get started here. Where would you recommend I begin?"

Gwyllym stood as well. "Anywhere you like. Feel free to use one of the carts, if you wish. The faculty is yours. To a point."

That stopped me. "Sir?"

Gwyllym smiled again, as chilling as a winter wind. "Every so often you'll see a door marked with a red diamond, Mr. Fleming. Those areas are off-limits."

I smiled back, with about as much heat. "I'm sorry, sir, but no areas are 'off-limits' to the E.P.A."

"These are," Gwyllym said firmly, then he softened his tone. "Mr. Fleming, please understand. I do not wish to appear stubborn, but some of what we are working on here has cost literally millions of dollars in research monies, with no net results as of yet. Those results may still be years away. And I cannot, and will not, compromise our secrecy, and possibly lose all of our work to a competitor." He went on, trying to sound conciliatory, "Of course, if you wish to secure approval from your department head in Washington, seeking the right to examine these areas, I will bow to that decree. But failing that, I must insist on the rules as they stand."

Well, that kind of tore it. Who was I going to call to secure that approval, Noodles? And the only department head I had was God Himself. So I figured that if He really wanted me to look at those areas behind the red diamonds, He would have to figure out how.

I smiled at Gwyllym. "Certainly, sir. This is your facility, after all. And if I later find I need to see those restricted areas, well, we'll address that as it comes. Okay?"

"Fair enough, Mr. Fleming," Gwyllym smiled in return, and he swept out a hand of dismissal. "Enjoy your tour."

"Thanks." A moment later I found myself back in the hall. With a whisper Gwyllym's door closed behind me.

Chapter 30

I don't play golf. But if I ever take up the sport--forbid it, Lord--I won't use a cart. I mean, why is it that I can run through the Goddess's gearbox without a hiccup, but I could NOT figure how to get that stupid cart out of reverse? I probably would have been still sitting there had a guard not approached me.

"Yes sir," he smiled (another smiler). "Having a problem?"

"You might say that," I scowled. "I've done everything but sing to it. What am I doing wrong?"

"It's not you," the man laughed. "That cart was built wrong. Boneless gave you good old number five. It's his idea of a joke."

"Boneless?" I frowned. "Who or what is Boneless?"

The guard laughed again. "Boneless is Boneless Chuck." I must have looked really lost, because he went on, "Chuck. You know, Charles. Gwyllym. The security chief. That guy that brought you here."

"Him." Now I started to laugh myself. "That's what you call him? Boneless Chuck?" I laughed harder.

"Sure," the guard grinned. "I mean, you saw the guy. Is he strange-looking or what?"

"He is that," I admitted with my own grin. "But why Boneless? He looked like he had plenty of bones to me."

I was hoping my questioning the guard this way would work, because I was trying to draw him out. The man appeared to be a talker, and seemed to be the first person I had met here--outside of Rae Ann the waitress--that could maybe give me some information I could actually use. So I let him ramble on.

"One of the guys that used to work here nicknamed him," the guard explained. "The guy was a fan of old Fred Astaire movies, and he said that when Astaire danced he moved like he didn't have any bones." The guard's smile faded as he lowered his voice. "See, our boy Boneless is kind of like Astaire, only he doesn't dance. With him it's martial arts."

Hah. Can I spot 'em or what?

"Boneless knows them all, and then some," the man continued. "Once I saw him tangle with another guard that had made fun of Boneless's voice. It was just a little joke; Tod had called Boneless the Breezy Wheezer. Like I said, it was nothing. But you don't do that, because Boneless really likes the sound of his own voice.

Anyway, one second Boneless is just standing there, calm, and the next he ties into the poor guy like a buzzsaw. I mean it. Every part of Boneless was flying. None of us ever saw anything like it. It was like...well, like the man didn't have any bones. Liquid. Like he wasn't human." The guard shook his head. "Tod never had a chance. He died the next day."

"Died?" I exclaimed. "So what happened then?"

The guard's laugh now held no humor. "You mean with our boy Chuck? Nothing. Not a thing. GeneSys can't do anything wrong in this town. Boneless's dad just spread a little green around, including some to Tod's wife, and it was all nice again."

I shook my head at that. "That doesn't sound like Sheriff Hardesty to me. Him just letting that go. I mean, I just met the man once, but he struck me as a pretty straight-shooter."

"Oh, he is," the guard admitted. "But a fight's a fight, and Tod did start it with his crack. It just finished different than he would have liked."

"Well. You know all that's interesting, but-"

"But you're still stuck with a cranky cart, and you need to get on with your business." The guard smiled again and motioned for me to get off. "Here, switch with me. You take mine and I'll take number five. I don't mind. She's crotchety, but you just have to show her who's boss."

Getting off my cart I thanked the guard, and then climbed in his. But before I pulled away I turned back to my gabby friend and smiled. "Wait a minute. I certainly appreciate your information, but you don't know me at all. How do you know I won't go running to your boss and tell him what name you call him?"

"Because he knows already," the guard smiled back. "And we think he likes it. But we never call him that to his face, of course."

"Of course," I agreed. "So then if that's the case, I would guess Boneless must really like the guy who nicknamed him."

"You mean Tony Mordetti."

"If you say so."

"That's the guy," the guard replied, and his smiled faded again. "But I don't know what Boneless thinks about him. The day after Tony named him, he disappeared." With that, the guard hopped in number five and drove away.

A minute later I was in his cart, gliding the other way back down the long hall. I needed a map, and since Gwyllym must have thought I could find my way around this little funhouse of his by osmosis, I figured the best place to get that map was at the desk where I had come in.

I followed the sweeping curve of the hall, and in two more minutes I was back at the dome's entrance.

"Yes sir, Mr. Fleming." That same guard who had greeted me earlier was still at his post, and still smiling like a man trying to sell timeshares in Iran. "Finished already?"

"Nope," I said. "I haven't even started. I need a map."

"Sure," the guard said, reaching down for something. "We keep these for visitors." His hand came out bearing a small, flat, charcoal-gray rectangular object, maybe eight inches by five, and he handed it to me.

"What is it?" I asked as I took it.

"What you asked for, Mr. Fleming," he smiled again. "A map."

"Really." I examined it. What I saw was mainly an LCD screen, a few buttons, a small touchpad mouse, and enough plastic to hold it all together. "If I didn't know better, I'd say this thing looks like a handheld computer. Like a Palm Pilot."

"It's similar," the guard agreed. "You'll see our workers with them, because they also contain an intranet hookup."

"Interesting," I said. "But don't you have just a simple map you can give me?"

The guard grinned at that. "Mr. Fleming, take a slow look around. What don't you see here?"

I frowned. "Is that a joke?"

"Not at all, sir," the guard said. "Give up? Okay, I'll tell you. What you don't see is paper. Not a scrap."

I gazed around. By golly, he was right. There weren't even any magazines next to the chairs.

"GeneSys is the most advanced facility of its kind in the world, Mr. Fleming," the guard explained. "And it should be. It cost enough. It was funded mainly by private endowments."

"Really?" Now that was interesting. "Like who, for instance?"

"Many diverse ones," the guard answered. "Have you heard of the Pew Charitable Trusts, Archer-Daniels-Midland, and the Gnostic Peace Center?"

"The first two, yes. Not the last one." I gazed around again. "So they're the ones that paid for this place?"

The guard smiled. Again. "Did I say that? No, GeneSys was funded by organizations like them. As well as some famous, well-heeled, socially-concerned Hollywood types, whose names you would know if I told you." He grinned. "Which I won't."

"I see," I said. "Lots of bucks, then."

"Yeah, lots and lots." The man was still smiling. "Everything here costs money, Mr. Fleming, because everything here is absolutely state of the art. And all geared towards one purpose: that of ending famine in our lifetime. True, it's costly. But we feel the payoff is worth every cent. Don't you think so, sir?"

"Oh my, yes," I said. "Go on. This is fascinating."

"GeneSys is completely self-sufficient," the guard continued. "As you may have noticed when you entered, most of the facility is located underground, because it was built using earth-berm construction. That's why we're still so cool in August. We have our own water from an aquifer, and the dome helps to generate our own heat. We also compost everything here, and I mean everything, and we utilize the heat generated by that composting to generate steam, which in turn powers our electric turbines. Even the toilets here are the latest incinerating type."

"Yow," I grinned. "That would give a whole new meaning to the term hot-seat."

The guard smiled thinly at that and motioned above us with his hand. "As I mentioned, the dome itself is active/passive solar, and is composed of hundreds of thousands of photovoltaic cells, again for electricity. All of this has been done for one simple purpose: to make sure we don't waste a thing. And Mr. Fleming, that includes not having anything made of paper. It again all comes back to waste. Mr. Gwyllym just can't stand the thought of it."

"I see," I said. "You know, that was very well done." Now it was my turn to smile. "What's your name, anyway?"

"Albert Trask, sir."

"Well, Albert-Trask-sir, you are a pure-dee treasure of information. Really. It's a wonder you don't lead tours here."

"I do, Mr. Fleming," Trask smiled. "I split my duties between 248 that and greeting people."

"But I would imagine your duties would also include keeping out the riffraff," I pointed out. "By whatever means necessary, correct?" I pointed at his sidearm. "Including deadly force?"

"Sure," Trask answered, and now his smile didn't seem so sunny. A bit brutal, as a matter of fact. "But Mr. Gwyllym's been real good to me. I'd do a job like that for free."

"Well." I cleared my throat. "Thanks for the information, and the map. I'm sure it's not as hard to figure out as it looks."

"Mr. Fleming," Trask smiled again, "an eight-year-old boy could make it work."

"Good," I said. Then I raised my eyebrows in hope. "You wouldn't happen to have one laying around, would you?"

Chapter 31

I must be smarter than I think, because I had that map going inside of a minute and a half. Or it could be that the thing was idiot-proof. Anyway, what I was seeing now was a shot from above, as if I was suspended high up in the dome's support girders. I honestly couldn't tell if what I was viewing was a real photo or computer-generated: the graphics were that good.

Here it is. Picture an oval racetrack, a thousand feet long by five hundred wide, with a huge field taking up the center. In that field, and filling it completely, were plants of all shapes, sizes and kinds, sitting up on racks of varying heights and being fed with hoses and watered by pipes hanging just above them.

That was the dome in a nutshell.

The racetrack, of course, was the hall running around the inside of the dome's perimeter. According to the map the offices and rooms that were coming off that hall were all angled in towards the center. I touched the mouse and titles appeared over the rooms: Supply, Data Entry, Information Systems, Clean Room, and so on. I even saw the universal symbols of man and woman, showing where the restrooms were; you know, the ones with the flaming toilets. I needed to remember to give those babies a wide berth. Then I spotted the door that read Security. Ah, the lair of one Boneless Chuck, he of the wheezy voice. That man and I were going to dance before this was over. I knew that as sure as I knew my name.

I also found his daddy's door. That door read simply A. Gwyllym, Director. Not to mention A. Kidnapper of children.

And then I saw the doors with the red diamonds.

There were three of those, at the dome's far end. Only three? So why had Gwyllym gotten so exercised about letting me see what was behind them?

I saw why. I had missed it at first glance. If this map was right, and I had to assume it was, those weren't office doors at all. They were elevator entrances.

But elevators to where?

I wasn't sure of the answer to that, but one thing I did know for lead-pipe certain: those elevators would lead me to Francesca Taylor. I knew it. Somewhere beneath my feet--how far down I couldn't even hazard a guess--she was waiting. For me.

But that rescue would need to wait just a little bit longer. I needed more information before I made my move, and so far all I had gotten was the tourist line. There simply had to be a person here with what I needed; I was new at this Christian stuff, but I could not imagine God had let me get this far only to hit a wall.

I bowed my head, as if fixing my shoe--I didn't want to tip off Trask--and prayed a short, silent prayer: God, what now? And with that prayer, the answer came.

I climbed back on the cart, map in hand, and with a wave to Trask I set off. I knew where to go now. I needed data. Where better to get it than Data Entry? Following the map, I turned left this time and headed down the opposite leg of the racetrack, towards that area. My pulse raced. I was on the hunt.

I started passing people now. The majority looked like townies, men and women dressed in jeans or business casual, and not a few of them were giving me dirty looks as I went by. I guess they figured I was here to cause trouble. If they only knew.

The remaining workers were men, older, and clad in white labcoats. Techies, I thought, and they didn't have a local look. What look these men did have I couldn't quite pin down, but the difference was there all the same.

These are the ones in the know, I mused, the inner circle. The townies were just earning a paycheck; these in the labcoats were true believers. And the gazes those men were giving me were different, too. Cool. Calculating. Dispassionate. Superior.

And suddenly something inside rose up with a roar. I waved at those old guys as I drove. You gents give me all the cold looks you want, I thought. Because you see this place? God's gonna tear it down. Yes He is. He's gonna tear it down, and plow it under, and sow the ground with salt. And you boys can die with it if you want.

Caramba, what WAS this I was feeling? I knew it wasn't my old nemesis; that was gone forever. No, this was different. This sensation was quite beyond indignation, or fury, or even wrath.

It was good old righteous rage. God was angry at this place. Exceedingly so.

I saw GeneSys now as He did. An abomination, a cancer, a blight on humanity. Because what these men were doing here was nothing less than spitting in God's own face and laughing. In effect they were cocking their thumb and telling Him, take a hike, rube. We can do it better than You.

Whoa, doctor. No wonder He was hot.

I smiled inwardly. New as I was at this, I would not want to be on the receiving end of God's judgment, like these yahoos were fated to be. It almost made me feel sorry for them. Almost.

A minute later I pulled the cart up in front of the door that read Data Entry and got out. The office door was open, so I wandered in without knocking.

The woman behind the desk was fooling with her computer as I walked up. She must have heard me approach, though, because she took her time as she slowly swivelled around in her chair to see who it was that had disturbed her work.

Wow. This lady gave new meaning to the term 'severe.' Rail-thin, the woman was dressed in a gray business suit that had been fastened clear up to her neck. She wore no makeup that I could detect, but then again maybe she had on the new invisible kind I'd heard tell of. Her jet black hair was plastered with gel, then swept straight back down and clasped. She'd pulled and twisted that hair so tightly into a knot at the base of her skull it was a miracle her brain hadn't imploded. The nameplate on her extremely neat desk read Alicia Bancroft. "Hi," I said. "James Fleming."

"Mr. Fleming." Bancroft folded her hands, her expression neutral. "We rather wondered if you would be stopping by here."

"Oh? Why's that?"

"You desire information about us here at GeneSys, correct?" This lady's smile wasn't nearly as good as I'd been getting from the security guards. "I would suppose that Data Entry would be the place I would start. Were I you."

"That's amazing." I spread my hands. "Alicia, what can I say? You're a wonder."

She frowned at that. "You are to address me as Ms. Bancroft, or ma'am. You don't know me well enough to call me anything else."

Brother. One of those. "My apologies, Ms. Bancroft. By the way, who told you I'd be stopping here?"

Bancroft motioned to the Palm Pilot-like thing I had hung on my belt.

"We've already been alerted by Mr. Gwyllym that you were in the facility, sir. We were also told to assist you in any way we can, provided it doesn't compromise our work."

That was a variation on the same line Gwyllym had given me. But I didn't know yet if dear Alicia was one of the inner circle or just a drone.

So I pressed on, "The guy up at the front desk, Albert Trask, has already filled me in on the genesis of, er, GeneSys, Ms. Bancroft. But I was wondering if there are any gaps you might be able to fill in."

Bancroft smiled thinly. "Albert is quite well-versed in our history here, Mr. Fleming, and I'm sure Mr. Gwyllym has told you about our purpose. By my estimation, you possess all the information you require. You have no 'gaps.' "

"But-"

"I'm sorry, Mr. Fleming," Bancroft broke in. "As I said, you know as much as I'm authorized to tell you. I have nothing more to add. Any further conversation would be counter-productive."

"Nothing more to add, Ms. Bancroft?" I gave her a look. "At all?"

The woman narrowed her eyes. "Sir. Appearances to the contrary, we at Data Entry are not the nerve center of GeneSys."

"No? Where would I find it, then?"

The look she gave me was aloof. "I suppose that Mr. Gwyllym himself would be our nerve center. Mr. Gwyllym is not only the founder, he is the driving force of GeneSys. And as I have stated, this office is only for data entry."

"Okay," I smiled. "Fair enough. Then how about letting me see some of that?"

That seemed to throw her. "Sir?"

"Open your heart wide, Ms. Bancroft, to this poor government hack." Maybe humor would thaw this biddy. "Make my life complete. Let me see some of your data."

"Some of-" Bancroft snorted. "Oh my... You-"

Then she started to laugh. And laugh. The woman began to gasp and chortle and snort, like Lily Tomlin doing her old "one ringy-dingy" routine on *Laugh-In*. I had gotten Bancroft tickled, all right, but it was not a pretty sound. She was laughing at me, not with me. I hate that. Her fit took some time. I just waited her out.

Finally she was done. Bancroft's eyes had teared and her face was flushed crimson by her exertion. "Is there anything else I can...help you with, Mr. Fleming?" She wiped her eyes, threatening to start it all again. Jeez, it wasn't that funny.

I blew out a breath. "No, Ms. Bancroft, thank you. You've been a peach."

Bancroft put her hankie back in her purse and gave me another cold look, her smile now gone. "Then I'll say good day to you, Mr. Fleming. I'll inform Mr. Gwyllym we were not able to be of service to you." With that she swivelled around in her chair and again started monkeying with her computer.

Well. Now what should I do? I couldn't figure it: had I or had I not been given what I thought was a clear leading that I was going to find somebody here at Data Entry that could, and would, help me? It was a cinch that person was not Alicia Bancroft.

I was still musing on this as I left her office and found myself back in the hall. I was shaking my head in confusion and consternation when I felt a tap on my shoulder. I turned.

And there before me stood a Waffen SS storm trooper.

I nearly stepped back at the sight. What in the world-? Then I realized from the shoulder patch the man was wearing he was simply another security guard.

But of what type?

I saw now that the similarities between this man's uniform and that of a Nazi's were only fleeting, save for a couple of things. His was black, true, in contrast to the gray of the other guards' clothes, but where they wore simple dark work shoes, this guard sported black combat boots. Well, Sieg Heil. And that wasn't the only difference. The other troops I had seen had all carried thirty-eight revolvers as their sidearms, much like mine. From the butt-end of his piece sticking out of his holster, I could tell this fellow had strapped on some type of a semi-automatic. Hm. Curiouser and curiouser.

Especially considering the greeting he gave me.

"Mr. Fleming?" The man was grinning. I nodded, and he grinned even wider. "Wow. This *is* a pleasure, sir!" It was? Why? Not that I was knocking him; his was the first genuine smile I had seen since I had arrived here. "Yessir," the guard continued, "it's a real pleasure. I really appreciate all the work the E.P.A. does. I'd like to shake your hand." Before I could reply, the man grabbed my hand and pumped it like a Chicago ward-heeler. He was still grinning tightly at me as we released our grips.

It was then I felt something slipped into my hand.

The guard's eyes met mine, and what I saw there was completely unexpected.

Desperation.

I palmed whatever it was he had given me and slipped it into my pocket. Without another word, the guard turned and walked away. My thoughts were spinning. I started to climb back onto my cart when I happened to glance back into Bancroft's open doorway. The woman was looking at the departing guard with the oddest expression, then she turned her gaze back towards me.

Bancroft raised one eyebrow and twisted her lips into another bloodless smile.

Chapter 32

As everybody knows, in mid-August the sun doesn't really set until after nine p.m. And one would think that at sunset the temperature would drop. One would be wrong. Not in this part of the country, and not at this time of the year. So here I sat in the Goddess, slowly baking in the humidity and listening to the insects as I waited for my unknown benefactor to show.

The party line at the complex had been wrong, on at least one count: there *was* paper at GeneSys, whether Albert Trask knew it or not. Once again I pulled the gum wrapper that the black-uniformed guard had slipped me from my pocket. The words on it still read the same: Sunset--Big Oak West. I was here. So where was he?

I had puttered around GeneSys for the rest of the day, doing E.P.A.-like things, peering here and there and going "Ah. I see." at the appropriate times, but had uncovered not one blessed new thing. And the receptions I had gotten from the other offices weren't as bad as dear Alicia had given me, but still I knew I wouldn't be winning any popularity contests there in the foreseeable future.

And try as I might, I still had not figured out a way to get into one of those elevators with the red diamond on the door.

So all that was left at the end of the day was to hop in the Goddess, go west out of the drive, start looking for a big oak tree, and hope for the best. I began passing sycamores, pines, and maples a-plenty, but didn't find an oak of any size until I had driven a mile further down the road. It was then I spotted one on the left, and it was a honey; towering at least a hundred and fifty feet in the air, the tree was absolutely crammed full of acorns, and it dwarfed anything else around it. This had to be it. I pulled the Goddess off the road, drove under the tree's leafy canopy, shut her off, and waited.

That had been nearly three hours ago. I guess in hindsight I should have gone back into town before coming out here and grabbed some supper, or at least some bottled water to bring back with me, but I didn't want to chance missing the man. So here I sat, oily sweat running down my face, and wishing for a breeze. I checked my watch again. Nearly nine-thirty now, and the sun was just about gone down behind that far tree line. So where-

I heard the car before I saw it. Whoever it was needed a muffler job, badly. A second later a rusted-out Plymouth Fury, nearly the same vintage as the Goddess, pulled up beside me, and the guard I had met earlier shut it off and got out.

I did the same and we walked up to each other.

Dressed now in civvies, the man held out his hand. "Glad to see you made it, Mr. Fleming," the guard said as we shook. "I didn't know if my note was too vague. About the big oak, I mean."

"No, it was fine," I replied. "Because here I am."

"Yeah." He swallowed. "No trouble, huh?"

"Nope." I waited.

"Yeah." The man nervously rubbed his face. "Okay. I guess I ought to tell you my name."

"That would be nice."

"Okay." He swallowed again. "It's Thornhill. Roger Thornhill. Like in *North by Northwest?"*

"What?"

"*North by Northwest.* The Hitchcock movie. I have the same name as that guy in that movie. Roger Thornhill."

"Son of a gun."

Roger wiggled his fingers, still jittery. "But I guess that's not really important. I guess you'd like to know why I asked to meet here."

"I guess your guess would be right."

"It's just that I can't take it anymore." The man gave me a haunted look. "You know?"

I crossed my arms. "Roger, maybe you'd better start from the beginning."

"All right." Roger rubbed his face again. This was one scared man. "It's like this. I've been working at GeneSys for the last two years. The first eighteen months I was a regular guard, assigned upstairs on Level One, but for the last six I've been a trooper below, watching over the dorm."

"Roger." My voice was steady. "I'm lost already. Just take your time and tell me what's going on."

"Keep your shirt on. This isn't easy. I'm getting to it." He took a deep breath. "Okay. Mr. Gwyllym heads up GeneSys, and his son Charles runs Security. But you know all that, right?" I nodded, and Roger went on, "Charles--we call him Boneless Chuck--hired me two years ago as a guard in the dome. What we call Level One. I was assigned to the third quadrant, greenhouse." The man pulled at his shirt collar. "Hot, ain't it? Anyway-"

But I stopped him. "Roger, hold it. I'd like to know what you prompted you to tell me all this. Why me, and why now?"

He gave me a sad, sick smile. "Aw, you'll just laugh."

I shook my head. "Roger, I may laugh at a lot of..." and then I stopped. This conversation was sounding strangely familiar. But I guess it should; it was virtually identical to the one I had had with Mike Taylor just a few days before. So I pulled in a breath and gazed at the guard. "Roger," I said, "why do you think I'll laugh at you?"

Roger's answer was terse, as if he was embarrassed at it. "Because of who it was that told me you could help."

"And who was that?"

Roger shrugged as he mumbled his answer. "God."

I felt a chill run up my back. But it wasn't an unpleasant sensation. On the contrary. It was if I somehow felt a Presence drawing near. Then I heard that Presence whisper something deep inside me: *That's why I had you go to Data Entry, Joe. Not to meet Alicia Bancroft. But to encounter this man.*

Roger looked back up at me and gave me another anxious smile. "Like I said, Mr. Fleming. Pretty stupid, huh."

"No, Roger," I answered. "Pretty smart. And call me Joe."

He frowned. "Huh?"

"My name's Joe Box, Roger, not James Fleming. And I'm not with the E.P.A. I'm a private investigator, and I'm looking for someone. A girl named Francesca Taylor."

Roger's mouth fell open. "I know her! She's one of the ones in the dorm, on Level Six. Been there a just a few days."

"And she's alive?"

He nodded. "Sure, last time I looked."

"Thank God," I sighed. "When was that?"

"Gosh, I dunno. Maybe four hours ago. Right before I clocked out." Then he frowned again. "But if you're not with the E.P.A., then why-"

"Oh, Roger," I broke in with a sigh. "My good pal Roger." I lowered myself to the ground beside the Goddess, and once I was down, I patted the grass next to me. "Make yourself comfortable, my man. We've got some stories to swap."

*****

So swap we did. I gave Roger the Reader's Digest version of why I was here, hitting the high points of the last few days, then he told me his side.

And what a tale it was.

GeneSys had been constructed over two years ago, Roger said, and its coming here had just about pulled Willisville back from the brink of bankruptcy. The story was as sad as it was familiar: a little farm village, miles from the nearest interstate, slowly drying up and dying as its youth fled the town in search of something better. But then Alexander Gwyllym had arrived. Gwyllym dazzled both the mayor and the town fathers with his charm, his money, and his promise of Willisville's rebirth.

How better to say it? They flat ate it up.

Construction on the dome began almost immediately, although a few folks wondered aloud why it was going up where it was, out on the old McAllister place. It was well-known that the land wasn't that great there, and everyone also knew that the farm was honeycombed with limestone caverns not too far underneath, but Gwyllym had merely smiled and wrote old man McAllister the biggest check for his place anyone around here had ever seen.

Another thing that gave some of the townsfolk pause was the fact that Gwyllym had used his own crew on the building of the complex, a firm that no one around here had ever heard of. But Gwyllym had smoothed things over with the local contractors, telling them that once the dome was up, there would be jobs aplenty for all who wanted one. And there were.

Gwyllym's builders worked around the clock, and six months to the day after ground was broken, GeneSys was done. A personnel company had then come to Willisville and set up temporary offices down at the courthouse. They hired for everything, including security, and that's where Roger came into the picture. He, like most of the guards that were hired, had grown up around here, and the pay that Gwyllym was offering made Roger's head swim. Nearly fifty young men had shown up that day, for only twenty positions. Roger was amazed that one of the requirements of being a guard at GeneSys was having a good personality. Roger also knew that let him out, so he wasn't surprised he didn't make the cut. He was just turning to leave when he heard someone call his name.

Roger turned. It was a really pale, skinny guy sitting at the far end of the review table, and he was smiling at Roger. "Wait, Mr. Thornhill," the scarecrow said, his voice strange and wheezy. "Before you go, could I speak with you?"

"I guess," Roger shrugged. The scarecrow pointed and together they walked down to an unoccupied end of the office.

When they got there, the strange man stopped Roger and motioned to some chairs. They both sat down, and the scarecrow had again smiled. "I suppose you're wondering about this," he wheezed. "Let me introduce myself. I'm Charles Gwyllym, head of security. Alexander Gwyllym is my father."

Roger's tone was sullen as he answered, "So?" He was still upset at having been passed over. That money sure would have been sweet.

"So," Charles replied, "I'm the one that makes the final call on my guards, not those people out there. They're good enough for file clerks and coffee girls, but not that. I'd like to make you a proposition, Mr. Thornhill. I'm bringing in some of my own men next week for some rather...delicate...security work, but I'm always in need of more of those." Charles pointed to some papers he was holding. "I see from your questionnaire that you've had some extensive military training, is that correct?"

"Yeah," Roger replied. "I was a hand-to-hand combat instructor at Ranger Training School at Fort Benning for eight years, but when I mustered out I came back to Willisville to open a bait shop." He scowled, "It didn't work out."

Charles smiled. "Here's my proposition, Mr. Thornhill. I need men like yourself who are not only good with firearms and their hands, but who are also especially discreet, owing to the work we are going to be conducting at GeneSys. These guards will be assigned special duties, and will of course receive extra pay. As I said, I have nearly a dozen of those men I'm bringing here next week, but I'm also looking for some locals that can serve a probationary period as a standard guard, with the incentive of possibly moving into one of these elite positions in the future. Are you interested?"

"Interested?" Roger shot to his feet, eyes alight. "You bet I'm interested!"

"Good," Charles smiled. "That's very good. I'll have Personnel fix you up. We'll give you a year or so doing regular duty, then we'll see if you're ready to move up. All right?"

"Yes, sir!" Roger said, and they shook.

*****

It was now getting a little hard to see the man. The sun was nearly all the way down by now, but I didn't want to drag my flashlight out of the car for fear of drawing more bugs. I plucked a blade of grass and rolled it between my fingers as I leaned back. "So far it sounds pretty standard, Roger."

"I'm getting to it," he replied. "I'm just trying to give you a feel for how it was around here then. Gwyllym brought the town hope, yeah. But he also brought something else." Roger stopped.

"Go on."

"It was..." Roger seemed to fumble for the words. "I guess the only word I have for it is evil. Twisted. Because Gwyllym brought something dark to Willisville, Joe, and with it the town started to change."

"Change how?"

"Everybody... I can't really describe it. It was like some heavy thing had settled on the town. Especially when Gwyllym's own people arrived. And not just his security guys, either. People like Alicia Bancroft. You met her, right?" I nodded, and Roger shuddered. "There are a lot more like her there at GeneSys. And worse."

"I know," I said. "I met some of them."

"And then don't forget the Germans," Roger said.

"Germans?" The hair on the back of my neck started to tingle. Oh boy. Not good. "What Germans?"

"You saw them, Joe. The scientists. The old boys in the white lab coats. Every one of them is German, and they're always chattering around with each other in that kraut dialect they do. And then the few times when they come into town they all hang together, not letting anybody else get close. The running joke around here is that they're escaped war criminals." Roger gulped. "But that may not be a joke after all. Not after what I've seen."

Now we were getting to it. "And what have you seen, Roger?" I asked him softly.

"What I've seen..." The rising moonlight was just bathing Roger's silhouette. He turned his face to me, and now it was all in darkness. "Joe," he said, "I've seen the back door to hell."

Chapter 33

There wasn't much to say to that. Roger and I had come to the same conclusions about GeneSys, albeit from different approaches. Neither one of us said a word for awhile, both lost in our own thoughts. But there was still an unanswered question.

"I'll say it again, Roger. Why me, and why now?"

"Okay," he replied slowly. "Since you didn't laugh at me about what God had said, maybe you won't about this either."

"I'm all ears."

Roger sighed and then drew his knees up to his chest, resting his forearms on them as he spoke. "As I said, I grew up in this town, but I had never in my whole life gone to church, not even when I was a kid. To me there wasn't one around here that was worth two cents. So I didn't grow up real religious, and neither did most of my friends. But then about eight months ago we got a new preacher in Willisville. Brother Ken Springer is his name and man, is he something." Roger looked up at me. "I mean that in a good way. Brother Ken is a walking Bible, but he doesn't lord it over you, like I've seen some preachers do. He knows his stuff and is real deep, but he's friendly at the same time, do you know what I mean?"

"Yeah I do, Roger. He sounds an awful lot like a preacher I met just this week."

Roger nodded and started fooling with his thumbnail. "Well, Brother Ken really shook this town up. He said he had gotten a 'call from the Lord' that we were gonna need what he was offering before too long, and he was right. It seemed like the man hadn't even gotten his bags unpacked when he started holding Sunday services down at the high school gym. Little by little people started showing up there. Within a couple of weeks even my wife Trish began attending." Roger again looked up. "Have you ever heard of 'getting saved', Joe?"

"Yeah, I have."

"That's what happened to Trish that first Sunday. She left the house one way and came back another, you know? Trish was all cranked up, but to tell the truth I couldn't make sense of any of it. At last, just to shut her up, I told her I'd go with her some Sunday, and I'd hear it for myself. Two weeks ago I did, and Joe," here Roger gave a short, disbelieving shake of his head, "don't you know that by the time that morning was over the same thing had happened to me." He quit picking at his thumbnail and shrugged. "You can laugh now."

"Why should I, Roger?" I said. "The circumstances are different, but I've experienced the same thing."

"Hey, no fooling?" Roger grinned, and now his smile seemed genuine, the first one from him I'd seen. "When?"

"Wednesday morning."

"This past Wednesday? You mean *yesterday?*" I nodded, and Roger's jaw dropped. "Holy mackerel. You've been saved less than a week and you're HERE?" He shuddered. "Man. Talk about getting tossed into the deep end of the pool."

"Yeah. Try telling me something I don't know."

"Okay," he said. "I'll bet you don't know this. I'll bet you don't know how to make the elevators work."

I sat up straight. "How?"

Roger reached into his shirt pocket and pulled something out. "With this."

I looked a closely at it. "A credit card?"

He shook his head. "Not a credit card. Key card. Only Boneless's special troops get 'em. They'll open any door in the place, except Mr. Gwyllym's."

"May I see it?" Roger handed it over, and I examined it. It was the size and shape of a credit card, white, with a large red diamond on one side and a black stripe on the other. "So you got one of these when you got promoted to Boneless's special squad?"

"Yeah, along with those black kraut uniforms he makes us wear. All the rest of the troops like 'em, along with the extra respect and the higher pay. But anymore...I dunno." Roger shrugged again. "Like I said, Joe, I got saved a couple of weeks ago, and the stuff at GeneSys that never bothered me before is driving me crazy now."

I started to hand the card back to him. "Like what?"

But he didn't take it. "Like everything. And that card, you can keep it. You're gonna need it. I won't. They don't know it yet, but I'm not going back. Trish and the baby and me, we're splitting tonight."

I pursed my lips and slid the card into my shirt pocket. "I can't say I blame you, Roger. If I had a family I'd do the same."

"I hate to leave you alone with this, Joe, but you know how it is. I've been living on borrowed time at that place for the last two weeks. If it was just me, I'd go back in with you. I would."

I sighed. "I know you would, Roger. You Rangers are tough. I met some in 'Nam, and I know you wouldn't skedaddle unless you had a strong reason. But if I'm to get the girl out, I'll need more information than I've got now."

"That's why I think my attention was drawn to you today, when I saw you go into Alicia's office. Brother Ken had called me two days ago and said that while he was praying that morning, God told him that someone was coming to Willisville to 'wield the scourge', whatever that means. I guess that person is you, Joe. Because as soon as I saw you, I knew we had to talk. That gum-wrapper thing was kind of spur-of-the-moment, but it worked."

"Two days ago?" I frowned. "I wasn't even a Christian two days ago."

"That's why He's God, Joe," Roger grinned, "and we're not. He knew already."

I sighed, "That He did," and then I nodded. "Okay, Roger, give. I need Intel. Tell me all you know about hell's back door."

*****

For the next hour, he did. It turned out that most of what I had deduced was right. GeneSys had two parts: the public side, and what was underneath. Level One, the immense greenhouse under the dome, was just what it appeared to be: a huge, living laboratory for testing new strains of DNA on plant life. It made good P.R., and a great cover for the other part, the hidden part.

Levels Two through Seven could only be accessed using those coded elevators. Boneless's black-clad troops carried key cards, as did the German scientists and the workers in those levels, whom I hadn't seen yet. Levels Two through Five held other labs and conference and computer rooms. Roger was told these levels also contained some kind of machines, gene sequencers and DNA splicers other things he didn't have a clue about. In Level Six was the dorm. There, up to a dozen young women resided.

"Prisoners or volunteers?" I asked him sharply.

"I'm not sure," Roger admitted. "The girls seem happy enough, but they're never allowed to roam far, and then only under escort from one of us. And I can't be sure, but from the way the girls act, I think they're kept under mild sedation."

"And you're sure Francesca Taylor is one of them?"

"Yeah. She calls herself another name, though. Felicity Smith.

But her real name is entered on her chart screen. And here's the worst, Joe. Level Six not only contains the dorm, but something else too." Roger swallowed. "The pod room."

"Pod room?" I asked Roger to describe it. Brother, did he.

As Roger told it, the young girls in the dorm had only one purpose: to furnish eggs, which were harvested from them on a regular basis. The eggs were then taken into the pod room. Roger had only been in there once, and asked to never do it again. It seemed the eggs that had been taken from the girls were fertilized *in vitro* and placed into vertical tanks of nutrient-rich fluid. Pods, if you will. And then, through some hellish alchemy I couldn't even imagine, in those pods...babies were grown.

I stopped him. "Wait a minute, Roger. These babies. You've actually SEEN them?"

"Yeah." He gulped again. "And I wish I hadn't. Because these little babies, Joe...there's something wrong with them."

I stared at him. "Wrong? How?"

"God, don't ask me that," Roger breathed. "You wouldn't believe me if I told you. The good thing is, none of those babies are alive, not like we are...I don't think. Boneless told us that's something the company was still working on. But then again, maybe he's lying. I wouldn't put anything past that man."

God have mercy. GeneSys was everything I had feared, and then some. And I was voluntarily going back inside? Pastor Samuels and his people had better be exceptionally good at prayer.

Roger looked at me. "So when are you figuring to spring the girl?"

I tried to get my thoughts under control. "Tonight, I guess. It'll never be any easier than now."

"Then if that's the case," he said, "there's one more thing I need to tell you about: Level Seven."

I felt Fear run its skittering fingers up my spine. Just from the way Roger had said it, it sounded bad. "So tell."

"Level Seven is its real name, and that's the way it's listed on the internal documents at GeneSys," Roger replied, "but we've got our own name for it: the Pit."

Now it was my turn to swallow. "The Pit?"

"Yeah. You know how Trask told you that nothing is ever wasted at GeneSys?" Roger nodded, "That's true, all right, but in a way the tourists are never told. See, you get off the elevator on Level Seven, and right across the hall is a door. You go through that into an airlock, and then through a last door. That one opens into a huge, circular, blank room, fifty feet across by twenty high, all metal, like everything else at GeneSys. But in the middle, right in the center of the floor, is this opening, like a"--Roger fluttered his fingers--"camera thing."

"Camera thing?"

Roger shook his head in frustration. "Yeah, you know, that thing inside a camera, right behind the glass, that thing that looks like a flower?"

Recognition dawned. "An iris opening."

He nodded again. "That's the name of it. It's like a big one of those, maybe fifteen feet across, set into the floor."

"But what's it for?"

"I guess you might call it a...disposal. See, when you come into the room there's things like gurneys against the walls. You fit your gurney into this track that leads to the iris, then you load stuff on it in bags, garbage or trash or whatever. You press this big red button on the wall next to the door and that iris opens up. You walk the gurney on the track right up to the edge and dump your stuff in. You bring the gurney back, press the button again and the iris closes."

I frowned at him. "So? What's bad about that?"

Roger's voice was tight. "When I said garbage, Joe, I meant more than just banana peels. *Everything* goes into the Pit: trash, sewage, medical waste, food. I can't even describe the stink that comes out of that hole. Like I said, everything goes in." Roger looked haunted. "And that includes bodies."

"BODIES?"

He shuddered. "Bodies. Did you hear the story of Tony Mordetti, the guy that gave Boneless Chuck his name?"

"Yeah, that gabby guard filled me in."

"Fred. Well, I was there the night Tony's body was dumped. Thank God I wasn't part of the detail, but I saw 'em wheel him in there. A press of the button, and Tony was history." Roger stared at me, remembering things best left forgotten. "But not just him. When I was first promoted one of the girls had just died, some kind of infection, and they put her in there. And last month when one of those old kraut doctors croaked, I personally saw Boneless shove him in with no more thought than you'd give a cat. And that ain't all, Joe." Roger's voice dropped to a whisper. "Sometimes they'll empty all the babies from the pods and toss 'em in and start over."

Sweet Jesus. Nightmare fuel. "But what's *down* there? Beneath the iris?" I wasn't so sure I really wanted to know.

"I don't know!" Roger shouted. "All kinds of stuff. It's like the world's largest chemical toilet, so they tell me. Everything down there gets rotted or dissolved or something, and as it does they draw off the methane gas and use it to help heat the dome."

I rubbed my fingers across my mouth. "Yeah, I can see how that nugget wouldn't go over real well with a Cub scout troop on a tour."

Roger gave me a wan smile. "Nope."

With a sigh I climbed to my feet, Roger doing the same. As I turned towards my car he stopped me with a hand on my arm. "Are you carrying?"

"Yeah, but obviously not on me. It's still in the car."

"What?"

"A .38 Smith and Wesson, four-inch barrel."

"A six-shooter?" Roger shook his head. "You'll need more than that to impress Boneless's boys. You saw what I had on my hip, right?"

"A Glock?"

"A Glock 23. It shoots a forty-caliber Smith and Wesson round, thirteen in the clip and one up the pipe. I checked mine into my locker at the armory on Level Two when I clocked out tonight. But feel free to grab it using the key card when you go back in."

I grinned tightly. "Thanks, but no. I know all about Glock 23's, Roger. I'll stick with the Smith."

"So you'll agree you're outgunned."

"Yeah. Let's just hope it doesn't come to a shooting war."

"You better pray it doesn't, Joe," Roger replied in dead earnestness.

"Because there's one more little piece of firepower Boneless has us all carry when we're underground: an FN P-90."

That was a new one to me, and I try to keep up. "What is it?"

"The P-90 is a personal defense weapon, from Belgium," Roger said. "Illegal as you can get. You've never seen anything like it, Joe. It looks like something out of a science fiction movie."

"A machine-gun?"

"Yeah, but smaller, with forward grips and downward ejection. It only weighs about seven pounds, but it shoots a 5.7 by 28 millimeter frangible armor-piercing round, and it fires those babies out of a fifty round magazine at the respectable rate of nine hundred rounds per minute. Oh yeah, frangible means the bullets break apart into pieces when they hit you."

"I know what frangible means, Roger." Vainly I tried to push the picture out of my mind of my body being cored by a slew of those things. It would look like a dragon had chewed me.

"And you still want to go up against those with a revolver?"

I smiled. "Now's not the time for me to be learning the feel of a new piece, Roger. Like I said, I'll just have to stick with what I know."

Roger shook his head at me. "Your funeral, man."

"Thanks, Roger," I said. "That's the spirit."

Chapter 34

"Do you know what time it is, sir?" The young guard at the gate was looking at me just about the way you'd think.

"Yeah, I do," I said. "My Granny taught me how to tell time when I was just four, using an old mantle clock that held my Grandpap's ashes in a little box underneath. There wasn't a whole lot left after the lightning had cooked him."

"Huh?"

"Well put, son. I can always spot a college man. Now are you going to let me in or not?"

He started to pick up his phone. "Maybe I ought to call Mr. Gwyllym..."

"You do that," I smiled. "And he'll tell you that as an E.P.A. representative I'm allowed to make spot checks of any facility just about any old time I feel like it. And then, in gratitude for you waking him from what I'm sure is a sound sleep, you and Mr. Gwyllym can discuss your career options here."

"Well..." The guard put the phone back down. "You at least need to sign in."

"Fine," I said. He handed me a clipboard, and a second later I had signed "James Fleming" for what I sincerely hoped was the last time. The guard motioned me on through. It wasn't until I had shut the car off that the shakes started. What would I have done if the guard had called my bluff and phoned Gwyllym? I wasn't sure, but I knew for a fact that Gwyllym would have been a lot tougher to buffalo than that pimply-faced post-adolescent at the gate. At any rate, one hurdle was done. I was sure I'd face another when I encountered the night guy at the desk.

But I was pleasantly surprised. After coming down the tunnel and into the lobby, I found the area unoccupied. I guess it only made sense: what group of tourists would be here at midnight? The answer was, None.

I made my way to the left and over to the golf carts, now noticing that each did indeed carry a number etched into a small brass tag attached to the bumper. Studiously avoiding Boneless's gag cart, number five, I picked the next one down, number six. I climbed on and a second later I was whizzing down the hall towards the bank of elevators. I didn't encounter a single soul during the trip. The entire place seemed as deserted as a lacrosse game, not even a skeleton crew.

Then I remembered the Pit, and tried to shut skeletons out of my mind.

At last I was there. Hopping off the cart, I strode up to the middle elevator, pulling Roger's key card out of my shirt pocket as I came. I shoved it into the slot next to the door, and when I did the red light above it instantly turned green. There was a soft ding. The door opened, welcoming me inside.

I swallowed.

It's not too late to back out, I told myself. I could just tell Mike that I was wrong and Francesca wasn't here. Who would know? I would, if nobody else, and I firmly shoved that gibbering, cringing coward back down inside. I squared my shoulders and walked in.

The elevator was an unadorned metal box, with its floor buttons recessed into a panel on the right. I pressed Level Six, and the doors slid smoothly closed. Then I started to sink. In less than ten seconds the doors opened onto a sterile hallway. I stuck my head out and peered up and down it. Deserted.

I crept out and the doors closed behind me.

There were no signs telling me which direction the dorm lay, so I mentally flipped a coin and turned right. I saw now that this floor I was on was quite a bit smaller than Level One--no surprise there--and I tried to picture GeneSys as a hideously huge mushroom sunk into the earth, the dome above being the elongated cap and the levels below, the stem.

As I walked, it seemed I could hear a humming all around me, but low, nearly in the subsonic range. I stopped and put my ear to the metal wall. The sound was louder now, and still as deep, like a Gregorian monk holding one long bass note. Machinery. Obviously the skunk works powering this little nightmare. But God willing, not for much longer.

Then I drew up short. I had rounded the curve, and now just a few feet away I saw a small cubicle containing a man in white watching a bank of video screens. It took a second before I registered what this was: a nurse's station. But what was the man watching? Not me, I hoped. I glanced up and around me. No, no video cameras, at least that I could see. One of the last things Roger had told me before we parted was that if somebody ever got down this far, Boneless felt a combination of his lethally-armed troops and his own physical prowess would be enough to handle any unfortunate sod.

Well, maybe. All things considered, I really didn't feel like testing Boneless's security measures if I could avoid it.

There was no way I could see to get around that station, and I wasn't about to do like Little Egypt and try crawling past the thing on my belly like a reptile, so there was nothing for it but to stride boldly up to the nurse and use a little country blather. If I still had any left. So that's what I did.

The nurse manning the desk was a swarthy, curly-haired cuss, and he narrowed his eyes when he saw me. "What the-! Who are you? What are you doing here? How did you get-"

The nurse's nametag read Mario Amonitos, R.N. "Hi, Mario! James Fleming, E.P.A." I lifted my lapel badge, which by now was looking a mite ratty. "I'm just having a little look-see."

But Mario didn't buy it. With a snarl he reached down and yanked something out of his desk. Being that he was a male nurse, and I was an old-line unreconstructed Southern chauvinist, I was almost too late as I saw Mario begin leveling the Glock 23 right at my sternum. But then my old unreconstructed reflexes kicked in, and before the nurse could bring the gun fully to bear I leaned across the counter and sent my fist crashing right into the bridge of his nose.

Nurse Mario's eyes went in two separate directions, and with a cry he crashed over backwards, chair and all, out.

I sucked my knuckles, muttering some not-so-nice words as I waited for the pain to subside. That was highly stupid. I could have broken my hand on that fool's head, and then what?

I leaned over and looked at the man. Mario was soundly gone, for what I hoped was a long time. Then I nervously glanced around and listened hard for black-clad reinforcements. Nothing.

Okay, enough screwing around. I was going to find that dorm, rescue the girl, and get in the wind.

I kept going the way I had come, only now double-timing it. The dorm had to be close to the nurse's station.

It was. In a few more yards, as I followed the curve of the wall, I came upon a door that read simply, DORMITORY. I stuck the key card in the slot mounted on the frame and held my breath.

Just like on Star Trek, the door slid back.

I paused for a few seconds while my eyes adjusted. In contrast with the bright, harsh light in the hallway, the dorm's illumination was muted. And why not? It *was* the dead of night, after all. Silently I crept three steps into the room and the door slid closed behind me. Timer or electric eye, I couldn't be sure which.

As Roger had said I would, I counted twelve beds, each holding a sleeping form. Then a crazy thought hit me: what if this was the wrong dorm, and instead of young girls, these bunks held instead a dozen highly-trained, ill-tempered commandos? Things would get interesting in a quick hurry.

But then I noticed something: at the foot of each bed there was a rack holding a softly green-glowing electronic pad, much like the one I had signed at the gate. On each pad was the name of the bed's occupant, along with bunch of medical lingo that meant less than nothing to me. I walked as quietly as I could down the row of beds, checking those names.

The seventh bed down, I found her.

Chapter 35

I bent down and pulled the covers away from the girl's face. Francesca--Felicity--looked pretty much like the photo Mike Taylor had showed me, minus the makeup. But there was something else there, a coarseness, that hadn't been evident then. Maybe it was the atmosphere here, what Roger had called that "heavy thing" that had "settled down" over the town, that had put those lines between her eyes and around the corners of her mouth.

Or maybe I was just exhausted and seeing things.

Gently I shook her, and as she awakened I clamped my hand firmly over her mouth. The girl's eyes grew huge in panic and I pressed my hand down tighter. "Shh," I whispered. "I'm a friend, Felicity. I've come to get you out." She rolled her eyes at me and I wasn't sure if she was getting it. "A friend," I whispered again. "My name's Joe."

Still staring at me, she looked as if she was considering my words, then she nodded once.

I bent down and put my mouth by her ear. "I'm going to pull my hand away, Felicity," I said softly. "Please don't make a sound, okay?"

She nodded again, and I began to remove my hand. This was the moment of truth. If Felicity had been brainwashed by Gwyllym and his goons, she would scream, the guards would appear, and the situation would turn terminally ugly. But if she really wanted a ticket out, she would realize I was it, and follow what I said.

I hadn't realized I was holding my breath until my hand was completely away from her. Then Felicity blinked and said in a very small voice, "Who did you say you were?"

"Joe Box," I muttered with a smile. "Your dad sent me."

"My father?" Tears began to well up in her eyes.

I patted her hand. "Shh. You gave everybody quite a turn, kiddo."

"But-"

I put my finger on her lips. "We'll talk later," I whispered. In the next bed over, another prisoner mumbled something in her sleep. I bent low. "Right now we need to leave."

"But the others-?"

"We'll come back for them, I give you my word." If all went well we would. The last thing I'd had Roger do was to promise me that he would delay his family's flight until dawn. If I wasn't out of GeneSys with Felicity by then, he was to call in as much help as he could muster: Sheriff Hardesty and his men, the Indiana State Police, even the National Guard if he had to. Roger agreed, and then we had prayed an awkward, halting prayer together, two rookies in the hands of God.

"Do I have time to change my clothes?" Felicity whispered.

"Sorry, kiddo," I whispered back. "The clock's running and we gotta go."

She nodded and slid out of bed. As she stood I noticed the girl was wearing a shapeless sweatsuit outfit as her sleeping gear, and I realized with a start how short and frail she was. Felicity really was still just a child, and my thoughts towards Gwyllym and Boneless Chuck grew even more dark and ill-intentioned.

Putting her small hand in mine, we began padding back towards the door, keeping a eye on the others and making sure we weren't waking them. We reached the door and I shoved the key card into the slot. It slid back as silently as before and I turned to Felicity with a smile. A short walk, an elevator ride, a golf cart ride, and we were home free. We stepped through the door and turned right.

And ran smack into Doctor Ernest Mangold.

Mangold and I rebounded off each other, both of us just barely able to keep our footing. But I didn't have time to register surprise, because at that instant something crashed into the back of my skull and the world turned black.

Chapter 36

Somebody--maybe it was Granny--had once said that there was nothing to life, really; all you had to do was to make sure that you woke up one more time than you fell asleep. Good advice, but right now sleeping was sounding pretty good. At least it beat the pain I felt when I opened my eyes. Bright, glaring light was everywhere, lancing through my eyeballs and darting through the highways of my brain like white-hot needles. I groaned. If I wasn't suffering a concussion, it was only by a miracle, because it sure felt like one. A blurry shadow crossed in front of my vision, shutting out a bit of that harsh candlepower, and I squinted up at him/her. It was only then I realized I was sitting bolt upright in a metal chair, and I was trussed to the thing as tightly as a county-fair hog.

I felt a stinging sensation and someone behind me withdrew a syringe from my tricep. With that pain another piece of news registered: before tying me to the chair, that possibly same someone had removed my suitcoat, tie, and shirt, leaving me only my pants, socks, shoes, and undershirt. And my BVD's, I hoped. My gun and shoulder rig were gone as well.

"Welcome back, Mr. Box." I squinted again at the figure standing before me. It materialized into that of Alexander Gwyllym. "That shot Charles just gave you should take effect momentarily. Until then, I would advise that you use the next few seconds to reflect silently on your possible future."

What future? I thought bitterly. I could see now that this whole "rescue" had gone completely too smoothly. Just like Sarge had said, I had gotten cocky, and now Felicity and I would pay for that mistake with our lives. The wonder of it was that we hadn't been tossed into the Pit already. I just hoped Gwyllym would have enough decency to shoot us first.

But that megalomaniac was right. Whatever his son Boneless had given me seemed to be working, and within another twenty seconds the pain ringing in my head had receded into a dull thud. And speaking of our good friend Boneless Chuck, there he was now, standing next to his father, both of them gently smiling at me like I was a long-lost relative, only now come home.

Looking around, I took stock of the room I was a prisoner in. I had no idea of what level we were on, but the room was maybe fifteen feet square, with my chair bolted to the floor right in the middle. The wall directly across from me was one solid mirror, top to bottom, side to side. I knew without being told it was two-way glass. On my right side, just out of reach, stood a long table on wheels, and resting on its surface there were spiky tools and long-handled ratchet gizmos and more sharp blades than you would find in a cutlery shop. I swallowed. I bet I knew what all those were for, and who they planned to use them on. And here was the worst part. Right at the end of that table, tantalizingly just out of reach, Gwyllym had placed my shoulder holster and gun. Just by doing that it was as if he was saying to me, "See? That's how little hope you have, and how little we think of you. We've placed your gun right where you can see it, but we know you don't have a snowball's chance of grabbing it and using it on us." Too true.

The wall on my left held, incongruously, two immense Morris chairs that faced mine, with a tall ashtray on a stand between them. It looked for all the world as if all three objects had been lifted whole from the smoking room at a London gentleman's club. Then it hit me what those chairs were for: a couple of people could sit comfortably and watch and smoke as tortures were inflicted on the poor, luckless wretch strapped down before them. Me.

Gwyllym smiled. "How are you feeling now, Mr. Box?"

"Oh, top-notch," I answered, with more bravado than I was feeling. "And I'll go ahead and ask, since I know you're dying for me to: what tipped you off?"

Gwyllym laughed. "Your thumb."

"Beg pardon?"

"Your thumb," he repeated. "There's a micro scanner built into the button next to my door. When you pressed it this morning, your thumbprint was scanned into our security system. By the time we were finished with our business your complete service and police records had been accessed. We knew all about you before my door closed behind you, Mr. Box."

"So I was dead before I started," I said flatly. "Why didn't you kill me right away? Why let me keep up my charade?"

Boneless answered for him. "Yours was the first serious security breach we've encountered here, Mr. Box," he wheezed, "and we wanted to put our system through its paces." His smile was chilling. "We found it works admirably."

"So you tracked me all the time I was here. But how? I didn't see any cameras."

"Cameras?" Gwyllym barked, and he and his son grinned at

each other.

"Cameras are so...twentieth century," the old man said. "Didn't you wonder at all the metal around here, Mr. Box? Did you think all that was done to make GeneSys appear evil and high-tech?" He shook his head. "Albert Trask told you that everything here is state-of-the-art, and so it is." Gwyllym motioned around us. "The floors, the ceilings, even the walls themselves, all carry the very latest in scanning technology. We were hoping someday to give our system a real-world, real-time test." Gwyllym showed his teeth. "For that we thank you."

"Glad to oblige." Then I swallowed again. "Now what?"

"Why, that depends entirely on you, Mr. Box," Gwyllym answered, the very voice of reason. "You know you'll die here, of course."

I gulped. "Of course."

"But when and how that death occurs depends solely on how cooperative you are with Charles," Gwyllym finished.

"I don't understand."

Gwyllym sighed, the schoolmaster with the backward pupil. "Charles will ask you questions. You will, in due course, answer those questions. The alacrity and straightforwardness of your answers will wholly determine how quickly your death will transpire. And my son is willing to take all the time he needs." Boneless grinned at that, and I felt ice pierce my heart.

"Then we're in for a long night," I said, "because I don't know anything about anything."

"I'd bet you'd be surprised," Gwyllym chuckled. "Especially around the fourth hour. Isn't that right, Charles? The fourth hour is usually the time when the cooperation really starts?"

Boneless was still staring me, a slight smile playing around the corners of his mouth. "Yes. About then."

My own mouth felt as dry as cornflakes. "I thought you said I was the first one you had captured."

"Captured on-site, yes," Gwyllym replied. "But this room has seen much use in the past two years. Many have sat where you're sitting, Mr. Box, and doubtless thinking what you are right this minute."

"Like who?"

Gwyllym's reply was airy. "Oh, the occasional drifter, train hoboes and the like. Charles brings those in himself. He does enjoy the hunt. And of course the girls. When they've reached the end of their usefulness, Charles brings them in here for one last session before they join the others in the Pit."

"But *why,* for God's sake? What's the *point?"*

Gwyllym genuinely appeared puzzled. "Why, to keep Charles's skills sharp, of course."

"No. I mean this." I motioned with my head around me. "Why all this? For what?"

"You're a hillbilly, Mr. Box," Gwyllym frowned. "And for all your well-turned words you're still just a corn-fed country boy at heart. I'd hardly expect a man like you to understand a man like me, or what we hope to accomplish here at GeneSys."

"Aw, give it a shot, Mr. Gwyllym," I grinned sickly. "What have you got to lose? You're going to kill me anyway, who could I tell? And besides," I leaned my head forward, "like I said before, you know you're dying to."

Gwyllym's eyes crinkled in fine humor. He looked for all the world like the president of the Kiwanis, if they had a chapter in hell. "Mercy me, Mr. Box!" he chuckled again. "You're quite astute, in your hayseed way." If this man continued to insult my lineage, I was going to get upset. "Very well, I'll answer you, sir," Gwyllym smiled. "As you put it, what have I got to lose?"

"Father..." Boneless's wheezy word carried a warning tone, but Gwyllym waved it away.

"Charles, I allow you to take pleasure in your own way, without interference. Please allow me the courtesy in kind."

Without a further word, only a subservient nod, Charles stepped aside. Gwyllym placed himself directly in front of me. "All right, Mr. Box, where should we begin?"

"Why don't you begin with telling me where you've stowed the girl?"

"She's safely tucked away back in her bed. Charles gave her a few different medications." Gwyllym smiled again. "By the time Felicity wakens in the morning, if she has any memories of you at all, it will only be as the broken shards of a forgotten dream."

"Quint was right," I breathed. "You really are a monster."

"On the contrary, sir," Gwyllym said. "I am God."

"Say *what?"*

"You heard me correctly. As Peter O'Toole put it in a film many years ago, if God could do half the tricks we do here, He'd be a happy man." Gwyllym sighed and pointed. "Mr. Box, take a look at my son Charles. A long look. Tell me, what do you see?"

I did, and then looked back up at Gwyllym. "A sadistic evolutionary U-turn?"

Boneless shook his head once and took a step towards me, but Gwyllym stopped him with a touch. "Patience, Charles. You can have him in a bit." Boneless relaxed, the tension leaving his body as quickly as it had come, and he smiled.

Gwyllym sighed again. "Mr. Box. Please." His tone was exceedingly reasonable. "In a few moments I'll be leaving you alone in here with Charles. How things progress from that point is entirely up to you. So take care, I implore you. Charles is a highly distinct individual, the first of his breed: a New Man."

That's just the way Gwyllym said the phrase, "New Man," all in quotes and large capital letters. "I thought he was your son," I said.

"He is," Gwyllym responded, "but not biologically. No, Charles's real father is someone I'll wager even you've heard of." Gwyllym paused dramatically, waiting for me to ask.

So I did. "Who's his father?"

Gwyllym chuckled, the soul of humor. "Josef Mengele."

"WHAT?" My jaw dropped. "Josef Mengele! The Nazi? The 'Angel of Death'?" Gwyllym and Boneless both grinned, and furiously I tried to process what I was hearing. "But...that can't be. Mengele escaped capture from the Allies at the end of the war, and ended up in South America. He was an old man when the Mossad finally got him. Boneless isn't old enough to be his son."

"Oh, but he is," Gwyllym argued. "You see, Mr. Box, even in the 1940's there was enough knowledge of crude cryogenics to be able to freeze sperm samples. And with all his shortcomings, Mengele was not a stupid man. When he saw the end coming in 1945, Mengele had some of his own seed flash-frozen, seed that he took with him in his flight. Thirty years later, and through medical techniques which I doubt you possess the brains to understand, an egg was fertilized with that seed. The result you see before you."

I nodded at the scarecrow. "Boneless Chuck."

The sadist smiled. "Call me what you wish," he wheezed. "At the end, you'll be begging me to stop your existence."

With an almost physical will I turned my face away from my future torturer and addressed Gwyllym. "Where does Mangold figure into this?"

"Doctor Mangold was an intern at Auschwitz, as are several more German scientists and doctors in our employ who served at other camps," Gwyllym replied. "We set them up in clinics around the country and they do the preliminary screenings for our young ladies. Occasionally those men come back here to assist in research work before they return to their home cities."

I digested that. "Okay, I'll accept that Josef Mengele is Boneless's real father. It makes as much sense as anything else to explain him. But who donated the egg?"

Gwyllym smiled. "Another person I'll bet you've heard of, Mr. Box." He seemed so happy to tell it. "Eva Braun."

Great...God...almighty. Incredible. Could it be? But then I looked again at Boneless, right into the depths of his eyes, and realized that Gwyllym was speaking the truth. This hellspawn grinning quietly at me and licking his lips was none other than the twisted offspring of two of the worst people in history.

Boneless Chuck's father really was Josef Mengele, the infamous mass-murdering demon-doctor of Auschwitz. And worse, his mother was the mistress of Mengele's employer.

Adolf Hitler.

Chapter 37

Gwyllym briskly rubbed his hands. "Well, enough of this, Mr. Box. I must be going. I'll be leaving you now, in my son's capable hands. Were I you, I would answer whatever questions he asks you, truthfully and the first time." Gwyllym turned to go.

"Wait," I said. I'll admit it, I was trying to keep the pleading out of my voice, and Gwyllym in the room, because the longer he stayed here, the longer would be the delay before Boneless started in on me. I hoped. On the other hand, it could be that one of those comfortable-looking chairs over there on the far wall belonged to the old man. "You still haven't answered the question," I reminded him. Gwyllym raised his eyebrows at me. "What all this is for," I said.

"I thought I had made that clear," Gwyllym replied. "Charles is the first of the 'New Men'." But I guess I wasn't getting it, because Gwyllym sighed at me. "It's quite simple, sir. Charles is different from anyone who has ever lived. You see, through some quirk of his birth, he was born completely without a conscience."

I shook my head. "That's impossible."

"Is it? Look again into my son's eyes, sir, and you tell me. Is it?"

I didn't have to look, but I wasn't letting my argument go that easily.

"How do I know it wasn't you that made him the way he is, Gwyllym?"

The old man's mouth twisted in amusement. "Perhaps I did."

"But I thought you said-"

"You heard me correctly," he smiled. "Let me explain, then I really must leave. My father's name was Anton Gwyllym. His mother was a German and his father, Welsh. By the time the war broke out Anton was a young man with a family and a thriving medical practice in the south of England. Believing strongly in the Third Reich, and the principles which guided it, in 1940 he took his wife and child--me--and defected to Germany. My father joined himself to the Reich, and in due course he found himself working under Doctor Mengele at Auschwitz. When the war ended and Mengele fled, my father and mother and I joined him. I spent my youth in the jungles of South America, watching and learning from both men. Years later my parents were killed in a laboratory explosion, and I took up where my father had left off, assisting the great doctor in his quest for Hitler's ultimate dream, the Aryan superman. In 1975, that dream was realized in Charles."

Gwyllym gazed affectionately at the monster, who shyly ducked his head in deference. "I knew from the start that Charles was something special," Gwyllym said, "and I set out to make him even more so. Using operant conditioning techniques first developed by the late B. F. Skinner, and methods I myself devised, I formed Charles and molded him into what you see here."

Frankenstein, move over. "But some of Skinner's work was controversial," I argued. "Sensory deprivation and the like."

"And so it is," Gwyllym answered smoothly, "only I refined it to a degree Skinner had only imagined. From his birth Charles was treated differently than other children. Until he turned twenty he lived in a glass room of my own design, under constant monitoring and supervision. He has only ever eaten a food paste I invented. When Charles was a small child I would periodically remove him from his room and then lock him in a sensory deprivation chamber. There he experienced no light, sound, or touch. Weeks later the first thing Charles would hear upon exiting that chamber was my own voice. He has been taught extensively, not only from the classics, but also in martial arts. Charles is now nearly thirty, and in all that time he has never had a friend, never enjoyed a woman, and has never known a teacher other than myself. Charles has a measured IQ of 168, is completely fearless, utterly strong, and absolutely loyal to me. And because of all that, I call him my son."

The light finally clicked on in my brain. "So that's what you're doing down here. You're trying to make more of...him."

"That's correct, Mr. Box," Gwyllym said. "We combine an egg from one of the girls with seed drawn from Charles, and then we take the completed product of conception and place it in a nutrition pod. Charles's development took an awfully long time. Now, with the pods, we are hoping to cut that time considerably."

"But it's not working," I said. "I've looked in that room." Which was a lie, but I didn't want to tell Gwyllym that Roger Thornhill was the one who had told me about it. "The only things grown in those pods are lifeless deformities."

"True," Gwyllym admitted. "But we have time, money, and a society screaming for order on our side. We will prevail. Now, I really must be going." Turning his attention away from me he addressed Boneless. "Don't dawdle, Charles. When you've finished here, meet me in my office. There are things we need to discuss." With that, Gwyllym walked out of the room and the door hissed shut.

Oh, boy. Here we go. I tried to swallow and speak. "Hey, Boneless." My mouth tasted like it had been wiped dry with a kerosene rag. "Listen-", but Boneless ignored me, instead turning to the long table on my right. Humming something familiar, he began picking each tool up and critically examining it before putting it back down. With Boneless's wheezy voice it took me a second to get what he was humming. Then I did. The song he was murdering was an old one, from the seventies: *The Needle and the Damage Done,* by Neil Young. Very funny. If Boneless was trying to make me nervous, he was doing an excellent job.

Boneless was still rummaging around on the table, not looking at me, when he spoke. "Do you like music, Mr. Box?"

I moistened my lips. "When it's done right I do."

My insult went right past him. "So do I," he said. "All kinds of music. Are you familiar with the song that I was doing just now?"

"Yeah. So was that to prepare me, Boneless?" I was going for brave. "Will needles be figuring in our fun?"

He turned. "Why, no. I just happen to like Neil Young's music, that's all." Boneless returned to his rummaging, and his humming, and a second later he found what he was after. He turned back to me and held the thing up. "Isn't that the way?" Boneless smiled. "It's always the last place you look."

A pair of locking pliers.

Boneless walked over and lifted my left hand, critically examining the diameter of my little finger. Then, humming again, he adjusted the knurled knob on the plier's handle accordingly.

Oh God. This was gonna sting.

Boneless placed the plier's jaws loosely between my knuckle and the finger's second joint, and he smiled again. "Now then, Mr. Box," the freak breathed, "this is how our session will progress. As my father said, I will ask you a question. I'll only ask it once. You will, without hesitation, give me a complete, factual answer to that question. Any delay, or hint of a lie, and I'll snap your little finger straight up. After that we'll proceed to the ring finger and try again, then to the middle finger, and so on. Is that clear?"

I didn't answer, and Boneless frowned at me. "That was a question, Mr. Box. Let's not start out on the wrong foot, shall we? I asked you, is that clear?"

"Crystal," I managed to croak.

"Fine," Boneless smiled again. "Now then, first question: who else besides the late Mr. Thornhill and his family knows who you really are, and why you're here?"

I could feel the color drain from my face as the words registered. Roger and his family, dead? My God. Boneless must have had Roger followed home and then killed, along with his wife and baby. But then with a sinking heart I realized that it wasn't Boneless's goons that had killed the Thornhills: it was me. First Linda, now them. They were dead because of me. My cockiness had killed those people just as surely as if I had shot them myself. I just hoped their deaths had been quick. When Boneless finally got around to taking me out, he would be doing me a favor. Then my grief was cut short as I realized the full import of Boneless's words. With Roger dead, there would be no rescue coming for Felicity.

Or me.

Chapter 38

Boneless tightened the pressure down on the locking pliers a hair. "I'll repeat the question, but I warn you, I don't plan to make a habit of that. Now, again. Who else knows of you besides the Thornhills?"

"Nobody," I said, and I closed my eyes.

The pain was worse than I had dared to imagine. In one fluid motion Boneless locked the pliers down on my little finger and then violently wrenched the digit vertical. The knuckle popped out of joint with the sound of a chicken leg separating from the thigh. And with it I howled like a hound with his tail caught in the door.

The pain climbed, and climbed, then peaked, and then slowly began to recede as shock and numbness took over. After a few seconds I opened my eyes and risked a glance at my hand; sure enough, my pinkie was standing straight up at military-school attention and was already turning red with swelling.

Tunelessly humming again, Boneless flipped the lever on the plier's handle, releasing it and moving it over one digit. Then without warning he tightened the pliers down again and did the same thing to that finger, snapping it up towards the ceiling.

My scream this time was as much rage as pain.

"Why did you do *that* one for?" I gasped. Lord almighty, what that man was doing to me hurt worse than just about anything I had ever felt.

Boneless gave me that same gentle smile. "Oh, that was just for me." He placed the pliers around my middle finger. "This one's thicker," he said. "Bear that in mind."

I couldn't take much more of this. Boneless still had the rest of my left hand to do, then the right. After that my toes and feet. And when he was done with all them, then what? The next logical place would be my eyes.

Fear flooded me. I knew I wasn't getting out of this one alone. I couldn't help it as I bowed my head and desperately whispered the next. "Dear God... Save me, please..."

Boneless narrowed his eyes and bent low with a chuckle. "What's that? A *prayer?*" He shook his head. "You surprise me, Mr. Box. I hardly pegged you for a religious man. I expected you to be stronger than that."

With an effort I brought my eyes level with his. "I'm not

religious," I said shakily, then I swallowed. "I'm a Christian."

"Real-ly?" Boneless grinned in happy surprise. "Well now! That's a first at GeneSys, I believe. I'll have to make doubly sure your time here is memorable. What little time you have left, that is."

As Boneless's words sunk in, icy hands closed around my heart. I guessed the freak was right; this was the end of the road for Joe Box, the failure specialist. Fail. Failure. That was me. At the outer edges of my consciousness I could feel despair rapping, insistently rapping, wanting in.

Sorry, Felicity. Sorry, Roger. Sorry, Joe. Sorry... In retrospect it would have been so easy to open that door.

But then with a soundless blast of light, something else suddenly pushed in. Whatever it was rudely shoved that despair aside, and then I felt that same something washing over me like warm oil. What was this? Then I knew.

It was hope. Sweet hope. Hope in the form of a Person.

And not just hope. What I was experiencing now, growing by the second inside me, was more: triumph. The victor's song. I knew, deep in the center of my being I knew, that God had heard the prayer of this raggedy briar, and this wasn't over, not yet. The pain hadn't left, no, it was still there, strong as ever, but now a stronger power was overriding it.

My veins began to swell. Roaring through me now was a heady combination of not only the power of Almighty God, but another thing nearly as good: five generations of stubborn, red-dog, always-spoiling-for-a-fight, Southern hillbilly cussedness.

I almost laughed. Sarge was righter about me than he knew.

Boneless bent low again, peering at me. "Smiling are we, Mr. Box? Perhaps you've already slipped over into madness. Pity, but it wouldn't have been the first time that's happened. I've broken stronger men than you." He removed the pliers from my finger and carefully placed them back on the table. When Boneless turned around what he was holding now was worse. A brace-and-bit, like an old-world carpenter would have used to drill a hole for a drawer pull. "Let's see how this does on your kneecap," Boneless smiled.

And at that second the power died.

For a moment the whole room was plunged into darkness, then the emergency backups must have kicked in and the lights came dimly back on. Boneless and I looked at each other. He furrowed his brow and frowned.

I was trying to ignore the pain in my hand as I grinned back. It wasn't easy. "Don't look at me," I said. "I didn't do it."

Before Boneless could answer the door behind him slid open and two black-uniformed men entered. Through my pain-dimmed eyes I couldn't make out who they were, until the bigger of them spoke.

"Power glitch, Mr. Gwyllym," the man said. "We were just going down to the cafeteria when the whole system dumped like a fat guy flushing the toilet." His partner went "A-hyuk-hyuk-hyuk."

Blakey Sinclair and his trained idiot, Chet.

Boneless sighed. "That's the second time in two weeks. I'll not have it again." He pointed at Blakey. "Is that clear?"

Blakey gulped. "Sure, Mr. Gwyllym, Chet and me, we'll get right on it, sir."

"Who was the electrical contractor we used?" Boneless asked. "Ballantine?"

"That's the one," Blakey agreed.

Boneless's speech was low and measured. "I was never happy with his work. I want him brought here, to this room." Boneless's voice was still soft, but mayonnaise-like spittle was beginning to collect at the corners of his mouth. "Do you understand me?"

Both men answered in unison. "Yes, sir."

Boneless sighed again in disgust. "I suppose I need to check this out. I'll be in Control. You two, watch him. And Sinclair," Boneless said with dark menace, "I heard about your row with Mr. Box at Jerry's. I don't want him touched, by you or Chet. He's mine. Is that clear as well?"

Again both men answered in the affirmative.

Boneless nodded once at them and started away from me. He was just walking through the door when I called out, "Hey, creep."

Boneless turned to give me what I'm sure he thought was killer look number six, but I just smiled at him. "You may think this is over, but you're wrong," I croaked, my voice raspy from screaming. "The next time we meet, it'll be under a black flag."

Boneless's lips curled in a condescending smirk. "The next time we meet, I'll be tossing your broken, living body into the Pit." Then he was gone, and the door slid shut behind him.

Blakey narrowed his eyes at me. "Well, as I live and breathe, if it ain't the funny man," he growled. "That was sure a funny trick you played on us at Jerry's. Chet and me, we laughed a lot as the docs were sewing us up."

Blakey wasn't kidding. He was sporting a puffy white bandage over the ear that my fist had cauliflowered, and Chet hadn't fared much better: his bandage covered the whole base of his skull.

"Those docs didn't do such a great job, Blakey," I observed. "You and Chet look like human Q-tips. Cute, though. You guys have the market cornered on cute."

Blakey snarled and took a step towards me but Chet grabbed his arm. "Hey, man." The skinny jerk sounded worried. "Remember what Boneless told us?"

With a yank Blakey pulled his arm free. "I heard. Who's gonna tell him? You?"

"Wait a minute Blakey," I said. "You go busting me up and Chet won't have to tell. Boneless will know with one look."

Blakey grinned at me. "So I'll leave your face alone. I'll just do a little body work on you." He turned to Chet. "Untie him and get him on his feet."

Chet, ever the obedient toady, did just that. As Chet was undoing the ropes, Blakey stayed out of reach, still grinning at me and rolling his shoulders in a tough-guy way. "You're mine, cracker," he hissed. "And don't think you'll get out of this with any fancy-dan tricks. That worked once. You won't get a second chance."

But Blakey was so engrossed in his testosterone posing he wasn't paying very close attention to what Chet was doing. And old Chet had made a classic error. He had untied the ropes from both arms and my left leg, but in the process of removing the cord from my right leg Chet never realized he was kneeling in front of me and was wide open...as it were. The last knot dropped away, and as it did I slashed out my left foot and planted the toe of my shoe deeply in the spot where it would do Chet the least good.

The color blanched from Chet's face. He sank to his knees, clutching at himself, and yelped like a puppy caught in the gears.

But I didn't take time to gloat. I shot from the chair and threw the table full of tools right at Blakey. He must have still been in shock over what he had seen, as he was a bit slow in blocking the thing. The table hit Blakey square in the midsection and both he and it went over backward with a crash.

Now I could gloat. But not for long. Because as I was heading for the door something grabbed my ankle and I went down, hard. I solidly hit the floor with my wrecked hand, and I thought the pain was going to black me out. With a gasp of agony I looked to see what had tripped me. Chet. The pin-headed moron was hurting from where I had nailed him, but not so badly he hadn't been able to reach out and snag my foot as I had gone past.

Well, if that boy liked my foot so much he could have it, and I savagely booted Chet in the noggin. As my foot connected, Chet whined like a dog and his eyes fluttered closed. When Chet woke up this time, I doubted if even morphine would help his headache.

I stumbled to my feet then, my hand throbbing like a football going for the extra point. But to my dismay I saw that Blakey was getting up at the same time, and he didn't look happy with me. In three running steps the thug was in front of me, blocking the door.

"Pretty good, funny man," Blakey panted. "Only you just screwed yourself. You're an escaped prisoner now. And that makes you mine."

"Come on, Blakey," I pleaded. "This isn't a fair fight, and you know it. Just look at what Boneless did to me." I thrust my left hand straight out and wagged it at him.

And don't you know Blakey looked. Again.

And when he did my right hand shot out, middle knuckle extended, catching Blakey dead on his Adam's apple, "right in the googler", as Granny would say. Blakey's tongue shot out and he grabbed his throat, eyes bugging. A split-second later my same right hand was now a fist, tearing into his jaw. Still clutching his throat, Blakey went straight down to the floor, gone.

I couldn't help it. I pointed at his prone form and whooped. "Twice. Twice!!" I sucked at my knuckles as I shook my head at him. "Criminy *dick,* Blakey, you are one dumb Hoosier."

I started to go, but stopped again. I was missing something here, something important...then it hit me. Evidence. Assuming I managed to get Felicity free with both of our skins still intact, I would need some hard proof of what was going on here. Otherwise Gwyllym would button the place up tight, and who in their right mind would believe me, a raggedy P.I.? But that proof had to be something small enough I could carry away easily... My eye was drawn to that two-way glass. Without thinking I strode over to it, grabbed one of those big old Morris chairs, and slung it through. When the glass had quit falling I looked in. On the other side was a room filled with computers and cameras, all presently dead due to the power crash. I supposed they were there to record the fun for Boneless's later enjoyment.

I gingerly stepped over the threshold and stopped at the first computer I came to. Dead like the rest, but I knew what I was after: a disk, any disk. I popped out the first one I saw and slipped it in my pocket. Whatever it held, it would have to do.

Then I crossed back into the torture room, pulled Blakey's key card off his belt, retrieved my gun from the floor, shoved both of them in my pocket, and ran.

Chapter 39

I didn't get far. As soon as I reached the hallway my hand reminded me I was still badly hurt, and I glanced down at it. No change there, not surprisingly. Through all my gyrations of the last few minutes my ring finger and pinkie were still pointed skyward. If I ran into any more trouble before I got Felicity out that could cause a problem...only I really didn't want to do what I knew I needed to do to get them laying flat again. Did *not.*

I sighed. Oh well. Don't think about it, that makes it worse, just do it. And without a second's more hesitation I grabbed those two fingers and snapped them back down into place.

Woo-WEE. I almost bit my lip through on that one. Then back beyond my pain I heard Granny's voice from my youth come floating by: "It'll feel better when it quits hurtin'." I almost laughed in spite of the throbbing; how could you argue with that? My fingers were still red and swollen and banging like Indian drums, but at least now they wouldn't get snagged on anything. With that assurance I started double-timing it down the hall.

Then I stopped again. Where *was* I, anyway? I looked up and around, and I finally spotted a small sign on the wall up near the ceiling that read Six West. Okay, I was still on Level Six. But which way was the dorm? I didn't have a clue, but I figured if I could find that nurse's station then I could get my bearings. I flipped that mental coin one more time, then I turned right and began trotting once more. The big thing now was time. I didn't know if the power dump had crashed the security scanners or not, but I had to assume that someone was watching me. If that was the case, my lifespan--and the girl's--might be measured in minutes.

I followed the curving hall around, searching for something familiar, and twenty seconds later I came upon the nurse's station. Hopefully it was unmanned. Maybe good old Nurse Mario was still conked out on the floor behind the counter. If he was, he could stay there. I sure wasn't going to stop and look.

But then I heard voices, and it sounded like they were coming my way. Without thinking I vaulted over the counter and landed on something yielding. You guessed it: Nurse Mario. I'm sure my hundred and eighty-five pounds landing on his chest from four feet up didn't do the man any good, but Mario didn't even grunt. He was still out. Or was he dead? As quietly as I could, I reached down and felt his wrist. No, there was a pulse there. Good. I really hadn't wanted to kill him. I hadn't taken a life since Vietnam. The truth is, I didn't want to kill anybody. Save for Boneless. In his case I'd be willing to make an exception.

Enough. The voices were drawing closer, and I held my breath. If whoever they were looked over the counter as they passed, I was toast. They approached, and I could now tell they were men's voices, older, and definitely German. One of them was Mangold's; I would have bet the Goddess on that. The other one I didn't know.

Mangold was speaking in a thick accent. "All these electrical problems we're having are driving me mad. Did you know, Fritz, in chust those few seconds I lost nearly three days work?"

As Mangold talked I felt a sneeze coming on--hang the man and his pheromones!--and I pinched my nose tightly shut.

"You must back up your files, Ernest," the other man--Fritz–replied. "I know you don't like it, but you must take the time to do this. Otherwise you will continue to lose data."

"Bah. If a certain skinny psychotic would not have overloaded the circuits with his asinine scanners, we would have plenty of power for all. And to what purpose? His beloved machines are yet again off-line, as are our computers, and all we have now are emergency lights. And does he care? No. He would rather waste his time torturing some idiot. Fritz, I tell you, it's madness. No good can come from this."

If Fritz made any reply, I missed it as both men passed out of my hearing. As they did I blew out a silent, relieved breath, my sneeze fading.

Idiot? I rather resented that. Mangold, you liver-lipped Nazi, we'll see who's the idiot when this little deal is done.

I waited another full minute to make sure they were really gone, then I came around the counter and started moving down the hall. In a few more steps I was back at the dorm. I took a quick side-to-side glance and then slipped the card into the door slot. It opened...and I hesitated. What if somebody had laid a trap? What if they did, I argued back. I sure didn't have the time to circumvent it. Besides, I had already sprung a Bouncing Betty and lived to tell the tale. They don't get much nastier than that.

So I just walked straight in.

It was if the previous events had never happened at all. The same girls, including Felicity, were still fast asleep in their same beds. I knelt down, softly placing my hand over the child's mouth, and she never stirred. I shook her gently. She still didn't come around.

Gwyllym was right. Boneless had given the girl something strong, that was certain, and now I saw our escape had gotten complicated. I had simply figured that when the time arrived Felicity would be able to come with me under her own steam; it never occurred to me I might have to carry her. Well, these were the cards I was dealt, and I had to play them. But it also seemed natural to mutter a prayer for strength as I lifted the girl from her bed and slung her across my shoulders in a fireman's carry.

God must have heard me as I stood with her; Felicity was a little slip of a thing, but even so it was if she weighed nothing at all. Who was that guy in the Bible that was so strong? Samson? Hadn't he killed like a whole slew of bad guys with just a bone or a stick or something? I wasn't in his class, but with God helping me I felt like I could carry this kid all the way back to Cincinnati.

I fumbled getting Blakey's key card out of my pocket, but thankfully I managed to do it without dumping Felicity on the floor. Then I slipped the card into its slot, the door slid back, and we stepped into the hallway.

And came face-to-face with Albert Trask.

Caramba. Was it always this hard to leave this room?

Chapter 40

I went into pure reflex mode. And I knew God was still helping me, because even though Albert carried ten less pounds and twenty less years than me, I managed to keep both my wits and my feet as I pivoted sharply and swung Felicity's legs hard across his head.

Albert grunted with the impact, but he was wicked quick as he shook off the blow and made a diving tackle at my gut. The man connected like a concrete truck hitting a bridge abutment, and we all three went down in a tangle. Somehow Felicity rolled free during the melee, still out. Being as he was younger, Albert was the first to recover his footing, and when he did he launched a vicious kick towards my face. I was barely able to pull away from his shoe as it whistled past my nose. That was close.

But I didn't have time to ponder my luck as I clambered to my feet, because instead of following through with me, Albert grabbed Felicity. He pulled her upright with a grin, then slapped her hard across the face. When he did that she whimpered like a three-year-old having a bad dream. My blood instantly boiled.

"Albert," I said through gritted teeth, "if you hope to live to see the next five seconds you'd best put her down."

The only reply Albert gave me was a smile as he whipped out his gun. It took a second to register that what he was now holding tightly to the side of Felicity's head was a Glock 23.

I narrowed my eyes at him. "So that's it. You're not just a regular guard pulling a paycheck. You're one of Boneless's special boys."

"Yep, I am," he grinned. "I told you before that Mr. Gwyllym's been good to me. He promoted me in secret a while back and asked me to keep him up to speed on who's saying what. I said sure."

"Who's saying what, huh?" I shot back. "Like ratting out that other guard, Tony Mordetti?" I began edging around to Albert's right as I talked, all the while keeping a sharp eye on his gun. Albert nodded, still grinning, and I went on, "You're an informer on your own friends, the worst kind of vermin. And you had a guy killed just because he made fun of your boss's voice." I shook my head. "You're quite a piece of work, Albert my boy."

"Thanks," he nodded again, "and you can stop right there."

By now Felicity was starting to come around. It was also beginning to dawn on her what was going on. She looked at me. "I know you..." the girl whispered, then her eyes opened wide. She rolled them fearfully towards the gun at her skull, then again over at me. "Help me." She sounded terrible. Little girl lost.

I stared hard at her, hoping to almost visually drive my words home in her fogged brain. "Pray, kid. This isn't over yet."

Albert laughed. "That's right, man. You have her pray I don't paint the walls with her brains."

"I really hope you won't do that, Albert," I said. "Because if you do I'll tear out your throat."

Albert sighed theatrically. "Strong words. Strong, strong words. But how's about nobody kills anybody. Let's all take a break." He seemed to brighten. "Hey, here's a thought. Since I have one hand around this girl's mighty fine waist, and since I'm using the other to hold my gun against her pretty skull, and furthermore since that leaves me no hands left to call for help on my communicator, how's about you follow us on into the pod room?"

"Now why should I do that?" I scowled.

"Because," Albert answered reasonably, "there's an alarm mounted on the back wall there, and I figure that while I keep the gun on the girl you can push the button for me."

I glared at him. "Albert, it's a miracle you've kept your job for as long as you have, seeing as how you must be on drugs to think I'd call in alarm on myself."

He shrugged. "Makes no difference to me. I'll just use my elbow to do it. Of course, I might twitch and shoot this pretty thing, and wouldn't that be an awful shame?" Albert began to crab back down the hall, keeping a firm grip on the girl as he went. He motioned at me with his head. "Come on Fleming, or Box, or whatever your name is. If you get out of my line of sight that'll upset me to no end."

I didn't have much choice. The three of us made our way down that curving metallic hall, Albert and Felicity walking backwards, me following at a discreet distance. Thirty or so feet of that, and we found ourselves approaching an open door. "Good thing for you it was open already," I said. "I don't think I would have done it for you."

Albert grinned again. "Where do you think I was coming from, smart mouth? I was just slipping into the dorm for a little quick fun, like I usually do this time of night, when you had to go and spoil it."

I blew out a breath. "You know something, Albert? You're a

tough man to like."

Albert's perennial smile fell away. "You don't have to like me. You just have to do what I say." He and Felicity began backing into the room, me not far behind.

Right at that moment the main power picked its time to come back on with a hum. The lights grew cheery bright...

And what I saw illuminated in those lights made me stop and stare in mute, disbelieving horror.

Lining both long walls were glass tanks standing on stainless steel tables. The tanks were big, maybe two feet across by five feet high, and were lit in a strange bluish light from below. But what had made me stumble to a halt was what was in those tanks.

The babies from my nightmare.

My God. It was them. Only these babies weren't the products of a fevered imagination. No, they were as real as a tax audit, and I prayed with all my heart that the poor, twisted creatures floating inside those tanks were well and truly dead, and not locked in some hellish limbo.

And here was the worst: even though those babies were all deformed in their own way, they all had the same thin frame, sallow skin, and lank blond hair I had seen on Boneless Chuck. There was no denying it. These were his unborn brothers and sisters.

Albert caught me staring and grinned. "Cute, aren't they? And don't worry about your reaction. The few people that have actually been allowed in here all do the same thing as you the first time." He looked around. "Me, I like it. There's nothing like seeing your mistakes up-front and personal to tell you that at least you're on the right road. It's...inspiring."

But Felicity didn't look inspired. Far from it. She was staring around with what I'm sure was the same look on my face, her mouth opening and closing but with nothing coming out.

My speech was clipped. "You're really a company man, aren't you Albert? You've bought into the full party line." I sneered at him. "What have they promised you? That if you're an obedient little stooge and do a good job you'll have a starring role in the Fourth Reich or Fifth or whatever number we're up to?" I could feel the derision leaking out. "You? Lieutenant Bootlicker?"

In reply Albert smiled and screwed the gun barrel in tighter. "You're going to hurt my feelings if you keep talking like that."

"I'll hurt more than that, Albert, if you don't stop."

Whatever reply Albert was going to make was drowned out in Felicity's scream. She had finally found her voice. And with that scream the girl wrenched violently out of Albert's grasp, heedless of what he or I or anybody else on God's green earth thought about it, and shoved against the nearest pod, doing her best to dump it.

This time I nearly beat Albert to the draw. In the next few seconds he had Felicity pulled back away from the pod and again clutched against him, his Glock pressed into her ear.

But as I said, Albert wasn't the only quick one in the room. He turned his attention back to me, and as he did his look was drawn to something that I'm sure was an unexpected and nasty surprise: my .38 Smith and Wesson, hammer back and lined up on his left eyeball from a distance of less than six feet.

Albert swallowed. He tried to put together a smile, but it wasn't very good. "Wow, I never even saw it. Quick Draw McGraw." He licked his lips. "Well this is some kind of a deal, isn't it?"

I tried to keep my voice as level as my gun. "You like sunrises, Albert? All you have to do to see the next one is to let the girl go, lay your gun on the floor, and walk away. Nothing could be easier."

"No." Albert seemed to be recovering some of his composure. "No, I don't think so. The problem with you is, you being a hillbilly is a worse condition than you know. You aren't familiar with physics."

I frowned, still keeping him lined up. "How's that?"

"Physics. One action affecting another." Albert slowly pulled his head back around behind Felicity's until only his left eye was showing. "How this works is really simple. If you shoot me, physics says the impact of the bullet will cause my muscles to contract, and I'll still be pulling the trigger even though I'm dead." Now Albert was grinning again. "The only way, and I mean the *only* way, for you to beat that is to shoot me so that my brain is destroyed faster than my finger will move. And I really don't think you've got the guts to see if that's going to work."

I centered the .38's iron front sight on his pupil. "Are you willing to bet your life on that, Albert?"

"That's not the question," he said. "Are you willing to bet hers?"

I sighed. "Then I'd say we have us a standoff. Sooner or later somebody's going to get an itch or a cramp or a quiver in their muscles, and things will turn messy." Now it was my turn to grin. "So here's my idea. What do you say about us both laying our guns down and finishing this like men?"

Albert shook his head a millimeter. "No way. I could tell from our tussle in the hall you're a tough old bird. That's what they do with you country kids, right? They teach you how to fight when you're young?"

"And shoot," I said.

"That's what I thought. So I won't fight you, but I'll tell you what I *will* do. I've decided to kill this girl." Felicity gasped, and Albert chuckled, "Quiet, baby, it'll be a hoot." His eye twinkled at me. "Yeah, hilljack, I'm going to shoot you both, double-tap, and I'll do it before you even realize how I did it. Then we'll know who the better man is." Albert's chuckle was now sounding a bit crazed. "How's that strike you?"

"Like somebody dropped you on your head." A bead of sweat began to roll down the side of my nose but I didn't dare touch it. Nerves. "Come on, man, it doesn't have to go this way. You can find better ways to make points with Boneless than to pull a fool stunt like you're talking."

"I don't think so," Albert breathed. "Boneless likes this kind of macho stuff." He grinned. "Now don't blink. You'll want to see this."

"Albert," I said. "Don't make me kill you. Please."

His voice now didn't even sound human. "Don't beg, briar. It makes my stomach turn. What's about to happen, you can't stop it. Nobody's that good."

I saw Albert's knuckle grow white as it tightened down on the trigger, taking up the slack.

Felicity moaned in fear.

Then everything stopped as my .38 roared, its round rocketing six feet across the room and flying straight into the man's eye.

The bullet mushroomed out as it hit, growing instantly from the size of gumdrop to the diameter of a golfball. That's what wad-cutters do. As the round exited Albert's head, the back of his skull vanished, and he slipped into what was in all likelihood a Godless eternity. The guard's gun flew free and unfired from his hand and his body slumped to the floor, deader than four o'clock.

"I am, Albert," I whispered. "I'm that good."

Then I threw up.

And Felicity began screaming again.

Chapter 41

"Shut up, girl." I hoped my words didn't sound too clipped or forceful, but with that gunshot I knew we had both crossed over into uncharted waters. What would happen next was anybody's guess. "Felicity!" She shut up her caterwauling and looked at me blankly. I was trying to ignore the acid burn of vomit in my throat, and the gore plastering the whole upper side of the girl's body. Easier for me than her, though. "Now listen to me," I said more softly. "We're probably about to get company, and I want you to do something for me. Take this." I reached into my pants pocket and pulled out Blakey's key card. I handed it out to her, and she slowly took it from me. "Do you know how to make the elevators work?" I asked. She nodded, still unspeaking; I wondered if she was so traumatized she would never talk again. "Good," I smiled. "Now here's what I want you to do. I want you to open the first elevator you come to, ride it to the top, get out, and then run like the wind. Don't stop until you get outside and on the highway. Flag down a car and have them take you to the police station. Sheriff Hardesty's a good man, and he'll help you get home. Okay?" Lord, I hoped she was getting all this.

Felicity again nodded wordlessly, and when she did I almost cried. This poor kid had been through unvarnished hell, and I had completely screwed up her whole supposed rescue. Now the least I could do by my death was to buy her the time to get clear of here.

"Good," I said. "That's real good." I smiled again, blinking rapidly, and went on, "Now you be sure to give your daddy a real big hug when you see him. Tell him...you tell him Joe tried." I took a quick look up and down the hall. She had time, if she was fast. "Go, kid."

And like a shot, she was gone.

I saw her disappear around the left curve of the hall, and it wasn't ten seconds later I heard the grim clatter of running feet headed my way and coming from the right. That idiot Albert hadn't needed to trip the alarm in the pod room; the sound of my .38's discharge had probably carried all over the metallic walls of GeneSys.

Okay, think. If what I was hearing now was any indication, there had to have been at least a dozen guards bearing down on my position, and I frantically weighed my options.

There wasn't much weighing to it. At the end I only had two: surrender to those men and find myself in short order back in the torture chair, or go down firing.

For the first choice, forget that. Boneless had done with me all I was going to allow; I wouldn't give him the satisfaction of killing me piecemeal. No, we Southern boys have a long and honorable tradition of making last stands against superior firepower, and I knew our blood-soaked soil ran all the way from Manassas to Chancellorsville to Gettysburg to here.

I readied myself, zeroing out everything but what I needed to do. A moment later the guards thundered around the bend right at me, guns drawn. Boneless was in the lead. He was smiling.

I held my .38 two-handed, just the way Sarge had taught me, spit to the side, and let fly.

Chapter 42

So that's how I had ended up in that dead-end hallway. I must have surprised them all with my Wild West act, because as I popped off the five rounds I had left, Boneless and his boys almost flattened themselves in panic, each trying to hide behind the other. Two went down right away, but before the rest had a chance to recover I ducked down the nearest branching corridor, empty gun in hand. It wasn't until I was halfway down the thing that I realized it ended in a smooth metal wall. Uh-oh. That was stupid. What could I- But there was no more time. Boneless's troops had taken a position flanking the hall's entrance, and as their bullets started to rip through the air my way I wedged myself tightly into a little alcove just off that hall. That's where this tale began.

I'll still never know how Boneless managed to get his hands on Felicity; all I can figure is that she was nabbed by one of his men before she ever set foot on the elevator. At any rate, Boneless had her, and he wasn't shy about rubbing my face in that. It wasn't until the freak had started to choke her, though, that I saw red and came up with that idiot plan. Since I was out of ammo, all I could do was to throw my gun up into the lights and make like Nate Forrest charging the Yankee line. As I said earlier, I knew right away this was a suicide run as I did it, because even with my rebel scream coming at them from out of the darkness, Boneless's well-seasoned men had merely hunkered down and opened up on me with everything they had.

In retrospect the whole action couldn't have lasted more than five seconds, but having been under fire before, I also know that time is a relative thing. All I can say for sure is that I found myself running *at,* and then somehow *through,* the darkness and the thunderous muzzle flashes from those nasty P-90 man-killers.

Then the emergency lights mounted in boxes up near the ceiling suddenly flickered and flashed and then came fully on, lighting the scene in stark relief. And as they did I stumbled to a stop and dropped my hands, staring for the second time this night in shock.

Boneless's men were dead. Gone. Shot to pieces. Somehow, some way their hundreds of bullets had missed me, and instead those troops were laying everywhere like broken dolls, like cracked-open cherry pies, every mother's son of them. How in God's name-?

Then I knew. It was His name, all right, and the power behind it. God had somehow caused those battle-hardened troops to ignore every rule of combat they had ever learned and completely miss an unarmed cracker--me--running at them from out of the dark. Those men had missed me, and instead killed each other in a crossfire.

Crossfire. Yes. That was the word for it.

The Cross had saved me...and God's own fire.

Well, stay with me Jesus, because we weren't done yet. The one body I had really wanted to see laying there wasn't, and now he was gone with the girl I had promised to save. But save her I would, and I again started to run. I had just seen a miracle; with it my fragile faith had leaped up tenfold.

I almost laughed at the sheer audacity of it. Boneless, I thought, you crazy mutant, you've seriously screwed yourself now. You've got God Himself about to cloud up and rain all over you.

GeneSys was a blight on creation, true enough, but no more. The seeds it had sown, the untold miseries it had so callously inflicted on so many innocents for too long were about to come up in its own destruction. And there would be no recourse for mercy, none. Executioner terms came into my mind. It was time to pull the switch, hit the plunger, drop the gallows door, and end it.

But as I hustled around the bend, bearing down on the elevator bank, my faith suddenly seemed to falter.

I was too late.

The doors of the first one were closing, and I saw Boneless grinning at me in victory, his strong hands tight around Felicity's neck. The look in her eyes seared my soul.

I reached those doors a second too slow. They sealed, and as they did the arrow above them blinked on, pointing down. Then I heard the elevator motor beginning to whine and my fingernails broke as I tried to pry my way inside.

No good. The sound faded away and it was gone. I looked in despair at the arrow. Down? Why? All that was down there was...

The Pit.

Oh my God.

Now I knew what Boneless was going to do, I knew it as sure as I knew anything. With the death of his troops, things had gotten personal between us. Boneless knew his plans to cap the evening's fun by tossing me alive into the Pit, as he had promised he would, were gone.

Instead he would throw in the girl.

Chapter 43

I was running as fast as I could back the way I had come. I needed another key card to follow Boneless and Felicity, and the only place I knew where I could get one quick was off of one of the dead guards. I reached the hallway where they lay and, without looking too closely at them, retrieved the card from the belt of the first one I came to. I also lifted his P-90, hoping I wouldn't need it. I'd just seen what they could do. Then I flew back to the elevators, my feet eating up the distance. With all my running I figured to be in pretty good shape when this was done.

Or dead, my cowardly self reminded me. I ignored him. God had saved me to this point; I knew He'd see me through to however it would end.

I was a little winded when I again reached the elevator bank, but I ignored that as well as I slid the card in its slot. When the middle doors opened I jumped in, punching the down button as I did. As the thing sank I wondered again that this place didn't have emergency staircases; I guess Gwyllym would have rather traded off lives in a fire than to sacrifice a little security. One more proof of the callousness to human life here.

A few seconds later the doors opened, but I was already squatting on my haunches near the floor against Boneless getting cute and waiting there in surprise. But no, the hall was empty. Boneless either thought I truly was too stupid to be able to follow him, or he genuinely didn't care. Either way, he wasn't there. According to Roger, that left only one place he could be.

I stood and ran out of the elevator and across the hall, to another door. This one was blank. No surprise there; everyone here knew what was behind it. Belatedly I checked the magazine in the P-90, like I should have done when I picked it up. And don't you know it was empty. Son-of-a- Well, this was just dandy. Roger had told me the thing held fifty rounds, and the only way I could figure it was that in that OK Corral shoot-out I'd been in, the gun's owner must have dumped them all into somebody else.

I tossed the thing away in disgust, checking myself for weapons. I came up with nothing, no surprise. My .38 was laying somewhere back in that charnel-house hallway, not that it would have done me any good, being empty as it was. No, the facts were deadly simple: I was an aging, weaponless ex-cop with a useless left hand going up against a trained martial arts expert nearly half my age. Sounded like a fair fight to me.

Okay, enough shallying. Behind that door, and then the next, Boneless had Felicity. I hoped. For all I knew the freak had thrown her in while I was still out here cranking up my courage.

And courage I needed. Again I ducked my head in a quick, heartfelt prayer. It was getting easier now; I just hoped I would live to get better at it. "God, this seems hopeless, but I have to believe it isn't. Give me strength, and save us both." I started to raise my head, then bowed it again. "Oh yeah, in Jesus' name, amen." The fragment of some forgotten Bible story Granny had told me as a kid came floating up in my thinking then. All I could remember of it was one line as I grinned and slid in my key card. "Gird up your loins, Boneless. We're gonna scrap."

Chapter 44

I went through the first door and found myself in a short hallway, not unlike the entrance to the dome. The mechanics were the same, any road, and I watched as the door behind me closed securely before the next one opened. As it did, I slipped past it as quietly as I could into the room.

Roger had been right. The room's diameter was nearly a sixth of the length of a football field. Why? I guess just because they could. I'll have to say the place was intimidating, in an *Aliens* sort of way, all metallic and oppressive and science fiction-y. And as Roger had also said, dead center in the room's floor there was the Pit itself, a huge, iris-like opening, closed for the moment. For some reason the thing struck me as faintly obscene.

But I didn't linger too long on that, because my attention was drawn to what was happening on the far side of that iris.

Boneless and Felicity both had their backs to me, and I could hear the girl's muffled cries as she struggled in his grip. Ominously I could also just barely make out something red and glistening on the floor between her feet. No. It couldn't be. *Blood?* What was he *doing* to her? Everything in me cried out to run towards Felicity, but I held back. The only card I had was surprise; if I tipped my hand too soon, Boneless would get us both.

I glanced to my left and there, as Roger had also told me, were gurney-like things with small steel wheels. Those wheels were obviously meant to fit into the narrow-gauge track set into the floor and running straight from the door to the iris.

As quietly as I could I went to pull the nearest gurney to me. My plan was that maybe I could fit the thing into the track, get a running start with it, leap on and ride it to the iris, and then jump off at the last second and nail Boneless from the back.

Stupidly creative I know, but I never even got the chance to try. As I latched onto the gurney and gave it an experimental tug, the wheels on the thing screeched like a mining car at the Comstock Lode.

Boneless heard the sound and turned to me with a smile. "Joe! It's about time you made it. As you can see, I had to start without you." I didn't answer, but flew over to see what he meant. As I approached the iris's edge Boneless stopped me with an upraised hand. "That's far enough. Let me finish with the girl, then we'll chat."

With a sick appreciation I could see now what he was doing to her. Somewhere Boneless had gotten a knife, and he'd used it to run a long cut down Felicity's left arm. I could tell from the rate of blood flow it wasn't deep or life-threatening, but the very fact Boneless felt compelled to hurt the girl without reason made my Southern-bred deference to women come roaring back. "I'll make you a deal, freak," I said. "Me for her." I gritted my teeth. "Come on, what do you say? A strapping young crazoid like yourself needs a better challenge than a scared kid." Grinning, I spread my arms to either side. "I'm the guy, Boneless. Let's dance."

"Taunts don't affect me, Joe," Boneless smiled again. "My father taught me many years ago to ignore them."

"Yeah, your father taught you a lot of things, didn't he?" I shot back. "Like how to inflict pain and feel no emotion and ignore the cries of the weak." And suddenly the words were there. "Just like your dad ignored your cries, right? Your cries as a child when he wouldn't let you out of that dark box he locked you in for weeks at a time. The stuff he made you eat and the things he made you watch. Is that how you learned, Boneless? Is that how you got to be the way you are, the man you became?"

Boneless's composure seemed to waver and his mocking smile slipped a bit. "That's a low blow, Joe. You being such a paragon of religion, you being a *Christian,* I would have expected better of you."

"Sorry to disappoint," I grinned again.

He shrugged. "No matter. You and I, we'll balance the books in a moment. Let me just do some things with the girl first."

"I'll bet you're disappointing her, too," I spit, and Felicity moaned. I ignored it; I was doing my best to keep my attention riveted on his eyes and not on hers. For some reason I couldn't fathom, I knew it was important for me to do that as I kept on drilling. "But I'd guess your whole life has been one long disappointment, hasn't it, Boneless? Yep, bet so. Does the fact that people fear you make up for them not liking you? Do you ever wonder that you've never had the love of a woman? Or a friend?" Then I went for the throat as I lowered my voice. "Or a father?"

That did it. With a feral scream of rage and betrayal Boneless slung Felicity to the side and charged me, hands outstretched. But I never gave him the chance to reach me as I turned and made a dead run back towards the doorway, and towards the big red button I had seen recessed into the wall next to it.

The one that opened the Pit.

I had never run so fast in my life; fear will do that. Gasping, I felt the ghostly touch of Boneless's fingers whispering across my back. Then I passed the button and mashed it home.

A motor far beneath the floor whined, slowly opening the iris wide, and when it did the most God-awful stench filled the room.

Imagine a Dumpster on a wharf outside a Baltimore fish market on a hot August day, then add Cincinnati's municipal sewer system, and top off the whole thing with all the Port-A-Potties at all the construction sites in the world all spilling over at the same time, and you might have a tiny inkling of how the Pit smelled.

Did I say it stunk? Yes indeed.

But I tried to ignore the furious burning in my eyes and sinus cavities and concentrate on what was important as I cut hard right and away from Boneless, making a beeline back to Felicity.

And that's a strange thing. Because I know for a fact that in reality there was no way that I, nearly fifty and in middling good shape, could be outrunning a thirty-year-old martial artist who I'm sure did miles of roadwork every day...but there it was. It was happening and I couldn't tell you how.

And then without warning Boneless had me. I felt a savage karate blow fall across my neck, much like the one I supposed he had used on me when I came out of the dorm that first time. But it must be hard to solidly land a blow like that while running full-tilt, because instead of the hit knocking me out, I merely stumbled and fell.

And almost rolled into the Pit.

Horrified, I slammed the fingers of my right hand into the track, digging deep. My broken nails tore loose as I slid to a shaky stop.

Caramba, *that* was close.

Then my breath was driven from my lungs as Boneless landed on top of me, and I started punching him like crazy. His hands probed underneath me as we fought, and with a start I realized what he was doing: the freak was trying to finish flipping me in. Desperately I wrestled back, my eyes streaming tears from the Pit's stench.

Suddenly I felt the floor beneath me fall away. Boneless now had my whole upper body leveraged out over that hellish opening, pushing me hard, and far in the background I could hear Felicity screaming for all she was worth. Whether for me or herself or for the whole nightmarish situation I didn't know, but the dim thought came to me as I struggled that if the kid could sing as well as she shrieked, she might give Celine Dion a run for her money.

Boneless's pale blue eyes burned down on me with insanity and his breath was hot and foul in my face as I felt him wedge one arm under the backs of my knees. Then my heels lifted. "In you go, Joe," Boneless huffed. "And mind that first step."

I couldn't help it as I screamed the next: "Jesus, help me!"

Desperately I formed my right hand into a rigid flat spear- head, and then I jammed that hand straight into Boneless's eyes.

His eyes didn't pop, but having been on the receiving end of a blow like that back in Vietnam I knew the pain I had just inflicted was right up near the top of the scale.

Sorry, Boneless. Mind my fingers.

Boneless nearly dropped me as he clapped both hands across his eyes and bellowed. I used those seconds to grab the front of his shirt and pull myself up and away from that putrid hole.

And then, of all things, my dad's voice came back to me, reminding me of one of the few things he had ever said that I could use. "In a fight, Joe, they ain't no rules," my dad had said. " 'Cause when it comes down to it, the meaner man always wins."

True enough, I guess, and with those words echoing through my mind I kicked at Boneless just as hard as I humanly could.

I heard the man's shoulder separate with an audible pop and he screamed again. Payback's a bear, ain't it Boneless? Okay, I saw he was done. Again I started around the opening towards Felicity.

But I was wrong. I had either underestimated Boneless's capacity for pain or the depth of his hate and madness, because I hadn't gone a step when he shot to his feet and rammed his good shoulder hard into my back.

And when he did we both went over.

The next few moments are a blur. I remember Boneless's roar of triumph suddenly sliding into a shriek of horror as he realized his error. I remember that metallic room tilting crazily. I remember my own cries for mercy as we tumbled in.

Then time seemed to stop.

The next thing I knew I again had somehow jammed the bloody pulps of my fingertips into the gurney rail. The rest of me was gone over the edge, dangling.

I felt absurdly heavy, and I looked down.

Hanging from my leg, pulling on us both, was Boneless.

I gasped. Oh my God. My mind screamed to kick the man free and save myself...but I didn't.

Instead I found my wrecked left hand reaching towards him.

Now *that* was a heck of a thing. Why? Why was I suddenly trying to save this man who fully intended on killing me? I didn't know, but I kept moving my hand his way.

Maybe...maybe this was what Christianity was all about, I thought as I stretched. Maybe this is what Jesus had tried to show us, and we were all too dense to get it.

But it was no use. Boneless had really done a number on those dislocated fingers, and I knew they wouldn't support his weight if I tried to pull him up. And Boneless couldn't help either, his left arm hanging useless from my kick.

So there we were, two enemies in a hopeless fix.

And now it was growing worse. I could feel the blood from my fingertips lubricating the track, inexorably causing us both to slide forward, and there wasn't thing one I could do to stop it.

Yes there was. Again I prayed.

"God," I groaned. "Help us."

Boneless squinted up at me and grinned. "Don't include me in that. If this is my time, all right, but I'll go my own way. I don't need your God."

"You moron!" I gasped again. "That's what started this whole GeneSys mess in the first place!" Then with a jerk I felt Boneless slip further down.

His cocky smile was gone, now replaced by stern concentration. Boneless began to swing his legs around, grunting with the effort. Once more I tried to stretch my ruined hand towards him, but my fingers just wouldn't cooperate. "Stay still!" I yelled. "You'll pull us both over!" I screamed up to the room. "Felicity! Get us some help!" But she didn't answer; the kid had either fainted or gone catatonic.

One last time I looked, and now replacing the smirk on Boneless's face was something I would have never expected: the beginnings of mindless fear. Boneless knew full well what was down in that Pit, what awaited him there.

And me too, if God didn't step in right now.

I saw Boneless slip again. Now he was swaying by his arm from the toe of my shoe, looking around wildly in hopeless panic. We locked eyes, and Boneless's last words haunt me still.

"Daddy!" he sobbed. "Daddy help! I'll be good, Daddy! I will! Don't let me fall, Daddy! Don't-"

Then Boneless's fingers slipped, and with a shriek he was gone into the darkness and the stink.

And I hung my head and cried for this creature who had never had a chance.

But the time for tears was done. As was my life.

With a small squeak my bloody fingers finally slid free of the track, and gravity took over. I felt myself dropping, and as I fell my mouth roared open with His Name on my lips. "JESUS!"

And with that scream...someone grabbed me. I felt a strong hand grasp my wrist and stop my descent. Was it-?

"Not him," a relieved voice above me grunted. "Just me."

Blinking, swinging, I looked up to see.

Sheriff Hardesty.

He stared down at me, his mouth twitching in humor. "I told you to watch your back."

Chapter 45

Hardesty had someone throw blankets across Felicity and me as he guided us through the mob of city cops and state troopers filling the room and the hall beyond. My mind was still spinning and I couldn't put together a coherent thought until we were on the elevator and it was rising.

"How-?" I began, but he waved it off.

"No talk until we get outside in some fresh air. That stink's about to make me puke. By the way, your hands are a mess. We have some doctors outside. I'll have one fix you up."

That sounded good to me, and Hardesty and I said no more as we rose. Neither did Felicity. I shot a worried look at her. The girl still hadn't said a word as she gazed ahead with the blank look and thousand-yard-stare I'd seen so much in 'Nam. She needed help, possibly of the psychiatric kind, to aid her in dealing with her nightmare.

But that could wait until she was home. Right now it was honey-sweet to be walking out of the dome with her and into a glorious, pouring rain that was washing the early dawn clean. I looked around at the trees. Showing silver, Granny.

I had thought the GeneSys complex had been filled with cops; out here it was worse. I hadn't known Indiana possessed these many law-enforcement types. But I was sure happy they were here.

The three of us found some shelter at last inside a SWAT van that had been parked under a tall sycamore by the chain-link fence, and as Hardesty shut the door I finally got to ask him the question that was chewing at me. "How, Sheriff? Who tipped you off?"

Hardesty poured us some coffee in styrofoam cups and handed us each one before answering. He was enjoying this; I hadn't pegged the man to be such a scamp. Hardesty and I sipped from ours but Felicity didn't even acknowledge what she was holding; I gently took it from her and set it on the van's floor before she spilled it and burned herself.

"Who tipped me off?" the sheriff answered at last. He cocked his thumb up towards the van's cab. "Him." The driver turned around and grinned.

Roger Thornhill.

I almost leaped over Hardesty in my haste to embrace the younger man. "Roger! But Boneless told me you were-"

"Dead?" he finished up, still grinning. "Well, it wasn't for his lack of trying." Roger settled back against the seat. "Here's the story, Joe, and it's a corker. After I had left you I went home, and I was just getting Trish and the baby ready to scoot when the phone rang. It was Brother Springer. He sounded real anxious, and said that he had been in prayer and the Lord had told him, clear as day, to call me and tell me my family was in danger. I looked out the window and sure enough one of the staff cars had just pulled up with four of Boneless's troops. I saw them step out with their P-90's cocked and locked." Roger stopped and looked at Hardesty. "Hey, Sheriff, you got any more of that coffee?"

"Sure," Hardesty said, pouring him a cup.

I was about to come out of my skin. "Forget the coffee! What happened?"

Roger sipped his coffee and smacked his lips. "I killed 'em," he said simply. "I keep a nine millimeter for home defense, and that's what I did. As they came up on the porch I stepped out and emptied the clip." He sipped from his cup again and looked at me. "I told you I was trained as a Ranger. The second those guys came onto my land to kill my family, they signed their lives away."

I stared at him. "I'm glad you're a good guy, Roger."

"Not good," he said, sipping again, "but improving." I turned my attention back to Hardesty. "So how come it took you so long to get here?"

He scowled. "What are you, complaining?" He pointed at Roger. "Just be glad I believed this guy. I've known him since he was a kid, and up until he got religion he was a rowdy punk."

Roger grinned and lifted his cup in salute. "Why thanks, Sheriff. I love you too."

Hardesty shook his head. "Anyway, I get a phone call from Roger telling me he's just killed four guys on his front porch. That was enough to get me up and moving. Then I get out to his place and he spins me this wild yarn about Nazis and experiments and mutant babies. I almost took him away right then, but something about his story rang true, especially considering the way the GeneSys people had taken over our town. So against my better judgment I woke up Judge Sanders to have him cut a warrant, then I made a call to Captain Bovard at the state police barracks and told him to bring company. He did, and here we are. Satisfied?"

"In spades, Sheriff," I smiled, then I looked at Roger. "How come you didn't come in to help guide everybody around?"

Roger gave a wry grimace. "I know the light in here's not that good, so maybe you didn't notice that our good friend Sheriff Hardesty has my foot handcuffed to the steering column."

Hardesty shrugged. "In case you were lying."

Roger pointed. "Well, now that you know I'm not..."

The sheriff sighed and tossed him some keys. "Just don't make a habit of killing people, Thornhill. You know how that aggravates my ulcer."

Roger, grinning, caught the keys and started to work on the lock.

Hardesty looked back at me and lowered his voice. "What about her?"

I glanced over at Felicity; the girl was still staring straight ahead, emotionless as a bass. "I don't know. She has a lifetime of bad dreams locked up in her head. But since her dad paid me to bring her home, that's what I'll do. I need to give him a call first, though, and tell him what happened."

Hardesty grimaced and pointed out the van's window. "I'd say he knows already."

I looked out the window and groaned. The rain had quit, and now TV news trucks by the score were pulling up on the grounds and discharging their pretty, plastic reporters. CNN, Fox, MSNBC were all arriving, not to mention local vehicles from the Indianapolis and Cincinnati stations. "Buzzards," I mumbled. "It sure didn't take them long." I turned back to Hardesty. "She doesn't need this now. Is there any way we can keep them away from her?"

Hardesty tightened his lips in resolve. "You leave that to me. If it comes down to it, we'll keep her locked in here. I've never heard of a reporter yet that could break his way into a SWAT van."

I opened the rear door. "Let me get my car. I'll swing around here and grab her and go."

Hardesty put a hand on my shoulder. "Whoa, not so fast, Tex. You're not going anywhere yet. I need to get a statement."

I rolled my eyes at him. "Come on, Sheriff. Look at that swarm out there. Buzzing like flies around an outhouse. I need to get Felicity on the road, now. I'll phone my statement in. Or fax it. I'll even come back out here, whatever. I promise. Okay?"

Hardesty blew out a breath. "Oh, all right. I guess you two have been through plenty." He waved his hand. "Go on, go. Get your car and bring it back here. I'll keep that crew away."

"Thanks, Sheriff," I grinned, and then I cautiously opened the rear door and peered out. The cloudburst was over, the sky was cool and clearing, the reporters were setting up their live shots outside the fence, and no one was looking our way.

I jumped out of the van and began moving as quietly as I could towards the lot, where the Goddess was. If I was lucky none of the newshounds would notice a battered man in suit pants and a T-shirt walking around in back of them. Right. Those reporters were a dumb, rude bunch but I doubted if any of them were legally blind.

But ten seconds later that was all a moot point. I hadn't gone twenty steps away when the sky was filled with a thunderous clatter. I remembered that sound from the war, and I looked up. Incoming slicks. Helicopters to you. Five of them, unmarked.

The reporters pointed up and their camera crews all aimed their gear skyward. The noise grew and I looked back at the van. Hardesty had stuck his head out and met my gaze. We both shook our heads at the same time. We knew who this was.

"Who invited them to the party?" I yelled at him over the din.

"It sure wasn't me," he hollered back. "I got no use for 'em. Maybe the staties, maybe Judge Sanders. Who knows?"

Any reply I would have made was drowned out as the helicopters set down on the wide swath of grass inside the fence perimeter. The rotors hadn't even begun to slow before their doors opened and a horde of well dressed young men with sunglasses and wrist radios poured out.

An older gent dressed in a suit that would have cost Roger or me a month's pay stalked up to the gate and spoke to the first reporter he came to. "Who's in charge here?" the man barked, no nonsense.

The young reporter, trying to hide her tremble, pointed. "I think he is."

The older man's head pivoted to a uniformed person walking up. "And you are-?"

The cop stopped at a respectful distance. "Captain Bovard, Indiana State Police. This is a secure area, sir. I'm going to have to ask you and your people to leave."

The man gave Bovard a wintry smile. "I'm afraid you're a bit confused, Captain." He flipped open the badge holder he was carrying. "Smith, NSA. We'll take it from here."

Bovard scowled. "Sorry, Mister Smith. I've got orders from the governor himself not to let any unauthorized person past that gate."

"Too late, Captain," Smith said. "We're in. And you and your people are out. As of this moment, this is federal business. But feel free to call the governor if you wish. He'll confirm it." Smith smiled, still cold. "And Captain? Thanks for your help."

"You bet I'll call it in," Bovard snarled. "I'll call it in right now." He turned to a young cop standing near. "Whitey, tell the troops to keep an eye on these...gentlemen. If they attempt to take any evidence before I get this straightened out, shoot them."

"Captain, captain," Smith soothed. "Let's not get into a jurisdictional turf war, shall we? If we do, I can assure you who'll win." Still smiling at Bovard, Smith snapped his fingers over his shoulder. When he did a man inside the lead copter leaned out with an M-16.

The kid Whitey gulped and turned even whiter.

Meanwhile as this little drama was unfolding, I was sneaking behind the row of state squad cars and into the lot. Who said justice is blind? Maybe just nearsighted. I reached the Goddess and was putting the key into the door when I heard a voice.

"Stop."

I did.

Turning around, I saw it was one of the federal boys, a tall young man with all the accoutrements: ash-blond crewcut, Raybans, and a tiny .32 aimed right at my heart. His lips barely moved as he spoke. "Drop the keys and lay facedown on the ground."

I sighed at him. "Son, you would simply not believe how the last twenty-fours have gone. I'm tired, I'm dirty, and I'm dripping blood on the only pair of suit pants I own. Now why don't you put that gun away before I shove it down your windpipe."

He took one step closer. "I'm afraid I can't do that, sir."

I sighed again. "Then all I can tell you, kid, is open wide."

Before the guy could answer, Smith walked up behind him. "Do we have a problem, Agent Pettit?"

Pettit still had the gun on me. "No sir. The situation is under control."

"What situation?" I asked, exasperated. "I'm just trying to get in my car and leave." I motioned with my hand. "This horror show is all yours, Smith, and welcome."

Smith smiled; he wasn't very good at it. "So you know my name. What's yours?"

"Joe Box. And I really would like to leave."

Smith's phony smile grew wider. "Box! I wondered if that might be you." He gave me an up-and-down look. "With your appearance I figured you had to be either a bum or the one I've been hearing about."

I scowled at him. "Nothing good, I trust."

"On the contrary. You're the man of the hour."

I rubbed a hand across my face, dragging more grime away with it. God, I was weary. "Well, that's fine. I'll have my agent send you an autographed picture."

"I'd rather you come with me." Smith turned to the kid. "Put that away, Agent Pettit, and go assist Erlandson." Without argument the kid holstered his piece and walked away. What a fine, mannerly young man. Smith smiled again at me. "If you would follow me..."

I started to fire off a smart reply when I saw something behind him: two of Smith's agents were putting Gwyllym into the lead helicopter, and he wasn't even handcuffed. "Hey!" I yelled. "Wait a minute!" I began to push past Smith but he grabbed the back of my arm, right in the tender spot. I hate that.

"We're not done yet," he hissed.

"Maybe not," I shot back, "but I've got something to say to that creep." I looked down at his fingers. "Let me go, now, or I'll snap your spine."

Smith huffed out a laugh but he did it. "Fine. Have your say. But when you're done with him, it's my turn."

"Fine." I began trotting towards the helicopter, where the rotors were just spooling up. The two agents on either side of Gwyllym saw me approaching and reached into their suit coats for their weapons, but I heard Smith call out to them.

"It's all right. My call. Let him see him."

The agents stepped aside from the doorway as I got there and I jumped in. Gwyllym was fluffing his seat pillow, but when he looked up and saw me his face blanched. Screaming out a strangled cry he started to rise.

I pushed him back into his seat. "So this is how it is," I snarled. "You're going off to spill all to Uncle Sammy." I spit the words at him like nails. "What did Smith promise you, Gwyllym? Immunity? A French villa? Hot and cold running boys?" I narrowed my eyes. "Or maybe it's not that. Maybe it's worse. Maybe GeneSys was really one of Uncle's black-box ops and you're headed back for a debriefing." I bunched Gwyllym's shirt up in my fist, oblivious of the pain in my hand. "Which is it, Gwyllym? Are you a grasping neo-Nazi, or just a fumble-fingered patriot? Which?

Which?" I didn't even realize I was strangling the man until I saw his face turning purple. I had to will my hand to let go.

Gwyllym gasped a few times before he sank back into his seat, then he gazed up at me with a quivering smile. "What...what does it matter, Mr. Box? In the end, what does anything matter?"

"Matter? I'll tell you what matters, Gwyllym. Family." I looked down on him, beyond disgust now, into the realm of something else. "Have you wondered where your son is? Has he even crossed your mind?" I shook my head. "Don't answer, I think I know. Let me tell you. He's in the Pit. But I didn't put him there. He put himself. Because the thing is, Gwyllym, at the end Boneless was just as much your victim as Felicity, or any of those girls." My lip was curling in revulsion. "You know, some of us will never be fathers. And some of us *should* never be. Because you want to know something else, Gwyllym? At the end, even as he was dying, your son was calling your name. That's what people do sometimes at death. They call out the name of the one they love the most. I know, I've seen it." I gulped. "I've done it. And even though you didn't deserve it, you were his father. And he loved you." I sighed, weary to the bone. "I just wanted you to know that."

I turned back to the guards who had followed me in. "Let me out of here."

As I stepped back onto the grass, Smith was waiting. His smile was quizzical. "Everything settled between you two?"

I looked at him. "Not yet," and I climbed back inside the helicopter.

Gwyllym was once again fluffing his pillow when he saw me enter. This time he gave a put-upon sigh. "Are you back again, Mr. Box? After that fine speech I would have thought you had made your exit."

I bent low and held my index finger in front of his face. "Wait," I said.

Then I balled that finger up tight with the rest and slammed my fist straight into the dimple on Gwyllym's magnificent Dudley Do-right chin. The blow snapped the man's head to the side and he tumbled heavily out of his seat onto the floor.

But Gwyllym was tough. He wasn't knocked out and he glared up at me with pure hate.

I pointed down at him. *"That's* for being the world's worst dad," I said. I remembered Junior. "And I should know."

Gwyllym dabbed at his mouth with a silk hankie as he spit out a tooth. "Incredible. All this effort, all this expense, all these years of planning, and in the end my work is brought down by a-" he shook his head it- "*...hillbilly.*"

I squatted down on my haunches and grinned. "That's all right, Gwyllym." I leaned in. "Southern man don't need you around, anyhow."

I stood up and stepped back through the hatch onto the verge. "Okay," I said as I came up to Smith. *"Now* it's settled."

Then I heard a noise behind me.

I turned, and when I did I saw a thing that made all the hell of these past few days worth the pain. It was Felicity, shuffling over to me, being gently guided by Hardesty.

And she was smiling.

I called to Smith, "I'll be right back."

"Don't roam far, Mr. Box," he called back. "We still need to talk."

I waved that away as I trotted up to the two.

"The girl started coming out of it a few minutes ago," Hardesty grinned. "She's got something she'd like to say to you."

I took Felicity's small hand in mine, and she looked up at me. "Thank...you..." Her words were halting. "...for saving me..."

"My pleasure, child," I choked out.

Felicity tilted her head back, examining me closely. "What's your name?"

I blinked back the tears. "Joe Box."

She squeezed my hand. "Would you take me home?"

Epilogue

"...and that's the story," I said. "Wild, isn't it?"

Pastor Luke Samuels ran a hand through his hair. "I've not heard a wilder one." He pointed to the pot on the table. "Are you sure you don't want some coffee?"

I grimaced. "Please. I'm not as stupid as I look." The rest of the people laughed.

We were in Harvard Pike's large conference room, Luke and I, along with some of the folks who had figured strongly in this case: Mike and Sophia Taylor, of course, (Felicity still being held at a private hospital for observation); Nick Castle and CT Barnes; Tony Jackson; and three of what Luke had termed his level one intercessors: John Bohe, Robert Baird, and Angela Swain. Luke had to tell me what exactly an intercessor was; I mean, I knew what the term meant in a general way, but he told me a level one intercessor was simply a well-seasoned, well-trained prayer warrior, just exactly the kind that Sarge said I would need.

Speaking of Sarge, he and I had already had one long phone call right after I had gotten out of the hospital to have my hands repaired, and Sarge told me he and Helen were going to be flying up the following week for a long visit. That sounded great to me.

"But here's the thing I don't get," I went on. "I know this church as a whole was praying for me, and I'm not denying the power of that, but does that also explain why Boneless's guards all managed to kill each other without me getting a scratch? I've never heard of anything like that in my life."

The others looked at each other, smiling, then Miss Swain spoke up. "Joe, what happened to you also happened a long time ago in the Bible." I leaned in closer, and not just because I wanted to hear this. Angela Swain was a beauty: tall, with jet-black hair, creamy skin, and the most startling violet eyes. She smiled again at me, and when she did I felt something trip deep in my chest that I hadn't felt for a long, long time. "Look it up in second Chronicles twenty," she said. "A righteous king and his people were facing destruction from three armies at the same time, but the king got a command from God that he and his people were to pray and praise on their way to the battle. They did, and when they got there, every enemy soldier was dead, each killed by the other."

"But I wasn't praising," I argued.

John Bohe smiled. "We were."

I cleared my throat. "And my outrunning Boneless?"

"Also in the Bible," Miss Swain said. "The prophet Elijah outran a horse-drawn chariot."

"Wow. That kind of puts me in good company, doesn't it?" My new friends laughed, and I leaned forward again. "That only leaves one thing left to do, I guess. I'll be needing to find a church." I smiled at them. "Can any of you recommend a really good one, with a friendly congregation and a pastor that knows his stuff?"

Luke grinned at that. "I could think of maybe one or two."

*****

So that's how the case ended. Not the way I had thought it would, and certainly not the way I would have chosen, but I couldn't squawk: I was a thousand dollars to the good, I had received reams of free publicity, and I had finally gotten some self-respect back. But that wasn't the best: now, at middle-age, I felt my life was beginning at last.

As for the principals, Mike and Sophia and Felicity, things are looking up. The girl seems to have weathered her ordeal better than could have been hoped, and she and her folks are starting to work through the problems that started this whole circus. But they aren't going through them alone; they have a ton of people praying for them, me included. They're going to make it.

Nick Castle has offered me a job as a corporate investigator for his company, running background checks on new hires, stopping industrial espionage, the usual. The only problem with it is that over all these years I've gotten pretty used to doing things my own way; I'm not so sure that if I tried shifting into a corporate lifestyle the fit would work. Nick has tried sweetening the pot by telling me that if I took the position I could set up shop just about any way I wanted, no questions asked, and that I would be reporting directly to him.

Steady pay, benefits, no one trying to kill me...he's making it sound awfully tempting.

CT and I have mended fences, pretty much. I still say I could take him two falls out of three, and he still says he could drop me like a bad habit. Try as I might, I find it impossible to dislike the gorilla. But I'll also say this: if I end up taking the job at Castle Industries, I'm glad I won't be answering to him.

By the way, it looks like Gwyllym is going to skate. Big surprise. After the way he was hustled into that government slick that morning I just knew he would. Uncle Sammy may be a wastrel and a scoundrel, but he ain't stupid. I have the feeling our leaders are mighty interested in what Gwyllym and his merry band were working on, and I'll bet they think they can turn him. Maybe they can.

So why doesn't that thought give me any comfort?

I guess it's true: sometimes, even after giving it your best, the bad guys win anyway. But as Sarge likes to remind me, Gwyllym hasn't been judged yet. Not really. Not by the only Judge that matters, and I suppose that's true.

On the other hand, if somebody takes it into their head some dark night to shove an icepick through Mr. Gwyllym's skull I can't say I would shed a tear. (Sarge tells me I have a ways to go with this salvation business.)

Speaking of croaking in a gruesome manner, they never have found Boneless Chuck's body. Take it from me, they never will. Two weeks after GeneSys folded, authorities at last got around to opening the Pit.

And closed it up just as fast. I think the man who first shined a light down in there might be having a hard time sleeping. I know I did.

But as I said, things have worked out, all in all. It's just that sometimes they work out in ways you could have never hoped.

For instance, Angela Swain, that lady intercessor from church? Son of a gun.

I'm dating her.

Printed in the United States
4005